BLAINE L

PATRONS OF TERROR

BOOK FIVE IN THE BLUE DAWN SERIES

Patrons of Terror

First Edition: 2024

Printed in the United States of America

10 9 8 7 6 5 4 3 2 1

ISBN-13: 978-1-963102-08-6 (Paperback)
ISBN-13: 978-1-963102-07-9 (eBook)

Cover Art by Cedar Sanderson

Published by Defiance Press and Publishing, LLC

Bulk orders of this book may be obtained by contacting Defiance Press and Publishing, LLC at: www.defiancepress.com.

Public Relations Dept. – Defiance Press & Publishing, LLC
281-581-9300
pr@defiancepress.com

Defiance Press & Publishing, LLC
281-581-9300
info@defiancepress.com

"The use of intimidation, censorship, and terror to force social change is the act of tyrants and fools. In the world's history, it has been proven that those who have thrown these levers of change are themselves, oppressors. Those that do not take a stand against these tactics or choose to remain silent are patrons of terror."

—Blaine Pardoe

ACKNOWLEDGEMENTS

I started writing this novel prior to the sadly inevitable Russian invasion of Ukraine. To be clear, our demonstration of weakness in Afghanistan led to the Ukraine, which will eventually lead to Taiwan, or worse.

During the writing of this novel, one of my publishers canceled me: Catalyst Game Labs … I was banned from writing BattleTech novels in the future. A very small, woke mob, led by an online activist/stalker who threatened my life (and whom I have a protective order against) whined enough for me to be removed from the list of authors after almost thirty-seven years. The person who led this was a criminal who had been fired from their last job for issuing Terroristic Threats, a charge he pled guilty to and was placed on probation. He was joined by others of his ilk.

I wasn't a victim; I was a *target* of woke ideology. Part of the ire raised against me was because of this book series, to which I offer zero apologies.

They made a critical mistake. You can't cancel someone who refuses to be cancelled.

First let me thank my fans who didn't succumb to the negativity spun up around me. I hope you are enjoying the ride.

I also want to thank my detractors for making the entire *Blue Dawn* series far more realistic and plausible. My former publisher bending to the whims of self-appointed social justice warriors only validates the concept of Social Enforcement in these novels. They failed to exile me to a Social Quarantine camp. Instead, I am bouncing back with a vengeance. I'm writing and publishing more and better novels than ever before. We call that winning.

Further, I appreciate the leftists out there giving me more fodder for my novels with your outrageous claims and demands; but please stop. You don't have to ruin the country to make me out to be some sort of Nostradamus.

I also want to thank the FBI and DoJ for their overt politicization. You are making the National Security Force in my books more tangible for my readers. For the social media companies that systematically censored conservatives until Elon Musk exposed your traitorous acts, thanks for making the Truth Reconciliation Committee appear so viable. As it turns out, the censorship by Big Tech that I wrote about in this series is all too real.

My thanks to my neighbor Jack for his technical advice and to Chad for giving me the inspiration for Stewart-Newburgh Airport and some specs on helicopters. Thank you as well to Scott McCullough for some advice on dropping trees on tanks and John Blair for his nuances on firing an Abrams tank and NC Scout for information on signals intelligence from his book, *The Guerrilla's Guide to Signals Intelligence*.

DEDICATION

Patrons of Terror is dedicated to my comrades in arms at the Council of Future Conflicts channel. If you're not watching the channel on Rumble and YouTube, you are missing out on some prime material. Thanks to Scott, Joe, Stan, Kyler, Sean, and Fred for producing top notch military, political, and economic content sans the spin of the mainstream media. Here's to another year of being insightful, entertaining, and informative.

THE KEY CHARACTERS

Captain Lauren Aguilar. Captain in the California Veterans Corps.

Alex – Short for Alexandria (no last name given). Former Congresswoman from New York; she sits on the Ruling Council and commands the National Security Force (NSF) as its Secretary. She removed her opposition and folded the Social Enforcers into the NSF. She is the Newmerica Vice President-Elect.

Randy Birdsell. Leader of the Sons of Liberty (SOL) in New Hampshire.

Trudy Ford. Member of the Sons of Liberty (SOL) from the Upper Peninsula of Michigan.

Andy Forest. Andy's father was a member of the Sons of Liberty (SOL) and Andy was instrumental in recovering the original copy of the Constitution and Declaration of Independence.

Arthur Forrest. Andy's father and a persecuted professor at the University of Mary Washington. His actions saved the Constitution and Declaration of Independence.

Frank Campbell. Private investigator in Virginia.

Rebecca (Becky) Clarke. The Director of the Truth Reconciliation Committee (TRC) and member of the Ruling Council. Was instrumental in seizing control of Congress during the Liberation.

Travis Cullen. Former Navy SEAL, now a covert operative supporting the American administration.

Jack Desmond. Former Director of the Secret Service and now the American President's Chief of Staff. Jack was instrumental in bringing the former American Vice President to power, and for years was the clandestine leader of the Sons of Liberty (SOL).

Lieutenant Duwe. Intelligence officer, New Hampshire National Guard.

Herb Fletcher. The leader of a cell of the Sons of Liberty

General Hank Griffiths. Commanding General of the New Hampshire National Guard.

Booker Hickox. Self-proclaimed General of the Free Texas movement.

Miley Hines. Supporter of Free Texas and a musician

Veronica Hinkley. Member of the People's Warden Program.

Gwen Holtz. Leader of the Sons of Liberty unit, the Witches of Wichita.

Deja Jordan. A Social Enforcer from Minneapolis.

Charli Kazinski. Current Director of the American Secret Service. For years she lived as an NSF officer named Angel Frisosky to avoid detection. She was with the last President when he died.

Faust Kidder. One-eyed mercenary pilot.

Caylee Leatrom. Former NSF Operative, she has flipped sides and now offers her skills to the Americans. She killed Alex's mother and brother.

Senator Earl Taft Lewis. One of the few surviving Senators after the Liberation.

Dr. Weber Liu. A deep-planted Chinese agent operating under the guise of being a professor at the University of Michigan.

Maria Lopez. Sister of Raul Lopez.

Raul Lopez. Former member of the Youth Corps, his murder of a man led to riots in Detroit. As a member of the Sons of Liberty (SOL), he liberated the Social Enforcement Camp at Valley Forge.

Aiguo Lung. Chinese spymaster in North America.

Salem Marshall. Self-proclaimed President of Free Texas.

Captain Judy Mercury. Officer in the Texas National Guard and the American Army.

Tate Palmer. New Hampshire patriot.

Captain "Lariat" Paredes. American helicopter pilot.

Sam Patheal. Leader of a Sons of Liberty cell out of North Carolina, Hell's Tarheels.

Daniel Porter. Former Chairman of the Ruling Council, and the President-Elect of Newmerica. Daniel orchestrated the overthrow of the government during the Liberation/Fall.

John Quang. Chinese agent.

General Trip Reager. Renowned and scorned for his actions in San Antonio several years back, Reager is a Texan who is loyal to the American cause and is the Commanding General of the American Army.

Thiago "Rumbler" Reese. NSF Operative, expert in overthrowing governments. Also known as **Luis Fernando**.

Kiffin "Kiff" Renner. A government cyber-security specialist and friend of Jack Desmond.

Colonel Dan "The Dancer" Ricketts. Officer in the American Army.

General Hollings Rinehart. Commending General, Newmerican military forces.

David Steele. Maddie's younger brother.

Grayson Steele. Former conservative member of the Virginia House of Delegates and Maddie's and David's father.

Ted (no last name given). Former Texas Senator held prisoner by Newmerica.

Pat Templeton. Reporter, MSNBC whom Trip Reager punched.

Darius Thorne. Veteran and member of the California Veteran's Corp.

Valerie Turner. Former New York City police commissioner, leader of a Sons of Liberty (SOL) cell from New York.

Rita Zhang. NSF Operative.

Hachi Zhou. Wife of Su-Hui, she is an active member in the Sons of Liberty (SOL).

Su-Hui Zhou. Refugee from Taiwan, he is a leader in the Sons of Liberty (SOL).

Ya-ting Zhou. Daughter of Hachi and Su-Hui.

Acronyms:

ADMAX – Administrative Maximum Facility – the Supermax Prison's official designation.

ANTIFA – Acronym for Anti-Fascists. These radicals violently rioted during the summer of 2020 in an effort to influence the presidential election. They evolve into the roles of Social Enforcers in the Newmerican nation.

ATF – Bureau of Alcohol, Tobacco, and Firearms. With the formation of the NSF, this agency is now part of that new organization.

CAB – Combat Aviation Brigade

BDA – Battle Damage Assessment

BOQ – Bachelor Officer's Quarters

CHOP – Capitol Hill Occupied Protest. The occupation of Seattle by protesters in 2020.

Fedgov – The Newmerican rebranding of the federal government.

FOIA – Freedom of Information Act.

IWB – The Immigrant Welcoming Bureau formerly Immigration and Customs Enforcement prior to The Fall.

JCS – The military Joint Chiefs of Staff.

NSF – National Security Force. This is combination of all federal and local law enforcement agencies.

SAC – Special Agent in Charge.

SE – Social Enforcement. Groups supporting the Newmerican government that operate beyond the law, inflicting their own 'social justice' as they see fit.

SOL – Sons of Liberty. These groups of patriot partisans fight for the restoration of America.

TRC – Truth Reconciliation Committee. Working with Big Tech and the mainstream media, the TRC determines what truth is and what is misinformation. It clears all official stories and either censors or blocks those that would be considered dangerous.

UP – Upper Peninsula of Michigan.

UVA – The University of Virginia.

PROLOGUE

"Occasionally history needs a nudge in the right direction."

Five Years Earlier ...
San Francisco, California

Darius Thorne had come to California for the weather. After his three tours of service with the Army, serving in Iraq, all he wanted to do was kick back, find a good job, and enjoy life. He had earned it, at least in his mind.

At first it seemed like things were going his way. He and two veteran buddies opened a coffee shop in a good suburb of San Francisco called Hayes Valley. They could have opened a ritzy place, but they opted for something that the everyday worker could afford. All Jacked Up Coffee had an industrial feel to it, a lot of steel furniture and live edge wood tables ... classy, but utilitarian. The transition from a military mindset to that of a businessman was a struggle at first, but he managed to wrap his head around it. For the first few years, things had been working out well. Darius and his partners were making a good income. There was even talk of opening a second location. Like he told his sister, "This is what the American dream is all about."

The riots during the summer of 2020 had been a trying time for their startup. Several nights Darius had taken watch over his business in case things got out of hand. "Activists," or at least that was what they called themselves, became more prevalent in the neighborhood. They were peaceful, at first ... little protest marches by purple haired college students on the streets with a myriad of signs for their various causes. It seemed innocent enough at first. Then their numbers grew, and the cries for social justice seemed to be louder.

Then they began to block the entrance to his business. His partner,

John Livingston, asked them nicely to move on. He was greeted with the middle finger. John had been in the service two tours longer than Darius, spending a lot of his career in Afghanistan. The thought that some young punk kids would simply flip him off was unacceptable. They called the police, but San Francisco's finest showed up—albeit two hours later—and proceeded to tell them they couldn't do anything about it. When they left, the protesters outside continued to mock the owners, throwing garbage at their front window and door, screaming obscenities. The fact that the police had walked away only seemed to embolden them. They marched on, looting and damaging other businesses along the street.

Now, though, things were different. The news was flooded with images of what had gone down in Washington DC earlier in the night. Parts of the city were in flames … federal buildings were 'occupied' by protestors. The images of the White House ablaze tore at Darius, as did the images of the American flag being stomped on by the armed insurrectionists, who the media were already referring to as, 'The Liberators.' *This is no damned liberation, it's an overthrow.* Darius had expected that kind of shit in Iraq, but never in his own country. *This is something far more sinister. There's an agenda at play here.*

Outside of his own business, he watched as the black bloc and masked children began to show up. Some carried clubs, others carried guns. He watched as one twenty-something walked by, his finger on the trigger, waving his gun about. *No goddamn discipline ...* Darius knew that this was going to lead to trouble.

There were a lot of problems in America. As a veteran, he had more than earned his right to have a list of bitchable items he wanted changed. *These punk ass white kids haven't suffered a day in their lives. They haven't put their lives on the line for anything of merit.* He didn't like the man in the White House, but to burn the building down … well, that was just damned un-American. The riots were unfolding in a number of cities now that Washington had been taken … including San Francisco. In the pit of his stomach, he knew what was coming and dreaded it.

Shut off the television behind the counter of the closed coffee shop and armed with a baseball bat, John, one of his partners, pulled his Glock G21 and chambered a round. Darius didn't protest. John had been an Army Ranger and had a knack for spotting trouble before it happened. His other partner, William, was a former gang-banger that joined the Army and straightened out his life. He held a shotgun at the ready. The three of them looked at each other and said nothing for a long moment. The commotion outside was growing, and all of them knew that there was a chance that things would go south. *I didn't fight in that forsaken hell-hole to come here and have a bunch of punk-ass kids trash my business.* To Darius and his partners, All Jacked Up was more than an investment—it was their lives. Their little coffee shop was a symbol of freedom, built by vets and supported by former brothers and sisters in arms.

The size of the crowd outside continued to grow, and their disorganized and often competing chanting of demands simply equaled the noise of a lot of people yelling random words and sounds. Darius took a position behind the bar with his partners on each flank. They had moved the tables and chairs away from the windows fearing they would be destroyed if the rioters rushed inside. Laying the furniture on their sides they formed a protective barrier that might slow anyone trying to get in to do further damage. As he looked at the barricade, he realized that he was still in the Army in his mind. *I'm still preparing for battle.*

For a few minutes, it looked like the crowd of angry rioters might thin out—that they had lost steam or had moved up or down the block. *Maybe this will blow over.* His sense of relief was shattered when a hurled brick slammed into the front window of All Jacked Up. The crack and cascade of glass falling like deadly guillotines, tinkled everywhere on the floor. It was followed by another object that broke the door window … then the crowd surged in.

The black-clad rioters spilled in through the holes, angry and vicious. They eyed the three veterans, guns in hands, and for a moment there was a weird standoff of sorts. John raised his gun towards the ceiling and fired, probably hoping that the shot would frighten off the vandals. The boom made Darius's ears ring with pain as a few of the rioters turned and ran out. Others looked at them as if they were a pack of hungry hyenas. There was a rush towards the overturned tables; then came the shots—fired wildly at the bar where the men stood their ground.

One woman stepped forward, waving a .357 revolver that was so big in her hands that it wobbled in the air as she took aim. Her face, what little he could see of it over her mask, was filled with rage. He could even detect the outline of a big angry smile of hate on her face as she fumbled with the weapon. She was a danger just trying to handle the gun.

John leveled his aim slowly at her. Darius opened his mouth to call out to him not to fire, but it was too late. His gun barked loudly, popping Darius's left ear. The woman was hit in the throat, thrown back, as the bullet sped through her soft tissue and into another rioter behind her. She dropped on her back, blood squirting in fast pulses upward as the crowd surged back through the open window, their feet crunched and ground the shattered glass as they fled. One young Asian kid bent down and scooped up her gun, fleeing with the others. Three of the protesters grabbed the young man that had been hit and pulled him into the street, leaving a smear of crimson on the black and white floor tiles.

Damn! He instantly wished that John hadn't fired that shot. The woman tremored on the floor as her life fled her. William vaulted over the counter, then the barricade of tables, kneeling in her blood and trying to treat her wound. Darius knew it was a lost cause.

After a few moments, William looked up. The ebony skin of his hands was slick with her blood. "She's dead," he announced.

Darius could see that the crowd was moving on outside, heading up Laguna Street. Even with his ears ringing and popping, he could hear the sounds of glass breaking at other businesses. He looked down at William; then the dead woman; then back to John. "Call the police. We need to report this."

John nodded, putting his weapon on the counter and pulling out his iPhone. Darius pinched his nose and blew, managing to pop his left ear back, though the ringing was still persistent. *This is bad ... real bad. William and I are black, and John is white. That might be the only thing that helps him when the police arrive.* Glancing around the battered coffee shop, he wondered what would happen to the shop if they were arrested. *I put my whole life into this place, and because of some idiot woman waving a gun at us, we might lose it all.* Dread and the fear of the unknown chewed his thoughts as he waited for the police to arrive.

Camp Peary, Virginia

Thiago "Rumbler" Reese was still wet from running the obstacle course with the new trainees when he was told to report to the office.

Running the course at night was a completely different experience than during the day, which was why he did it. Camp Peary, the CIA's illustrious 'Farm' existed to train US and her allies on covert operations. Technically it was considered a myth, the stuff of urban legend, but in reality, everyone knew what it did and where it was.

That was the kind of weird contradiction that made up Reese's life. He had been born in Guatemala and had been smuggled across the US border by a coyote who had loaded him down with bags of drugs and directions about where to go. His mother had promised to follow, but she never came. He had been an illegal alien for years, eventually joining the military, getting his citizenship, then being recruited by the CIA. His job, unofficially of course, was to discreetly eliminate threats to the nation he called home. He did this by toppling governments, a unique specialty that he loved. Reese often joked with his new trainees, "I came here as a criminal, went to war, got paid to be a criminal, and now I train people to do criminal actions."

As he entered the office where he had been summoned, he saw the big screen TV was on, and the light from it illuminated the semi-darkness. Only one desk light was on; its dull white light cast long shadows on the gray-green walls that dated back to WWII. Images of the White House in flames stunned him for a moment, but he said nothing, simply letting himself be transfixed by the images. A number of his superiors encircled the television. They were mesmerized by the footage.

Bob Thompson—all of the senior people were called 'Bob'. It was an inside joke with the agency personnel. Everyone turned to him, "Thiago, you seeing this?"

He nodded. "How bad is it?"

"Bad enough," Bob replied.

"Did they get the President out?"

Bob shrugged. "We have zero info on that. Word is that Congress is either being held hostage, or they have been killed."

What the hell? "How was this allowed to happen?"

"Somebody screwed up," said Bob Jones, Thompson's counterpart who was sitting next to the TV.

"Where in the hell is the military?" Bob Smithers, another man in the room, spoke up.

"They must be sitting this one out," Thompson said.

"Can they do that?" Jones asked.

He got a shrug from Bob Thompson. "I don't see any soldiers on the ground there restoring order."

Reese had been in some unstable countries as an employee of the CIA. It was an environment that he thrived in. Military involvement or lack thereof spelled one thing out for him—*this is a coup ... here, in the US!* His mind processed the images with cold calculation.

"This is a pretty big, damned intelligence failure," Reese said.

"Not ours," Thompson replied. "FBI and DHS handle domestic shit. Those aren't Russians dancing around the burning White House; those are Americans. I wouldn't want to be the Director of DHS tonight."

How do we know that there wasn't outside interference? To Thiago, it seemed like a massive assumption to be made as events were clearly unfolding. "Are we just going to sit here? I mean, DC is only a couple of hours away. Do we have orders?" He was no fan of the President, but by the same token, he loved the country he had made his home. Seeing the White House in flames—the protesters seeming to celebrate over the carnage they had wrought—it tore at him. He was a person who always felt that strong action was better than none at all.

"We have no orders. I think all the bigwigs are probably shitting themselves right now. No doubt Langley is still trying to piece together what all of this means and how to respond. In the absence of any direct orders, we are to remain here."

It felt wrong to Thiago Reese. While he was not fond of the current administration, he had no desire to see it go up in flames. Yet the White House was lost. Having toppled governments himself, he wanted details. "Do we know where the President and VP are?" he asked.

"The situation is too fluid to get a solid response to that," Thompson said. "As much as we are an intelligence agency, you know we are outward facing. This is internal."

"I hope they killed both of those SOBs," Smithers snarled. "The Orange Man was a travesty. We are all better off with him dead."

He's already talking about him in the past tense. Talking about politics within the Federal Government was risky from a career perspective. To hear Smithers say what he did made Reese hold his words for a few moments, choosing them carefully. *I've seen coups,* he thought. *Hell, I've orchestrated a few of them. If this is one, they follow a pattern. One is to identify and remove anyone connected with the previous regime. If this isn't one, people like Smithers, who spoke up, might find themselves facing retribution. It's best to not voice one's opinion at this time.* "There are a lot of bad guys around the globe that are going to be pretty happy that this is going down. It makes us look weak, and they are likely to take advantage of it," he said, keeping the focus on their profession.

"You are right about that," Thompson said. "I'm sure the bobble heads up in Northern Virginia are going to be checking signal traffic from the usual troublemakers. Chances are we're going to be needed now, more than ever."

The TV camera changed to a view of protesters swarming the Capitol, waving ANTIFA flags and cheering. To Reese, he shook his head at the sight, attempting to remove the image from his fresh memory. Reese had spent time in Venezuela helping destabilize the government there and knew that when governments were toppled, even partially, that heads would roll. He had seen it before, enough to know that this was both an opportunity and a risk.

Things are going to be turbulent. If the President is alive, he will want vengeance, and based on what Reese saw on the TV, that would be fair. If he were dead, then the new regime would want to remove the remaining opposition. *They don't have a choice. If they allow resistance to grow, then they risk being overthrown.*

Experience had taught him to be observant and to take advantage of the emerging situation. *I have skills that they are going to need ... I eliminate people that pose a risk to governments.* There was a wave of pride at that thought. *I do it and do it well. I'm invisible ... undetectable. When my targets drop, I'm right there, always beyond suspicion.*

As he crossed his tattooed arms, he eyed the TV image and knew that if he played his cards right, he could turn the coup to his advantage. *I need to make sure that I come out on top of this.* It was beyond the Agency ... this was about being an asset that the new powers-that-be would depend on.

CHAPTER 1

"What makes us strong is our trust in our government."

Smyrna, Tennessee

Raul held the rubber, practice knife in front of him with his right hand, holding his left back and up near his face. Caylee held her practice blade in front of her as well, shifting her position to his left, forcing him to pivot also.

These were practice weapons, the dull edges covered in blue chalk to track the simulated damage. As much as Caylee had been drilling him, he was still nervous going up against her. His heart pounded in his ears as he stared into her narrowed eyes. Her expression was anything but friendly—she looked as if she would strike to kill.

Raul and his sister Maria had been living with Caylee, secure in the Tennessee National Guard base in Smyrna, Tennessee since she and their friends had broken him out of the Supermax prison in Colorado. They worked out every day, and she dedicated time to teach him to fight and defend himself. Maria, who had been withdrawn, had asked just a few days earlier to learn as well. Raul knew that something had happened to her while she was a prisoner in Social Quarantine ... something that she couldn't bear to talk about. The fact that she wanted to learn to protect herself was a good sign. He didn't like to think about what it could have been, and so far she had not opened up to discuss it. In their makeshift gym, Maria sat cross-legged on the floor watching them, taking in every move they made.

Caylee's feet glided back to where she had started. "Keep your focus," she said. "Remember, every attack is a block; every block is an attack." Raul nodded, feeling the beads of sweat forming on his brow as he shifted his stance to adjust for hers.

She came at him, striking like a cobra. With his free hand, he made a fan-like gesture, hitting her forearm and deflecting her knife thrust past him as he stepped forward and off to her flank. His wrist hit her arm hard, moving her blade away as he brought his own knife in, hitting the underside of her thrust arm.

He maneuvered to pull the blade in a fast thrust across the front of her neck, just as she had trained him, but Caylee had changed the routine on the fly, pivoting back towards him. Raul knew he was supposed to gain control of her arm, but in the moment's flurry he lost it. She moved past him, throwing off his footing. His knife barely hit her left breast as he fumbled to get back to a good fighting stance.

Caylee didn't let up. She switched the knife to her left hand and brought it down across his chest diagonally, leaving a blue streak of chalk to mark the cut. Raul went to lunge back at her, but she was low, coming across his groin area with an upward thrust. It was over. He knew that, but he wanted one more stab at her; he lunged downward. She turned, catching it with the thick muscles of her shoulder.

Then, it was as if the attack had never taken place. Caylee rose to a non-combatant stance, checking her arm where he had hit her. "That first cut was perfect. You caught the soft tissue on the underside of the arm. That forced me to switch hands."

"That felt like cheating," he said, grinning and rising to his full height.

"This is a knife fight. People are not going to attack you like we do during training, all smooth and controlled. There is no cheating in a fight to the death."

Looking down he saw the blue line of chalk across his torso and in his groin. "Pretty bad eh?"

"I would have lost a lot of blood and the use of that arm. You would have bled out by now," she said in a very calm tone given the subject. "Chances are I would have survived," she said, double-checking the chalk. "But honestly, if you nicked the artery, we might have both died."

"Not exactly a win," Raul said, brushing his hands over the chalk to remove it.

Caylee tipped her head. "I tend to agree. You are getting better though. Your cut was good. I just happened to have more experience. You will get better." She checked her watch. "It's been an hour and a half; that's enough for now."

"She is very fast," Maria said, handing both of them a towel. "Very precise."

Caylee turned to his sister. "It comes from practice. I learned from two masters of the craft. I am slow compared to them."

Maria eyed her as if to say, *I doubt that.*

Caylee wiped the sweat off of her brow, then turned to Raul. "So how goes Seraphim?" she asked.

Raul lowered his towel. Seraphim was the name he and the former Senator from Texas had chosen for the plan to attempt to rescue prisoners in the Social Quarantine camps that were behind enemy lines. Raul had been enlisted to help lead the effort, mostly because he had liberated a camp at Valley Forge months earlier. That had been easy; he had been simply one of the rescuers. Seraphim was daunting—not as much because of the scale, but because of what the Newmericans were doing in the camps.

Things were changing, and not for the better. Intelligence reports said that the camps were being used as death factories. The prisoners were being worked or starved to death. Conditions had always been atrocious, but in recent weeks, it was clear that the Newmericans had come to think that the best way to deal with their problem prisoners was to simply eliminate them. With each passing day, Raul knew that more people were dead.

"You were right about one thing," he conceded, thinking back to prior discussions on the matter. "This is all about logistics. It's not enough to take out the guards and free the prisoners ... we have to find a way to get them back to safety. Many are going to need medical attention, and some won't be able to walk on their own."

Caylee nodded slowly. "I know. And once you liberate a single camp, the others will accelerate their murder of the prisoners."

Her words hit him as solid as any kick to the stomach, right down to his wincing. "We need to save them all, but no matter how many times I review the information, no matter how many people we bring in to consult on this, we just can't come up with a way to do it on a massive scale."

"Then don't," she said.

Raul cocked his head. "What do you mean?"

"It's a common mistake," she said. "People get drawn into thinking about things on a grand scale. When you do that, it introduces too many problems, some of which are insurmountable. The key may be to think smaller."

"I heard you clearly," Raul countered. "Once we start, they will start killing more of their prisoners."

Caylee's face rarely showed an emotional depth beyond anger and rage, but he saw in her eyes something that was rare—sadness. "I don't like it any more than you do Raul. Think back to when we broke you out of the Supermax. Did we take all of the political prisoners with us? No. We took you and Ted—and we only took Ted because you insisted. If you had tried to push to take any others, I would have said *no*. Why? Because it would have jeopardized the plan to get you out. You knew enough not to ask us to do it."

She paused for a moment, giving him time to remember when she, Andy, Travis, and Charli had pulled off their prison break. He had tried not to think about his time in prison, awaiting a Tribunal and death, but now the memories flooded back. *Why didn't I ask her to take them all?* In that moment he knew the icy cold truth … because it would have put him at risk. Drawing a shallow breath, he looked over at Caylee's eyes again. *Sometime I wish she were wrong more often. This is one of those times.*

"So I must accept that people are going to die because we can't free them all at once?"

"They are dying now. You are focused on the dying. The purpose has never been about that. It has been about those you can save. You need to come to grips with the fact that not everyone can be saved, Raul. We are at war, and people die during wars. That's the reality of how the universe works. No one likes it, but it is reality. The enemy you are going up against is ruthless; they have no boundaries and will take extreme measures once you start this. Andy says it is the nature of revolutionaries to use violence to hold onto power while preaching peace. He's right. I was an operative. I *did* their dirty work. As such, you need to fight for the people you can save and embrace that."

Raul turned and saw Maria, still standing at his side. She nodded to him firmly. "She is right. I was in a camp. I saw how they killed our mother, working her to death. I hate that people may die, but you need to save the ones you can. You *have* to."

Dipping his head slightly, he said nothing for a few moments as he gathered his thoughts. *They are right. It's not what I want, but that doesn't change the fact that it is right.* Convincing Ted would be difficult, but he knew he could do it. *The sooner we start, the more lives we will save. We have to show the world how evil Newmerica really is.*

Carroll, New Hampshire

Su-Hui Zhou felt a sense of dread as he stood in front of the Patio Motor Court looking at the emerging grass out in front of the motel. The warm front that had come through lasted days, melting off a great deal of the thick snow, to the point where grass was starting to poke out defiantly. While he had been assured by the locals that winter was still lurking, the warmth of the sun seemed to confirm that the winter months were coming to an end.

The thaw, however brief, worried him. The Sons of Liberty and the New Hampshire National Guard had been using the winter weather as a willing ally in their struggle against the Newmerican occupation force. Their insurgency had engaged in only a few stand-up battles because the odds had been against them. Most of their attacks were IEDs, sniper attacks, or ambushes of enemy patrols. *Now things will change. No more hiding in the snows ... they will come at us with all they have.*

General Hank Griffiths of New Hampshire National Guard moved to Su-Hui's side; the General was cradling a hot cup of steaming coffee and Su-Hui caught the aroma. The General was a slender man, the same height as Su-Hui, five foot eight at most, hardly imposing at first. While sinewy in build, the General was not physically imposing, but had an air about him that commanded respect. Perhaps it was the way he always stood rigid, as if he were taller. "Winter isn't done with us yet. We sometimes get snows up here as late as May," he said, surveying the vast yard to the old motor court.

"But it is ending," Su-Hui countered. "And with it, the war will change."

"It already has," the General conceded, taking a long, loud sip of his coffee. "Thanks to your venture into New York, the governor there has pulled back a lot of their ground troops that were in New Hampshire. Connecticut has pulled a lot of their force to their border because of fear we will come after them next."

The mention of the raid against the New York National Guard Headquarters outside of Albany was something that Su-Hui and his harasser force were deeply proud of. He had led his mostly Sons of Liberty force to the outskirts of the state capital and had devastated the facilities there. As much as the Truth Reconciliation Committee attempted to downplay the damage done; word had spread, stories were passed on and exaggerated over time. The TRC had paraded out the 'brave guard that had been ambushed by the terrorists,' who talked about the attack and how he had feared for his life. Thinking about him made Su-Hui chuckle ... *I can't believe we forgot about him in the guard shack.* "So you think it won't be as bad as I do, when the weather clears?"

Griffiths shook his head. "It will be worse." The tone of his voice had dropped an octave.

"What should we expect?"

"Our so-called Defiance is something that Newmerica needs to stamp out, or they risk other states rising up against them. Standard military doctrine would call for a surge. Surrounding states may have withdrawn or reduced their National Guard presence, but Newmerica will bring in other forces. These people are demonstrating much in the way of creativity. A lot of regular army troops have chosen sides, which gives them a pool of resource to dip into. We've picked up some, but it is clear that the Pentagon is favoring the Newmericans."

"Then there's their biggest advantage—air power. New York, Vermont, and Connecticut may have withdrawn ground troops, but they can still fly missions against us from the safety of their states."

"Do we have a plan for dealing with this?" Su-Hui asked.

Griffiths cracked a grin, if only for a moment. "We are getting some anti-air defenses smuggled in. I have an idea or two for using them. The ground forces, well, as much as we can, we need to dictate where and when that fight is going to happen. As such, we are moving our heavy armor and support to the White Mountain National Forest. We have built a redoubt there, dug in deep."

Su-Hui had seen the huge forest when he was in Gorham. The huge, rolling mountainous terrain and thick forest would not make for large open areas to fight in. *Maybe that is part of the strategy.* "Will we be going there?" he asked.

Griffiths nodded, taking another long sip of his coffee. "Yes. We'll need you to move discreetly, not on the roads. We've seen a lot more recon work out of the forces that are already in-state. They are looking for us, trying to catch hints of where we might be concentrating, if at all."

It sounds like we are being hunted, which is too close to being true. "The snowmobiles we have are not going to be of much use. We have been outfitting recreational ATVs with gun mounts and racks for carrying gear. The locals are more than willing to donate them to the cause. Combined with the Humvees we have captured, in a few days, we should be able to begin moving out."

The General nodded in response, saying nothing for a few moments. "There's no rush. They haven't figured out that you're here. When you come, bring every bit of your ammo and gear with you. Also, you might want to leave your noncombatants here. This isn't going to be like a raid. When they come, and they will, this will be a full-fledged battle royale." Griffiths turned to him, making sure they were looking each other eye-to-eye.

Su-Hui said nothing for a moment, realizing the gravity of what he was being told. *He's going to lure them up there for the fight ... and he's doing that for a reason.* He didn't want his wife Hachi or any of the other spouses or children in harm's way. They had already been bombarded when the Newmericans attacked their base in Lisbon, and leveled the small town in the process. *I will not put her at risk again.* He knew his wife would resist it, but the gaze in the eyes of General Griffiths told him it was necessary. In the back of his mind, he dreaded the conversation with his wife far more than passing on orders to his resistance cell.

"General," he said in a calm tone, to belie his worst nightmares. "Can we win?"

Griffiths took a long sip of his coffee, no doubt to gather his thoughts on a response. "The war? The coming battle?"

"Yes."

Sighing slightly, he gave a single nod as he responded. "General Reager handed the Newmericans a bloody nose in Knoxville a few weeks ago. They have fallen back to a line from Norfolk to Charlottesville. If we were now in the best position, we would have pushed harder already.

"That raid in Illinois forced them out of Iowa, but they still hold Chicago and Springfield. It was a great operation, and it sure shook them up, but in the end, it's not the kind of ground you want to hold.

"They still hold St. Louis and a chunk of Missouri as an 'autonomous zone,' whatever the hell that is. We have slowed shipments of food into St. Louis to a trickle. New Mexico and Arizona are still a hot-damn-mess, but at least that whole Texas rebellion has resolved itself." Su-Hui had heard about the revolt of several counties in Texas declaring themselves the Republic of Texas. For a while, it looked like it might spread, until it was revealed that they were being propped up by China and Newmerica. That had made many of their supporters lay down the arms. The locals had taken matters in their own hands, locking up the leaders of the rebellion. *The Texans wanted to rule themselves, not be pawns of a foreign government.*

"We are facing this challenge. That is the essence of what it is to be an American, rising to face threats to your way of life. The Newmericans know that if they lose, they will be brought to justice for a lot of their bullshit. Desperation makes people take extreme risks to win. Likewise that drive on Knoxville taught us how fragile the American government is." Su-Hui understood that all too well. *If they had taken Nashville as they had tried to do, the nation's morale would have collapsed.*

"The bottom line is that the war is far from over. When the stakes are high, the risks and dangers rise proportionally."

It was a fair response—without overstating anything; something that Su-Hui appreciated. "And the coming battle?"

The General flashed his grin once more. "New Hampshire has become an ugly embarrassment to the Newmerican government. They want a big damn battle to wipe out the opposition, so they can subjugate the New Hampshirites and punish them for refusing to agree with their election results. As long as New Hampshire is free, it's a problem for them. It tells people that they can resist—and totalitarian regimes cannot allow that kind of thinking."

Pausing for a moment, the General drew a long breath before continuing. "They will come at us with everything they can muster. No quarter asked for or given. We win by not letting them win; and they win by a crushing defeat of our forces—no one getting away to fight another day."

"You have a plan, I take it?"

"I do," he said proudly, finishing off his cup of coffee. "And I am counting on the Sons of Liberty to help us achieve a victory."

"We won't let you down General," Su-Hui said, slightly puffing out his chest.

"You never have," Griffiths replied. "So let's go and review your troops. We have a lot of work ahead of us."

The District

The Vice President of Newmerica had a smirk on her face as she entered the interrogation room in the Department of Homeland Security facility on H Street in the District. The building itself was nondescript, wholly unremarkable—a dull gray façade with no official markings at all, just dull, dark tinted windows and the kind of blandness that one associated with a government structure. She was ushered into the room by her new Secret Service detail. *After they failed to protect me when Becky tried to kill me, I had no use for them.*

She was in the building because of Rebecca Clarke. Becky had been instrumental in the overthrow of the corrupt administration of the Traitor President and the establishment of the Ruling Council. Her control of the Truth Reconciliation Committee made her powerful … and a rival. The Vice President was brutal to anyone posing a threat, either in the present or the future. She had framed her for the fake assassination attempt on the Ruling Council. Becky was supposed to have faced a People's Tribunal, like Senator Lewis before her … but things had quickly gone awry. Becky managed to attack her at one point, something that the VP had used to garner sympathy from the public. Then, before she could face social justice, Becky had taken poison and killed herself. *She cheated me of my moment … and these men are responsible for that.*

The Vice President made a point of looking at the urn with Becky's remains every day. Her political foe was kept on a shelf in her office. Having her former ally cremated and placed in an urn where she could see them gave her as a sense of pride. Taking down Senator Lewis had not been personal, he had merely wanted to pry open the clandestine world of the NSF and make some of it public. Becky was a challenger … someone that might one day pose a true threat to the Vice President's empire that she had carved out of the bureaucracy of Newmerica. *If she was half as smart as she thought she was, she would have tried to take me down earlier.* Just thinking about the urn on her shelf in her office gave her immense satisfaction.

The room had dull gray, foam padding on the walls to cut the sound. The floor of the room was tiled, large squares, with a drain in the center—no doubt used for other means of interrogation. She could smell their commingled sweat in the air … something she had been warned about when she had insisted on seeing the two guards. A pair of DHS personnel, wearing face gaiters, black T-shirts, pants, and boots stood behind the two guards. They too were wet with perspiration.

The Vice President surveyed them as each raised their head on hearing her heels click on the tiled floor. The female guard was missing a spot on her scalp where her dishwater blonde hair had been pulled out—the bloody patch was dried but visible. Her left cheek and lower lip were swollen, no doubt from a blow. Her left eye was surrounded by a large, purple bruise.

The male guard was worse. There were marks on his neck, red gouges surrounded by purple bruises. A piece of his left ear lobe was simply missing. Both eyes were badly bruised, clearly from the bruised and broken nose he had suffered. His nose was still off-kilter with a trickle of blood from both nostrils down to his mouth. The Vice President was not stunned at the sight of the two guards. In fact, she had ordered their brutal interrogations. The DHS was hers to use as she saw fit … it fell under the umbrella of the National Security Force, which she controlled.

I would have thought the waterboarding would work. Both exhausted guards looked at her, seeming to struggle to hold their heads up. Their hands were zip-tied behind them, and when the female saw the VP looking down at her, she seemed to wince. *That's right. I'm here in person.* It wasn't that the Vice President savored seeing people in agony, but she did adore the power that allowed her to command such actions.

For a moment, she looked to the pair of interrogators. "Have either of them admitted their role in the crime?"

The female shook her head. "No Madame Vice President," she said. "Both claim they did not sneak Ms. Clarke the suicide pill."

For a moment she said nothing, but did a slow pace in front of them. "This is most disturbing. We know one of you did it. You were the only ones that could have done it. We have reviewed the videos, and only you two had the opportunity to pass on that poison to Becky."

"I didn't do it," the female said with a cough that followed. "I'm innocent."

"No one is innocent. Innocence is a lie the guilty tell themselves to justify what they have done. I'm sure whichever of you did it thought you were doing the right thing. I'm sure you have convinced yourself that it was for the better that the tribunal did not fully expose Becky's treason. Maybe you tell yourself that you're some sort of patriot. I don't know, and I don't care. I simply want to know which of you did it, and I want to know who else might be involved."

The man spoke, and when he did, she could see two freshly broken teeth. His gums were still crimson with blood from the blow he had taken. "I would never betray the country. I've been part of Newmerica from the start."

"So was Becky Clarke," she snapped. "That didn't prevent her from trying to seize power and broker some sort of deal with the Americans." The lie flowed across her lips without a hint of regret.

"I didn't do anything wrong," the male sputtered as the female sobbed. A bubble of snot formed under her right nostril.

The VP turned to the interrogators. "I'm very disappointed that you have not gotten either of them to admit their complicity. Clarke's suicide denied our people the justice they deserved. They needed to see the evidence against her."

"We are both sorry, Madam Vice President," the male interrogator said. "They have both stuck to their stories, despite our best efforts."

"Clearly this is not your best effort," she countered quickly. "This is a fairly simply matter. The guilty party simply needs to admit their wrongdoing. You would think that all of our experience in torturing people would have gotten us further than this."

The female interrogator spoke next. "Some people are so committed to their beliefs and their cause that it is impossible to break them. There are, alternatives that we can pursue."

"Go on."

"Both of them have family and friends. True believers, people committed to their cause, will often weather physical and emotional pain. When they see it done to people that they care about, well, that is a different matter altogether."

I like her, she is creative. "Then by all means do that. Let's round up their mothers or fathers, whoever they care about."

"No!" the female guard flexed against her restraints, still unable to move. "My family hasn't done anything!"

The Vice President bent down in front of her, reaching out and lifting her chin so she could look her in the eyes. "If you are indeed innocent, then you had better hope that your partner here admits his guilt quickly." She released the woman and glared over at the man who worked hard to avoid looking at her.

"We will need some written authorization to do that," the male interrogator said. "They are being treated as domestic terrorists. If we start bringing in people that had nothing to do with this, it can create some legal messes that I don't think any of us want."

I AM the law! That was what she wanted to say. Working with Social Enforcement was so much easier. They didn't whine about due process, people's rights, or other meddlesome things; they simply took action. While she had maneuvered to have Social Enforcement roll up under the NSF, she was reluctant to include them in this matter. While they were effective, they could be sloppy at times. "You want something in writing? Something that you can use to cover your ass? Very well. You'll have it before I leave here."

His face reddened at her crisp words and tone. "It's not like that at all. We just need to do this right," the male interrogator said.

"Understand this clearly. You will get your little piece of paper. In exchange for that, I want results. I want a confession from whoever usurped our social justice. If that means a little torture on the part of their families or friends, so be it.

"But," she said looking at both of the DHS interrogators with an icy stare. "If I don't get what I expect, then you may find yourself in those chairs, with your replacements standing over your beaten forms." With that, she pivoted in place and marched out of the room.

CHAPTER 2

"Everyone has a duty to support the state.
Some duties are greater than others."

Mt. Carmel, Tennessee

General Trip Reager took a seat next to his lawyer in the makeshift courtroom as the judge advocate entered. The Mt. Carmel Tennessee National Guard Armory was a relatively new facility, and the big conference room that had been taken over for his hearing was much nicer than most facilities that he was accustomed to. It had not been designed for court proceedings, with its big conference table and dull green carpeting. A part of Trip was embarrassed that he was even in the hearing in the first place. He was thankful that it wasn't a public courtroom, where the media would have been tracking every twitch of his eye.

The judge advocate, a colonel, was at least a decade older than Trip. The judge advocate wore a perfectly trimmed, white goatee. He banged the gavel once. The corporal standing as bailiff spoke loudly and clearly as he said, "All rise."

"At ease," the judge advocate said, and Trip took his seat at the end of the reddish wood table that dominated the room. Trip remained standing with his lawyer who stood beside him on the side of the table near the draped windows. The trial counsel, the prosecutor in the case, a young red-headed captain, was poised on the other side facing Trip. He glanced at the young officer, and despite his rigid demeanor, he could tell that the trial counsel was nervous … a bead of sweat showed near his sideburn. *No doubt he's wondering if prosecuting the commanding General is good for his career.*

The Article 15 Hearing was not as career crippling as a full court martial, but it still had serious ramifications. Article 15s were designed for these situations where senior officers had violated the Uniform Code of Military Justice. There was quick dispensation of justice without long-term damage to an officer's career.

Trip wasn't worried about his career. He had been put in command of the American Army and had been fighting a vicious civil war for months. There had been victories, but they had come at a cost in terms of human lives. Even if he were busted down to private, he would continue to fight. *The Newmericans destroyed my business and split my family apart. They are owed this.*

"General Reager, you have been charged with conduct unbecoming an officer. How do you plead?"

"Guilty," Trip said firmly. It had been negotiated in advance with the judge advocate. Trip had been accosted by a reporter named Pat Templeton, in Nashville, and he had punched her … hard. Of course she had sued him, but the case had been thrown out because the reporter had actually profited from her taunting him and goading him into hitting her. Her ratings had soared, and she had landed a book deal, which had demolished her claims that she had 'suffered' as a result of their confrontation. The Newmerican media had wailed that it had been a miscarriage of justice, that it was proof of America's corrupt legal system, but Trip had ignored those cries. *She benefited from me hitting her and everyone knows it.*

That had left the military for her to extract her justice. Trip could have been court martialed for losing his temper; he knew that. By the same token, he had liked hitting her. *She brought up my daughter and got decked as a result.*

The judge advocate looked over the case file for a moment, flipping silently through the paperwork. He then turned to the trial counsel. "Does the prosecution have a recommendation for sentencing?"

"Yes, your honor," the red-headed captain replied. "We recognize that Genera Reager's role in the current conflict is vital and do not wish to see the war effort damaged as a result of these proceedings. As such we recommend that the defendant's wages be garnished for a period of not more than six months."

The judge advocate turned to Trip and his lawyer. "This court concurs with this sentencing guideline. General Reager, you are first and foremost an officer in the United States Army. Your actions of punching that reporter were undignified and beneath your standing as a General. It is my hope that this punishment serves as a reminder to you as to the role you serve in representing the service of our nation."

"It does your honor," Trip said.

"And I trust that the General will apologize to the civilian in question?"

That was a twist Trip hadn't anticipated. He felt his face go red with embarrassment. *Apologize? That is destined to be a media shit-show! She should be apologizing to me.* The thought of facing the reporter again was cringe-worthy, but a quick glance at his lawyer only got a single slow nod in response. "I will your honor," he said flatly—realizing there was no real alternative.

"Very well, then these proceedings are concluded," the judge advocate replied, dropping his gavel again. Trip thanked his lawyer and gave a courtesy nod to the opposing trial counsel, as if to say, 'You did your duty.' That got him a return nod from the captain.

Outside the doors, his intelligence officer, Captain Paul Harnessy, made eye contact with him and entered the room, passing the judge advocate on the way in. Once they were alone, with the doors closed, Harnessy moved in close. "General," he said.

"Paul, you usually don't just show up. I trust you have some news."

He nodded. "Yes sir. General Rinehart showed his face just an hour ago."

Since the Battle for Knoxville over a week earlier, the Newmerican commanding General had been quiet. There had even been rumors that he might have been killed in the retreat back in central Virginia. "So he made it out alive. What did he have to say?"

"His press briefing was short. He maintained the lies that the TRC has been putting out—that the thrust into Knoxville was a diversionary attack—one that had gone exactly as planned. He denied that we had taken parts of southern Virginia; he claimed that our forces were insurgent cells, not the regular army."

The lies of the Truth Reconciliation Committee were always

entertaining, a twisted perception of the nation. Their spin was that Newmerica could do no wrong—that the war was going just as planned—that they were winning. *Sadly, most of their people believe them ... probably because they are telling them what they want to hear.* "Did he say anything useful?"

"California is raising a 'volunteer veteran corps,' which may point to some activity in the west. When he got a planted question about the so-called insurgency in New Hampshire, he assured the media that 'the New Hampshire issue would be resolved in a matter of weeks.' He followed that with, 'the usual traitors and terrorists would be dealt with harshly.'"

Trip admired that Harnessy didn't have to consult his iPad to rattle off the quotes. "As we expected, an early spring surge."

"Yes sir."

New Hampshire had been a meat grinder for the Newmerican occupation forces. Trip and his people assumed that the enemy would surge when the weather began to clear. He had been in contact with General Griffiths and had approved of his plan for fighting that engagement, but he knew that the forces in New Hampshire were going to need some help. *That's where Major Mercury comes in. The enemy will want to deliver a hammer blow, and we need to blunt that.* "We will need to get more arms, some Javelins, in there. Any chance of that?"

"The surrounding states have reinforced their borders, especially after that strike on the New York National Guard HQ. Patrols have increased. It's possible, but tricky and slow. We have a number of owners of small aircraft that are loyal to America. They have been making runs over the border, coming in below radar and landing on roads rather than at airports, bringing in equipment and ammunition. It's slow, but it's happening."

They have been forced into creative solutions—a measure of how desperate the fight to come was bound to be. "The more forces Griffiths can tie up on the border, the less they have for their surge."

"Agreed. Word from the west is that now that this Republic of Texas thing is over, the locals are starting to patrol and defend the border with New Mexico. There are reports of some skirmishes in several spots."

"Any sign of a troop buildup?"

Harnessy nodded. "Some. Some SE volunteer units have been

deployed to the border, not to mention some positioning of units of their national guard. Word from civilian intelligence sources say that California is preparing to send some forces there. The Arizonians are mad as hell about it, so they blocked the highways forcing them to resort to aircraft for transport. The enemy is 'leasing' assets from the Air Force, flying sorties out of Cannon Air Force Base, which is troublesome."

"We haven't got a lot to toss into a new front in this war. Our refitting from Knoxville is going to take a few more weeks, and the Southern Virginia lines are stretched thin in the meantime. Set up some time with General Stinson of the Oklahoma National Guard and Roger Hash of the Kansas Guard. We are going to need them to deploy to the New Mexico border, just in case the Newmericans decide to press the matter."

"Yes sir," Harnessy said. "Anything else?"

"Tell Major Mercury she better get her plans pulled together and fast. The enemy has suffered some losses, and they need a reversal. I don't expect them to give us a lot of breathing room … I wouldn't do it with them. New Hampshire is vulnerable, so I expect them to hit there … hard." New Hampshire, New Mexico, Iowa … the war was everywhere, and it felt as if everyone needed his time and attention. *We've been lucky so far ... but how long can that luck hold?*

Mt. Diablo, California

To Darius Thorne, the California Volunteer Veteran Corps was an utter contradiction in terms. There was no 'volunteering' involved, other than the name. Their recruiters had come to the Tiny Town that Darius and many other veterans called home, and had told them that their food and medical cards would be revoked if they didn't volunteer. *What choice did I really have?* To him, it was the California Blackmail Corps. Like the majority of the veterans that were living in the Tiny Town, formerly called Veteran Rehabilitation Camp #43, they signed up … not so much out of loyalty to the state government, but to simply not put their health and welfare at risk. The FedGov liked to say they were all volunteers, but in reality, their joining had been an act of extortion. It reminded him of the COVID days and the mandates to take the vaccine. *Personal freedoms mean nothing to petty tyrants who seek to impose their will. It was never about the vaccine, it was all about the control ... the ability to force people to do something that they were opposed to.*

It was all perfectly normal in California, Newmerica. Right after the Ruling Council had come to power, they had "restructured" how veterans' benefits were paid. It was a nice way to say that they had been cut, replaced with stuff. Free cell phones, clothing allowances, even government cheese took the place of real money. He did better than most. Under the Freedom Scale for pay, he got points for being black; his years of service; his "homing challenged" status. Everyone knew that the compensation levels were not fair, but no one heard the voices of those impacted. *Little did I know that those were the good times of the Ruling Council's reign.*

At first, the Veteran Corps wasn't like real military duty. Yes, there were uniforms, made in Thailand, a dull, tan color to avoid confusing them with the regular army. Their only saving grace was that they were free and hid the dirt fairly well. Their food was mediocre at best. Meat was replaced with plant protein substitutes that were, in his opinion, the equivalent of Grade D meat. California loved to dictate terms on people's lives—everything from what food you ate to where you could live. *At least they aren't shoving roach burgers down my throat.*

The officers were of the National Guard variety, young men and women sent in to "whip the vets back into shape." Calisthenics had been a train wreck. It wasn't just a matter of the men and women being out of shape ... which many were. There was no drive, no motivation. Threats made to young kids who had never seen a day in real combat fell on deaf ears. The only thing that seemed to motivate some was the threat of not being fed. Desertion was rampant in the first few weeks, but the NSF showed themselves to be adept at rounding up those that tried to flee the service. The vocal leaders of the resistance were removed—what happened to them was still a mystery. It was presumed they were tucked away in penal units or shipped off to Social Quarantine camps.

Slowly the men and woman were worn down and started to fall into a more military routine. His unit, Bravo Company of the Third Veteran Corps had good people in the ranks. Vixen, an Hispanic woman in Bravo, had been a Humvee driver in Iraq and got wounded twice in battle. She had been in rehab twice fighting the heroin demon. Lucius had been a gunner in a Bradley fighting vehicle, unable to hold down a decent job because of PTSD. Now he served as the company clown, quick with witty and biting commentary on just about anything. Justin, who went by the nickname Fax, didn't talk about his service, just about his drug addiction and his hatred of the Marine Corps where he had served. The State of California made sure he had access to "drug supplements" which were just state-manufactured meth in tiny doses. Fax was barely functional as a member of the unit, but he showed up which, in the Veteran Volunteer Corps, counted for something.

Their days were filled with drilling, which came back to Darius far too quickly. They worked with their weapons, which consisted mostly of NSF confiscated AR 15s, part of the 'Disarming of Newmerica' program. Darius was lucky; his weapon was in good condition from the start. Vixen's was a hodge-podge of parts and jammed despite her having the Corps armorer work on it several times. The veterans tended to get the shoddiest of equipment, which did not bode well if they were ever called up for action. When that came up, the commanding officer's response was a five-mile run for the company.

Captain Lauren Aguilar, the company commander, ordered the unit to assemble. Their camp site was dominated by Mt. Diablo just forty miles east of San Francisco. The park had fairly inhospitable terrain and as Darius moved out, a gust of breeze hit him with dust, which stuck to the sweat on his skin. That was part of living in the park—the constant dust, the hot days, and the cold nights. Captain Aguilar stood in front of them, with a fresh set of tan fatigues and a cold, passionless look on her olive-skinned face.

"We have gotten our first assignment," Captain Aguilar announced proudly. "We are deploying shortly to the Presidio. A group of squatters, housing disenfranchised, have set up a camp there. Their presence there is causing some problems, so we are going to clear them out. We are going in with the NSF to help relocate them to a Tiny Town. The NSF has tried before with these folks, but they are apparently unwilling to cooperate."

"How many are we talking about sir?" Vixen asked from the second rank of troops.

"Estimates vary," the captain replied. "Upwards of five hundred, maybe more. They have built themselves a little community there. The locals are complaining about the crime issues they cause, so action is called for. We are going to tear down their little makeshift town and get them out of there."

Fax spoke up from behind him. "Captain, why not send in the SEs?"

Darius knew the answer even before the captain's politically correct response: "Simply put, they are absolving themselves of that duty. The governor believes this will be a good test of the Veteran's Corps. That means the job falls to us."

Darius heard the words and cringed. It was a lie, contrived for the media. The truth was that social enforcers often profited from their actions. When a family was shipped off to Social Quarantine, they would enrich themselves with what the family left behind. Often times the house itself would be taken over by an SE or a family member. They kept the cars and sold off whatever they could to make some side-cash from their action. With a Tiny Town and an 'economically displaced' homeless population, there wasn't any profit to be made. *Why risk themselves for zero gain? It's easier to send us in to do the dirty work.*

He had been forced to live in a Tiny Town and understood why people didn't want to live in them. The state government built villages of tiny houses, believing that people that were labeled 'shelter-dependent' simply needed a place to stay. In a matter of weeks the Tiny Town becomes a dump. *A typical government program ... applying the wrong solution to the wrong problem.* The problem with most of the homeless wasn't that they didn't have a place to live; there were plenty of shelters with space. Many of them had drug issues, or were suffering from mental illness, or lacked the skills to operate in normal society. Putting them in compact homes on top of each other changed nothing. Garbage piled up; several units burned down; fights were common—and the drug use didn't diminish; it actually increased. *Now they want us to go in and inflict the same shit on these people.* Darius cringed at that thought.

"Are we going in with weapons?" asked Jaxson, a Private in the front rank of the company..

Captain Aguilar nodded. "The last time the NSF went in, there was some bloodshed—so we go in armed. We will load up non-lethals but carry full live ammo if things get out of hand."

Jaxon smiled at that response. He liked violence far too much for Darius's taste. *That ass will enjoy this far too much,* Darius thought.

As the company dismissed and went back to their tents to rest and prepare, the others talked about what they might be facing. Some of the troops were nervous, but most had seen combat before and worked with steely resolve. Darius said nothing as he stripped his weapon, carefully checking to make sure it was clean and fully operational. Where a few of his comrades were wondering if there would be a fight, Darius knew there would be bloodshed. *They wouldn't be bringing us in if the NSF could handle this. They want to keep their hands clean of what is coming. They want us to do it so that if things go south, they won't be blamed.*

"You're being damned quiet since assembly," Lucius said as he shouldered a weapon.

"I got forced out of a camp and put into a Tiny Town," Darius said. "I don't have fond memories of that. We aren't doing these folks any favors. Giving them a new place to live won't solve their problems, it just creates new ones." His mind momentarily went to his former partner, William. When he pictured the last time he saw William's face, his brain cut off that memory, pushing it down into the recesses of his mind.

"We're helping law enforcement."

Darius shook his head once. "Don't kid yourself. We're doing their dirty work for them. These people haven't done anything wrong. They are on the street because that is where a lot of them belong. They're only real crime is living in a place that is inconvenient for the locals."

"We have to do it. We are in the army."

"We are in *an* army, not *the* Army. I got forced into enlisting, and I know you did too. We are being used. The moment you forget that, you become part of the problem—you know what I am saying?"

Lucius paused. "I've been played by the man most of my life. This isn't any different. At least I get three squares a day and a roof over my head."

Darius glanced at the tent above him that served as their home. "I'm here because I don't have a choice. What we do out there—I *will* have control. Don't let yourself be part of the problem Lucius. Some of these others … they are going to fall back on their darker habits once this shit goes down. This isn't some Iraqi insurgent you are going up against. These are people just like you and me."

Lucius nodded as they finished. Darius dreaded what was coming.

Nashville, Tennessee

Charli Kasinzki woke up with a jerk. The T-shirt she slept in was soaked in sweat. In her head were only bits and fragments of what had jarred her awake. She had been reliving her bombing of the NSF facility in Virginia months ago. Swinging her legs over the edge of the bed, she sat up for a moment, taking long, deep breaths trying to lower her blood pressure.

Andy Farmer stirred next to her. "You OK?" he asked wearily.

"Just a nightmare," she said, half-lying. It wasn't just a nightmare—the nightmare was one of the symptoms of her PTSD. She had gone to counseling over it, but she felt like it didn't help.

Charli carried a lot of burdens from the last half-decade. At the time, the life decisions she made came with little guilt. Now, as time passed, the weight of that guilt seemed to grow, chewing at her sleep, sowing it with nightmares. The list of deeds she did in the name of freedom was long.

The worst of those actions had been when Jack Desmond asked her to bomb an NSF facility, killing hundreds in a matter of seconds. Other acts were her choice. For years she had been fighting her own war against the Newmericans. Posing as an NSF officer, she did what was necessary to set things right. There was the man who lost his wife to an SE gang—Charli had shot two of their members with a sniper rifle—swift and clean retribution. She had set fire to the house of a rapist who had been released with no bail for what he'd done. Charli had avenged the brutal rape and assault on a young girl named Zhou by killing three members of the SEs that had assaulted her. When several fellow officers were hauled off by social enforcers, Charli/Angel dealt out brutality either with her bare hands, or with the end of a gun. Justice came in a lot of forms, and Charli often simply created her own justice with icy precision.

The problem was it came back at her in the form of nightmares causing constant tossing and turning, and stress. Andy sensed it, sitting up in bed and putting his arm around her. "Same nightmare?"

She shrugged. "I can't be sure. There's a boom and I wake up."

He pulled her a little closer. "You did what you had to do," he said. "We're at war. That is one of the universal truths about war, or so my dad used to say. "Wars mean people die—some more innocent than others.""

Charli said nothing for a moment. "Your dad was pretty smart."

"He would have loved you," Andy replied, stretching slightly as he came more awake. "He was a patriot, and so are you. Dad always had a soft spot for true believers in the cause of freedom."

"I don't call myself a patriot. It feels awkward, old-timey. For a long time, I was just a vigilante, striking back at the people that went after innocents. I don't think that makes me a patriot."

"Righting wrongs, making sure real justice happens—that seems patriotic to me. Think about this, every Founding Father knew when they signed the Declaration of Independence that war was coming. They knew that people were going to suffer and die. The Founders had to have known there'd be bloodshed. They also knew that if they failed, *they* would be strung up by the British as traitors. Still, in the end, not a single one of them hesitated to put their name on the document."

"I'm more of a foot soldier," Charli countered. "Jack's the true patriot. He held together the Sons of Liberty, found the VP alive, and restored him as president. I'm just the Secret Service Director—a glorified bodyguard for the biggest target on the continent."

Andy offered a smirk in response. "You took a bullet for the previous President. If you hadn't done what you did, they would have put him in a kangaroo court and humiliated him in front of the world. You focus too much on the negative stuff, the things you had to do. You saved this President's life. That operative that tried to blow him up, you took that guy down. You're not a glorified bodyguard; you are a part of this. Look at what we did with breaking Raul out of the Supermax. That was bona fide action hero shit. More importantly, I think you have a bigger role to play."

"What makes you say that?"

Andy shrugged. "A suspicion—a hunch; a gut feeling. Look at our circle of friends. Raul—a freedom fighter; Caylee—an operative; Travis—a former SEAL; Jack—the Chief of Staff; Ted—an ex-Senator. I mean seriously, we run with a group that practically draws in trouble and deals with it. I believe that the universe brings together the right people for the right cause. It can't be coincidence. And you—you are built to handle the pressure that comes with your calling."

She smiled thinking of their friends and soaking in the words. She slid her arm around him and pulled him even tighter to her supple torso.

"I don't deserve you."

"I like to think that you do," he chuckled. "We will get through this like we do everything—together. Whatever it takes."

"Whatever it takes," she echoed.

The District

Thiago Reese entered the Newmerican Vice President's office walking so that his footsteps barely made noise on the polished hardwood floor. The knit polo shirt he wore was stretched under his chest and arm muscles. He wore an inexpensive, generic, navy blue sport coat. It had been recommended that he dress professionally, but he wasn't going to put on a tie for anyone—even the VP.

She sat behind her desk, barely looking up as his escort peeled off and left her guest. Her fingers furiously stabbed at her keyboard. She gestured to the chair opposite her desk without even looking up, and he moved in front of her, taking the chair. It was deliberately lower than most guest chairs, clearly some sort of subliminal intimidation on the part of the Vice President. Reese was unimpressed. He'd seen the ploy before, from people that had just as frightening a reputation as the VP.

As she finished her work on the computer, he allowed himself a glance around her office. Opposite his desk was a shelving unit of deep walnut. There was an urn on the top shelf. He had researched the Vice President as much as anyone that he ever was called in front of. *Her mother and brother are buried at Arlington ... so who's in the urn?* He would have to do some more digging to ferret out that nugget of information.

Turning back towards her he saw that she had set aside her wireless keyboard and was in the process of sliding her Chopard glasses up on her nose. "Mr. Reese," she said, clearly eyeing him as if he were a slab of meat. "Thank you for coming by."

"The pleasure is all mine ma'am," he said.

"Use Madam Vice President when addressing me. It's a little more fitting," she corrected him—another power play.

"Very well, Madam Vice President."

"I presume you know why I have asked you to meet with me."

"I have a fairly good idea. My specialty is destabilizing and toppling foreign governments." He wasn't bragging. He had been a disrupter; that was the title that the CIA gave him, for years. In the occupied part of the Ukraine, he had turned half of the government against itself, much to the chagrin of the Russian occupiers. He had been the force behind the overthrow of the Venezuelan government two years earlier, in what looked like a popular uprising and coup. Brazil—that had been outright fun for him. Thiago was proud of his work around the globe.

"I've been told you have a gift for this kind of work."

The VP had been part of the overthrow of the original American government, so she came to the subject with experience. "It is as much of an art form as a process. Yes, I have a knack for success in that realm."

"The target I want you to go for is obvious. The resurgence of America out of Nashville has become intolerable. This charade of theirs needs to be brought to an end. From what I hear, you are the right person for the job."

The moment they had summoned him to meet with her, he suspected that the Pretender President's government would be his target. "Their victories of late had given them momentum."

"Minor setbacks," she responded.

She is downplaying how bad it is Reese thought.

"You sent an assassin to kill the Pretender," he said bluntly, more to measure her reaction than anything else. "It is a bit of a classic mistake, if I may say so. In doing that, your failed attempt has made him a sympathetic figure. People love an underdog, someone who is defying the odds. Surviving an attempt to kill him had solidified his support."

"Killing him would have killed his cause," she said, crossing her arms.

"It might have. It might have given his supporters greater resolve." Reese paused for a moment. "Have you ever played chess?"

His question caught her off guard but only for a moment. "Yes, I think so. When I was a kid. Why, is it relevant?"

"It is. Your assassination attempt was an attempt to take out the king."

"Isn't that the goal?"

Reese gave her a slight shrug before continuing. "Ultimately, yes. But in chess, the most powerful piece is not the king. He is a goal, an objective. The most powerful piece is the queen. Taking out the queen leaves a player devoid of their most powerful asset. It often sets the course for the rest of the game."

"So you propose to take out the queen?"

"In a sense, yes."

"So who is the queen?"

"Jack Desmond."

"The Chief of Staff? That's a glorified secretarial role. He's a troubleshooter, yes, but I don't think of him as a power player. He's never even held a political appointee position before now."

"You think too much like someone who works in the FedGov. The title means nothing. Jack Desmond is the brains behind the Sons of Liberty. He was responsible for finding the former VP and getting him sworn in on national television. He was behind the selection of General Reager for his role. Desmond is the real power behind the throne. If he is taken out of the game, it leaves their President without his most trusted advisor. In many respects, it leaves them blind."

She said nothing, which meant she was contemplating his words. She templed her fingers in front of her on the desktop, then spoke. "So you intend to kill Desmond."

"Desmond needs to die, yes. The key with these sorts of acts, however, is to not simply kill him. His death needs to implicate someone else, another person in the administration. You see, to topple most governments, it isn't about the killing—that comes later. What is more important is to pit their leaders against each other. Let them accuse and point fingers and place blame on each other. If you want to make a government impotent, erode the people's trust in it. It hamstrings the support of the people. They are reminded that they cannot fully trust their leaders or the government itself. Their infighting will consume any morale burst they got from their recent battlefield victories. We need to get people questioning their leaders once more, wondering if there is a greater deception in play. Distrust. Lack of confidence in the people in charge—these are the things that initiate the fall of governments."

The Vice President looked at him and cracked a wicked little grin. "How long will it take?"

"Weeks, months … maybe more."

"We need something faster."

"I cook as a hobby. One thing I learned a long time ago: You can't rush a soufflé. It takes as long as it takes. If you want it faster, I can suggest other personnel for this op. They won't be as effective as I am, but you will get some results that may or may not meet your goals. If you want me, you need to give me time to do what I do."

"If you are captured, there can be no ties to me," she said. "This has to look as if their government has collapsed on its own."

"I understand the rules of the game. My only concern is that this is above the CIA's mandate. This is a domestic affair. We are only able to operate against foreign threats."

"This *thing* called America is a foreign government," she countered.

"From your perspective, that is the case. Others might not feel that way."

"I can have you made an operative in the NSF. The NSF is not burdened with such technicalities of the law."

It made sense to him. "That sounds reasonable."

"Good. I will ensure your transfer is made immediately. Understand this, Mr. Reese, if you are successful, I promise that you and your family will never need to concern yourself with wealth. Newmerica takes care of those that are loyal to the cause. If you fail, however, there is no hole deep enough for you to hide in."

He ignored the threat. *She talks about family—I have so very little of it left. She thinks money alone motivates me. It is useful, but I am more focused on the thrill. A chance to take down something truly historic. This is a challenge that is worthy of me.* "I haven't failed yet."

"Very well," she finally said. "You claim to be a cook. Then fire up your oven and begin mixing your ingredients. Our people are hungry for a victory."

CHAPTER 3

"If you expect less, you will receive more."

Littleton, New Hampshire

The tiny burg of Littleton was nestled to a hillside. One side of the main street was on the upward slope; the other on the downslope. The stately buildings were quaint, old twentieth century structures, some far older than that, with stone and woodwork that looked like they came off of a New Hampshire postcard. From Su-Hui's vantage point, many looked like they had started their life as cottages that had been added to over time and slowly converted into contemporary homes. It was the kind of place he thought about living in before the war.

He crouched behind a tombstone of the Dell's Park Cemetery with several other members of his Sons of Liberty team. At the intersection of Farr Hill Road and Main Street, there was a vehicle convoy consisting mostly of Maine National Guard troops, but with a mix of Maryland, and Massachusetts troops as well. One truck had the markings of the Michigan National Guard. They had paused their convoy in the road, fanning out and securing a perimeter—apparently waiting for more forces to arrive or for some other reason. He eyed them cautiously with his binoculars, noting that some vehicles had made the transition from the white camouflage of winter to the dull green and brown digital woodland patterns. Another winter squall was expected. Mother Nature rarely released New Hampshire from her icy grip so soon, but the snows were far less frequent and the air temperatures were creeping upwards.

They had found the route of the convoy thanks to basic signals intel. The Newmericans were sloppy when it came to hiding the signals they broadcast. Soldiers were using their cell phones, and the spikes by cell tower showed their route. Even with frequency hopping gear Su-Hui's people had used homemade Yagi antenna and had triangulated the convoy's path.

It was tempting to push forward an attack, but his mission was one of observation. Littleton was only a few miles from his base in Carroll. General Griffiths had asked him to reconnoiter the enemy, conduct surveillance—not attack unless it was deemed advantageous. That had been left to his discretion. The temptation was there for Su-Hui, and he knew that the others were bound to be feeling the same way.

A few minutes passed as the MPs took over traffic control. Then he saw it, a long convoy snaking in from the west. Trucks, Humvees, towed trailers; all were in tight formation. Local traffic was stopped, and were routed up Farr Hill Road heading north. As they turned, he could see that many were filled with ammo crates, where others were loaded with infantry and support troops huddled in the back of the vehicles. "Count them by type and what you can see in them," he said to Trudy, the burly northern Michigan woman who had proved herself quite adept in the Sons of Liberty operations. She nodded and made tick marks with a pencil on a small pad of paper.

"That's a shitload of trucks," she muttered as she worked.

"That," he replied softly, "is what a surge looks like."

"You don't say," she quipped with heavy sarcasm. "Pisses me off that some of them are from my home state. For the record, I don't like it. You get the distinct feeling that they intend to kill us."

"That's their plan."

"I hate their plan, chief."

We all do. He squinted through the binoculars and could see that the troops were deploying on a small piece of pasture about a half-mile up the road. "It doesn't look like they are deploying to move against us," he muttered, more to himself than to Trudy.

"Still, they're awfully damn close to our base," she replied.

She spoke a bitter truth. By roads, it was twenty miles to their base in Carroll. If they went cross country, it was even shorter. *Could they be staging here for a thrust directly against us?* That was something he didn't want to contemplate, but was forced to. He knew that his force were irregulars. The Sons and Liberty excelled at hit and run attacks, ambushes, and raids. Individually, the troops had skills, and many were veterans, so there was some experience in his ranks. They were not trained in straight-up infantry assault tactics … not to the extent of the National Guard.

The biggest advantage he could see was that they were a mix of National Guard units. Coordinating them would be tricky, but they had leaders that would sort that out. Su-Hui felt comfortable that they were not deploying to assault his force immediately, but that time might not be too far in the future.

As he watched them fan out in the pasture, some already pulling out tents and setting them up, he wondered if they even knew where his SOL teams were. Both sides lacked military satellite intelligence. The Regular Army had sidelined itself in the civil war. *Their perimeter security would be a lot tighter if they knew we were so close.*

The last of the convoy slowed to a stop at the intersection. It was taking time to move vehicles into their new camp location. The six trucks extended out on Main Street, stopped, belching diesel fumes as they waited to make the slow turn up Farr Hill Road. Leaning back behind the tombstone, he lowered his binoculars and glanced over at Trudy.

"You know," Trudy whispered from behind two grave markers that concealed her and Su-Hui. "We have two IEDs at that intersection. Two phone calls, and I can seriously fuck up these guy's afternoon."

It was tempting to give her the word, but he held himself in check. "Trudy, they have a lot of troops here. You set that off right now, and they will fan out fast to find us. They have the numbers on their side."

"They have had the numbers on their side since the beginning," she reminded him.

"True. I merely have no desire to get caught."

"I can trigger them once we are a few miles away. Will that work for ya?" Her unique Upper-Peninsula-of-Michigan accent came through at the end of her question.

"Yes, that will be much better."

He gave the word for the recon team to pack up. Crouching low, they moved between the weather-stained stone and granite markers to the back of the cemetery and into the surrounding woods. About a half mile away, they uncovered their ATVs from where they had been hidden and started them. Su-Hui led the trio of vehicles through the woods, up hills and across muddy creeks that were still clogged with snow and ice.

After several minutes, he reached a thinly wooded hilltop that barely gave him a view of the intersection, and only then when he stood on the seat of his ATV. Between the pine boughs, he could see the intersection through the binoculars, over a mile out. The convoy had only advanced by a truck length. Two local vehicles were being held back from the intersection by an MP, his white gloves stood out at this distance. One local was backing up and turning around as he squinted at the progression.

The chance of injuring the civilians was low … he knew where the explosives were planted. That had been one hallmark of the Sons of Liberty—they had avoided causing harm to innocents whenever possible. The enemy had no issues with civilian casualties, and that had led to more people supporting the Defiance against the Newmericans.

"Alright Trudy, you wanted to mess them up … now would be the time," he said lowering his binoculars and turning to her.

She flashed a wicked grin and pulled out her burner cell phone. Her sausage-like fingers pulled up the number and she stabbed at the dial button.

The delay was agonizingly long—it always was. Suddenly there was a distant crack and booming sound. It was enough to stir some birds into flight in the trees above them. Su-Hui once more looked out at the convoy. One truck was on its side and ablaze. The bodies of two guardsmen lay on the pavement. Two other trucks were on fire. Troops were struggling to climb out of the vehicles.

Then the second explosion came, just up Far Hill Road. Two trucks were flipped; one fell on the troops that had just deployed out of them; black, oily smoke rolled skyward in a churning ball. From the first blast site, there was a secondary explosion that went off as ammunition on board the toppled truck exploded. Shrapnel erratically blasted outward, taking down at least three more of the Newmerican infantry.

A glance at the camp showed a flurry of activity. Troops assumed defensive positions, weapons at the ready. A pair of Humvees rushed down the snow-covered, grassy side of the road, heading towards the site of their attack.

The troops still alive in the intersection fanned out quickly, to their credit—forming a circular perimeter. Three of them moved into the graveyard where Su-Hui and his people had been just a few minutes earlier. Spreading out made them less of a target if there was another blast. They were huddling behind trees, mailboxes, anything that would provide cover. Clearly they anticipated a follow-up assault.

In a strange way, he admired them. They were moving quickly and professionally. They had come from their homes to New Hampshire, no doubt fueled with the propaganda from the TRC about the resistance. Now they found themselves facing war on the terms of the Sons of Liberty. He climbed down as another explosion went off from a burning truck.

"Let's roll back to Carroll," he said. "We need to redeploy from there. They will come looking for who did this, and I have no desire to hand them when they want."

Nashville, Tennessee

Raul stood over the massive poster-size aerial photograph of Social Quarantine Camp NM028 that Ted had laid out before him. "It looks like very rugged ground," Raul said as he eyed the camp.

Ted stroked his gray beard as he circled the table and glared down at the same image. "The Santa Fe National Park is very isolated. I went hiking there once decades ago." There was a longing in his voice, perhaps remembering better times when recreation was possible.

Andy Forrest stood next to Raul with his arms crossed. "When you look at this image, something doesn't look right. What is that big area outside of the camp?" He pointed to a blackish, dark green blob that covered acres.

"Unknown," Ted conceded. "There are trucks; it looks like they're dumping whatever that stuff is."

"So what is the factory for?" Raul asked.

"We have limited intel on that," the former Senator said. "There seems to be a pretty long line of trucks coming in and out of this place."

"Given the number of barracks, they could have a thousand or more people there," Raul said as he surveyed the image again.

"Word is that buses come in with more people every three or four days," the former Senator said.

"Replacements?" Raul asked.

Ted shrugged. "Unknown. We just know they are bringing in more folks all of the time. Ever since this conflict started, there has been an uptick of activity by the social enforcers. They are rounding up anyone that is even remotely suspected of having a non-Newmerican perspective."

Death camps. No one liked to say the words, but it was the implication. Raul's mother had died in one, and his sister had been rescued from the same fate. He had dedicated himself to saving others that were imprisoned, waiting to die under the rule of the Newmerican leadership. "There are several phases of this kind of mission. One, we have to get there—not easy to do though. The New Mexico Army National Guard has sentries and defenses along the Texas border, fairly thin. They rely more on SEs to patrol. Once we get there, we have to deal with the guard. The prisoners have to be taken back to safety—again, forcing us to cross the border." Just saying the words out loud made him realize the magnitude of it all.

Andy spoke up. "To move that many people, you are talking about a lot of buses or some large aircraft."

Ted leaned over the photo image of the rooftops of the buildings and the surrounding fence that had been scraped clean of vegetation and possible cover. "With that many prisoners, we can expect at least a hundred SEs guarding the facility."

Raul looked over at the older man. "Any chance that the Army can support us?"

Ted frowned. "They have priorities elsewhere." Raul felt like sighing with those words, but Ted continued. "That doesn't mean we won't have help."

"Go on—" Raul prodded.

"Two different Sons of Liberty groups from Kansas and Arkansas have volunteered their people's time and resources. The majority of them are combat veterans, which will give us a leg up. Also, the Texas Director of Public Safety has canvassed volunteers from the Texas Rangers. This morning I got word that the Arizona Maricopa County Mounted Posse has offered to pitch in as well. While they are older folks, they are skilled law enforcement officers and experts at traversing rugged terrain."

"Mounted … you mean on horseback?"

"That's right Raul," Ted said with a smile. "How they got to Texas is a bit of a story all of its own. I couldn't refuse their help though. They are experienced trackers, and we need all the help we can get."

"I'd argue with you, but you're right. Any help is better than none."

Andy spoke up. "Travis gets his cast off in a week. Maybe we can convince him and Caylee to do some snooping for us. We need recon of this place. That strange area outside the camp—I want to know what they are dumping there. One thing I learned from breaking the two of you out of the Supermax—good intelligence is priceless. Going in blind would be an invitation to a disaster."

"In the meantime, we need to figure out how we are going to transport the prisoners safely," Raul said. "At Valley Forge, we were lucky; there were not a lot of prisoners in the camp. This is a big facility. Once we get on the move, the New Mexicans are going to react. They will try to stop us." He knew he was stating the obvious, but he also knew that someone in the room had to mention it.

"We could cause a diversion," Ted said. "That forest is prone to fires, especially in the spring. If we set off a few forest fires, it would give them something else to think about."

Those comments elicited a snap-response from Andy. "Let's not go there. Yes, it's tempting, but that is a National Park. I've been tasked with protecting our culture, and that park is part of it."

"Isn't getting the prisoners out more important than a few trees?" Raul asked.

Andy shook his head as he spoke. "No Raul. The Newmericans have no problem with destroying art, architecture, or anything else that represents who we are as a people. We are better than that. We have to be. If we don't fight to preserve the things that make us Americans, we are no better than they are."

"He's right," Ted said. "This war is not just about victories; it's about the *right* victories. It's about taking and holding onto the moral high ground. That's why Andy is here, to keep us in check. I agree we need a diversion of some sort, but destroying a national park would be the wrong thing to do. Worse, it would give them a public relations coup."

Their arguments were compelling enough to make Raul blush with embarrassment for even suggesting it. "I just want to get those people out alive."

"And we will," Ted said.

"We all want the same thing," Andy said offering him a thin smile. "We just want to make sure we do it the right way, Raul."

He nodded back to his friend. *My madre would agree. She would not want me to do something that would cause greater harm simply to win.* "Let's look at the roads, the airports, everything. We need to find a way to make this work. The people in that camp are counting on us. We are their only hope. We can't afford to leave anything to chance." He knew that what they were facing was daunting, but the thoughts of his sister and mother and what they endured gave him determination to succeed. *We will find a way! We have no choice!*

Texas Military Department (TMD) HQ,
Camp Mabry, Austin, Texas

Major Judy Mercury was happy to be back in Texas. She had quickly grown tired of the media. The stunning raid she had led across the State of Illinois which culminated in the capture of the Governor and Lieutenant Governor of that state, had earned her all of the attention she ever wanted. While she simply wanted her next duty assignment, the Army had used her as a publicity piece. She felt that her story was being blown out of proportion. *It was never about me; we did it as a team.* She made a point to say that in every interview—even calling out members of her Grab Asses. The moment she realized she was really a thing, was when she passed someone wearing a Grab Ass T-shirt on the street. *This shit is getting out of hand.*

Two days ago she had been presented the Medal of Honor and a promotion by the American President at the Southern White House. General Reager assured her then, at her insistence, that her days of doing media tours were over. "Give me a chance to do what I do best." Reager told her to report to Camp Mabry shortly thereafter.

When she came to his makeshift office, Judy saw her former CO, a man she revered, looking as if he had aged several years. He had lost weight, and his skin sagged a little under his chin. The wrinkles on his forehead, which used to surface from time-to-time, were now permanently etched there. His smile and the gleam in his eyes were the only parts of General Reager's face that seemed to defy the stress he was under. He gestured for her to take a seat.

"How are you holding up, Major?" he said as she sat down.

"Tired of cameras and reporters."

"Me too. It could be worse; you could have to apologize to one of them. I think it's safe to say we've milked all we can out of your stunning raid. I take it you are ready to climb back in the saddle again."

"Sir, that is an understatement."

"Good. I need your help. A battle is coming, a nasty one, fraught with logistical challenges. I need someone to figure out how we can help win the fight."

"Where are we talking?"

"New Hampshire."

Judy leaned back in her chair opposite the plain, government-issue desk where Reager sat. New Hampshire had been a tinderbox for a while. The Sons of Liberty and their National Guard had been waging a guerilla war against the Newmericans for months. The TRC had labeled their effort The Defiance, and that was an apt description … and for the people there, a rallying cry. "What's the situation?"

"General Hank Griffiths is leading the effort there. The Newmericans are taking a page out of our Middle East strategy, and now that spring is here, they are planning a surge. Griffiths' folks have been fighting an insurgency, but now that spring is barreling in, they are going to face an actual war, a shooting war.

"His plan is simple. He wants to consolidate his forces in the White Mountain National Forest. He's dug in tight there, good field fortifications, etc. For now, the Newmericans don't know where he's at, but once they find him, they will build up and hit him hard. He's going to face a laundry list of problems. First, they will have air superiority. He's got some jets and has converted some roadways to act as runways, but even he admits they can't hold out for long. As you know, maintenance of aircraft is an enormous challenge. Second, the Newmericans are going to come with at least two-to-one numbers on the battlefield, possibly more. This is their chance to squash this insurgency once and for all."

"General, New Hampshire is surrounded by enemy states. What

exactly do you need me to do?"

"We are smuggling in some special forces, but that alone isn't enough. We have given Griffiths some Stinger anti-aircraft missiles—which will help level the playing field a little."

"But ..."

"But that isn't enough for me," Reager conceded. "You know me; I want to win. I want to hand the Newmericans a staggering defeat in New Hampshire. If we can do that, it will weaken them politically. Their own people will start to question whether they can win this war. I want New Hampshire to be a bright light of hope that we can take back this country."

Judy understood his feelings and the candor with which he shared them. "This is all about air superiority. You and I both know that Stingers are only good for 3000 meters or so. They are great against low-flying aircraft, choppers especially, but not for anything above their ceiling. The Newmericans will know that just as well as we do, and will do high altitude bombing, so they don't risk their air assets."

"My thoughts exactly. I believe that if Griffiths can lure them into the forest, he can bleed them dry. He can't do that if he is being bombed into the Stone Age. We need to negate their airfields and, if possible, give Griffiths close combat air support."

"In New Hampshire."

"That's right."

Judy paused for a moment, leaning forward in her seat, looking down. *The enemy controls all of the airfields in the state*. That means we need to either wage this war from a long distance, which puts our efforts at risk, or we take and hold an airfield close to the state and fly our missions out of there. "Do we have air resources for this? I'm taking attack helicopters, jets, bombers."

"I can allocate the aircraft. Wright Patterson is the closest big field under our control, and we control several other air bases. We don't have a lot of aircraft, but neither does the enemy. With most of the military on the sideline, we have what we scrounged from National Guard Air units. It's not a lot, but I can get you the assets you need."

"I'm going to need some assistance. I'm not an airman. The logistics involved with this is big." It was an understatement. Judy had some experience in joint operations, and one thing she knew was that while the Army traveled heavy, the Air Force carried massive requirements in terms of equipment and gear.

"I will give you Captain Juanita Hill, my Air Force Liaison. She's damned good at her job. Anyone else you need, you will get."

"I want Lieutenant Colonel Mihalek from the Oklahoma National Guard. He helped plan the op in Illinois. We work well together."

"Done. Anything else?"

"What's my timing?"

"As usual, you're already late. Hill has come up with some rough ideas already, but I'm not sure they will work. Parts of them you might be able to use though. With the temperatures starting to warm up, I think this surge is going to be coming in a few weeks' time. They have started pre-positioning troops already."

"So I'm behind the 8 ball."

"As always. If it helps, you're a victim of your own success. What you pulled off in Illinois was so fantastic, I had no choice but to hand you this one."

"I'd thank you, but you'd just promote me again," she said with a hint of sarcasm.

"Not for a while. I'd like you to get used to those oak leaves for the time being. I've already heard the mumblings about nepotism and you getting bumped up the ladder twice in just a few months."

"And what did you say to that?"

"I told them if any of them want to lead an operation behind enemy lines, and capture a rebellious governor, I'd be happy to promote them right on the spot."

"I'm sure they think it's because we're both from Texas and served together in the war."

"Frankly, I don't care what they think. I don't play favorites. Their problem is that they look at everything through the lens of it being equitable or not. They are starting with a flawed premise when they do that."

"I'd hate for the Army to do anything based on merit," she quipped. It was an ongoing joke. The former US Army had implemented a massive diversity and inclusiveness program aimed at identifying radicals, i.e., conservatives. Then came the inevitable equity program. That had pushed the service branches to promote people based on preferred status, rather than their true skills and ability. Warriors like Trip and Judy had argued that it only promoted mediocrity, and as the General had said, "Mediocrity doesn't win wars any more than diversity and inclusiveness." That had been one of the few positive things about America not having to deal with the regular Army out of the Pentagon.

"What else do you need?"

"Maps, sleep, and someone smarter than me to figure this out."

"Set up shop here," General Reager said. "Get yourself an assistant, some second lieutenant that wants to make a name for themselves. Delegate the shit out of this. Have that person get your team assembled and get yourself over to the BOQ and grab some sleep. You're going to need your head clear because this is going to come fast and furious."

A small part of Judy wanted to complain, but she knew better. First off, Trip Reager wouldn't listen to it. The small, dark bags under his own eyes spoke to his own lack of sleep. That was part of his character; he never asked people to do something that he wasn't willing to do himself. Second, complaining never solved anything. All it did was lower the morale of those around you. "Good idea," she finally replied. "Sir, there is one thing you haven't asked me."

"And that is?"

"Is this even possible?"

Reager smiled. "I try not to ask for the impossible. You're smart. You'll figure out something that can help those poor bastards up in New Hampshire. I know you well enough to have faith in what you can do."

She rose from her seat and gave him a silent nod in response. *That was the best possible answer that he could have given me. Now all I have to do is pull off a miracle or two.*

CHAPTER 4

"Those foolish enough to cling to the past are the most determined to bring it back."

The Southern White House
Nashville, Tennessee

Thiago Reese adjusted his name badge as he sat through the orientation session. The badge read, "Luis Fernando," an alias that he had carefully crafted prior to his arrival in the self-proclaimed Southern White House. Luis was an immigrant, having come to Newmerica three years earlier. Reese had put down two traffic violations in his record—a perfectly clean record might have drawn a little too much attention. Luis had a good job history. Newmerica's open borders had allowed millions fleeing poverty in their countries to flood into the nation. Many had become dependent on the FedGov for survival. Luis had not fallen into that pattern. He had gotten a job, first as a lawn care person, then as a janitor at Heritage Christian University in Florence, Alabama. If anyone called there, they wouldn't remember him; his employment record was on file though, and showed he had been promoted twice.

The Vice President's credentialing him with the NSA also gave him access to tools perfect to make his persona more believable. The security background check was something he monitored, courtesy of his own cyber expertise. The CIA had put him through the National Cyber Academy, and armed with a number of NSA tools, he had hacked in and tracked the Secret Service checks on him, making sure that none had set off any alarms. The Secret Service had been keenly thorough, even placing a call to the University where he claimed to have worked. They confirmed his employment, but could offer little more. With the turnover of janitorial staff, the man in charge admitted that he didn't remember Luis Fernando, but his records showed him to be a good worker. The Secret Service probe was more cursory. Their Director, this Charli Kasinski, was on her A game. The Service's poking at his past was the only element he was concerned about.

He had chosen a janitor role because of their near invisibility. People didn't remember the cleaning staff, if they even saw them at all. It gave him broad access to the Southern White House where he was going to work. Dumpster diving through the trash was easy for getting intel. His badge would give him access to a big portion of the old Federal Building, enough for him to be able to penetrate other non-authorized parts with ease. Thiago/Luis would be able to study the security systems first hand and find ways around them. Yes, the work itself was demeaning, but his experience in toppling governments showed that the best way to take down the enemy was from within. It didn't take a significant character to sow dissent and distrust.

The orientation dragged on far too long for his taste, but he kept up the façade of being honored to work in the Southern White House. They toured their assigned location, got their security badges, and listened to a talk by a Secret Service agent about the rules governing the building. All along, Luis Fernando played his role perfectly, asking almost obvious questions to show that he was paying attention. *When you take on a persona, it is all in the details.*

The most important part of the orientation was the discussion about security. Individuals had to pass through a metal detector with bomb-sniffing dogs nearby. All personal bags were to be searched going in and leaving. Electronics, especially phones, were tucked away in small lockers before you even got through the detectors. The new employees were told that they were constantly monitored and should assume no privacy. It made sense of course; only a few months earlier there had been an assassination attempt by another Newmerican operative. From what Thiago/Luis heard, the barriers for security were formidable.

The high profile personnel in the building had their own elevator. The garage in the basement was limited to senior staff, and their vehicles were checked for explosives. The presence of the Secret Service was everywhere.

He was introduced to his supervisor, a lanky African-American named Rosa Johnson. She had incredibly short, curly hair dyed blonde, and she wore brilliant red lipstick. She ushered him into her office in the basement of the building, a dull gray painted affair, cramped with a desk and a single chair. The computer on her desk was at least twenty years old, but he did notice that despite the rough-looking quarters, the desk and everything on it were organized in neat piles with sticky notes. Rosa's pens were lined up in a neat row. *Order is everything to her.*

After the initial pleasantries, Johnson got down to business. "I'm assigning you to the third floor, evening shift starting tomorrow. You will work with Dot. She will show you the ropes. Once you get your feet wet, you will handle the west side of the floor while she handles the east. It's fairly standard stuff. Trash and recycling pickup every day, clean restrooms, the usual stuff. There's a detailed schedule for carpet cleaning. We hit different parts of the hallway floors on different days. You meet down the hall in the meeting room, and Dot will review the schedule with you each night. It's not complicated work, but it is important."

"What kind of space is it? Offices? Conference rooms?"

Rosa nodded once. "There are two secured conference rooms; the rest are for non-classified meetings. There are twenty closed offices. The rest of it is open office space, highly flexible. Movable wall units, white boards, desks on wheels—that kind of thing."

He made note of every opportunity in what she said. *Those secured conference rooms are useful. They are overflow, when the other rooms are occupied. That brings class one targets down to this floor.* "What kind of security is here? The last thing that I want to do is trigger some sort of alarm."

She grinned. "Don't worry about that Luis," she assured him. There's cameras in the secured rooms, and a few operating in the workspace. There's not a lot to trigger. Building security comes through fairly regularly. They will check you when you leave the building, fairly standard stuff. Once they get to know you, you'll hardly notice them.

"This building was never designed for classified work, so they have added security systems. Those rooms have classified disposal bins, but you don't have to deal with those—that is subcontracted through the Secret Service. The most you'll have to do is empty the trash and recycling. You'll be expected to bus any glasses, plates, or utensils used as well. Those are sent down to the kitchen on the first floor for cleaning. With the heightened security here, they don't allow food deliveries."

Every word that Dot said was of use to Luis, if not now, perhaps in the future. Each detail he gathered was a potential weapon in his arsenal. To Luis, this job would allow him to plant voice-activated listening and recording devices. Without broadcasting, they would be immune to most bug sweeps but would provide him a wealth of information. Discreet local phone taps would give him a myriad of data. Taking down a government wasn't as much about firing bullets as gathering the right intelligence and using it properly.

Yes, there were risks, but he liked to believe he was smart enough to minimize them. The key was finding the nooks and unseen crannies in their security and exploiting them. Dot would no doubt think the smile on his face meant that he was happy about his new job. In reality, it was all about the opportunities to hamstring the Americans.

When I am through with them, their supporters will question why they back them. I will erase their victories on the battlefield with dissent and distrust.

The Presidio, San Francisco, California

When Darius got off of the olive, drab school bus, he could feel the sag of the body armor on his shoulders. Despite the drills, the exercises, the PE routine, his body had been through a lot in life and protested the tactical gear with a series of aches and nagging reminders of his age. He paused for a moment and tightened the strap on his transparent riot shield, so it was snug on his left arm. *The NSF or social enforcers should be doing this shit, not us.* A part of him knew the answer as to why the NSF wasn't there, though he would never say it out loud. *They probably tried and failed. That's why all of the riot gear for us. They don't want to look like they are beating up a bunch of homeless people who they know will resist. They just don't want to get dirty—or worse.*

As he walked away from the bus with the rest of the members of his platoon, he detected a distinct aroma. It was a mix of urine, garbage, feces, and filth. This was the stench of a squatter town. He knew it well from experience. It was the stink of failure and despair.

"Alright," Captain Aguilar said to grab their attention. "We are at the Fifteenth Avenue Gate. The transports for these squatters are at the Lombard Gate. We will deploy north, herding them as we go, then turn them east to Lombard where they will be loaded and taken to their Tiny Town." She paused for a moment, looking around, then continued. "We aren't expecting trouble. If things get out of hand, non-lethal force is authorized."

"Loaded?" That sounded less like people and more like animals to Darius. Aguilar ordered them in a standard tactical advance formation as two other companies of the Veterans Corps unloaded from their buses. Darius looked at the number of armed troops and wondered why there were so many. *The Captain says they aren't anticipating trouble, but then why have so many of us here?* His experience was that you could create different problems by putting too much force in place. *Overkill can trigger reactions these officers can't anticipate.*

Glancing off further down the road, he saw several Youth Corps buses. The Youth Corps was a social work program that the Newmericans had kicked off. The press they got was usually very positive—removing urban blight, building housing, etc. He saw the Corps as a more active form of indoctrination, beyond what the young got forced into at school. Seeing the buses, he knew why they were there. These camps are trash pits—they already have the Corps lined up to clear out the mess. While it made sense, he worried about the youth being so close to the proximity where there might be trouble.

The Presidio had been a beautiful park when he was a kid, and parts of it were still. The city had cut back on the maintenance; that much was obvious as they started their slow march into the park. While the golf course was still pristine, the other areas had not been cut or trimmed. Garbage was nestled with the dead leaves and brown grass of winter. As they moved along the roadway, Darius found himself longing for the days before the Liberation.

Jaxson moved alongside of him, clutching a tear gas launcher. His eyes were ablaze as Darius glanced over at him. He had seen that look before—the adrenal rush before going into battle. "You think we're going to mix it up with them?" Jaxson asked, as if he wanted the answer to be *yes*.

"They didn't give us all this gear to look pretty."

"I haven't seen action in a long time. Nothing like looking down the sights at the enemy."

"Enemy? These are squatters—economically-displaced folks. They are not the bad guys you fought in the Middle East." While the distinction may not mean much to Jaxson, it meant the world to Darius.

They marched along the perimeter of the Presidio's golf course. Their formation was sloppy; Darius and the others all knew that. Like him, the majority had been forced into the Veteran's Corps. Guys like Jaxson worried him. *He wants to fight. He wants to relive his experiences. I've seen it before.* As they proceeded north in the vast park, he began to catch something on the wind. The aroma that had the smell of a squatters' camp, a trademark of such sites. He watched as Vixen pulled a black kerchief up over her nose, hoping to diffuse the stink.

As they turned slightly to the west, he saw the camp. To a casual observer, it looked like a dumping ground for trash. Filthy tents, cardboard box homes, garbage everywhere. A muddy path snaked through the hundreds of makeshift shelters. As soon as Darius came into sight of the massive encampment, he saw the occupants stirring. Some grabbed clubs, little more than scraps stolen from construction sites. Others held glass bottles. They were not kowtowing at the presence of the Veteran Corp. If anything, they looked as if they were more than willing to engage in a fight.

A piercing male voice from the Corps sounded over a bullhorn, punching through the trees and garbage. "Attention. This camp is in violation of city ordinance. You are required to gather your personal belongings, and we will escort you to transportation."

Grumblings from the squatters grew quickly. "We don't want to go," a burly man in a filthy, gray wife-beater T-shirt replied.

"You are ordered to evacuate this park immediately," the bullhorn barked back.

Then it came, a lone rock thrown in a high arc at their line. It hit the shield of one of the soldiers with a cracking thud further down the line from where Darius stood. It was followed a heartbeat later with a volley of bricks, rocks, bottles and one flailing piece of wood. He raised his shield in time to intersect a bottle which exploded in shards of glass around him. Three people to his left, Fax cried out when a brick hit him in the helmet. Staggering, the younger man was shaken by the kinetic force, but moved back to his place in the line.

"Gas 'em!" came the command from Sergeant Ingersoll of the Veterans Corps, a skinny vet with a deep, southern voice that almost sang when he barked out commands. Jaxon raised his tear gas grenade launcher and began to fire shells that rained down on the encampment. Smoke rolled, and the troops paused, pulled out their gas masks and put them on. Darius pushed the mask against his face and made sure it sealed to his skin. He hated the mask just slightly less than the sting of tear gas.

Another rock slammed into Lucius's shield forcing him to recoil a half-step. Then came a crack—a sound that was unmistakenly gunfire. It came from in front of him, and he saw someone in the next company of troops drop down and back. *Damn it!* He twisted his body sharply, bringing his weapon to a more easily accessible position at his side.

Another gunshot went off from the camp. Suddenly, without orders members of the Veterans Corps opened up. There were a few at first, but within a few seconds, everyone was dropping their riot shields and opening fire. Darius was stunned that he did the same thing, without even thinking.

The non-lethal rubber bullets were unleashed with each squeeze of the trigger. He hit one man craning back to throw a brick. His shot caught him in the jaw and sent him toppling back hard, falling into a dirt-smeared yellow and blue tent as he dropped.

A surge of satisfaction hit him, but he reined it in quickly. Another rock hit him, but with the shield down, it slammed hard into his chest. For a moment, he struggled to catch his breath, reeled around and moved behind the person on his right for cover. The tactical vest and blast plate had prevented any real damage, but it was a reminder of what they were up against.

Gunfire from the camp suddenly increased and with it, the screams of men and women being hit. "Live ammo!" Captain Aguilar called out, her voice muffled by the gas mask. *Shit ... we are going to kill these people!* He pulled his magazine of rubber bullets out and found the one he had marked with red tape to indicate live ammo. He tried to assure himself this was the right thing to do, and the moans of two of the wounded seemed to help him as he slapped the magazine into place. *They started this. All they had to do was leave.*

Swinging around he heard the order to advance. Gunfire now filled the air between the two groups. The veterans were controlled in their shots, small bursts at most, aimed. The incoming gunfire was erratic and deadly.

They moved forward, into the dwindling haze of the tear gas, to the edge of the encampment. He didn't fire his weapon indiscriminately like some of the others. Darius knew from personal experience what a bullet could do to a man,. He had gotten shot in Iraq and his shoulder still bore the ugly scar from that. As much as these people were fighting him, he had no desire to fight back. *I'm here because the State of California didn't give me a choice.*

The line of battle came up against a wall of brush, and he had to twist as they passed through the brush. On the other side was the edge of the squatters' village, clouded in a diminishing haze of tear gas. He saw the occupants, some fifty feet away, retreating but still facing them, lobbing anything they could get their hands on. A few brandished handguns, wobbling, firing but not aiming. Darius stepped forward onto a pile of debris next to a half-collapsed tent as one of his company fired, taking down one of the armed, homeless people.

As he struggled with his footing, he was stunned when a figure emerged from the tent and threw a punch at him. Darius had boxed in his youth, but he had never done it while wearing a gas mask. While his assailant's blow missed his jaw, it caught the filter on the mask and spun it hard. The mask twisted enough to block his vision almost entirely. Panic gripped him in that moment, and he staggered back into the bush, struggling to get his mask off, so he could see his attacker.

Ripping it free, another blow hit him hard on his right side. His ribs caught most of it, but it was a solid punch.

The mask came off, along with his helmet. Stepping another half-step back, he saw his attacker, a squat muscular woman. Her eyes were wide open and as wild as her brown hair. She was missing a lower tooth in the front, but what remained were gritted and ready for more of a fight. She said nothing, and in that moment, they looked at each other, unmoving.

"I ain't leaving!" she growled. "Damn it—I'm one of you!" Her left hand went down to her front pants pocket, as if to pull something.

Darius's body seemed to act on its own, without his thoughts. As she moved for what he thought was a weapon, he raised his rifle. She fumbled for a millisecond, then seemed to spring towards him. His gun wasn't fully up, but it didn't have to be. A shot rang off to his side. The woman was hit mid-flight, in her neck. Her body pivoted mid-air squirting blood in every direction, and she collided with his thighs as she dropped by his feet.

Darius didn't see who had shot her; it didn't matter. He knelt down and rolled her over so he could see her face. Her eyelids fluttered as he looked at her face, now wet with her own crimson gore. She struggled to speak as he tried to put his hand over her wound only to find a significant piece of flesh ripped from her throat. There was no flinching as he put his hand over the tore area and applied pressure. "Hold on … stay with me!" he ordered.

For a fleeting moment, her eyes somehow gained focus and looked up at him. "Medic!" he called as more gunfire popped and cracked around him. His attacker opened her mouth but could not form the words; instead she gurgled. Then suddenly she froze—her eyes looking straight up at him, devoid of life.

He pulled his blood drenched hand from her throat, knowing full well that she was dead. The sounds around him seemed to be muffled in that moment as he leaned slightly back from her limp body.

His eyes caught a glimpse of her hand, the one that had been diving for her pocket. Darius saw something familiar in her hand, bronze with a white, red, black and green ribbon. It was an Afghanistan Service Medal. She had not been reaching for a weapon, she had been pulling out her service medal to show that she was, indeed, just like him.

Slowly he reached down and pulled the medal from her dead palm. He wanted to curse at her, tell her that if she hadn't attacked him, she might still be alive. His clenched jaw prevented the words from coming. *I am a vet—I was 'shelter-dependent' too.* Her last words stung at him still, "I'm one of you!"

His big hand clenched the medal tightly. *Damn it! What have I done? What am I now? What is it we are doing here? What in the hell am I fighting for?*

The District

Alexandria, the Vice President of Newmerica was flanked by her Secret Service detail as she walked through the checkpoint at the Walter Reed Medical Center. The emblems of their self-perceived prestige were everywhere. Each branch of the service had a flag on a pole along one wall. The current Newmerican flag was there as well, a black banner with a single blue horizontal banner that intersected an oval. Inside the stark white oval was a black chain that was broken. She had personally selected it, not so much for its symbolism but as a reminder to the people that the Ruling Council, and now the current leaders of Newmerica, had freed them.

Seeing the flag there, while somewhat pleasing, was also an irritant. The military was taking a sideline role in the current civil war. *For all of their pomp and bluster, they are afraid—afraid of backing the wrong side.* The majority of the military stood down, citing the need to be ready should the country be attacked by a foreign threat—and God knows there were plenty of those. Some units had broken with the Joint Chief's stand and had sided with both sides in the civil war. It made for a mess, one that the Vice President intended to rectify once the war was over. *They stood by in our time of need, and I won't forget that—nor will the people.*

The Vice President hated hospitals, and Walter Reed was no exception. Even now she could detect the hint of disinfectants in the air. The wood paneled walls were dated and far too dark for her taste. The terrazzo floor had a utilitarian look. To her, these were not places of healing. This was where people came to die.

She was greeted by a Navy officer, a doctor, who offered to escort her to the room. There was no small talk in the elevator ride, nor in the halls. Her interpretation was that either the officer was intimidated by her, a common reaction—or he simply was under orders to keep quiet. They stopped at the patient's door, holding it open so she and her security team could enter.

General Hollings Rinehart sat in his bed; the back of it was elevated. His arm was in a black fiberglass cast, and his face had a small scar on his left cheek, held together by a trio of stitches. His chiseled chin wore a day's worth of grayish-black beard stubble. When he saw her, his eyes narrowed slightly, and he adjusted himself in the bed.

"Madame Vice President," he spoke slowly. "I was unaware that you were coming to visit me."

She nodded to her Secret Service detail who understood and left the room to stand in the hall. "I don't generally make it a habit to transmit my agenda in advance. A few assassination attempts will do that to a person."

The General nodded once slowly. "To what do I owe the pleasure?"

"I wanted to see if you are on the mend. I also wanted to pass on the President's sincere wishes that you recover quickly so that you can put an end to this war."

"Thank you. I'm checking out in a few hours and returning to duty," he said.

"Good. So what is your immediate plan?"

He eyed her for a moment, clearly wary. "I was going to go to the President and lay out that strategy."

"We have made some adjustments as to who you report to. The President has appointed me as his primary liaison with the armed forces. With the current state of the nation, I'm sure you understand the demands on his time."

It had taken some persuading to have Daniel turn over the military to her. While he could easily override her as Command-in-Chief, she doubted it would ever come to that. With her staging of the false-flag bombing of the Capitol and the framing of other former members of the Ruling Council, she remained one of the few confidants the President had left. She relished the power she now had, with the SEs the NSF, and now the military. At the same time she never allowed anyone to see that expression on her face. What she let them see was the burden she had been 'forced' to carry.

There was something in the way General Rinehart looked at her that conveyed that deep down, he understood the might she wielded. "Very well then," he slowly replied. "As you are already aware, we are increasing our forces in New Hampshire. It is our intent to crush this so-called Defiance there once and for all.

"In Virginia, we will be keeping up the pressure and start to retake some of the territory we lost. I have shifted Wisconsin National Guard troops down to Illinois to the south. I'm hoping that will get the locals off of our back after that little stunt the enemy pulled there."

"They captured the Governor and the Lieutenant Governor," she stated flatly. Her words conveyed an entirely different message. *It was far from a stunt. If they can go for politicians, no one will be safe.*

"I am well-aware," Rinehart countered. "Militarily however, aside from the destruction of their National Guard HQ, it was little more than a rambunctious raid. It's not the kind of operation they can pull off again."

"I disagree. This is not just a war fought with armies. It is about the hearts and minds of the people. That raid has made people in Illinois afraid. It made us look weak. It cost us the Rock Island Armory. As a result, every governor in our loyal states is pulling troops to protect them and their capitals. That gives you fewer troops to deploy in the field."

"Madame Vice President I assure you, I am well-aware of that, which is why I am concentrating our forces. That is why I intend to take the war to the enemy, fight on their soil."

Those words intrigued her. "What are you talking about?"

"We've got a plan, code-named Star Burst. It isn't a knock-out punch, but it is enough to make them shift their resources to a new front."

His words were encouraging and intriguing. "Where will it take place?"

"Out west," he said. "It's time that California put some skin in the game."

The Vice President smiled broadly as the General outlined the broad strokes of his plan of attack. She savored the turmoil it might cause. Better yet, she might be able to entice some allies to add to the carnage. *Our enemies will never know what hit them ...*

CHAPTER 5

"Our greatest enemies might be your neighbors."

The Southern White House
Nashville, Tennessee

It impressed Raul that General Reager was willing to meet personally with him and Caylee. He looked weary; there were small bags under his eyes, a sign of not sleeping. His short, cropped gray hair was old-school military. Other than that, Reager had an almost father-like demeanor. Where many people peppered them with questions, the General listened and let him and Caylee talk before interrupting them.

When he was done, Reager shifted in his seat slightly, then spoke. "You need my forces to open a roadway for you to get these people out."

"Correct, General," Caylee said. "Getting in can be done covertly. We will have a small convoy of trucks coming out. The New Mexico and Arizona National Guard troops on the border, will be alerted to us, so getting out will be … problematic."

"That's an understatement."

"It is a reality," Caylee said. "We are hoping to neutralize their communications. If we do, they will not be aware we have liberated the camp. If we do not, they will be unsure of where we are heading."

"You have to assume that you are kicking over a beehive when you pull this off," he said. The NSF will throw up roadblocks all over the place once they figure out what is happening."

"We realize that," Raul weighed in. "That is why we are splitting up, using back roads. They will expect us to keep the convoy together; it will be easier for us to blend in by splitting up. The only time we need to come back together is when we cross the border."

Reager leaned back in the chair, then took a sip from the glass of water that sat in front of him, as did Caylee. *She's mirroring his gestures ... doing it to psychologically get on his side.* She had taught him the technique, but now he was witnessing it for the first time. "Obviously, I can't go into the details of our current military deployments."

"Obviously," Caylee replied. "We would not think of asking you to do so, General Reager."

"If I support this plan of yours, the only way to open a road for your return to safety is to apply military force. The enemy might very well mistake a minor border skirmish as a pretense for an all-out incursion. While I won't confirm or deny our plans, opening a road for you might very well tip our hand on something we would prefer to keep secret."

Tipping our hand ... they are planning to attack out west. Raul now understood the reluctance that the General was expressing. *He doesn't want to ruin his own plans by executing ours.* "General, we don't require much assistance. We can come back on a roadway of your choosing, one that would not provide the impression of a full-blown invasion. The roadway would be some distance from your planned operation."

Reager nodded his head at those words. "It's not just that—there is a matter of timing. If we implement a military operation along that border, and you are on the other side, we could inadvertently leave you trapped behind enemy lines in the middle of a war."

"I don't suppose you could tell us when such an action might happen?" Caylee asked.

The General shook his head. "That wouldn't be my first choice ... hypothetically of course."

"It was our intent to start our attempt in two weeks," Raul stated.

"You'll need time for recon, to secure your vehicles, etc.," Reager said. "That kind of timing might just work. That presumes, of course, that the Newmericans don't have plans of their own."

"Is there any indication of a troop buildup?" Caylee asked.

"No," Reager conceded, "but the Texas border is a big piece of land, and our enemy is showing themselves to be a crafty bunch of asshats. We are limited in reconnaissance drones and aircraft, which means they could be planning something that we do not know about." It was a frank admission on the part of the General.

"What I am hearing is that we'll need a fallback plan," Raul stated. "One that gets those prisoners to safety in case something goes bad."

"Always advisable," the General said. "I will assign Major DeYoung as your liaison with the Army. He's good, and he can help you with anything you might need. I will tell him to provide any assistance necessary to aid your little raid, as long as it doesn't compromise our plans."

"Thank you."

"No, Mr. Lopez, thank you."

Raul was surprised by his words. "Sir, for what?"

"For reminding me why we are fighting this war," he said, rising to his feet. "The Newmericans have been imprisoning and killing our people for years. Things like what you're doing—going and rescuing these folks—it is why we are fighting this war. How we treat each other is so vastly different than the enemy, and sometimes we need a reminder of that." Reager reached across the conference table and extended his hand.

Raul felt his face blush as he gripped the hand and shook it firmly. "Good luck," Reager said.

"To all of us," Caylee added. As the General left the room, she said nothing until the door closed. "He seemed impressed with you."

"He's impressed with the plan," Raul countered.

"It's a good plan, but we need good eyes on the ground there. Executing this is all in the details, and right how we have very little to work with."

Raul paused for a moment. "You are going to go. Is that what you're saying?"

"I was going to take Travis with me," Caylee replied. "We both are experienced in this kind of reconnoitering."

"It's risky."

"Everything in life is risky. We need this intel, and if I'm going to be on the ground in there, I want to know exactly what I'm up against."

As with many things in her life, she had clearly thought this through. Raul knew her well enough to know that any attempt to change her mind was going to be wasted effort. "When do you go?"

"Soon," she assured him as she opened the door to leave. Raul stepped out into the second floor hallway and saw a janitor waiting patiently to go in. He and Caylee walked right on by him and towards the elevators.

The Southern White House
Nashville, Tennessee

Luis Fernando saw the trio leave the conference room, General "Butcher" Reager was followed by Raul Lopez and Caylee Leatrom. Reager had been featured many times by the TRC, painting him as a traitor commander, a vicious killer and an enemy of Newmerican freedom. Lopez was a terrorist, one he thought was in prison, from the last he had heard.

Caylee Leatrom's face had been well publicized. She was an operative—a *former* operative. She posted hundreds of pages of incriminating information about the NSF operative program on the internet. The Vice President had issued a kill-on-sight order for her. While he had never met her, her reputation was well known in the tight-knit circle of operatives. *She is dangerous and relentless. If the rumors were true, she had something to do with the deaths of the VP's mother and brother.*

He didn't have a gun on him, so shooting her was not an option. Even if he struck her from behind, there was a good chance she might recover, and, with the help of her terrorist friend, overpower Luis. Killing her will have to wait for another time. I have the advantage. I know who she is, where*as* she has no idea who I am.

He entered the conference room and pulled on his blue, rubber gloves. Since the waves of COVID, they were commonplace with the cleaning staff. He moved to the water glasses and carefully picked them up, and put them on his cleaning cart. These fingerprints could be very useful.

Then, in the dark recesses of his mind, an idea formed. There were many ways to create distrust in a government. Internal conflict was one of the best ways. It generated distrust, and regaining the trust was difficult for even the strongest government. As he plodded through his menial tasks, he was careful not to disturb the glasses that he had recovered.

Implementing the plan would be tricky, but parts of it were already underway. With a few modifications, he could twist the Americans into a knot that could not be undone. *I need to pit them against each other. Once that's done, the will of the people will crumble. They will see their government like any other, just another corrupt entity.*

Luis wiped down the table and allowed himself a moment to grin with satisfaction. The aroma from the disinfectant made his nose burn, not as much as it did when he had first started the job, but it was still noticeable. He took a small amount of pride in his work, mostly because it was in character. Luis Fernando, the fiction he was living, was a hard worker, thorough and diligent. Deep down, however, he was still Thiago Reese, the man that toppled governments, the man that brought down dictators.

This twist to my plan is perfect—a way to tear the enemy down from within ...

Texas Military Department (TMD) HQ,
Camp Mabry, Austin, Texas

Judy Mercury was tired, mentally and physically. For the last four days, the team she had assembled had been huddled in a secured room, attempting to figure out how to provide the close combat air support the defenders in New Hampshire were going to need. It wasn't that they didn't have aircraft that could fly that far and back; the problem was that it was a long journey, and getting that far undetected was a challenge. Also, at those long ranges, it meant that by the time they got called in to bomb or strafe the enemy, they would still be hours away. Her experience was that battles were fluid. While you could circle your support aircraft, that exposed them to enemy fighters. It was best to get in, blow shit up, and get out fast. Loitering spelled death.

Their working sessions had dragged on into the evening hours. No one complained. There was no point. They were on a military base. There was no place to go after hours, so they plowed on ahead every night. Each scenario they came up with was too complicated to execute. Her frustration was intense and there was a feeling that they might not come up with a solution.

At one point Captain Juanita Hill had proposed using long, flat sections of highway as runways. They had spent several hours batting that idea around. While aircraft could land and take off, highways weren't equipped with lights for nighttime operations. Nor did they have fuel supplies or the munitions for rearming, or the facilities for flight crews to repair aircraft. While for long minutes the plan seemed to have potential, the logistics fell apart quickly. One thing Judy knew: The key to victory lay in the logistics.

As the sun set, Captain Hill stood and cracked her neck, an annoying habit but one Judy was getting used to. "It's starting to look like we don't have any option but to use Wright Pat and risk our support aircraft over the battlespace."

Lieutenant Colonel Mihalek crossed his arms and shook his head. "Let's not go there. We'd be sending those pilots and crews on missions that we know would entail huge losses. Worse. Even if we win on the ground, we'd be crippling our air force for future operations. There has to be another way."

"We need a forward air facility, one that allows us to get on the deck quickly and support what we require for the missions we will fly," Judy said, going back to the parameters. "That means fuel, maintenance gear, parts, the works."

"There are none," Captain Hill replied.

"What if we took one?" Judy floated.

"Took one what?" Hill asked.

"An airport."

The Air Force Captain winced at her words. "All of the National Guard airfields are going to be set up with air defense systems of some sort, at least the ones that are immediately surrounding New Hampshire."

"What about a commercial airfield?" Mihalek asked.

Is there one? "You have something in mind?"

"I graduated West Point," he stated factually, with no bravado or pride in his voice. "The nearest airport to the academy was Stewart Newburgh."

"I never heard of it," Judy said.

"That's the thing. Most people haven't. Only a couple of airlines even service it. It doesn't have a lot of gates or personnel. While the commercial airport isn't big, the actual airport runways were massive. I remember we would land, and the planes wouldn't slow down at all, but drive for what seemed like forever, before getting to the gates. A pilot once told me that the runway was an emergency landing strip for the space shuttle. It's a small facility, but has the kind of runway and resources we are going to need."

Judy turned to Captain Hill. "Any military presence there?"

Captain Hill's fingers were a blur on her laptop. "That's the best part. There is. The 105th Airlift Wing of the New York Air National Guard uses that as their base. A Marine Corps Reserve Refueler Transport Squadron is there as well. If I remember right, there's a small Defense Investigative Services office too. The good news is that it's close enough for us to get our planes on the deck for missions, but far enough from New Hampshire that it isn't likely to be heavily defended."

"What's the surrounding terrain like?" Judy asked with a hint of excitement in her voice.

"Hilly. It's the Hudson Valley region. If my memory serves, there's one road in and out of the place."

It almost sounded perfect to Judy. *Could this be made to work?* "If we were to take the facility, what kind of counterattack might we expect?"

Neither of her fellow officers responded at first. Hill squinted at her laptop screen, and Mihalek simply paced. "Not military. The NSF has an outpost nearby, but I don't think they have the kind of firepower to repel a military force."

Judy assembled her thinking, finding new focus with this concept. "Okay, let's clear our heads for a moment. Let's focus on Stewart Newburgh as a potential target. First, we'd have to seize it, then control it."

"Correction, first we'd have to get there," Mihalek said. "We take off from Wright Pat, we are going to show up on radar. They are going to see us coming. This is far more effective if they are unaware of our presence."

Hill cracked a thin smile. "We don't have to show up on radar."

"We have stealth transports?" the Lieutenant Colonel asked sarcastically.

"No. But we can come in low, under their radar. It's called nap-of-the-earth flying. I'm not saying it isn't risky and tricky as all hell, but it can be done."

"I'm not familiar with that," Judy said.

"Ever watch the old film, *Dr. Strangelove*? You can come in low, under the radar. You might pop up every now and then, but if we fly low, I'm talking 1700 meters or less."

Judy knew of the movie, but had never seen it. *I know what I'm watching tonight.* "What kind of risks are we talking about?"

"Pilots are trained in nap-of-the-earth flying. It's trickiest around mountains and over cities. There's always some risks, but we should be able to send in transport aircraft loaded with troops. We could start our approach, and the ground crew might assume it was a technical glitch or some unscheduled incoming aircraft—not necessarily hostiles."

"So they land, deploy, and secure the airport?" Judy asked.

"Why not?" Captain Hill said. "Surprise would be on our side."

Judy liked what she heard. Yes, more planning was needed, but she wanted to play out the scenario to see that it was workable. "Assuming we can secure the airfield, then what?"

"We bring in our forces. C-5s with assault helicopters and crews … flight crews, munitions. Then we shuttle in our attack aircraft. We make Stewart-Newburgh our own base, right under their noses," Mihalek said firmly.

"They may bomb us," Hill cautioned.

"We stick to nap-of-the-earth flying," he replied. "They won't know we are there for a day or two at least. We can use the assault helicopters to hit their airfields, and our aircraft can kill their air superiority in New Hampshire."

The coordination required by the plan was staggering. Judy knew she had to time their operation when the Newmericans were making their push—which required solid intelligence. While using a secret airfield could tip the scales of the fight, it could also invite disaster. Risks and rewards swirled in her brain—punctured by the thought that this plan just might succeed.

"Goddamn it," she muttered, half under her breath. "This might *actually* work."

"We're talking about moving a lot of heavy equipment and personnel," Captain Hill said. "The good news is that the airfield has a military refueling station there already. Once we negate the Marines, we won't have to worry about fueling operations."

"Negating the Marines won't likely be easy," Mihalek said with a sly smile.

"We do it right," Judy said. "And they won't have time to respond. Oh, they'll suspect something is amiss, but they won't have time to mount an armed response."

"It's big and bold," Hill said.

"It's a fighting chance for those folks in New Hampshire. It gives us an airfield in their rear area. We can pulverize their own airstrips and get on deck over the battlefield quickly. They'll know something is wrong, but it will take hours for them to even piece together where we are and what we have there." Suddenly the weariness was gone, replaced with a sizzling energy that flowed in her veins. *Damn—it might just work!*

Smyrna, Tennessee

Caylee was in her room packing when Maria, Raul's sister, rapped lightly on her open door. "Please, come in," she said, folding a sports bra and putting it in her bag.

Caylee and the rest of their small cadre of friends had rescued Maria. Caylee had taken to Raul, mostly because his thinking had saved her life. Maria had been suffering from PTSD, and while she was coming out of her defensive shell, a part of her was still deeply reserved. "Raul told me you were going to leave."

"Just for a few days," she said, putting a pair of climbing boots into the blue gym bag.

"I wish you wouldn't," Maria whispered.

Caylee paused and looked at her for a moment. *The kid has been through hell. She's afraid of losing someone else in her life.* It was understandable. Her mother had died in a Social Quarantine camp. "Maria, you are in favor of the mission that Raul is planning."

"Yes."

"Well, to successfully pull that off, we need to know what we are up against. All I'm doing is going in and observing, making sure we don't walk into a trap. What I am doing will save lives."

"Someone else can go," she said in a low tone, just above a whisper.

"That's true. At the same time, I am best equipped to do this. It is my job—my duty. You don't have to worry. I'm taking Travis with me."

"Is he good?"

She nodded in response. "He's a former Navy SEAL," she paused. "Yes, he's good at his job." Acknowledging Travis Cullen's skills was a rarity for her.

"You won't be in danger, will you?"

It was tempting to lie to Maria. Caylee knew it would ease her concerns. She had learned long ago that lies came easily while the truth often came with struggle, but the struggle was worth it. If something did go wrong, she didn't want Maria's last memories of her to include a lie. "Everything we do has risks attached. It is the nature of our work. I am accepting these risks to help reduce the dangers to your brother and the others when we go in and save these people. My risk might very well save lives."

Maria nodded slowly. "I've lost a lot to these people. We did nothing wrong, but they arrested us to get to Raul. They killed my madre. Two of the men in the camp …" her voice trailed off for a moment.

They raped her. She can't say it, but this is as close as she has ever come.

Caylee dropped her desert camouflage top on the bag and moved over to Maria. "They assaulted you, didn't they?" she said, reaching out for Maria.

The young girl leaned into her suddenly, wrapping her arms tightly around her. Caylee was not a hugging kind of person, but instinct took over, and she held Maria back. She could feel her sobbing into her T-shirt, so Caylee awkwardly stroked her hair. Saying nothing for long minutes, she found tears forming in her own eyes.

Finally she formed words again. "It's okay. It wasn't your fault," she assured Maria.

"They did things," Maria said; her face was still buried in Caylee's chest. Slowly the young woman pulled back from her. Maria's eyes were red; her face wet; her cheeks a bright crimson. Caylee bent her knees, lowering herself slightly to be eye-to-eye with Maria. "None of this was your fault. The people behind this—they are bad people—evil people. They can't hurt you here. You're safe here."

She sniffed heavily, wetly, wiping the tears from her face. Caylee could feel the wetness on her own shirt from Maria's crying. "I'm safe because you are here."

"No. You're safe because this place is safe. This isn't Newmerica. It is *America*. The SEs don't have control here. The NSF is being dismantled. This is a free country. Your safety doesn't depend on me. Freedom is never about a person; it's about a people."

"They kidnapped Raul—"

That was true. Social Enforcers and the NSF *had* kidnapped Raul. Caylee thought her friends had freed him from the Supermax prison as a result. "That was a fluke. The people that did that are either dead or wishing they were." Her memories of Deja Jordan lying crippled at the Supermax prison rushed back at Caylee, along with the satisfaction of the moment. "You won't be alone. Your brother will be here while I am taking this little trip. Charli and Andy will be coming by as well."

"It would be better if you stayed."

"No," Caylee said. "If I don't do this, if I don't scout this camp out, your brother and a lot of other people might get killed. I'm doing this to make sure he stays safe. You understand that, don't you?"

Maria nodded, once more wiping the tears from her eyes. "I understand," she said, sniffling again. "I don't have to like it though." She stepped forward and hugged Caylee once more, quickly, then left.

Caylee rose to her full height and looked at the empty doorway to her bedroom. *It was a big step for her to say she had been assaulted. She's healing, and that admission was a leap forward.* As Caylee contemplated that, she also had a moment of icy shame. *I was in the NSF. I inflicted harm on a lot of families out there. For a long time, I was part of the problem.*

Turning back to her packing, she refolded the camouflage shirt. *I have a long road of redemption to walk.* With Raul, Maria, and her small circle of friends, Caylee realized that they were her family now. She had felt that before, but now she fully accepted it. Being part of a family meant support—like she had just done with Maria. It wasn't easy; it was hard.

It was a part of her life she had been missing, that sense of being. As an operative, she had always been on her own. Rarely did she bring in assets to work with her. Being a part of something important, something that might erase some of the blood on her hands—it felt good. For a long moment she did nothing, simply stood there, over her bag, looking downward.

What she found, staring into the nothingness, was a sense of determination. *I will set things right. I have to. It's not about me. It's about all of the Marias out there.*

CHAPTER 6

"It is important that we all share the same definition of Liberty."

The Southern White House
Nashville, Tennessee

Charli stood in Jack Desmond's rather plain office. She had planted her fists on her hips. She noticed he had a picture of his family on his desk, with a small black ribbon stretched diagonally over the corner. Desmond had refused to talk about what happened to Barbara and the girls the night of The Fall, let alone put up a photograph of them. That he now had a photo of them in view was oddly comforting to Charli. *Maybe he's finally coming to terms with their deaths.*

"Jack, we've known each other for a long time. Hell, you were my boss in the Secret Service back in the day, so you know the drill. You have to tell the President that going to Ohio is too risky."

Jack shrugged his shoulders slightly. "I can tell him, but I can't promise you he won't do it."

"It was madness when he went to Baltimore before the election. Fortunately, he listened and did his speech from Fort McHenry. Going to Ohio—that's even worse. Half of the state is siding with Newmerica."

"He's going to friendly territory Charli."

"There *is* no friendly territory any more. The risk is too great."

"He's a headstrong man," Jack conceded.

"You're the Chief of Staff. If anyone can convince him of the risks, it's you."

"You're acting as if I haven't tried already."

"Try harder," she demanded. The determination in her voice, that rigid tone, was one of the many things he respected about her. "I'll make another run at him on this later today."

"Good. We've come too far to have him get shot at this stage of the game."

"Agreed," Desmond replied, leaning back slightly in his seat. "I'll try to get him to do something from Kentucky, near the border."

"That's better," she admitted, removing her fists from her hips. "I appreciate it."

"Good," Jack said. "Anything else?"

"Yes, there is." Carli moved to a chair in front of his desk. "I hear you've been trying to ditch your protective detail recently."

Jack offered her a rare smile. "You know, back when I was the Director of the Secret Service, I got pissed as hell when someone tried to sneak off on their own. I couldn't figure out why anyone would put their life at risk to run to CVS or to go pick up dinner. When the tables are turned and you're the one being protected, you feel differently about the protection."

"You know what I'm going to say."

"Yes I do. Look Charli, I just need a little privacy now and then. Having your guys shadowing me doesn't allow that. It's just Sunday mornings. I need that time alone. Surely you understand."

"You're the Chief of Staff. You hold this place together."

Desmond shook his head. "That's not true. I just smooth over the rough edges. We have a functioning government."

"Barely," she said. "The parts we have are a tenth of what we used to have at our disposal, and you know it. You can drop the humility bit with me Jack. We've been through too much together for you to get away with it."

"I'm *just* the Chief of Staff."

"Ha!" Charli chuckled. "You and I both know how important you are. So do the Newmericans. Yes, they went after the President, but my job is to protect the government—not just the man. You're a target Jack. There's nothing that you can be doing on Sunday mornings that is so important to drop your security coverage."

"I go and see Barbara and the girls," he said in a low tone. "I—I just need some time alone with them."

Jack's wife and daughter had been killed by the mobs that rampaged through the District during The Fall. The family members of the Secret Service had been targeted by a traitor, Drake Barker. He had doxed them all, hoping to use their deaths to compel surrender of the leaders of the Department of Homeland Security. Their deaths were something that Jack would not talk about, but Charli had done her own digging into their fates. The mere fact that he admitted that he was going to their gravesites was substantive to her. For a long moment, she said nothing. "I assumed they were buried in the District."

"There wasn't much to bury. What was left was cremated by the family while I was in hiding. Barbara's sister kept their ashes … she suspected that I might have made it out alive. She reached out to me and got the urns to me. I had a private ceremony, and I had a memorial marker erected here—where I can be close to them." His chiseled face reddened as he spoke.

"Shit. I had no idea. I understand that. You have earned that privacy. You don't have to ditch your security detail though Jack. I will give them orders to stay outside of the cemetery. At least they will be close in case something goes south. Will that work for you?"

"You drive a hard bargain."

"I learned that from you."

Desmond gave her a nod of concession. "Fine. Your people need to give me some distance though. I don't want them where I can see them when I go to the cemetery. That time is my time."

"I'll give the orders myself," Charli said. "I'd prefer you let them stick close, but we all need time for our personal lives."

Carroll, New Hampshire

Su-Hui was in the pavilion area of the Patio Motor Court, which had been converted into temporary housing for his resistance fighters. Where the pavilion had been a large open area for picnics and parties during the summer months, they had put up walls and had converted it into living space. There were grumbles and complaints, but most of the Sons of Liberty and National Guardsmen kept it to a minimum.

He had been there talking over their current stock of gasoline and diesel fuel with a trio of National Guard troops that had been assigned to work with him. Suddenly a winded woman burst in. "Sir, we just captured an enemy scout!"

"Captured? Where?"

"Across the street from here," she said.

That's close ... too close. "Take me," he said. He followed her out with the National Guard close on his heels. The snow under his feet was churning into a muddy mess, and despite the brisk air, the warm sun was slowly whittling away at the remnants of winter that still blanketed the area.

When they reached the main lodge, she led him into the office area where the prisoner was. He wore an almost green uniform with strips of white cloth tacked on to make a ghillie suit of sorts. Aside from some wet mud on his knees and boots, his attire was almost pristine. The man was blindfolded, and he jerked his head toward the door as Su-Hui closed it. He saw the start of a bruise on the man's forehead, just swelling up slightly under the crude blindfold that had been pulled across his face.

"What do we have here?" Su-Hui asked slowly.

"We caught him a half mile from here. From the looks of it, there were three of them. His buddies must have bugged out," Valerie Turner, leader of a cell of the SOL from New York said. "He had this on him," she said and handed Su-Hui a notepad. On it was a crudely drawn diagram of the Patio Motor Court that was their base. The notations seemed to indicate their snowmobiles at the rear of the complex had been spotted, which meant that the captured man had gotten closer to their base than Su-Hui would have liked.

Lowering the notepad, it put it on the counter in the motel office. "Who are you?"

"Private Rocknee Woodford," he sputtered, craning his head to try to locate the source of the question. "Serial Number MNG-2-1-5—"

"Spare me your serial number," Su-Hui said.

"I demand fair treatment as a prisoner of war," Private Woodford responded.

"You are not in a position to demand shit," Valerie said, before Su-Hui could respond with the same.

"Where are you from?" Su-Hui asked.

"Serial Number M—"

Valerie jabbed the butt of her assault rifle into his stomach—not devastatingly hard, but enough to stop him.

He coughed, gasping for air. "You can't treat me like this. I have rights."

"You've invaded New Hampshire," Su-Hui said. "Your people killed the elected government. You have brought war to these people. Do not presume to lecture me about your *rights*." He was surprised at how angry his own response was. He reeled in his frustration and rage for a moment. "What unit are you with?" Su-Hui asked in a much calmer tone.

"I won't answer that," Private Woodford said.

Valerie pointed to the green and black patch on his shoulder. "Maryland National Guard," she said, responding for him.

"You are a long way from home," Su-Hui said. "Tell me, what did your friends see of our operation here?"

"You know I can't answer that," he said with more fake bravado than true bravery.

"I could beat it out of him," Valerie assured Su-Hui .

It was tempting … which was also a surprisingly new sensation for Su-Hui, one of brutality. A part of him wanted to see the arrogant Private get beaten. He was the enemy, sent to find and destroy them. Somehow, it made his foe seem less-than-human. Reining in those feelings was easy, if not somewhat disturbing. "We have to assume that if he knows where we are, his superiors do as well. Beating him is tempting, but it only wastes time.

"I don't know," Valerie replied with a thin smile. "It might make me feel good."

"We need to prepare to move out," Su-Hui said. "I want IEDs rigged around the complex. We have to assume they will come in-force. When they come, I want them to pay dearly.

"In the meantime, we need to move our non-combatants and our supplies out—immediately. They need to go in small groups. I don't want to risk the enemy engaging them."

"Do we mount any kind of defense here?" asked Tate Palmer, the stocky owner of the motor court.

Su-Hui shook his head. "If we dig in and fight here, your business will be destroyed."

"It's already ruined," he countered. "There is no tourism. We are in a war zone, behind enemy lines. The economy was shit even before the election. The FedGov was more worried about pollution than businessmen like me that were trying to make a living."

"Regardless," Su-Hui countered, "this base has served us well. You do not deserve to have it levelled. Our actual fight is elsewhere." He was careful to not say where, not in the presence of Private Woodford.

"Should I let the General know we are redeploying?" Corporal Abernathy, one of the National Guardsmen, asked. Abernathy had been more than helpful in coordinating with General Griffiths.

"Only after we start to move out," Su-Hui replied. "The enemy will be monitoring radio traffic. Even if our messages are encrypted, they might interpret a spike in signals as a sign of us redeploying." The only assumption he could make was that the enemy knew where they were and, at that moment, were preparing to strike.

Tate Palmer moved from behind the counter of the motel. "If you don't mind, me and the locals, we are going to dig in here. This is my home. We can slow them up if they come."

"It may cost you everything," Su-Hui cautioned.

Palmer nodded once, deeply. "This is my land. This is my state. If they decide to come here, I intend to make them pay dearly." His words signified deep commitment.

Part of leading the Sons of Liberty was understanding that each cell had some autonomy. While Tate Palmer was not a true cell, he and the loyal citizens of Carroll were under no compulsion to follow his orders if they opted not to. It was a balancing act that he had to walk—and a delicate one at that. "You have to do what you have to do," he said. "We appreciate any time you can buy us."

"What about him?" Valerie said, nodding at the prisoner.

Su-Hui eyed their captive. *We have a lot to move, and I will have to dedicate someone to watching him.* The temptation was there to let Valerie do what she wanted, to kill him. His people had all watched the execution of Herb Fletcher, a rogue member of the SOL, along with his comrades. *The enemy would have no compulsion about executing one of us if they caught us.*

He said nothing for a moment as he looked at the blindfolded man.

If we act like the enemy, we lose who we are. "Assign someone to bring him along," he said. Leaning forward, he hovered near the Private's ear. "If you try to escape, we will shoot you. Do you understand?"

Rocknee Woodard nodded fast and nervously with those words. "Yes," he said. His voice was filled with fear.

"That is settled then," Su-Hui said, standing straight and locking gazes with Valerie Turner. He could see she wanted blood, but gave him a nod of respect instead. "Get the word out. We are redeploying. We need to be out of here in less than three hours," he said, estimating that it would take a while for the enemy to come up with a plan and deploy their troops to attack their base.

I do not like giving up this place ... but we have no choice. We need to get to White Mountain National Forest and join up with General Griffiths. As tempting as it was to dig in and fight in Carroll, he knew the real battle was yet to come.

Quay County, New Mexico

Caylee sat alone in the beat-up pickup truck as she crossed the border from Texas into New Mexico. Travis Cullen had gone across the border six hours earlier, so he could assist her if she needed it. "It may look desolate, but these guys aren't stupid. They will be prepared. Let me go first to ensure we do this right."

On the Texas side were a handful of state troopers guarding Bell Street, a long, desolate stretch of highway that ran from Dalhart to Tucumcari. Her ID, fake of course, was checked, and she was warned that the New Mexican authorities were often arresting anyone crossing into the state, or at least holding them until their intentions were known. Rather than get embroiled in a debate, Caylee gave them a copy of her authorization, signed by the American President.

"Are you at least armed?" one young Trooper asked.

She had smiled coyly, "You can guarantee that."

She crossed the border into the state, and there was no reception committee. New Mexico was a state that seemed unsure which side of the civil war to join. Sometimes they were openly hostile to America, while at other times they seemed passive-aggressive. Their governor, a career politician, was clearly attempting to avoid a hard stand one way or another, so he could join the winning side when the time was right.

The American states were dismantling the NSF, turning authority back over to local authorities and arresting Social Enforcers and shutting down the camps. In New Mexico, the NSF was still in place, and the camps were still fully operational. Social Enforcement were still dangerous entities that had to be dealt with. As much as the terrain was flat and barren, she could feel eyes on her. *There is no way that they would leave the road open and unguarded.*

As she slowly drove down the flat stretch of road, she carefully surveyed the surrounding terrain. Then, from behind some sage, men emerged wearing desert camouflage and armed with AR-15s. Defiantly, they strode out on the road to block her truck. She saw several others rise on either side of the road. In all there were five men. Caylee mentally categorized them by their potential threat.

She drew a deep breath through her nose and forced a thin smile to her lips. There could be no hint of fear or concern when she spoke to them. Caylee brought the truck to a stop and rolled down the window as they approached.

"Where are you heading?" a tall man with a reddish beard asked as he moved up to her window.

"I'm visiting family," she said, keeping her lie deliberately short. She handed over her fake driver's license."

The man shouldered his weapon and looked at her ID. "You *do* realize that travel between Texas and New Mexico is discretionary, don't you?"

Her gaze narrowed slightly. It was always better to answer a question with another question when you were being challenged. "Are you NSF?"

The man glanced at one of his associates who stood in front of her front bumper and chuckled. "No. We are a Social Enforcement team—the Sidewinders." He was proud of the association with the SEs. She could hear it in his voice.

She glanced at the man in front of her and saw his trigger finger extended on the guard in a safety position. *They are military trained, but not operating under proper authority. Probably veterans. Cocky given their numbers.* "I don't want any trouble."

"We are going to need you to step out of your vehicle," the bearded man said.

Slowly, she reached down and shut off the engine. Caylee eyed the others as they seemed to surround her vehicle. Mental calculations began to go through her head. *If this gets out of hand, two of them are on the wrong side of the vehicle, too far to intervene. I would have to disable the two on this side, then the one in front of the truck.* The odds were not entirely daunting, but with guns involved in the hands of capable people made matters more complicated. Opening the door slowly, she stepped out, leaving the door open to act as yet another barrier to the man standing in front of the vehicle.

"Turn around," the bearded man said. "We need to pat you down."

Caylee had left her pistol in the truck. Coming from Texas, they shouldn't be surprised to find a weapon. The Ruling Council had ordered the surrender of all guns after The Fall. The weak complied, out of fear of jail or social enforcement. Many simply hid their weapons. *We were told it was for our general safety, but in reality, it was a means of control.*

She had taped a switchblade to her shin, before leaving. Given her boots, chances were high they wouldn't find it. Turning her back to the SEs, she put her hands on the roof of the truck, and leaned into it.

The man patted her down, and he was groping far more than he was searching for weapons. She felt him grip her breasts from behind, squeezing them. She wanted to clench her jaw at the obvious action, but she settled for a blush to her face. His hands slid down the inside of her thighs, stopping just short of the switchblade.

From the other side of the truck, a stocky man opened the door and found her gun. "Weapon here, boss," he said, pulling her pistol off of the passenger side of the vehicle.

The bearded man spun her around. "So what would a lady like you be doing with a gun?"

"Self-protection."

"Possession of guns is against the law; you had to know that."

"You saw my ID. I'm from Texas. Traveling alone, a gun seemed prudent."

"And dangerous," the bearded man countered. "That's why they are banned in Newmerica."

Guns don't make people dangerous, she thought. "You have guns."

"We are Social Enforcement."

"You have no position under the law."

"That isn't the issue," he said, clearly getting flustered—which had been her intent. "You don't have a right to have a gun in your possession."

"So what happens now?" she asked.

The bearded man glanced over at two of his comrades, then back to her. "Well, we should take you into custody and haul you into the justice in Tucumcari."

"You can't arrest me," she said. "You don't have the authority."

"I *can* do a citizen's arrest." The bearded man stroked his beard once, eying her as if they were in a bar. "Of course, you might be held for days, maybe a week, before getting a chance to see the judge. It's hard to say." His voice had a ring of coyness to it, one she didn't care for in the least.

"I haven't done anything wrong."

"Well," he said grinning slightly, "we could work something out." His right hand drifted down to the fly of his pants. One of the other men chuckled loud enough for her to hear.

Caylee's eyes swept the surrounding ground. Travis had come across six hours earlier. There was a chance that he was out there, able to help, but she saw no sign of him. Being a former SEAL, he would be hidden. That, or he was under arrest and she was on her own.

Drawing a deep breath through her nose, she would have to assume she was on her own. She advanced a half-step slowly. "Are you serious?"

His grin broadened. "It's your choice. It can be lonely out here. You either help us out, or spend time in jail."

Her heart roared in her ears as she assessed the situation. The leader would go down first. His buddies would scramble. She could use his rifle on the closest one—they would be too stunned to just shoot her at first. That would take care of two. Moving to keep the truck between them, she could probably take out the one in front of the vehicle. *That would still leave two. They will panic fire at first because the situation has gotten out of control. They have experience and will recover.* If she went low, she might be able to shoot one from under the truck … most people forget that as an option. That might leave her with one, with at least one or two wounded. They weren't the best odds, but she felt confident that she could pull it off.

Her face unleashed a mask of disgust as she looked the leader in the face. He spread his legs slightly, unzipping his fly. His penis flopped out, already rigid and purple as Caylee knelt down in front of him. As he shuffled closer to put it in her face, she looked up at him, making eye contact. His smile had become downright sinister as he anticipated the fellatio. Even in the cool breeze, she could feel the heat from his crotch.

With his eyes locked on hers, he did not watch her hand drift to her boot, and pull off the switchblade. With a stunning fluid motion, she snapped the blade and brought it up and across his left thigh, then doubled back across his penis. She didn't cut it off entirely, part of it dangled as his blood squirted into the dusty, orange dirt.

The pain came a moment later, and he wailed dropping to his knees as she rose. She still held the knife, using it to cut the nylon strap for his AR-15, dropping it as soon as the weapon was free; then she turned the gun on the nearest of the men as the bearded leader wailed in agony at her feet. She fired three bullets, two of them slapping into the next assailant, one in his shoulder, the other in his chest. His mouth puckered in shock. His own grin disappeared as he twisted and dropped.

A shot rang off to her right, and she moved, firing at the man in front of the truck. He ducked as she fired, one shot missing, another hitting him in the temple. Brains and white bits of bone sprayed out in front of the vehicle as she dropped low.

One of the remaining men was standing behind a tire; the other wasn't. He was running to the rear of the vehicle to come up behind her. She heard another crack-bang of gunfire as she aimed at the feet of the man trying to flank her. Four bullets, fired rapidly, tore into his left ankle mid-stride, and he fell, kicking up dust as Caylee rose, turning to the front of the vehicle where she sensed motion.

Beyond her truck's open door, she saw a figure approaching. She raised her weapon, but saw she wasn't going to be fast enough. He loomed over her, his muzzle tracking her as she prepared to jump, hoping she could throw off his aim.

Suddenly, his head exploded. Chunks of gray matter hit her legs as she kicked off. The bang of the shot came next, somewhat distant. Her attacker's arms fell limp, and his assault weapon fell, followed a millisecond later with him dropping to his knees, then falling towards her. Half of his head was missing, splattered on the dry dirt.

The leader was still alive, in agony. His face was white as he tried to quench the severed artery in his leg. His half-severed penis was covered with wet crimson gore. As she stood over him, his eyes seemed to plead for mercy, or pity, or help. She opted for mercy, putting a bullet between his eyes.

Another crack rang off in the distance, followed a heartbeat later with another. She crouched low, moving to see if the target was the man she had shot in the ankle. As she rounded the bed of the truck, she saw him dead.

All five Sidewinders were accounted for. She drew a deep breath in through her nose and released it slowly through her pursed lips. Looking off in the distance, some fifty yards away, Travis Cullen rose and waved to her. He wore a ghillie suit of dead brown brush and grass. "You okay?" he called out, his weapon with its big scope still at the ready.

"We're good," she said, moving to her third victim to make sure he was as dead as she assumed he was. Relaxing her breathing slightly, she felt perspiration on her face in the cool breeze.

Travis moved up next to her. Caylee looked at him with a hint of a scowl on her face. "You took your sweet time."

Travis grinned. "From where I was, it looked like you had all this under control. At least until the end. Besides, I couldn't risk shooting and missing. You were in my field of fire and on the move." He walked up next to her and glanced down at the leader. When Travis saw the mostly severed member, he flinched. "That's a hell of a way to go."

"We need to clean this up," Caylee said. People will come looking for them after a while."

Travis nodded. "It's a big ass desert around here. We can put them in the truck and drop them off—far enough away that it will take a while to find them. Let's secure their weapons too; we can hide them near the camp in case we need them." Her mind was already moving past the vicious encounter to the true objective—scouting the SE camp.

She nodded and with the back of her hand wiped a spot of coagulated blood from her cheek. "One thing is for certain, we won't be able to leave the way we came in. Even if they don't find these guys, they will know they're missing and assume the worst. They'll be prepared."

Travis paused. "You're right about that. Are you sure you're okay?"

Bending down, she picked up the switchblade and wiped the gore off it and onto the dead leader's pants leg. It had not been the first time in her life that someone tried to force sex on her, and few ended this way. *Am I okay?* "I'll be fine," she said. "I hate this part of the job."

"From what I saw, these guys brought it on themselves."

"True," she said, putting the captured AR-15 in the bed of the truck. "That doesn't make it any easier."

CHAPTER 7

"Our Forefathers were white privileged men, slave owners and oppressors. None possessed redeeming qualities. They are icons of white supremacy."

Mt. Diablo, California

Darius finished cleaning his weapon for what seemed like the hundredth time. It didn't need it. Cleaning the gun was never the point. Doing the task quickly, crisply—that repetition seemed to give him comfort. It calmed him, and calm was scarce since the events at the Presidio a week earlier.

The operation had taken the better part of a day. Skirmishes had popped up all over the Presidio grounds as they herded the squatters to the waiting trucks. Of the "housing disenfranchised," as Captain Aguilar referred to them; ten were killed and nearly twenty were wounded. There were a lot of injuries in the ranks of the Veteran's Corp, but only two fatalities. They had a ceremony for the dead two days after, but it felt like a hollow gesture to Darius. Getting killed to remove homeless people from a park was not some glorious military victory that it was portended to be. I have been in combat. What we did was to be nothing more than thug park rangers.

When he finished cleaning the weapon, he carefully stowed it and returned to his bed. Reaching up to his right breast pocket, he pulled out the Afghanistan Service medal that he had taken from the hand of the woman he had seen killed. He rubbed the medal between his thumb and forefinger, feeling every ridge and contour. Closing his eyes for a moment, he remembered the scene as clearly as any memory of any battle he had fought in. The despair in the woman's face and her last desperate words … "I'm one of you!" tore into him.

As he opened his eyes slowly, looking up, he noticed that his breathing was rapid. His face was wet with sweat. He didn't move, simply lay there, arms on his chest, the medal in his right hand. *She was right. I lived in those camps. I was made to move to a Tiny Town. I went from owning a profitable business to being homeless in a matter of months.*

Darius knew he could weather the loss personally, but it had cost him his buddies as well. They too were driven into poverty. He still remembered being with both of them for the last time. Both of their deaths were tragic. John had blamed himself for their plight, something he took with him to his grave. William had surrendered to his demons in a death spiral of drugs and depression. Darius had tried to help both of them, but had failed in each instance. *We had been to the other side of the planet in battle together, but the war didn't kill them; the peace did.*

He heard the footsteps on the plywood flooring near his bed and then a crisp voice. "Yo, Darius, you okay?" Vixen asked.

Sitting up slowly, he tucked the medal into his breast pocket and swung his legs off of the bed. Vixen was short, with an almost barrel chest and small breasts. Her body didn't have a bit of fat on it; she was all sinewy muscle. She wore her hair cropped, two inches tall, standing straight up on her head. "I'm fine," he said as she took a seat on the bed across from him.

"Whenever my mom used to say that, we all knew it meant the opposite," she said half-jokingly.

"Really," Darius said with little emotion in his voice. "I'm okay."

"You've been moping around ever since the Presidio. I'm not the only one to notice it. You were in here striping and field and cleaning your rifle for three hours, over and over. That's not normal."

What is normal anymore? He eyed her silently for a moment, contemplating if he could trust her. It had been a long time since he had given another person trust. The losses of his life had made him naturally reluctant to confide in others. Still, Vixen was like him in many ways. She had served with honor, had been housing displaced, and had been coerced into joining the Veteran's Corps. With a deep sigh, he started. "That whole thing felt wrong to me—going in there and forcing those people out. The NSF should have done it, not us. We are supposed to be military, and that was not a military operation. We killed civilians."

"They started it," she countered.

"Did they? We were the ones that showed up with guns and started rounding them up like cattle."

Vixen nodded. "I didn't like it either. You know the drill, though. Orders are orders."

"We killed civilians."

"In case you don't remember, they fired at us first. A lot of them were chucking rocks and bricks. A guy tried to waylay me using a bat with a nail stuck in it. They were far from peaceful."

"We came with guns and tac gear to evict them. It was excessive."

Vixen seemed to pause, thinking about what he said. "We had a job to do, and we did it."

"I didn't join the Corps to be used against our own people," he said.

"I didn't as much join as I was forced to," Vixen offered. "They were going to cut off my government support. I had some outstanding bogus charges against me, you know, a bench warrant or two. If I joined, they would make all of that shit go away, and I could keep my benefits."

"They threatened my benefits too," he said, patting his breast pocket where the medal rested—just to make sure it was still there. "It makes you wonder, doesn't it?"

"Wonder about what?"

"If our cause is just. Why did they have to force us to join?"

Vixen nodded once. "Yeah. I try not to think about it much. It's easier to just assume that orders are orders and do what I'm told."

"You've been in combat—*real* combat. You know that sometimes the officers in charge couldn't find their ass with a flashlight and both hands. Blindly following orders is right most of the time, but sometimes it is not. Good soldiers know the difference."

"You don't trust Captain Aguilar?"

It was Darius's time to pause. Trust was always a complicated matter. *She's done nothing that made me distrust her—but how much do I really know her?* Eventually, he settled on an answer. "So far, I trust her. I don't trust the officers that are giving her orders, though. Something about how they are using the Corps sticks. We should have never been sent into the Presidio in the first place, and you know it."

"So what can we do?" Vixen asked.

It was a pointed question. *What can I do?* Walking away was not much of an option. He could feel her dark eyes piercing his own gaze. "I don't know. But when the time comes, I will."

Texas Military Department (TMD) HQ,
Camp Mabry, Austin, Texas

General Reager crossed his arms as he stood at the far end of the conference table, looming over the built-in table display map. The computer image was stunning, a mix of greens and grays and splashes of red showing various deployments. The tabletop display was more than a map; it was a full-blown presentation, right down to the details of what equipment would be on which aircraft. He expected nothing less from Judy Mercury.

"I want to make sure I understand this. In order to provide air support in New Hampshire, you plan to seize an airport in New York State."

"I would call that the short version, General, but yes," Mercury replied.

Trip paused for a moment. The other options were far less appealing. Trying to fly ground support from friendly air bases would give the enemy ample time to intercept. Reager had to factor in that he did not have an inexhaustible supply of aircraft. Lockheed Martin's plant in Fort Worth was still operating, but it was not a rapid assembly line. Helicopters were also a carefully husbanded commodity. *We would be putting a lot of precious resources at risk.*

There were aspects to the plan he liked, though he hadn't said them out loud. Stewart-Newburgh looked easily defendable. If the Newmericans wanted to take it back, it would drain their resources and take considerable time. Also, from what they could tell, there were ample supplies of fuel, parts, and munitions at the National Guard base there.

"What are your thoughts, sir?" Mercury asked.

"It's audacious. I'll say that much," he conceded, telling her his favorite part. "They will never expect us to try it."

Lieutenant Colonel Mihalek, standing next to Mercury, spoke up. "Sir, they will never see this coming."

"Agreed. I think we should shuttle in additional air defense systems early after we occupy the facility," Trip said. "They may not be able to send in ground forces quickly, but they will attempt to bomb the base."

"Yes sir," Mercury said. "We can modify the plan accordingly."

"You'll need a top-notch Combat Aviation Brigade, outfitted with aux fuel tanks. Stewart-Newburgh is at the limits of their range to get to New Hampshire."

"I've got a unit in mind," Mercury said with a thin smile.

"Lariat?" he said, referring to Captain "Lariat" Paredes. He and his American First CAB was a volunteer unit of the American Army. Mostly Texas men and women who had defected from the Pentagon's controlled military, Paredes has crafted them into a tight-knit, hard-hitting helicopter assault team.

"He is one of the best," she said with a nod.

Trip couldn't hide his own satisfaction with her choice. "Even if you get him in, you're still facing some range challenges."

"In terms of the range, we hope that the Defiance movement can pre-position some fuel at a discreet location to help us refuel, if needed. With the auxiliary fuel tanks on the Black Hawks and the Apaches, they have enough to hang for a few minutes over New Hampshire. It is our intention to use them closer in, at least at first, to interdict enemy air bases," Mihalek answered. "That will allow us to use our Warthogs and AC-130s primarily over the battlefield."

"If you take out a few airfields, it will put the pinch on their logistics," Trip said.

"That's the plan. It will make them pull combat resources from the battlespace back to protect their airbases, which will help level the playing field for our folks on the ground," Mercury added.

Trip's instinct was to let his people talk, rather than to nitpick their hard work. *It's clear they've thought this through a great deal, right down to the logistics. Let's see if they will own up to the risks.* "Alright, Major, you and your people have a plan. So what are the risks? What's the downside to this?"

Judy Mercury shifted on her feet ever-so-slightly at the question. Her thin smile faded as she shifted to a parade rest stance. She cast a darting glace at Lieutenant Colonel Mihalek who gave her an assuring nod. "We've looked at this six ways to Sunday. Simply put, we are talking about seizing and using an advance airbase in the middle of enemy-held territory. We will be surrounded by potentially hostile forces the moment we arrive. Eventually, the enemy will learn where we are and either try to destroy us, or take the base back. Good people are going to die; there's no way around that." Her voice was deeper than before, a bit less cocky.

Trip appreciated her blunt honesty. "Agreed," he said, sighing momentarily. "They won't be expecting this. Even after your little jaunt through Illinois, they will not anticipate us doing something like this. That will work to our advantage. I like the fact they will be forced to look behind their backs…to know we can strike at them from any direction."

General Reager paused for a moment, then looked at Mihalek, then back to Mercury, locking his gaze with hers. "We are in a civil war. People are going to die. Even if a shot isn't fired at you, a hundred things can go wrong with a low altitude approach like you are proposing. Our job is to use the resources we have to achieve our objectives, while minimizing our losses. We are not going to win this war by playing it safe. Taking big risks for even bigger gains—those are the kinds of actions that can give us victory. The fighters up in New Hampshire are going to need every bit of help we can give them. You are one of those lifelines."

Mercury nodded. "So you are green-lighting the operation?"

Trip nodded in response. "You'll need a code name for this op. Something less colorful than your last one." While Trip had liked Operation Grab Ass, the enemy media had labeled it, "A tribute to toxic masculinity," despite the fact that a female had led the mission.

Lieutenant Colonel Mihalek weighed in. "We were thinking Green Lantern."

Trip couldn't think of any way the TRC might try to twist that into something bad, but somehow he knew they would. "Very well. You have your approval. I'll fill in the President. Go and assemble your team. Double-check your security—if the enemy gets wind of you loading choppers on C-5s, they might put two-and-two together."

"Yes sir," Mercury replied, her grin slowly returning. "We won't let you down."

"You never do Judy. Get up there and tear these bastards a new asshole."

Percy Warner Park
Nashville, Tennessee

Thiago Reese/Luis Fernando sat on a bench looking down the long cascade of steps known as the Allée. It was twilight, and the park was almost empty. He zipped up his blue windbreaker slightly to keep out the evening chill. Spring was coming; there were signs of buds everywhere, but the nights were still cold enough to keep people out of the park.

Things were progressing in his undermining of the American government. His hidden recording devices had picked up information about a possible military operation west of Texas, which he had passed on via a dead drop. Some notes he had recovered in the trash had pointed to strains and struggles in the American economy; he had shared the notes with the TRC, who had already run stories about how the American government was covering up their economic shortfalls. Such stories amplified issues, gave people pause, and made them wonder if they were being told the truth. Distrust in one's government was easy to foster, and once it was in place, it was nearly impossible to change.

The use of the media to undermine a government was an old concept and one he had used before. In this case, the media hated America, making their involvement easy. They wanted the rebirth of America to be aborted. They had reveled in the death of the Traitor President and had painted themselves martyrs when the Pretender had been sworn in… the victims of a terrorist attack. *America is fighting its own free press as much as the soldiers in the field.*

As he sat on the bench, he saw the woman work her way up the long row of steps towards him. She wore a black trench coat and a hat that hid her face from a distance, almost cliché in his mind, He knew her well, Pat Templeton of MSNBC. He had chosen her to be the recipient of his information because she had an axe to grind with the Americans. When she taunted General Reager, he had hit her. The public had not been on her side when it aired; many felt that she had gone too far. Her civil suit against Reager had died in court. *She will want revenge, and I will give it to her.*

Templeton sat on the bench with him, leaving a foot between them. "Alright," she sighed. "I'm curious as to who you are and what you have for me."

Luis cracked a smile. "Who I am is unimportant," he assured her. "What I have for you is a scandal." Unzipping his windbreaker slightly, he pulled out a large, yellow envelope and handed it to her.

The reporter took it, opened the flap, and pulled out the photograph he had taken. "What am I looking at exactly?"

"That is Caylee Leatrom," he said. "She's in the Southern White House often. She's working for the Pretender's administration."

Those words made Templeton's head tip down on the left, and she pursed her lips for a moment. "They have a wanted terrorist working for them?"

"There have been rumors for a long time that she's responsible for things here, but for some reason our friends to the north in the TRC haven't said much. Now you have a picture of her in the building."

She pulled the image further out of the envelope and looked at it. "Why would you do this?" she said, casting him a questioning glance.

"I am a patriot, just like you. If these Americans are working with a terrorist, well, the people should know. They should know the kind of man that their President is and the individuals that he is surrounding himself with. Don't you agree?"

She nodded, carefully putting the image back in the envelope. "This is big. I mean yes, there have been rumors that she's about and working down here in Tennessee, but this … this is something that big. What is her role here?"

"I don't know that. I do know that she meets with military and civilian leaders in the administration. You can see she's a guest, a visitor; there's no guards or handcuffs."

Templeton paused for a moment, looking away from him, apparently talking out loud to herself. "I'll have to get the TRC to clear it. They aren't likely to ask for verification or confirmation—not for something this big." Slowly, she turned her head back to Luis. "This is remarkable. How can I thank you?"

"You don't have to," he assured her, zipping up his windbreaker, and then standing. "Just run with the story. People that associate with such domestic terrorists need to be stopped, no matter what it takes."

"Agreed," she said standing, and extending her hand. Luis shook it. "Thank you again!" With those words, she started down the long stairs of the Allée. Luis watched her as she went. The press was always easy to manipulate, especially when they carried a grudge or a conviction to a cause. Having been in many foreign nations and taking them down, he saw the TRC and the press for what they were, tools of propaganda. The public didn't care because they assured the people that everything that was happening was good, that they were better off. When they reported bad news, it was always targeted at the enemy—and if the enemy didn't exist, they simply made one up.

Ms. Templeton is working for me, even if she doesn't realize it. She thinks she is breaking a big story, but she's really doing my bidding. Just thinking about that made him smile as he turned away from her and started back towards the parking area.

Luis had bigger targets in mind. He wanted to hamstring the Pretender's Administration, but getting to Jack Desmond was proving a challenge. He had hoped to use the parking garage and strike at Desmond as he got into or out of his vehicle. The problem he faced was the stringent security. Luis had tested it, 'accidentally' hitting one camera with a broom handle in the garage while taking out the office trash. By the next day, it had been readjusted. It wasn't enough to strike at Desmond; he had to do it correctly. Moreover, he had to get away.

The garage was too secure, and a pair of Secret Service agents protected his apartment, meaning that getting to him there would be a bloody affair. Luis knew this had to be a surgical strike, done with grace and precision. Armed guards of a security detail made taking Desmond out of the equation challenging. He knew he would overcome it, and when he did, he intended to plunge the American government into chaos.

Caylee Leatrom fits into my plans perfectly. Mine will be a bigger story that Templeton's ... one that will shake apart this little house of cards they call a government down here.

The District

The Vice President rose to her feet slowly as Veronica Hinkley entered her office. Veronica stood rigid before her desk, most likely out of respect rather than fear. She wore the new gray uniform of a People's Warden, replete with a gold braid that arched from her left shoulder epaulet over her bosom to her front buttons mid-chest. The Vice President was pleased with the uniform's look on Hinkley. *It is military-ish, but different enough. I'm sure the old men of the Pentagon will chafe at it, but they are fossils of a long-dead era.*

"Madame Vice President," she said in a crisp, quick voice. The Vice President extended her hand and Hinkley shook it firmly. As the VP slid back into her seat, her guest took a chair across the desk from her.

The People's Warden Program had come after the defeat in Knoxville a few weeks earlier. The pretense was simple—put loyal civilians side-by-side with the military commanders to ensure that failures like that battle didn't happen. They were political officers, answering to her. Military officers that were disloyal, or those that did not act in the best interest of Newmerica, could be identified and removed.

Of course, with the People's Warden's answering to her control, the Vice President had gained a new level of control of the military. *The military is supposed to be under civilian control; all I am doing is making sure that those in command have the right priorities politically—as they should. As more wardens are assigned, my grip on the military will grow. I will root out those that do not fully support our cause and eventually lead us to victory.* It was difficult for her to suppress a grin, so she didn't.

"I take it you reviewed your assignment?" the Vice President asked.

Hickley nodded. "Indeed I have. I am to shadow General Rinehart, monitor his and his staff's operations. Anyone not showing loyalty to the nation is to be removed from command and arrested for Tribunals. I also understand that I have full discretion to administer justice on the spot, as I see fit, as if I were an SE."

"Exactly. We have suffered far too many setbacks with the military in this little uprising by the Pretender President and his minions. We need a victory. Your presence there is a reminder to the General and his people they work for—*the people*. You will keep them in line, ensuring proper behavior and thought."

"I look forward to the chance to serve."

"I thought you might. I picked you for this assignment myself."

Hinkley's face reddened in her high cheeks. "I am honored."

"They treated you poorly. You were drummed out of West Point your freshman year."

"Plebe year," Veronica corrected her. "Yes. According to them, I could not meet the physical requirements required of a cadet. I petitioned the Commandant to lower the standards, and he refused."

"Typical male supremacist response," the Vice President quipped. "The military has always treated non-males with no tolerance. As I recall, you went to ROTC and were a lieutenant when you finally resigned your commission. They have long hidden behind their standards and doctrines, using them to suppress others. I chose you because of that—because they wronged you—they demeaned you—they cost you years of your military career."

"It was unfair." The bitterness still hung in her words, which was what the Vice President was counting on. *She's motivated and not likely to put up with any bullshit from the General.*

"It was unjust," the Vice President lightly corrected her. "You know what that makes you?"

Hinkley shook her head and the VP continued. "It makes you incentivized to do your duty."

Her words brought a smile to the lean face of Warden Hinkley. "Does the General know I am coming?"

"He has been informed about the program, and that we will be putting Wardens with this officers. He raised concerns, but they are irrelevant. Progress will not be slowed because their little empire is being threatened. Even the Americans believe that the military serves at the whim of the civilian authority. Putting in People's Wardens merely affirms that."

"And how much authority do I have?" Hinkley asked slowly.

"All that you need. You are there to make sure they do the will of the people. To do that, you may do whatever it takes. If that means eliminating disloyal soldiers to make an example, then do so."

"Where will I be going?"

The Vice President leaned back in her leather chair slightly. "We are preparing to finally eradicate the threat of this Defiance movement in New Hampshire once and for all. Also, we have recently gotten some intelligence that the Americans are planning some sort of offensive operation into New Mexico. The good General has been planning a little surprise of his own there. As such, you may be all over the country. It may be awhile before you see your family and friends, but that is the nature of the assignment."

The General's 'surprise' was not as bold as she would have hoped. The military always seemed to think inside of their box, rather than looking at the big picture. *That's okay. We have allies that can help us in ways he could not imagine. I will use Ms. Hinkley to augment what he has planned.*

Her own mention of the intelligence made her jaw set. Her operative that had infiltrated the Southern White House had seen Caylee Leatrom … he had used resources in the NSF to confirm her identity. She knew that the rogue operative was working for the Pretender in some capacity, and the Vice President wanted her dead. The problem was there was no way to get a message to Thiago Reese while undercover without putting him at risk. *He had better take care of her once and for all. That bitch killed my brother and mother.* Reese was good; his intelligence was already making people doubt that Pretender's administration … but the fact that he had not simply killed Leatrom was infuriating.

"That is fine. My family has never been supportive of me or my life choices," she said.

"Then this is your chance to prove them wrong along with all of the others in the patriarchy that have conspired against you."

Veronica Hinkley slowly cracked a smile, and it only broadened the one that the Vice President wore. *Everything is unfolding exactly the way I wanted—the way it must for us to be victorious.*

CHAPTER 8

"Righteousness is more than a state of mind; it is a purpose."

Santa Fe National Park, New Mexico

Caylee moved in the pre-dawn darkness, maneuvering from bush to bush for cover. Her night vision gear made everything green, and the weight of the optics dug into her lean cheeks as she maneuvered on the uneven terrain. Looming in the distance was the Social Quarantine camp, surrounded by a tall, chain-link fence. There were no signs of active patrols, which didn't surprise her. The camp was in the middle of the Santa Fe National Park. It was isolated, surrounded by miles of unforgiving terrain. Anyone escaping would be not only dealing with social enforcement pursuers, but fighting the elements and lack of water.

Squatting down, her eyes swept the rear of the camp, drinking in details. There were two-story barracks, crude wooden structures with little evidence of comfort. She had watched the camp in daylight and saw they were little more than plywood shacks with a sloppy coat of dull, gray paint applied to them.

There were larger structures, clearly industrial. One was four stories tall with massive smokestacks that jutted skyward. Even from where she knelt, a quarter of a mile away, the stench still stung her nostrils. It was a strange, almost toxic aroma, chemical-smelling with a hint of ash, as if someone were burning garbage. Clearly, the camp was part of the source, but the stench extended far from the potential source.

The enormous building was clearly some sort of processing facility.

A steady stream of trucks came in and left the camp. The trucks pulled in and were often there for hours at a time. Travis was working his way around the front of the camp to see if he could learn what was going on.

She had seen groups of prisoners earlier in the afternoon. They walked like zombies, shambling almost; no doubt their energy was spent. They didn't have uniforms like normal prisoners; they wore filthy clothing that they may have brought with them. Most of it seemed too large, baggy, an indication they were not being fed well. A single thought kept gnawing at her, a burning curiosity. *What was going on in that plant?* She remembered the camp where Raul's mother and sister had been exposed to toxic chemicals as they manufactured solar panels. The prisoners had been slave labor, intentionally worked to death as part of Newmerica's way of dealing with anyone that did not support their cause.

The night air was chilly and made her arms prickle with goosebumps as she took a sip from the tube connected to her Camelbak. In the distance, on the far side of the fence, she saw a pair of guards leaning up against one structure that was clearly not a barrack. They wore face masks with big, round filters, and when they moved into her field of vision, she saw them pull the masks off. A flash of light showed that they were lighting cigarettes. *Trading one health risk for another.* The detail she focused on was the masks. The social enforcement guards were wearing them, but not the prisoners.

She paused for a moment to make notes on a pad she carried in a right thigh pocket. The guards were wearing small side arms, but not rifles. *They are not worried about people escaping or revolting.* Only the guards in the wooden towers at the corners of the complex seemed to be armed with assault rifles. Their attention was not outward, but focused inward. *That's right; there's nothing to see out here but coyotes and snakes.*

Caylee secured the pad and pencil and rose slightly to change position, skirting to the northeast of the camp. She came across a set of tire ruts in the desert, leading away from the facility. The road path was well worn. It was not a surprise. Part of her mission was to find the large patch they had seen in surveillance photos out past the camp. Turning, she followed the roadway from the facility.

She could smell the site before she saw it. The chemical aroma that she had detected near the camp seemed to get more pervasive. It wasn't a stench she knew, and despite breathing it through her nose, Caylee could taste it.

Following the road over a hill, in the darkness, she saw a great blackness suddenly emerge before her at the end of the roadway. It stretched far and wide. With the night vision gear, it had a strange shimmer to it, like a pond of water. It was odd though; the pool seemed to rise off of the desert floor, in some areas three feet. Pivoting, she made sure she was out of the line of sight of the camp as she continued closer to it.

At the edge of the material, she bent down and touched it and found that it was hard and smooth. Caylee shut off her night vision gear and removed the headset. It took a moment for her eyes to shift from the shimmering green light of the optics to true darkness. With her gloved hands, she could feel ripples in the surface, and as she traced it in the night's blackness, it rose to nearly two feet in height.

Killing her night vision and pulling out her Maglite, Caylee made sure she was between the light and the camp, just in case some reflection might give up her position. The substance was black, glass-like. Touching it again, she realized that it was some sort of plastic. The color of it was a swirl of black and dark green. There were air bubbles in the material, along with strange little bits of what looked like charred paper or some other substance.

She stepped out on it and it was solid. The top showed signs of puddling and settling, as if the molten material had been pumped there and the heavier material had settled. Caylee checked her footing for a moment—the top was cracked in a few places, but otherwise it was not slippery. The top was pitted with embedded dust, and in other places it was like a sheet a glass.

Walking out further, she swept the vast field with her Maglite. Images deep down in the surface reflected back at her. Cautiously she made her way out to them. In one case a crushed metal barrel was entombed in the hardened plastic. She saw a few trash bags as well, sealed deep under her feet.

Then she saw something else … a human face. Its eyes were closed, but there was a body. Dropping to her knees, she looked at a female who was middle-aged. She was not on the floor of the desert, but seemed to be floating between layers of the plastic. The woman was naked. Near her was another body, that of an emaciated young man. A few feet away was the body of an older white-haired man with a beard.

Her jaw set in revulsion. *Why have they done this to them?* She knew that people were dying in the camps, but why not bury them? Why leave them this way? Taking out her camera, she took photos of what she saw. There was no choice. Without proof, people would claim that it was a lie, that she had been mistaken. *I wonder how many dead are out here?* In the black of the night, the shimmering area seemed to stretch for acres.

From the road, she heard a faint footfall and doused her light. She put on her night vision gear and saw the crouched figure of Travis Cullen approaching her. He crept down the hill, and she pulled the optics off again, motioning for him to join her.

"What is this?" he asked in a low whisper as he removed his own night vision gear.

She aimed the Maglite where she had seen the bodies, and showed him. "God damn," he muttered. "It makes sense though."

"How does this make sense?" she said, shutting off the light and plunging them into darkness once more.

"I checked out those trucks. They are hauling waste plastics in there. It's some sort of recycling center. They have the prisoners sorting the stuff when it comes in. From what I saw, they are grinding it down, then re-melting it into new bottles that go out."

"How does that explain this?"

"That plant isn't big enough for that kind of operation. That means they are cutting corners. There are pumper trucks at the far end of the facility. My guess is that they were short-cutting the process. When they melt this stuff down, there are impurities—mostly because they are not cleaning the stuff when it comes in. I checked out one of the trucks at the rear of the plant—it has this stuff on it. They must be scraping off the waste residue and dumping it out here."

"And the bodies?"

"Like I said, I've seen a recycling plant before. It should be bigger, with heavy duty air scrubbers, chemical cleaning facilities, and the means of dealing with this leftover slag. This place is skipping all of the safety measures, including personal protection. The prisoners work there, and they die there." His voice trailed off as he looked out at the massive field of waste plastic.

"So they just dump them here."

"And tell the world they are green … that it is clean recycling."

It was the lie of the green movement, that it was actually good for the environment. *Every so-called green solution they implement creates a whole new set of pollution problems.* "They're killing people in the camp to produce bottles," she said coolly, holding her rage in check. It was the same as the solar plant where Raul's mother had died. Newmerica was the master of telling the world that they were good and cared about the environment while running death camps to achieve their goals. "This place is a death camp—they work people to death here. I wonder how many people are out here, entombed."

"Probably hundreds," Travis said in a low tone. "I saw a truck come in and unload thirty prisoners in the late afternoon. So they must have some sort of high turnover to warrant that many replacements."

Caylee said nothing for a moment as she thought through the implications of what they had found. "The world needs to know about this place," she finally said.

"They will," Travis said. "When we get the people out of there."

Nodding, she put her night vision gear back on. They had a long way to go before the sun came up. As they moved out, each footfall seemed to jar her body a little. There was a numbness to her as she moved. Caylee thought back to her time as a NSF operative. *While I was there, I worked for the people that authorized this slaughter. I never bothered to look into what kind of government I was working for. It was easy to just live for each mission. I was a part of all of this and never knew it .*

She struggled with the revulsion of the preserved bodies trapped in solid plastic discharge. *They didn't cremate them; they didn't bury them; they threw them out as trash.* She remembered the camp where Maria and Raul's mother had been held. The bones of the dead were used as fertilizer. *These are people—not commodities, not garbage.*

The truck drivers going to and from the plant probably didn't know that the goods they were hauling were tainted with the blood of the dead.

The guards though, they knew, even if the general public had no inkling of what was happening in the camps. *People look to their own prosperity and choose to ignore what it took to get there. People opt to look the other way to preserve the illusions they embrace—they ignore the lies, deceit, and deaths so that they can sleep at night.*

The image of the bodies encased in waste plastic demanded justice. Caylee was sure that she could not sleep for a few nights—that those faces in the darkness were going to haunt her. While their eyes were closed, hers were wide open.

Carroll, New Hampshire

Su-Hui Zhou cringed and hunkered down as the mortar round slammed into the rear of the Patio Motor Court. The concussion from the blast made his chest throb and threw chunks of sod skyward. His ears were ringing from the two previous hits, but the last one made his left ear pop. Glancing at the motel, he saw that all the windows were shattered, and the siding was deeply pitted from shrapnel.

He and his people had been evacuating their base. Su-Hui remained behind, as one of the last to depart. The Sons of Liberty and their support teams from the New Hampshire National Guard had fled cross-country, using ATVs and rugged four wheelers. They had begun the evacuation before the enemy forces started their attack. Turning to the last ATV, hiding further back in the wood line of pine trees, he saw the bulky form of the motor court's owner, Tate Palmer, rushing over to him, his head ducked low as another mortar round exploded further to the east, blasting apart a pine tree.

"Your people out?" Tate asked with a yell as the two men moved towards the last remaining ATV. His voice was muffled, half-drowned out by the explosions, the rest suppressed by the concussion in Su-Hui's ears. The big man swung his rifle around from his back and into his hands as he moved, something he had clearly done dozens of times before.

Su-Hui nodded and raised his voice in response, "I have room for you with me."

Tate Palmer stood fully upright, towering over Su-Hui. "No sir. I'm going to remain here." The more he strained to hear Tate, the clearer it became as he filtered out the ringing in his ears.

"Tate," he barked loudly over the echoes of distant explosions. "The enemy is coming here in-force."

"I know. This is my place. I aim to stay here." There was dignity in what he said as he puffed out his chest.

Su-Hui shook his head. "You need to come with me," he said as they closed in on the ATV. Another explosion brought down a rain of dead pine needles over both of the men as they moved.

"My family built this place. It is my land. I'll be damned if I am going to run away."

What does he think he can do? Su-Hui knew the answer to his own mental question. *He intends to fight to the death.* It was a noble act, honorable, but foolhardy. In the distance, he could hear the throb of diesel engines, a sign that enemy tanks and vehicles were approaching.

"This is just a place" he insisted. "If you chose to fight, here you are throwing your life away."

"It's my land."

"And it will be again," Su-Hui insisted. "We need you—your son needs you. Dying here, now, accomplishes nothing." Another distant explosion made his joints throb with the reverberation, and both of them instinctively ducked, albeit too late.

"I can make my stand here," the larger man said proudly.

"You can, and you will be dead. Come with me, and you can live to fight another day. Isn't it more important to see them defeated once and for all? You can come back, rebuild. If you die, that is it—you're dead."

Tate paused for a moment as more pine needles rained down on his red and blue flannel coat. "I will take a hell of a lot of them with me."

He's committed. It is suicide, but he refuses to see another path. Su-Hui respected it. It was the same sort of determination that had kept the Granite Staters continuing to fight during the Newmerican occupation. The counterbalance to that was the senseless waste. *He will hate me for what is to come, but I would rather have his living hate than know that our presence here led to his death.*

"Come, I need your help with the ATV," he said moving along the vehicle.

Tate followed him, putting his rifle down on the rear of the ATV on the packs that were already strapped there. "What's the problem?"

"There," he pointed to the floorboard.

Tate leaned in and Su-Hui struck. He had trained in karate for six years and after college. He eyed his targets on Tate carefully, then committed—both mentally and physically. It was rare that he used the techniques, but the muscle memory was there. He struck with two blows so fast they were a blur. One hit Tate's jawline, snapping his head hard and away. The other, a blow to his neck, just below the ear, struck the nerves there.

The first blow did not hurt the larger man, but it twisted his head hard. Inside his skull his brain was sloshing hard to one side. The hit to the neck made his head snap back, adding to the trauma inside Tate's skull.

His eyes rolled back, and he fell across the passenger seat, limp and unconscious. Su-Hui climbed into the ATV and pulled him forward, head on the floorboard, wedging the man between the driver and passenger seats. It was ugly and awkward, but there wasn't time for formalities. Moving to the rear of the ATV, he grabbed Tate's rifle and slid it under two of the straps, securing it. Another explosion went off, this time hitting the motel directly. Bits of wood and roofing shingles flew into the air, and a plume of black smoke billowed skyward as the mortar round devoured the office area. Bright orange flames shot up through the damage, licking at the sky.

Su-Hui turned over the engine of the ATV and gunned it, following the path leading northeast as Tate's unconscious body flopped into a more secure place. A blast behind him caused wood fragments from a motor court to fall around him. Roaring up the hillside, he didn't glance down at his unconscious passenger. Behind him was the sound of cannon fire, mixed in with mortars, destroying the place his people had called home for much of the winter.

He glanced down at Tate whose neck was bent, doubled over the space between them. He was going to have a massive headache and was likely to be furious for being sucker punched. *I can deal with your rage, but I could not forgive myself if I let you die for nothing. You may hate me for what I did, but it was for the cause. Your son will understand, and in time, I hope you will too my friend.*

The Southern White House
Nashville, Tennessee

Charli Kasinzki was almost as frustrated as Jack Desmond when she slid the device across his desk. It looked like a simple, flash memory drive, dull, black, with a USB port at one end. The Chief of Staff picked it up and looked at it. "Where did you find it?"

"You told me there was some sort of leak coming out of the building, so we went to a Level 3 sweep of all conference rooms. It was in a drawer in Room 215. We assumed someone had gotten careless with their data and confiscated it. I had the guy you recommended, Kiff, take a look at it, so we could identify who had gotten so sloppy with their data. While it looks and functions as a flash drive, it had a lot less memory that it should. The geek knows his stuff. He opened it. It is a voice-activated recording device."

Jack held the device in his fingers, then tossed it back to her. "Pretty clever. It just records?"

"Yes."

"So it would not show up on our sweeps for bugs."

"That's right. It doesn't transmit; it simply records. No transmissions made it harder for us to find."

"Any thoughts as to who planted it?"

That was the one question Charli didn't want to try to answer. "We can't rule out a traitor. I would also have to assume a spy, someone who has infiltrated our facilities."

Jack said nothing for a moment, holding the faux flash drive in his fingers, then tossing it across his desk in front of her. "Someone has been leaking information to the press. The TRC has been making public things that we hadn't released yet, spinning it to make us look like we are in turmoil. I'm willing to bet that the mole who planted that is the same one who's leaking sensitive data to the media."

"Leaks in government are nothing new," Charli said, picking up the drive and pocketing it. "When the last President was in office, there were leaks almost every day."

"He warned us of a deep state in Washington, and they only proved him right. I like to think that the people we brought into this administration are loyal to our cause. There's always one or two who are misguided in their allegiance. That or they seek their fifteen minutes of fame."

Charli understood. She had been part of a mole hunt in the Secret Service before The Fall. *Leakers also wrap themselves in the cloak of patriots. Even when they are caught, it is rare that anything bad happens to them. Congress set up laws to protect the traitors, giving them the glorious title of whistleblower.* She saw them for what they were, hypocrites of the highest order. This, however, did not feel like the work of one of them. "Given that this is a sophisticated recording device, I think we are dealing with a professional. Whoever was using this to record discussions had access to some fairly high-tech resources. They knew our processes—that our standard bug sweeps would have picked up a traditional device. They knew us well enough to find a way around our security defenses."

"An agent then?" Jack asked as he narrowed his eyes.

"Maybe worse."

"An operative then."

"We already prevented one presidential assassination by an operative. It makes sense that the Newmerican Vice President would send another at us." There was resolve in her voice. She knew Caylee, which meant she knew the caliber of people that the enemy throw at them. "As such, I have augmented the President's detail."

"Good," Jack responded. "Whoever this person is, they seem to be aiming to undermine us. Their leaks to the press about the economy have gotten people to question if we are being entirely truthful with them. If this person was an assassin, he would have put such plans at risk by leaking information to the TRC."

"If that person is an operative, they are extremely dangerous."

"Agreed. Matters are more complicated now that you have discovered their recording device."

"We are going to replace it," Charli replied. "I have had some of our people add new cameras, much more covertly hidden. We are reviewing all of the personnel that had access to the room, and we are looking into their emails and cell phones to see if they reached out to the press."

"Hopefully whoever this person is, they haven't already discovered it missing."

“Agreed. Kiff rigged one of the recordings. If it played at all, it sent the IP address to him. That will allow us to track the person playing it down. The trigger is well-hidden, so it may help. In the meantime, I will have our people tighten the noose around this agent’s neck.”

Jack gave her a warm, almost fatherly smile. “Nail this bastard Charli. We need to send a clear message to people that we are not the government of the past … that we will not tolerate this kind of behavior.”

CHAPTER 9

"Anyone claiming the moral high ground is deceiving you as to what is truly moral."

Smyrna, Tennessee

The kitchenette table was covered with two maps—one of Texas and the other showing the aerial photograph layout of Social Quarantine Camp NM028, now augmented with Sharpie's to designate what buildings were for. Raul looked at the maps and felt nervous. The data that Caylee and Travis brought back was invaluable, but it also seemed to impress just how daunting it was going to be to assault the facility. He didn't waver from his conviction that the prisoners there had to be rescued.

Andy Forrest was there, along with Sam Patheal from a Sons of Liberty cell assigned to the mission. Patheal's family hailed from Bosnia, but he was a true patriot if there ever was one. His cell of the SOL came from North Carolina, Hell's Tarheels, and they had already earned a reputation for overrunning three camps in that state once it had pledged support to America over the Newmerican oppressors. They were former truckers, forced onto the welfare rolls when they refused to retire their diesel trucks in favor of smaller electric or natural gas vehicles. The Tarheel's reputation was one of brutality against Social Enforcers that crossed their path. Patheal's sandy colored hair was short, standing almost straight up as he loomed over the maps. His crossed arms appeared to be attempting to rip through the sleeves of his shirt as his eyes squinted at the details.

Andy Forrest stood next to Travis, opposite of Patheal. Andy studied the map, no doubt looking at it from a different perspective than the others. Raul liked Andy in that the two seemed to share one thing—they had stumbled into their roles in fighting for the American resistance. Andy had been with Charli and Caylee when he recovered the original Declaration of Independence and the Constitution. He was pragmatic, and like Raul didn't think in terms of military parlance.

In the room was another man, a pilot named Faust Kidder. He looked like a pirate. A patch covering his left eye had a target outlined in glitter. Travis had introduced him as "the best damned pilot to come out of the Army." From the grin on Kidder's face, he relished that description of him.

Caylee stood at the far end of the table alone with her hands planted on her hips. She and Travis had returned the day before. Raul had tried to get her to talk about how it went, but she was more silent than usual. Her evasion had a grim overtone. When she had called the meeting, she specifically asked that Maria *not* be in attendance. *She has seen something out there in New Mexico—something bad.* Maria had protested, but Caylee could not be swayed. Raul's imagination could only conjure what might stir the iron will of Caylee Leatrom. She left the room with her head hung low, like a scolded child.

"Alright then," Caylee finally said. "The code name for this op is Rabid Fox." Her eyes swept the participants of the planning session. "It is our intention to enter New Mexico by means of stealth; assemble our transportation locally; liberate the camp, and return to Texas. Travis and I have scouted the camp, and the map you see in front of you is our best estimate for the function of the buildings, location of barracks, etc. In your op packets, you will find where we recorded incoming and outgoing trucks, details of defenses we were able to observe, etc."

"What are we looking at in terms of the number of prisoners?" Andy asked.

"We didn't get an exact count," Travis weighed in. "My estimate is that there are a minimum of 400 with upwards of 900 still alive in the facility at any given time."

"Still alive?" Sam Patheal asked, cocking his right eyebrow with skepticism.

Caylee suppressed an inaudible sigh, then explained. "This camp is a labor camp. They are doing recycling of waste plastics. It appears they are not exactly OSHA compliant. We found dead bodies beyond the camp, entombed in waste from the recycling process." She didn't give time for a follow-up question. Instead, she tossed on the maps several images, taken in the dark, of the dead that she had found there.

Andy picked up one image, that of a woman, whose icy gaze was trapped in greenish plastic on the desert floor. "My God," he said. "They're killing them." Raul reached out and found one of the pictures as well. It was of a young boy, frozen in the plastic. His mouth was slightly open and an air bubble was trapped behind his head.

Caylee nodded as she clearly was suppressing any expression of emotion. "It is a work camp, like the others we have encountered or heard about. Without safety constraints, the workers die there. We were there at night, but that field could be filled with hundreds or more dead bodies."

Raul felt rage swell in him, and he tossed the photograph back, sending it spinning on the maps. "This must be stopped—*they* must be stopped. This is a murder factory. They are killing these people because they don't think or believe like the Newmericans do. They work them to death there. It is the same as putting a gun to their heads and pulling the trigger."

"They tell the world that these camps are for the safety of the people held there. They claim they are for reeducation. They claim that their recycling efforts are Environmental Equity," Raul said in disgust.

Andy spoke up. "When I was a kid, I would watch those old documentaries about WWII with my dad. I thought to myself, 'How could the Germans and the Japanese people believe all of that propaganda when the truth was right in front of them?" Now I understand. People work hard to believe the version of the truth that best suits their sensitivities. The Newmericans love the propaganda because it tells them what they want to hear. They don't care that their environmental efforts actually cause damage. All that matters is the crafted lie." It was a harsh truth, one that Raul understood.

Calyee continued, "We need to plan this carefully. If we blindly rush in there, a lot of innocent people will die."

She was correct, but that didn't mean he had to like it. "Every day, more die," was all he offered in rebuttal. Caylee gave him a nod showing that she had listened, but was prepared to move on. "Our getting back will coincide with a military operation along the border. We can slide across any time—in fact, the longer we are in New Mexico, the easier it will likely be to blend in. The military operation will draw the attention of the SEs and any NSF along the border with New Mexico and Texas, which should give us the necessary cover to get the survivors back to safety."

"What kind of military operation?" Patheal asked.

"That's classified," she said. "If I knew the details, I would share them. I don't. All I know is that they are going to give us a go-signal anytime from one to three weeks prior. That means we need to be ready to roll on relatively short notice." That seemed to satisfy Patheal enough, based on his nod in response.

"What about getting into New Mexico?" Andy asked. "How tricky is it?"

Travis chuckled slightly. "It was easy for me. Caylee, however, may have made it a little more complicated." All eyes shot to Caylee.

"I may have been forced to take lethal action against a few SEs," she said, giving a momentary glare at Travis.

"How many did you kill?" Faust Kidder asked with a twisted grin on his lips.

"She got four. I got one," Travis said. "Technically she got five. I just finished the one off. Regardless, that is one SE unit that has ceased to exist."

Raul looked at her, and she locked his gaze for a moment. "They were lining up for blow jobs, Raul," she said in a low, almost growling tone. "They brought the thunder down on themselves."

His face reddened at her admission. "They picked the wrong person for that," he said.

Caylee forced a grin. "It's a mistake they won't make ever again." She then turned to the others. "Needless to say, we won't be crossing the border at Quay County again. And—because that team was taken out—if they have found the bodies, they will be stepping up patrols."

Travis spoke up. "We should go in one at a time. Most of us can probably pass with no problems; we just need to have legitimate reasons for going to New Mexico. That kind of paperwork can be forged easily enough. They will be looking for groups, but if we do this properly, they will never piece together what we are up to."

"Where do we rendezvous?" Andy asked.

"Abiquiu," Caylee said. "It's small, discreet. Georgia O'Keeffe was from there. Her house used to be a museum, but it's been closed since just after The Fall. It's out of the way, a perfect place for us to assemble."

"We'll need vehicles and weapons," Patheal said.

Raul nodded. "We used dump trucks and buses at Valley Forge. The dump trucks are hard to get folks into, but they provide a lot of protection."

Caylee cut in. "Raul's intuition is right. We'll need some heavy haulers if we get more than 500 out of the camp. Buses are good, but they have limits. Also, we aren't sure just how we are going to cross back over the border, so the more rugged the vehicles and their ability to go cross country, the better. We intend to use a few heavy trucks, like the ones they use to bring plastic waste into the camp, so that they don't draw attention. We will get assignments for all of you to secure what you need. Travis will handle getting weapons over the border—you will simply need to focus on vehicles."

She spent several minutes outlining the assault on the camp—the diversions, everyone's objectives. There was a lot more planning involved than Raul's rescue at Valley Forge, but he expected that from Caylee and Travis. Everyone had a schedule, cover identities, and routes for getting into New Mexico. From what he could tell, all angles of the operation seemed to be covered, right down to the firebombing of the buildings, so that the camp would not be able to reopen. Andy's role was not only to assist, but to gather additional evidence of the crimes that had taken place there.

The presentation took two hours. The plan was rehearsed on paper so that everyone was called upon to recite where they were going and what they would be doing. Raul liked the fact that he would be driving one truck right into the front gate at the beginning of the attack. *They will never expect that.*

Faust Kidder spoke up. "I'm the only one here that doesn't seem to have a job in this. I can't chopper out hundreds of folks. Why exactly am I here, pretty lady?" he asked, winking with his remaining eye.

"Your resume says you can fly anything. You're our fallback plan. If something goes wrong, we may need you to fly in and get us out. You'll go in separately, and be in position if needed. Flying out will be our fallback plan."

"That doesn't seem like a lot of fun," he chided with a wicked smile. "After that little incident at the Supermax, I feel like I owe you a ride." Raul shifted where he stood, if only an inch or two. *He likes Caylee. I can see it.* A part of Raul took a dislike to Kidder in that moment. It was a mix of protectiveness and a hint of jealousy. While he and Caylee were close friends, there was nothing romantic between them. In that moment, seeing Kidder flirt with her so blatantly, he wondered if his feelings were a bit more.

"Mr. Kidder, as I see it, you got a new chopper out of the deal and got paid, but didn't extract us as planned. You owe us one."

Kidder grinned even more. "If you need me, I'll deliver."

"Good," Caylee said. "I'm governed by the old military adage—no plan survives contact with the enemy. In other words, we have to anticipate that things are going to go haywire at some point. Being rigid to a plan could be our downfall. Everyone needs to be sharp and able to adapt to a changing situation." Raul understood that thinking, and was glad that he had people who were looking over every angle.

As the group broke up, Sam Patheal walked up to him and extended his hand. "I saw the videos of what you did at Valley Forge. My people won't let you down."

Raul shook his hand. He didn't see himself as a leader, but in that moment, he knew his own view of himself didn't matter. "I just did what I had to."

"You were one of the people that set things in motion," Patheal said. "And you're the only guy to ever escape the Supermax. You're a rock star in the Sons of Liberty."

"These people got me out," he said, nodding towards Caylee and Travis who were talking at the other end of the table.

"Well, it's a pleasure. I'm sure glad as hell you're with us."

Sam's faith in Raul struck him as odd, if only for a second. As a Catholic, faith was part of his life, or so he had been told. He had heard the word used almost every Sunday in church. Now he understood it. He had faith in God, faith in Caylee, and Sam had faith in him. Faith was not about religion—now he understood it. It was something to be cherished … and shared. *It is not about our trust in God alone, but our trust in each other. It is the thing that separates us from our enemies. They have no faith. They are fighting to simply hold onto their perceived power.*

We are going to do this. We are going to pull this mission off. Those people, their souls, demand it.

Cannon Air Force Base
New Mexico

Darius was used to barracks from his time in the Army. The ones at Cannon Air Force Base were nicer than the ones he had stayed in before. Over his life, he had bedded down in far worse places. Even the Tiny Town, where they had moved homeless people, had been a bit of a letdown—unfinished plywood with an inflatable mattress … LA's 'solution' to what they often referred to as "housing insecure." There were days when you felt like you needed a dictionary for the new words and acronyms that the Newmericans cranked out. *They can call the problem whatever they want. Renaming it didn't solve anything.*

The problem was that they were far from safe. Many of the homeless were drug addicted, aided by free needles. Robberies, rapes, and drug-induced violence were commonplace. No one cared what the occupants did to each other in the Tiny Town, just as long as they didn't bring their crime to the streets. That was why their small homes were surrounded by chain-link fences topped with razor wire. It wasn't to keep people out, but to keep the homeless inside.

They had been loaded up on olive, drab, painted school buses two days ago to come to New Mexico. No one had been forthcoming about why they were heading there, but it didn't take a genius to figure it out. Cannon Air Force Base was almost on the Texas state line—and Texas was American territory. Some assumed they were there to defend the base, but Darius felt differently. *We're going on the offense. If we were going to be defending this place, they would have us digging in, preparing fire positions.*

A part of him dreaded going into actual combat. Members of his platoon were all combat veterans, but they were not a team. While he could count on some of them if the situation got hot, others would easily abandon him if it meant risking their lives. *This isn't at all like fighting in the Middle East. Over there, we were brothers. We protected each other. A lot of these troops will go into survival mode the first time they come under serious fire.*

"Alright people," Sergeant Ingersoll said as they entered the barracks. "Assembly in the parking lot outside in fifteen minutes. Put on your dress uniforms for this."

Darius didn't complain out loud, but instead rolled his eyes. *I hate those damn Captain Crunch uniforms.* He went to his footlocker and pulled out the dark dress uniform. It was like an Army dress uniform, but with a dull plainness to it. There were no brass buttons; instead they had dull, black, plastic affairs with the raised lettering of VC for the Veterans Corps. A single silver braid draped from his left epaulet over his heart to the chest button. His two rows of campaign ribbons and awards from the military were still there, a reminder of the man he used to be. When they had first formed the corps, there had been resistance to allowing the vets to wear their military decorations. If rumors were true, one company of the corps protested, trashing their barracks, and attacking prisoners. Eventually the California officers in charge capitulated.

"This is bullshit," Fax said. "They haul us out into the fucking desert, and now we put on our Sunday best. What are we going to do, have a parade?"

Darius was polishing his dress shoes and cut off the younger man. "Would you rather be digging latrines or foxholes? So we play dress up for a while. It is better than sitting here doing nothing." His words seemed to suffice enough to prod the handful of malingers to put on their uniforms. Sergeant Ingersoll gave him a nod of thanks in response from his own bunk.

He stepped out on the parking lot in the bright sunlight of the New Mexico afternoon. Spring was coming; it was already a warm day, amplified by a black dress uniform. They assembled in formation, and even a quick glance told him that the veterans looked almost impressive standing around him. Darius looked forward and saw that a low stage had been set up with a rather plain podium.

A woman slid onto the stage and up to the podium; she was dressed in a white pantsuit. Captain Aguilar barked the order, "Ten-hut!" As he snapped to attention, he recognized the woman as the Lieutenant Governor of California. Her skin was bronzed, not so much from the sun but from chemicals or a booth. She wore her hair short, almost masculine—no doubt a virtue signaling her stance against men.

"Good day," she said at the podium. "You may relax."

Captain Aguilar barked, "At ease," and they returned to parade rest in unison.

The Lieutenant Governor leaned a little closer to the microphone jutting up from the front of the podium. "It is my distinct honor to be here with you today. Your actions from several weeks ago at the Presidio drew the attention of all of Newmerica. The housing disenfranchised crisis was caused by the corrupt policies of the former administrations as part of their war against the weak. They did not care what happened to the downtrodden. The old, white leaders mocked those that were forced to the streets.

"In California, we care. We are solving the problem by providing these people with a place they can call their own. To date, we have created seventy-eight Tiny Towns—places where these people can regain their dignity.

"Some have refused our generosity. Those that you deployed to assist at the Presidio represented them. We don't blame them for not wanting to go. Many had been corrupted by outdated thinking. Others still do not trust what the government can do for them, thanks to the contamination the white patriarchy imposed on our society. Like an undiagnosed cancer, they do not realize that they have been corrupted until it is too late."

Darius felt his jaw lock at her words. I remember when she ran for office. *She's white, but claimed to be LatinX in the last election to get votes. That spray-on tan isn't fooling anyone. Old white men are not to blame for people not having homes. Race didn't put me on the streets. There is no one thing to lay the blame on. She probably sleeps in a nice mansion with security guards and safety while the rest of the state has to deal with a problem she never sees.*

The Lieutenant Governor paused and took a long sip from a bottle of water hidden in the podium. "Your efforts have made California, and all of Newmerica, safer. You have allowed us to begin development in the old Presidio Park where low-cost housing will be erected for the city's underserved. You have made a difference."

As Darius heard her words, he knew they were lies. *All we did was evict a bunch of homeless people against their will. She makes it sound like we landed on the beaches of Normandy on D-Day.* Memories of the victims, especially the one that gave him her service medal, tore at him as he stood there, wishing the speech was over.

"As such, the governor has awarded your unit a special citation and ribbon—the Presidio Award. It recognizes your gallant contribution to making our state and nation a better place for all." A Warrant Officer stepped forward with a case, standing next to the podium. Inside was a set of ribbons, from what he could tell, light blue with green stripes. There were medals as well, dull bronze with the same colored ribbon.

Each rank of the troops was brought up on the tiny stage, and the medals were pinned on, and followed with crisp salutes to the Lieutenant Governor. Darius marched up, falling in line with the others, moving almost numbly. *I don't need another medal ... I have one from the woman we killed.* A part of him wanted to take a stand, refuse the citation. It was the right thing to do. He was sure of that. He was also sure that spoiling the photo op was a dangerous thing. Living in Newmerica he saw what happened to those that dared take a stand against the imposed order. *They might not send me to Social Quarantine, but I sure as hell am going to end up in some sort of military prison if I refuse.*

Is this fight the one worth starting? Darius decided no. Conformity helped keep him in line, following the rank of soldiers in front of him. Mindlessly, he walked up on the stage and stood before the shorter Lieutenant Governor. She reached up with a smile and pinned the medal, somewhat crooked on his chest. He saluted her, more out of instinct than true respect. He was then handed the ribbon that he would add to the colorful salad of ribbons on the breast of his uniform.

His face was feverish with frustration as he stepped down and assumed his place in the formation. After a few long minutes, they were dismissed amid the snapping of photographs. *This isn't about what we did; it's a public relations exercise.* In silence, he made his way back to the barracks, where he quickly pulled off his dress uniform jacket, removing the medal.

"Not too shabby," Vixen said. "Another medal for the collection."

"We didn't earn anything," Darius mumbled as he stripped off his pants and folded them.

"We got medals, didn't we?" Fax asked.

"Medals should have meaning. We cleared a park of a bunch of homeless people. A lot of them got killed in the process. This wasn't some glorious battle. It will never appear in history books. We didn't win any glory. We rounded up an inferior force, killing some."

"What's bothering you?" Fax pressed.

"I don't like false honors," Darius said. "I don't like being part of a lie."

Sergeant Ingersoll seemed to wince at his words. "What does it matter if it's a lie? They just pinned a medal on your chest and now you want to get all bitter about it. What is your issue Darius?"

He glared over at the sergeant. "My problem is this. Most of us were forced into re-upping. They blackmailed us into joining. I didn't ask to be here. I certainly didn't ask to open fire on a bunch of folks that weren't bothering anybody. Getting a medal for it doesn't make what we did right."

"The concept of right and wrong is not something you should concern yourself with, Private," the sergeant said with a half-snarl. "Your job is to follow orders. It's as simple as that."

"I know, Sergeant," he said, trying to curb his anger. "It's just that so far, none of this is what I thought we'd be doing."

"And that bothers you? That you were persuaded to enlist again?"

Darius sensed a verbal minefield, but couldn't skirt it. "Something like that."

Ingersoll moved face-to-face with him, close enough for Darius to smell the stale coffee on his breath. "Not everyone was tricked into enlisting, Private. *I* wasn't forced to join. My welding shop was about to go belly up. I joined because it was a great opportunity. This is putting food on my table and a roof over my family's heads. I'm glad that Newmerica and the good state of California had the foresight to create the Veteran Corps. I'd tell you I'm sorry that you felt you were coerced into joining, but frankly, I don't give a flying fuck at a rolling donut about how you feel. I know you owned a fancy coffee shop at one point—upscale place from the way you talk. Newmerica provided you with every opportunity to get ahead. I had to build my business from scratch. No one would give me a loan when the economy tanked. I had no choice but to scrounge to keep my employees paid. Finally, it was too much for me. So I *am* thankful that Newmerica came along with this offer."

"What I *do* care more about is someone that appears to be screwing the morale of the unit. I suggest that from now on if you have any gripes, you find a way to work through them silently. Otherwise you will find yourself digging the deepest goddamned latrine in New Mexico. Do we have an understanding?"

He wanted to snap back, fire off something like, "I'd prefer digging a damn hole than being part of a massacre," but he held his tongue. Years of experience told him that NCOs rarely were looking for a retort. "I understand completely Sergeant."

"Good," Ingersoll said, leaning back to a less aggressive stance. "All of you need to get into your fatigues. We are going to be mustering in the mess hall in an hour for a briefing on the upcoming operation."

Darius fumed. His face was hot with anger and a hint of embarrassment at being called out in front of the rest of the squad. He could feel the eyes of everyone on him, boring into his soul. What hurt most, was that Ingersoll was right in many respects. Newmerica had helped some groups more than others. As a white male, he would have found getting loans nearly impossible in the years that followed the Liberation. That didn't abate his feelings of shame for getting the medal. Instead it would serve as a reminder of what was wrong with any country that would turn on its own people. It was a lesson he was not likely to forget anytime soon.

Nashville, Tennessee

Thiago Reese hid in the darkness of Sarah Topper's pantry as she came into the kitchen and tossed her leather briefcase onto the white marble-topped island. Thiago had shed his guise as Luis this night … tonight it was all him … the Rumbler. He rather savored what was about to come. It was one of the fun aspects of his job.

Topper moved over to a small cabinet and poured herself a drink—gin and tonic. She got a handful of ice from the freezer and put it in, stirred it with a plastic stir stick, then drew a long sip. She was at ease; he could tell by the way she unbuttoned the top of her blouse and leaned casually against the island. *It has been a long day for you at work—but don't worry Ms. Topper—it will be your last.*

Topper was an American Senator , one of the new ones that supported the Pretender President. She had been appointed by the great state of Kentucky, a state whose governor was a traitor to the Newmerica cause. She had positioned herself with the media as a firebrand, a daring and vocal advocate for the destruction of the government that Thiago served. Many members of Congress were all but invisible; people didn't know their names or faces. Not so with Sarah Topper. She seemed to savor her time in front of the camera. *That will make her death all the more impactful.*

Reese wore a synthetic body suit, one dubbed an *assassins suit* because it reduced the amount of DNA or other traceable evidence at a crime scene. His hair was cover with a skullcap, and he wore gloves that would be disposed of far from the scene of the crime that was about to unfold.

She turned away from the pantry, and he knew the time had come.

Opening the door silently, he quickly took three long strides to come down behind Sarah Topper mid-sip. The garrote that he had chosen was a scarf, stolen three days earlier from the home of the American Supreme Court Justice Truman Burns. Someone monogrammed it with his initials, which made it perfect to leave as bait at the scene.

The long, white scarf whipped around her neck, inadvertently catching the hand with her drink in the process. She tried to spin around to see her assailant as her glass fell and shattered on the dark hardwood floor. Thiago pulled it tighter, and she flexed her pinned arm and hand in a vain effort to get air. He knew it wouldn't work, but applauded her refusing to die without resistance. Rocking hard side to side, she dragged the struggle out for several agonizing seconds. Muffled grunts and gasping for air continued until her body went limp. Thiago didn't stop choking her though. He had to be sure that she was dead; that, and a part of him enjoyed the task.

His heart was thundering in his ears as he waited out the minute more; then lowered her body to the floor, face down. Moving to the trash, he casually discarded the scarf—knowing full well that the police investigating the crime would find it. He had already placed a few other bits of trace evidence in her bedroom, all of which would point to her being connected to Justice Truman Burns. He reached into his belt pouch for several hairs he had taken from the Justice's comb which he had stolen. A few were placed on the body, further linking Burns to the Senator.

It would be a scandal, one he would leak to his media contacts in Newmerica. There would be an implication that the conservative justice had been having an affair with Turner. The scandal would further erode the people's illusion about the rekindled America. Their messages and narratives would be eaten by the press who would dedicate time to the scandal.

Oh, they'll prove that he had nothing to do with it; he'll have an alibi, but once the story is out there, it can't be erased. It will make the leaders of this rebellious blight called America look twisted and corrupt. There will be conspiracy theories that will last forever about the murder and the cover-up, and he knew that there would always be a percentage of the people that would believe the good Justice was behind the murder.

Eroding faith in the government was a key pillar of his plan to take down America. It was key to his strategy. If you simply took out the leadership, people would want to continue on—they love continuity. He knew that if they thought their leadership was broken, immoral, or corrupt—there would be less of a cry to continue it. *Most people think that taking down a government is a lightning strike, a quick string of assassinations. It's more like giving someone cancer and watching them die slowly, rotting from within.* Otherwise taking down a government requires far too much time and resources. You need to set things in motion, and let nature take its course. There was an element of pride in his work that he refused to be ashamed of.

Avoiding the shards of broken glass, he made his way to the back door of the house and slid out into the darkness of the night. As he clung to the shadows, he made his way to his car that was parked three blocks away, Thiago contemplated the next stage of his plan. There are always key figures that hold a nation together. *Take out the right ones, and everything unravels all on its own. Even the people on the inside—they never can connect all of the dots, and see what is coming, and its inevitability.*

Texas Military Department (TMD) HQ,
Camp Mabry, Austin, Texas

General Reager's command staff stared at the map outlined on the digital wall display. The image showed the border of Texas with red dagger arrows that plunged into New Mexico and beyond into Arizona. For a long moment, he said nothing, letting his people drink in the details. *Sometimes saying nothing is far more powerful than talking—it makes people think on their own.*

"It's called Operation Diamondback," he said after two long minutes. "Its goal is to wage offensive operations against Newmerica on multiple fronts, and force them to try and manage multiple ops at the same time. As such, we will send a token force towards St. Louis, making them think we are finally pushing to retake that city. Several other ops will happen at the same time, mostly tied with ops in New Hampshire. While they are focused on those efforts, we will kick off Diamondback—driving through New Mexico and into Arizona."

Lieutenant Colonel Platt spoke up. "Sir, we've had feints towards St. Louis before. They might not bite on it."

Trip nodded once. "True. By the same token, they can't ignore it. I want St. Louis back in our hands, but not right now. When they see armor and trucks heading that way, they will have to respond."

"Why Arizona? Why now?" Brigadier General Ricketts asked from the far end of the table.

Trip appreciated his blunt questions. "New Mexico and Arizona are stepping stones. Ultimately, we need to drive into California. All three of those states are still running those damned Social Quarantine Camps. They are killing people by the dozens every day. We need to liberate those two states to give us a springboard for operations into Southern California."

"So, the rumors are true—about the camps," Colonel Bressel, his new logistics officer, asked.

Captain Paul Harnessy, his G2, spoke up. "The rumors are more than true, Colonel. I wish they were propaganda, but they aren't."

"Son of a bitch," Bressel said, dipping his head and shaking it.

Trip slid back into the dialog. "A civilian team is going to execute a raid that coincides with Diamondback. Our crossing the border should give them cover to get the prisoners back to the safety of Texas."

"As to why we are going now," he said, turning his head to Ricketts, "It is spring and the temperatures are already starting to climb. The longer we wait, the hotter it is going to get. If we can secure our supply lines west now, it will make our drive into California easier. Also, the enemy is leasing drone coverage out of Cannon Air Force Base. We need to put that to an end. Hence it is on our early list of targets." Memories of serving in the Middle East stirred in Trip as he spoke. The heat could be as deadly as incoming fire during the peak summer months. *I don't need troops fighting dehydration and heat stroke as much as the enemy.*

His words seemed to satisfy General Ricketts. "Very well, sir. What intel do we have on the enemy?"

Captain Harnessy spoke up. "Not a lot. We have had to shift our air assets for other operations which limits us getting a full picture of the enemy. We've had some rangers doing reconnaissance. Reports show very few New Mexico National Guard units. The belief is we will be SE units, many outfitted with stock from the NG armories."

Harnessy's words seemed to slightly dampen the enthusiasm in the room. Trip understood why. *We are going in with even less intel than we had in Virginia. They know the risks involved with going in blind.*

After a few seconds of mental processing, Rickett's spoke up again. "When is kickoff, sir?"

Reager adjusted his stance slightly. "Two weeks. Our forward units are already shifting to position. The sooner the better. The plan calls for us to be in Albuquerque in less than three days; then on to Flagstaff in a week. As you can see, we are bypassing Phoenix and Tucson with a lateral thrust to their north. Once they are cut off from Newmerica, their capitulation will come easier than us trying to lay siege to those cities."

"Two weeks is short," Colonel Bressel said. "I'd prefer three."

"I'll take imperfect and fast any day over slow and perfect," Trip countered. "We won't win this war with perfect planning. It's going to be won by being bold … and with the blood of patriots."

CHAPTER 10

"A society that rewards individual merits ignores what is best for everyone."

Wright Patterson Air Force Base
Dayton, Ohio

Major Judy Mercury moved into the hanger and was greeted by the smell of oil and other chemicals that lingered in the air. The hanger echoed with the sounds of talking airmen, tools being used, and the dull hum of the heating system. She ignored the ambiance as she strode up to the C-130 that had returned just an hour earlier. The gray aircraft's starboard wing tip was gone, leaving bits of jagged metal and a big of dangling wire in its place. Walking under it, she surveyed it with a sense of frustration.

Lieutenant Colonel Chad Mihalek slid in beside her. She caught him from the corner of her eye and saw that he too was looking upward at the damage. "You should see the other guy," he quipped.

She turned to him, far from amused. "We could have lost the aircraft and the crew."

His face was a solid muscle as he turned to her. "That's why we are doing the test flights."

"What did they hit?" Judy asked, returning her attention to the missing wingtip and the damage that remained.

"A wind turbine in Nazareth, Pennsylvania," he said. "They were following the mission parameters … seeing if it would trigger some sort of response if we came in low. We didn't have the turbine farm on our map; courtesy of the New Green Deal Part III. They hit it and turned back."

Judy shook her head. They thought they'd factored in everything—

cell phone towers, high tension power lines, but somehow the wind turbine farm in Pennsylvania had slipped through the cracks. *We were doing the flights to test our people flying so low, and we almost lost a plane and crew in the process.* "I take it we are compiling the wind turbine sites and adding them to our flight plan database?"

"Of course," he said.

"How's the crew?"

"They are fine," Mihalek said. "Rattled them for a few minutes—but not much else."

"When they go to find what damaged the turbine, they are going to find the wingtip," she said thoughtfully, turning her full attention to the Lieutenant Colonel. "Is that going to pose a problem for us?"

He paused and thought for a long minute before responding, which was one of the reasons that she liked working with him. *Most people just blurt out words in response. He thinks things through carefully before opening his mouth.* "The power company might not even look for the cause; they may just go and do the repairs. If they start looking around, they may find the debris. At most, that's going to tell them they got hit by an aircraft, but they aren't going to know what type or where it came from. If they decide to try and track down the source of the airplane, they will get the FAA involved. If the FAA determines that it was from a C-130, they will need to reach out to the military—which could be either the Air Force, or the National Guard units that are fighting for the Newmericans. If they check their damage lists, that will tell them it wasn't one of theirs."

"That's a lot of ifs," Judy said.

"Exactly. And all of that takes time and coordination from a number of different bureaucracies, civilian and military. In this case, bureaucracy is our ally. Even if they piece it together, we are still talking weeks before they could even consider that it came from one of our aircraft. Then they will argue over who has what authority over the investigation."

"We will be in Stewart-Newburgh by then."

"Correct."

Judy sighed, then turned to him. "Our test flights have shown we can operate under their radar. They aren't scrambling fighters after us. Aside from this incident, we have been able to act with a high degree of impunity in their airspace. Danger is a part of this mission."

Agreed," Mihalek replied. "The ground element has been practicing on a mock-up of the base. We were lucky to have someone who had served there who could give us some approximate schematics. Our people are ready, or as ready as we can get them. All we need now is a go date."

"It will be soon," she assured him. "I met with our G2 today. The Newmericans are starting ground operations, starting to probe where our New Hampshire forces are dug in. They will move to encircle their positions. The last thing they want is for anyone to slip out."

"They think they have them trapped."

She nodded. "Arrogance is an excellent weapon of war. They'll move to try and obliterate them. Then we make our play, so we can provide them the air support they are going to need."

"Hopefully they can hold out long enough for us to relieve the pressure."

"What choice do they have?"

"None," she said solemnly. We need to suppress the air strength being applied against them and provide ground support. Being close to the battlefield allows us to be nimble and respond quickly. For those folks on the ground, there will only be hours and minutes between life and death. "The balloon could go up on this thing at any time. Starting tonight, we should be on standby for departure. Assuming you concur, let's have all heavy gear loaded, planes prepped and ready to rock at a moment's notice."

"Agreed."

We were damned lucky we didn't lose a crew. Next time we go, it will be for real.

Union County, New Mexico

Raul Lopez laid low in the long, dried out coulee that ran parallel to State Highway 406. He and Travis Cullen had walked across the border between Texas and New Mexico, carefully snaking their way into Newmerican territory. Travis had halted them along the north-south highway that cut across their trail. They were hiding in the creek bed. At first Raul was unsure why. Then he heard the rumble of a pickup truck coming down from the north. It slowed to a stop not far from where he and Travis huddled down. The driver was a black woman, wearing reflective aviator sunglasses and a dour expression. The four men in the back of the vehicle stood, sweeping the scrub brush with their eyes and looking for something … *probably us.*

The engine shut off, and the men peered down both sides of the road, clutching their firearms tightly. Only two look like soldiers. It wasn't just their lack of uniforms, it was their body build. One man easily weighed 350 pounds, and another was a youth dressed like he belonged in a rap video. He was standing in the bed of a pickup glaring into the harsh New Mexico landscape.

The other two clearly were soldiers; their uniforms and identical weapons were a dead giveaway. It struck him as odd—military personnel operating with Social Enforcers in that manner. *What are they up to?*

After a few long, tense moments, the truck started up, and the men sat down. It took off, slowly, almost methodically, heading south. Travis said nothing as he squatted next to Raul and rested his hand on his shoulder. "That's damn peculiar," he finally said in a voice just above a whisper.

"What do you mean?"

"Those SEs," he said, nodding off toward the truck as it became a speck on the road in the distance. "What are they doing out here, in the middle of nowhere?"

"Watching the border," Raul offered.

"For what? I mean think about it. Aside from Caylee and I coming over the border and having an incident, why are they here? And did you see that one kid? He's not some local Social Enforcer out looking to cause trouble. He's inner city. That means he came a long distance to be out in this freaking desert. Add in that soldiers were with them, and the whole thing looks and feels suspicious."

Raul listened carefully to Travis. The man knew a lot, and he could learn from him. "So what do you think?"

"It's unusual and that can mean something is going down," Travis said. "Maybe they got wind of the upcoming military operation, or they are planning something of their own. They are here by choice. They wanted to be here." He rose slightly and checked the road both ways.

"Alright, let's get across. Keep low and move fast. The road exposes us. We'll move to that patch of scrub brush off to the right. It's not much, but it will give us some cover."

Ducking down, they both scurried across the highway and made their way to the patch of brush. Raul saw something white on the ground, and as he leaned in, he saw it was a small skull with fangs—probably a rattlesnake. It was enough to make him back away from the brush a few inches. Travis took a sip from his CamelBak drinking tube. "We've got a few hours before sundown. If we keep heading southwest, we should be able to reach Clayton by nightfall. There's not a lot there, but we should be able to get a room for the night, and there's a chance to get a vehicle."

"Rental car?"

Travis grinned devilishly. "No. One of the locals is going to donate their vehicle to our cause."

"Donate?"

"Raul, I'm going to hotwire and steal a car."

"Where did you learn to steal a car?" Raul asked as they walked briskly out into the desert.

"SEALs. It wasn't part of the former training, but my former CO said it would come in handy sometime. The man was always right."

It made sense to Raul from what he imagined. He knew about the SEALs. "Won't that be risky? I mean we will be traveling in a stolen vehicle. The NSF might be looking for it, and if they find it, they find us."

"No problem," Travis assured him. "First off, crime has been increasing for the last five years, ever since The Fall. The NSF isn't going to look for a vehicle; they will use their plate recognition systems to look for a vehicle match. We will switch license plates with a non-stolen vehicle. Easy peasy."

"You *have* done this before."

"After shit went down during The Fall, and I left the Navy, the pickings were light for employment. My benefit checks got cut courtesy of the Newmerican government. They preach a love of veterans, but behind closed doors, they stick it to us. Anyone complaining gets a visit from Social Enforcement, which isn't convenient for them. I had to do a lot of things just to get by for that first two years. I'm sure it didn't help that I had spoken out against the military response to the events. The night things went to shit."

"I'm surprised you didn't end up in Social Quarantine."

"They tried," he said, again flashing a wicked grin. "Four of them showed up at my father's house one night looking for me. They said they wanted to talk. I asked them why they brought guns and zip ties for a conversation. Things went downhill from there."

"What happened?" Raul asked. He had to know.

"My dad went out the back and circled around with his hunting rifle while I talked with them. They got mouthy—then pushy. One guy tried to take a swing at me with a baseball bat. Damn fool didn't factor in the tight space. He swung, but I deflected it. I used my knife to take him out of the equation first. They tried to come through the door at once, one waving a gun and firing."

"Did you get hit?"

Travis shook his head. "You shoot, so you understand. You just jam a gun forward and start finger-fucking the trigger, you miss unless your target is right in front of you. I faded back and moved laterally. I knew that would screw up his shots. Dad popped the one who was running around to the back."

"What about the two that came after you?"

"I'm a firm supporter of the Second Amendment, Raul," he smirked. "As far as the government was concerned, my guns had been stolen, but I kept them positioned in the house. I drew as that moron kept firing randomly in my directly. He missed, a lot. I don't miss. Took him and his buddy down; then put the kill shot in the one with the knife wound."

The story was believable—he knew Travis. "What happened next?"

"We had to dispose of the bodies and the evidence. They got so much blood on the carpeting. We simply cut it up and rolled their bodies in it like big-ass cigars."

"Did they ever find the bodies?"

"Not yet," Travis said.

"That is incredible! You and Caylee should scare me, but you don't."

Travis shrugged as they maneuvered around another patch of scrub brush. "We are well-trained. Enough of my stories about being a bad boy. What about you?"

"What do you mean?"

"Tell me all about Valley Forge."

"There isn't a lot to tell, really. I mean, you saw it on the news."

"That isn't the same, Raul. Tell me how it went down."

Raul suddenly felt a swell of pride. This was a former SEAL asking about his exploits. Raul began to tell the story of how they planned for the relief of the Social Quarantine Camp; how they had used fireworks as a diversion. Travis asked a lot of questions, extracting details that Raul had rarely spoken about. Every question made him feel more confident—more equal to the man he was walking with.

"That is seriously impressive," Travis said as he finished the story.

"Not compared to what you've done."

Travis stopped and looked him square in the eyes. "Don't ever sell yourself short, Raul. Yeah, the military turned me into a finely honed killing machine. What you did took guts, mostly because you didn't really have the skills to do something like that. Many people would have frozen, or shit their pants, or run the other way. You didn't do that."

"I never thought of it that way." His words were true. He was always comparing himself to people like Travis, Caylee, and Charli and was envious of what they could do. It never set in with him that what he had already accomplished was in the same context as *their* accomplishments.

"What separates us is confidence, Raul. Training does that for you, as does experience. You need to show it more. Everyone in our little circle respects the hell out of you. It's time you start doing the same for yourself." Travis then turned and continued to walk.

Raul followed him. *He's right. I question myself all of the time. I have faith in God, and my friends, but I don't seem to have any for myself.* As he strode through the stark New Mexico landscape, he vowed he would change. *I need to trust myself as much as I trust my friends, and I will from this point on.*

White Mountain National Forest
New Hampshire

Su-Hui was amazed at the warren of trenches and obstacles in defensive rings that filled the forests and foothills of the White Mountain National Forest. General Griffiths and the New Hampshire National

Guard had concentrated there for months, purposefully hiding from the Newmerica forces. Clearly, they had been busy. It wasn't just the depth and complexity of the field fortifications; it was the fact that most were carefully camouflaged, almost invisible. The air had a twinge of fresh cut pines and dug soil. The last remnants of un-melted snow covered many areas, a reminder of the chill still clinging in the air.

A few of the bunkers were barely concealed. When he asked why, he had been told they were decoys—set apart from the actual defenses. Radios were buried deep in them, non-encrypted, rigged to draw their attention. His escort was proud of them. "The enemy will expend a lot of effort to blow them up, and they are nothing more than empty shells. We even rigged a few of them with firecrackers, so it would sound like someone firing guns from them." It was ingenious, but this was no game they were playing. *When the Newmericans come, they will destroy them and everything around them.*

Twice, Su-Hui had almost fallen into a ditch as he followed the soldier that was leading him through the warren of defensive positions. One time, the soldier grabbed his arm as he fell, preventing him from falling into a trench that he had not even seen two feet away. "Happens all of the time," the Private said as Su-Hui got his footing and balance back.

The command bunker was of concrete construction, with thick walls, covered by growing pine trees and brush that would make it invisible from the air. He took the steps down and went through the thick, steel, blast door. The inside was far more spacious than he expected. Long hallways sloped downward into the stone and dirt of the New Hampshire park. He went through a maze of hallways, down another two flights of steps to reach a room he assumed was the command facility.

General Griffiths was leaning over a digital table that had a map of the region. When he spotted Su-Hui out of the corner of his eye, he turned, walked over to him, and extended his hand. "I'm glad you and your people are settled. I'm sorry it's been a few days before we met, but we have a lot in play."

Someone handed him a steaming cup of coffee, which he appreciated. "These defenses you have here are incredible, General."

"The actions of the Sons of Liberty bought us the time needed to reinforce our position here. For that, we are in your debt."

Su-Hui didn't realize that the SOL forces he had been leading had been buying time. He had always believed they were simply fighting the good fight against a ruthless enemy. A part of him was surprised at what the General had said, while another part of him was proud. "We have done our part."

"And we'll need more of you in the fight to come," he said with a nod towards the map.

As Su-Hui leaned over the illuminated tabletop display, he saw the full extent of the defenses that were dug into the White Mountain Forest. Lines and marks showed minefield, trenches, gun positions, and other intricate defenses. "Where do you need us, and what do you want us to do?" he said after a long time spent drinking in the details.

General Griffiths smiled. "I like that, up front and direct." He gestured to the map with his hand. "They were on your tail for an hour, but stopped in their tracks. I think they are worried about being lured in, which is what I intend to do to them." Pausing for a moment, he made sure that Su-Hui was following him. "Most of your people will take up position in the second line of defenses. They are going to hammer us hard, and they are going to be bringing air assets in on us, and frankly, we may not have a counter to them just yet." It was a grim admission. Su-Hui remembered when the Chinese had blasted his homeland, Taiwan, with their air force. The bombings had been devastating, leveling entire city blocks in a matter of minutes. *How will we fare against heavy air power here, in the wilderness?* It was a chilling thought.

"You said most of us," he replied.

"Like I said, for this to work, we need to get them to come at us on the ground. To do that, we need to bait them—get them to initiate a pursuit. If we can bring them onto our ground, we can inflict a hell of a lot of damage before they can even try to pull out of the trap."

"That makes sense. You see us playing a role in that?"

"I do. Our people are good. We have armored vehicles, some fast-moving recon stuff. We know the ground in and around our defenses, but not much farther than that. I need people that know this ground, can navigate the logging and hunting trails, so that we don't get blown to bits before we can spring the trap. Seems to me that a number of your people are pretty familiar with the surrounding terrain."

Several names came to the forefront of Su-Hui's mind. "We would be honored to be your guides."

"It's a dangerous op," the General cautioned. "This isn't about inflicting damage, it's about hitting them and staying just ahead of them enough that they are willing to follow."

"I understand. We are not here for the sightseeing or the hospitality. Most of us left our jobs; some left their families; others lost everything to come and fight. The Sons came here to defend New Hampshire. We lost a lot of good people in the cowardly attack on Lisbon, and the many raids we have launched. We are not strangers to danger. That is the life of a partisan warrior."

"This is going to be a different kind of fight. We have a lot of surprises planned, but the enemy has the numbers on their side. Not only that. The efforts of your cells and the others around the state have made the Newmerican forces scream for blood. They want payback for all of the people they have lost. To them, this is vengeance and a chance to put an end to the Defiance here."

"So when they come, they will be all in."

"I believe so. They think this will be our end. I intend to make it theirs. New Hampshire needs to be free." There was a deep, steely resolve in the older man's voice. To Su-Hui, it oozed with confidence."

"Tell me whom to coordinate with. We will make the Defiance proud," he said. His cheeks tingled with commitment and a flush of patriotism.

"Major Segal will liaise with you on the details. First we need to get your non-combatants tucked away in our deepest shelters. Then we can get your combat forces in position and arrange for you to help scout for the harassers."

"Sir," Su-Hui said coolly. "If this is the last battle here, my people will want to fight. All of them. We have long moved past the time where there were noncombatants in our ranks. If this is the final battle for the survival of this state, then we all fight." It was not a boast. The losses suffered from the Newmerican destruction of Lisbon had transformed the survivors. *None of them will want to sit on the sidelines when the shooting starts. They all have skin in this fight.*

Griffiths turned to him and planted his fists on his unformed hips. "I won't sugarcoat this for you. This is going to be a vicious battle. Are you sure this is what your people will want?"

Su-Hui was sure. They were tight as a unit. No one would be willing to send off a loved one while they hid somewhere. *With bombs falling, will anyplace here really be safe?*

"I understand. The Sons of Liberty will fight."

"Damn," Griffiths said, cracking a smile. "How can we lose with people like you fighting with us? I almost pity those stupid sons of bitches that come at us."

Nashville, Tennessee

Charli Kazinski sat in her office in the old Commerce Union Bank Building as one of her agents, Curtis Boyne, pulled up the video feeds on her monitor. The images were of various cameras positioned in and around the conference room where the flash drive recorder had been discovered. Her office felt cramped between the three big monitors that dominated her desktop and the stacks of paperwork she had carefully positioned on the desk. To some people, it might be seen as clutter, but to Charli, there was an invisible level of organization that only she understood.

It had been two weeks since its discovery, and so far, no one had made a move to recover it. Charli had feared that their investigation had been compromised, or that the perpetrator had discovered that the room was being heavily monitored. Agent Boyne opened two more video windows on her left monitor, then spoke. "Madame Director, we have had the room and corridor outside under tight surveillance. So far, the room has only been accessed by individuals that *need* access to it." As he spoke, the videos began to play showing an array of people entering the room, sitting down, talking, presenting … it was boredom on fast-forward for her.

"Has anyone recovered the recorder?"

"We didn't think so at first," Boyne said, pausing to slide his horn-rim glasses back up on is nose. "We checked daily, and it was in the drawer where we left it."

"So he's on to us?"

Boyne smiled, if only for a moment. "That's what we thought

initially. I then took the precaution of putting a tiny little mark on the drive … nothing that might be noticed. What we learned is that someone was grabbing it, replacing it with a duplicate recorder." As he stopped, she noticed his grin broaden.

"Tell me you have this person on video."

"Indeed," Agent Boyne replied, fidgeting with his remote and on seven different screens. Then a janitor appeared. In three of the images, he was opening the drawer that held the recording device, while making it look as if he were cleaning. There was no direct image of him touching the device; whoever he was used his body to block the camera angles as if he knew where the cameras were hidden. As he turned away from the credenza where the drawer was located, she hit pause on her keyboard, giving her a good look at his face for the first time. *This is the traitor. We have him.*

"His name is Luis Fernando. He started last month. He passed our background check and even cleared his poly," Boyne said. "Though a few of his responses were close to the threshold."

He must have had help with that polygraph. While polygraphs were not infallible, some people were far less susceptible to triggering a negative response. "He's a plant—which means his identity is bogus."

"Agreed," Agent Boyne replied. "We dug deep, and it seemed pretty legitimate. Whoever crafted his background was thorough as all hell. For a while we thought we made a mistake. Then we started looking into the backgrounds of the people that he used as references. Their backgrounds were not nearly as well built as his. In fact, we found evidence that two of them didn't exist until a year ago."

"Like I said, he's a plant."

"Indeed he is, ma'am."

"Someone who had the means to create false fingerprint records, immigration paperwork, everything."

"Yes."

"He's an operative," she affirmed.

"Can you be sure?"

"This level of sophistication and tradecraft is the validation."

"I can assemble a team and arrest this guy in the matter of an hour," Agent Boyne said confidently.

"Hold on," she said, thinking it over for a long moment. "As far as we know, he doesn't know we have identified him."

"Correct. If he knew we had him, he wouldn't have gone anywhere near the recorder."

This gives us an edge. "If this Luis Fernando is an operative, taking him down will not be easy. As it is, he doesn't know we are on to him. That is something that I think we can leverage."

"Isn't that dangerous? If this is an operative, they can cause a lot of damage."

"It *is* dangerous. This is the Secret Service—everything we do is dangerous, especially in the middle of a civil war. I want him followed, but it has to be done delicately. If this is an NSF operative, they will be checking constantly for shadows." *I wish to hell that Caylee wasn't off in New Mexico. I could really use her expertise in this.* "He needs to be monitored twenty-four seven, with people that have the firepower and skills to deal with him if he turns on them. In the meantime, we need to take advantage of the fact that we know about him."

"What do you have in mind?"

Charli grinned. "If he wants to steal conversations and secrets, we will give him some … just not anything of value. In fact, some wonderful fabrications."

CHAPTER 11

"Good people aren't cancelled. Only dangerous threats are."

Nashville, Tennessee

Custodian Luis Fernando sat on the well-worn couch that dominated the flat that he had rented. The tiny, one-room apartment was exactly the kind of place that someone working as a janitor might live in. He had the trappings to fit the persona of his character—photos of fake relatives, letters from loved ones still living in Mexico. Anyone covertly tossing his living space would find no evidence that he was really Thiago Reese, NSF operative. Like every other aspect of his life, it was a lie.

He picked up the small package that had come in the mail and used a knife to carefully cut the edge of the padded envelope. Inside was a book, some sci fi drivel. Anyone opening it would assume he had ordered it from Amazon, and if they checked his phone, they would find the order. Taking the book out, he thumbed through it slowly, carefully.

This was how he received material he needed from the NSF … ordered from his bogus account and fulfilled by a special group within Amazon that were NSF tradecraft experts. Big Tech had been allied with the Newmerican government before it even had come to fruition. They were a part of the government but were oblivious to that reality. They still thought of themselves as independent corporate entities that had good relationship with the government. Their ignorance as to the realities of the relationship and freedom they had was a tool that Newmerica exploited. As such, their cooperation with the NSF was a foregone conclusion.

When he reached page thirty-two, he got what he wanted. Thin, semi-transparent sheets tucked between the pages. Sealed in a clear transparent sheet, Luis held them up towards the light and looked at them. *The folks up in Langley came through for me as usual.* It had cost him a favor or two, and getting access to the source files was tricky, but now he had what he needed. Fingerprint transfers—exactly what he asked for. There were nine of them in the small sheet. All he had to do was take them out, peel off the cover, and press them against the object he wanted to transfer the false prints to. They were treated with an oil solution that ensured that the prints would not smear or be obscured if handled, ensuring they would be detected at the right time. He knew they would have the person's prints on file … but it still had taken two weeks to get them delivered.

He had intended to use fingerprints recovered from the glassware he'd taken from the conference room where he had seen Operative Leatrom. The problem was there were multiple prints on the glass; some were likely from other staff who had handled glass, or even other occupants in the room. For him, it was more important to have a clean set of prints to work from—which meant leveraging his resources back in Newmerica.

Reese/Fernando had assembled the rest of the disguise that he would need from materials he purchased at Hobby Lobby and online. When he struck, he needed to appear to be a different person, and a different gender. The disguise didn't have to be perfect. He had checked the cameras at the location where he planned his attack and found them to be older models. *I don't have to have an exact disguise, just enough so that on a blurry camera it will convince the Secret Service as to my identity. Combined with the fingerprints, the truth will be lost in a flurry to demand justice.*

Tucking the fake fingerprints back into the book, he sat it down next to him. *I won't be needing them for a few days.* His plan to cripple the American administration was still being completed, but had taken form. The target had a weak spot on his weekly agenda, a place where he was vulnerable. The detail that protected him was small, two Secret Service agents. Done properly, they would be negated swiftly, leaving their charge exposed.

It wasn't enough to kill the man. It had to be something that generated strife far beyond his death. To do that, blame had to be laid. Using a gun with fake fingerprints pointing to someone else in the American administration would be perfect. *I will leak it to my media contacts well, not allowing them the luxury to investigate the truth. The media will stir the proverbial pot for me. Once the story is out there, it will be impossible for them to recall it. Even if they put up the truth, millions will never believe them—never trust them.*

He got up and went to the older refrigerator in the nook that served as kitchen and pulled out a can of Coors. He popped it open. The first sip was always the best, biting cold on his tongue as he savored it and swallowed. *Everything is going according to plan. The material that I have gotten about the upcoming American offensive is in the hands of the Newmerican military, and they are prepared for it. The leaks about information to the media are already eating away at people's confidence in this government. Already their surge of patriotism at the swearing in of the Pretender President is starting to fade. They are starting to wonder if they are backing a government that might just restore the corruption of old.*

Luis/Thiago took another long sip of his beer and smiled to himself at his success and at what was about to come.

Forward Deployment Area Alpha
Adrian, Texas

General Reager entered the Adrian Rock Island Depot and surveyed the room. The tiny former train station had been a local history museum for years. After The Fall, funding had fallen off, and the building had been mothballed. Now it served as one of his forward deployment headquarters. As he made eye contact with the officers present, he removed his beret and tucked it into his belt as he approached them.

"I'll cut to the chase," he said. "What did our recon teams learn?"

Captain Paul Harnessy shifted on his feet but stood erect and ready. "We are seeing more SE and National Guard presence across the border than ever before. They have almost tripled their patrols. More importantly, they are more heavily armed. We found three teams armed with Javelins protecting the road to San Jon on I-40. Those are the ones we found."

"That is disturbing," he said slowly.

"There's more. We found teams with night vision gear and machine guns—Ma Deuce's. Their positions are not the kind of stuff dug by inexperienced troops. These are field fortifications, professional, perfectly placed," Harnessey added.

"It sounds like they don't want us to come over and play on their field," quipped Major Suarez of the Kansas National Guard. His comments brought a little chuckle from the officers—but not from Reager.

His intelligence officer's words gave Trip pause. He didn't like the sound of what he heard. The thought was that they would be facing SEs or local militia. This had the sound of professional troops. "Anything else?"

Harnessy shifted on his feet slightly. "I'm afraid so sir. Our team that was assigned to recon the Cannon Air Force Base perimeter was ambushed. Two of our people were wounded and taken prisoner."

"Did we get a good look at what they have at Cannon?" Trip asked.

The captain shook his head. "Sir, our team got pegged a mile from the base."

Brigadier General Ricketts spoke up. "Cannon is just across the border. We shouldn't be surprised that they have a pretty tight defense there. They have been using it to fly drone missions." His words were supposed to play down the ambush, treat it as something expected. If anything, it raised more questions in Trip's mind.

Trip crossed his arms. "They had to know we would make a grab for the air base, but intercepting us that far out is unsettling. Just a few weeks ago, we could get eyes on the base. It sounds like they have extended their defense perimeter. The question we must grapple with is simple: Do they know what we are planning with Diamondback?"

There was a prolonged moment of silence. His intelligence officer, Harnessey, spoke up to end it. "Since the attack on Knoxville, we have seen a general reinforcement all along the border states. In Pennsylvania, the defenses around Philly and Pittsburgh are being enhanced. In Virginia, we have seen troop concentrations and anti-tank barriers being erected along I-95 south of Petersburg and on I-81. Illinois has turned Springfield into a bunker after the capture of the governor there. Colorado's border defenses now include razor wire and trenches—where a month ago there was nothing."

"That's there," Trip said. "What about here?"

"Sir, this could very well be part of a general defensive posture on the part of Newmerica."

Trip's eyes narrowed in deep thought for a moment. He had hoped to catch the enemy off guard with an offense into New Mexico and beyond, opening a southwestern front in the war. Now he heard that the enemy was preparing, digging in. *I wish we had more air assets for this. I want to know just how strong their forces are.* Trip knew that a fight was coming, but the question that tore at him was not knowing how big a fight it was going to be.

He sighed before speaking. "We all knew this war would not be a cakewalk," he said, sweeping his gaze over to Ricketts and the other officers in the room, then settling back on his G2. "They are expecting something, whether it is our offensive or some other use of force. I take it there are no other indications of enemy buildup?"

Harnessey shook his head. "None we've detected," he said with careful wording. *That opens up a lot of interpretation. He's smart—there would be a lot we haven't detected yet.* "We need to review our plans of attack. If they have ambushes staged along the major roads, I want to consider going cross country in some places. We won't play into their hands. If they expect us to come with blunt force, we will swing around them and hit them in the flanks. I want our plans revised along these parameters."

There were nods of agreement from his staff and as they broke, many scattered to their duty. General Ricketts came up to him. "You're worried."

Trip nodded and spoke in a low tone. "I am at that."

"You think we are getting suckered in?"

Trip shrugged slightly. "I'm not sure. We've been able to predict the enemy's offensive operations up to this point. Maybe they have learned from that and are now starting to predict us. It's hard to say."

"You could call it off," Ricketts reminded him. Saying those words wasn't easy for the older officer. Trip respected it. Going along with the crowd was always an easy choice. Offering the option to back down took a margin of guts, something he admired from the man that saved Knoxville.

No. Hitting them here will change the balance of the conflict; it will draw forces that might otherwise concentrate in the east or north. "I could, but I won't. We will rethink our axis of attack. We will plan this out a little more, factoring in what we have learned. We need this southwest front."

"What if the enemy knows that and has a plan of their own?" whispered Ricketts.

"Then we will adapt. We can't afford a rigid adherence to a plan. When the enemy reacts, we will react as well."

"Very well," Ricketts said with a nod.

"But to be sure," Trip said. "I want you to work with the Kansas National Guard. Give me a response force, something fast, a mobile. Nothing big, but something nimble. If they do come at us, I want to throw an uppercut."

With those words, General Ricketts' semi-grim expression gave way to a broad smile. "It would be my pleasure."

Cannon, Air Force Base
New Mexico

Darius Thorne climbed the wooden wall in full gear, his muscles protesting each agonizing foot of the hurdle. There had been an increase to PT exercises in the last few days, more running, more drilling. While everyone complained, the veterans of the Veteran's Corp understood what it meant; they were going into action sometime soon.

There were other clues as well. Arizona Army National Guard (AZARNG) units had set up camp at Cannon. Their arrival had forced the Veteran's Corps out of their barracks and into tents, which brought more grumbling. The Arizona troops brought assault helicopters, the Desert Hawks. These were hidden under desert camouflage netting near the runways, clearly poised to avoid damage if the Americans struck at the hangers. *Some shit is going down soon. All of the signs are here.*

When he finished the course, he paused and got some water. He had to admit he liked the dry air. His sinuses had only been this clear once in his life, during deployment overseas. New Mexico's sand was not as fine and deeply penetrating as it had been in the Middle East. It was just as desolate though. Miles of nothing stretched out from the base in every direction. No one complained about not getting leave, simply because it was clear there was no place to go if they had the privilege.

April meant the days were getting warmer, but the nights still clung tight to the last remnants of winter. Sergeant Ingersoll dismissed them, and the unit began the short hike back to their tents. Darius drifted away from his comrades to dodge any conversation.

April was always like that for him. The memories of an April a few years ago were something that he didn't like talking about. Every year at this time, the thoughts came back to him, pushing and shoving him into an angry cantankerous mood. As he walked, those memories surged forward once more—taking him back in time both mentally and emotionally.

Four Years Earlier ...
San Francisco, California

The courtroom was filled with defendants, their families, and other onlookers. Darius sat behind his partner John Livingston as he rose to hear the verdict. The judge sat above them all, looking down dispassionately at his business partner.

The trial had been short. John had shot the protester and owned up to it. His lawyer had convinced him to plead guilty to manslaughter with the assurance he would get a light sentence. Darius had tried to get him to fight the charges, plead innocent—but John would have none of that. "I own my shit. I pulled that trigger. I wish to hell I hadn't, but I did. Fighting it would not be fair to that kid's family." John's honor was one of the reasons he and William had gone into business with him in the first place. Now it felt like his greatest asset was being turned against him by the legal system.

"Mr. Livingston," the judge said firmly. "Having pled guilty to manslaughter, do you have anything to say before sentence is given?"

John nodded. "I only want to say that I am sorry for what happened. It won't bring the victim back, but I am truly sorry for what happened."

"Very well. You are to be remanded to the authorities for incarceration in a state penitentiary for a period of not less than two years." The gavel came down hard with a crack that seemed to penetrate Darius.

John turned around, his face drawn and solemn. He looked to his partners. “Any word on the insurance?” Their coffee shop, All Jacked Up, had been targeted by the mobs in the streets after the shooting. While John’s shooting had driven away protesters that night, they had come back, trashing the place. William and John had pleaded with the police to move in and protect what was left of their business, but the officers had demurred. No one wanted to engage the rioters; they were bent on destruction and violence.

The question dug deep at Darius. He wished that John had not asked the question because he was compelled to answer it. “They have denied our claim,” he said as the bailiff came in behind him and handcuffed him.

“Why?”

William spoke up. “They say there’s some clause in our policy—if a crime is committed as part of the claim, they don’t have to pay a dime.”

John’s face sagged even more. “You have to fight them. This was a riot.”

Darius nodded, “I will John, I swear.”

The bailiff led off their partner, and he and William shuffled down the center aisle out of the courtroom. “You should have told him we already appealed, and that had been denied,” William said.

“He’s having a shitty enough day as it is.”

“We lost everything,” William said angrily. “We busted our asses building that place, and these rioters destroyed it all.”

Darius felt his shoulders sag. It wasn’t just losing their massive investment; the city had leveled fines at them for having an open storefront. So they had to board it up, hammering shut the place they had built their future dreams on. Gone as well was their source of income. They had to lay off the ten people that worked there. Darius had given them a small severance, draining his bank account in the process. It didn’t seem right to lay them off with nothing in their pockets.

Now he was drained—financially, emotionally, and personally. One of his best friends was being taken to prison for simply taking a stand against a band of looters. *I fought for this country, and when it came time for the country to respect that, they screwed me over instead.*

“Telling him how bad things are would have only made things worse.”

“Worse?” William blurted out as they stood in the foyer of the court, beyond earshot from the next case being called up. "How could they be worse? I am going to be evicted, Darius, and you will be soon too. We lost every penny we saved in that business."

"John lost his freedom."

"And we are going to lose our apartments. Damn the insurance companies! You pay and pay them, and when it comes time to collect, they are nowhere to be found."

"You can't blame them alone," Darius said. "The entire system is fraudulent."

"That doesn't help. What are we going to do now?"

The question tore at him. For a long few seconds, he said nothing. "We will do what we always do—survive. It was that way in Afghanistan, and it is that way here. We will rebuild … somehow. We'll find a way."

William nodded. "I sure as hell hope you're right."

Present day ...

Vixen bumped him as he walked, stirring him out of his memories from four years earlier. "You with us Darius?"

"Sorry," he muttered. "Just remembering some shit that happened a while ago." He continued to walk, suddenly realizing that he was almost to his tent. He didn't remember a thing about the steps he took—he had been so lost in thinking of John and William. A part of him wanted to weep at the memories of his friends. *We were family ... the three of us. We did everything together.* It felt as if the entire world had conspired against them. *Now he was the last man left. I wish you guys were here with me.*

"You going to be okay man?" Vixen asked.

"Yeah," he said reaching up and wiping the moisture that was forming in his eyes. "Just memories, that's all."

"Well, you'd better get your stuff together. Word is we are moving out tonight."

"Word from who?"

She grinned. "I have my sources. They are trucking us south."

"We are south—we're in New Mexico."

"Apparently there's some place further south where they need us. Some sort of big operation against the Americans." Vixen was the kind of person who thrived on gossip. It was understandable. Often it was the only form of entertainment for soldiers, next to griping. "It doesn't matter to me," he said in a low tone. "I just follow orders."

"Don't we all?"

They stopped at the flap door of the tent and paused. She reached up and put her hand on his forearm. "Hey, you look all shook up. If you want to talk, I have two ears."

Darius shook his head. "I've said it all before, down at the VA with my counselor, with other folks. Talking doesn't help the pain. It's just something I have to deal with."

"Alright," she said. "You know, you don't have to cope all on your own." With those words, Vixen walked away.

Yes I do ... I'm the last man standing.

CHAPTER 12

"Don't buy into the lies. No one is spying on you. We don't surveil innocent people. We are protecting you by watching possible dissidents."

The District

The Vice President slid into the seat opposite of President Porter. She crossed her legs at her ankles and produced a warm smile. She had been summoned to meet with Daniel, a rarity. The few times she had in the past, it was because of trouble, and he was seeking her input—something she considered intelligent on his part. Daniel looked frustrated, or angry, or both. His brow was wrinkled and red as he lifted his gaze to meet hers. "To what do I owe the honor?"

"I received a rather tense call from General Rinehart a little while ago. Apparently you saw fit to put one of these People's Wardens on his command staff personally." His tone was that of someone making a formal charge.

Ah, the good General is pissed. So much the better. "That is correct."

"Well he's furious. I was a bit surprised as well. I looked like a fool because I didn't know you had done that without giving me a heads up."

"I was unaware that you wanted to be informed of individual warden assignments Daniel."

His gaze narrowed. "Alex, don't take that tone with me."

"What tone are you referring to?" she said with a hint of innocence in her voice.

"Putting a shadow on Rinehart is only going to make him distrust us."

"If he's doing nothing wrong, he has nothing to worry about."

Daniel shifted in his seat, resting his arms out in front of him on the desk. "If you are going to be putting these Wardens on key military personnel, I think that is something I need to be made aware of—in advance." He stressed the last two words with her, enough to make it sound like he was scolding her. Alex didn't like it, not in the least. *I think sometimes he forgets who I am, and what I can do. Like most others, he needs to be reminded of that.*

"As the head of the NSF, the People's Warden Program falls under my prevue. I have no problem sharing information with you, but I need to run this program as I see fit."

He sighed, and his jaw adjusted forward. "There are times Alex, that I think you forget I am the President and you are just the VP."

"Just?"

"You know what I mean."

"I think this conversation has been long in coming. I have to admit, I'm a little surprised that you are letting Rinehart get under your skin. He should welcome a representative of the people looking over his shoulder, validating his loyalty."

"You are going too far. We talked about this as a means to ensure loyalty and control of the military. When you approved it, you were all fired up. Now you are backpedaling. What has changed?"

"What has changed was that I thought I would be more in the loop with this. You started right out putting someone on Rinehart."

"The best way to manage this is from the top down."

"He's furious. He's threatening to resign his commission."

Posturing and bluffing—pure patriarchal nonsense. She shook her head as if to dispel the threat. "He won't do that."

"What makes you think so?"

"One, my Warden there has told me that it is a bluff. Our good General is on the verge of whipping out the Defiance in New Hampshire and striking a blow in the west. Men like that don't walk away from their shot at military glory. Second, if he does resign, he'll be in Social Quarantine in a matter of hours." The last part was not a threat, it was a fact.

"I agree that we need to monitor the activities of the military, especially in light of our recent setbacks. Pushing around men like

Rinehart is risky. That's exactly why I should have been consulted first, before you took action."

"Need I remind you Daniel that we took incredible risks to get where we are today."

"I know. But this isn't the Liberation—it's about us finishing what we started then. These people are ungrateful for all we have done for them. They resent the enlightenment we have given them. The military has always distrusted us. They have only half-heartedly backed our war effort. With what we have going on in the camps, the enemy is salivating for a chance to impose their justice on both of us." Frustration rang in his words; she could smell it on his breath from across the desk. He's afraid of losing. He knows what they will do with us if we are defeated.

"We won't lose because we can't. The Wardens are a vital part of ensuring loyalty."

"I want more oversight regarding the key officers," the President demanded. "I just want it done correctly."

She paused. "Daniel, you must trust me enough to do my job."

"You are doing more than your job—more than any Vice President ever. You have the TRC, the NSF, and the SEs under your thumbs. A few people have gone so far as to suggest that you are accumulating power to usurp me."

"And who was it that made those accusations?" she asked.

"That isn't important."

"I think it is. Look Daniel, if it wasn't for me, neither of us would be where we are now. You know that. Yes, I am doing more that my predecessors. Once we have a new constitutional convention, we can make the role of the Vice President something more than a placeholder position. I do what I do for the good of the nation we created. Newmerica needs a firm guiding hand ensuring its security—and that is what I do."

"I think you may be taking on too much," Daniel countered. Perhaps you can off-load some of your responsibilities. Perhaps you can divest yourself of the TRC or the NSF."

Someone has gotten to him. They have been planting fear in his ears, fear about me. "What if I refuse?" she asked, deliberately baiting him.

"I'm more than within my power to announce appointments to the leadership roles."

It was rare for Daniel to assert himself as of late. The swearing in of the American President and the loss at the polls was something he had never expected. "You could do that Daniel. Certainly it is within your authority. But you won't."

"I won't?"

"No," she said, leaning forward slightly to close the distance between them. "We both know that you have slept with your underage babysitter on at least three occasions."

His fate went from pink to hot crimson. Daniel's nostrils flared, and his mouth opened to speak, but no words came for a second or two. When he spoke, it was in a lower tone. "You would dare to blackmail me?"

"Blackmail is such a racist word; don't you think?" she said coyly.

"Is extortion better for you then?" he said in a growl.

"I prefer to think of this as me expressing the risks of you taking such action. If I know this little nugget of information, imagine who else may know about it. Your little dalliances are putting your entire administration at risk."

Daniel fumed, but silenced his voice. When he finally spoke, it was through gritted teeth. "This is unbecoming of you."

She leaned back in her seat and smiled. "This is who I am, Daniel. Now, I know this infuriates you. You were ANTIFA—you hate career politicians. You see us as obstacles. By the same token, you *need* people like me to keep things running effectively. You want good administrators. You crave order. I respect you for standing up to me, but you must understand I have no intention of surrendering what I have created here.

"That doesn't mean I can't be amiable. You have created a security problem with this babysitter you slept with. I run an agency that deals with such problems."

"What do you mean?"

"I will clean up your mess. Your babysitter problem will simply go away." She spoke of it so glibly that it glossed over what she really intended.

"You're going to send her to one of the camps?"

"Oh no," she said. "There's too much of a chance she might talk. Her silence needs to be ensured. There is only one way to do that effectively and permanently."

The bright red color drained from his face as he realized what she was saying. Her thoughts were equally a flip. *That's right Daniel. I will have her killed. It's the only way to be sure.*

"Alex," he said in a softer tone. "She doesn't have to die."

"Daniel, just like the warden program, it is best that you not know the details."

He nervously closed his eyes and nodded his head.

"Very well then," she said rising from her seat. "I take it we have no further information to discuss."

Daniel nodded again, and she walked out of the room with long defiant strides. *This was a good meeting—productive. Daniel knows what I am willing to do. He won't risk challenging me, not for some time. And if he does, he will find I have more leverage—such as his approval to have his underage mistress killed.*

Springer, New Mexico

The Broken Arrow Motel was a dull, light brown with a faux adobe exterior. Springer, New Mexico was tiny. Not a tourist hot spot, not by a far stretch. The tiny town was flat with scrub trees and a few rundown gas station convenience stores. There wasn't a fast food place in sight. The nearest Subway was ten miles north. Caylee didn't care; she wasn't there for the sightseeing. This was nothing more than a waypoint when traveling to the Social Quarantine Camp in the Santa Fe National Forest.

So far, Operation Seraphim was going well. Raul and Travis had reached out to her to confirm they were across the border. Her own journey had involved going through three checkpoints—far more security than on her last trip across. Some of that might be because she and Travis had killed an SE team that had tried to assault her the last time they were there. Still, the increase seemed more militant. National Guard were traveling with the SEs. Her instinct told her that something was going on, and the New Mexico authorities were keeping a tight lid on it.

She sat against two pillows stacked where the bed hit the wall. One of her phones chirped, and she picked it up. Charli sent her four photos. Caylee muted the television which was spewing the nightly TRC-approved report. Her focus went to the photos.

Her first thought: *I've been in that conference room.* Turning her attention to the custodian, she studied the enhanced images of his face. It was familiar to her. There was something about the jawline, the shape of his nose, that stirred some memories. *I've seen him before.*

Usually her memory was excellent when it came to faces and places, but this was proving elusive. *I need some context.* With a few stabs of her fingers, she called Charli.

"Caylee," came the voice. "You got the images."

"I did. What am I looking at?"

"Our security in the White House has been compromised; we think by this guy. I was wondering if he was a former colleague."

An operative ... that was what she meant. Suddenly she had the context. A wave of memories came back to her.

Camp Peary, Virginia
Two years earlier ...

The CIA's infamous Farm was familiar ground for Caylee. She had trained there for three months during her stint with the Agency. She had been there during the winter, when the wintry winds came off of the York River, and she remembered it as cold. Now she was there in summer, and the humidity and blistering heat made her clothing stick to her as if it were painted on her skin.

The lecture was being given outdoors, barely shaded by the trees that dominated the area. Sitting next to her was Michelle Riley, a peer with a deadly reputation that rivaled her own in the operative program. Caylee surveyed the others that were gathered, focusing on a short man that stood rigid at the front of the group, awaiting his time to speak. His skin was dark, past bronzed. While he was stout, she could see his muscles straining under the tight, gray Under Armor shirt that he wore. His black mustache was thick, and he had a short goatee. His dark eyes seemed to sweep the room, and just for a moment, she made eye contact with him.

"Who is that?" she asked Michelle, nodding at the man.

"They call him Rumbler. Last name Reese. Thiago Reese. Deep operative. They say he overthrows regimes ... something of his specialty."

"I never heard of him."

"Remember that shit in Ukraine, when the Russians came in?

Remember how Zelenskyy and his thugs and the others got out on the last plane to the US. Well, that was him."

She remembered the news well, right down to the looted treasury they had brought with them. The Newmericans didn't want any part of propping up the Ukrainians. One rumor, which she had seen evidence of, showed that several politicians were using Ukraine to enrich their personal wealth, laundering funds through the corrupt regime. Letting the government fall, buried countless illegal acts. Letting it stand opened them up to blackmail. Another rumor was that the Newmericans had brokered a deal with the Russians—to let them have Ukraine for a promise of better crude oil prices to help shore up the US's struggling economy. NATO leaders whined that the loss of Ukraine meant nothing other than it helped prop up the economy after the first Green New Deal. Everything had happened so quickly; no one gave it a second thought. Now though, it made sense. *The civil war that followed—that is probably Reese's handiwork.*

Caylee nodded silently as the lecture started. His portion was on precautions that should be taken for long-term assignments. For her it was not very applicable—operatives tended to have a target or objective and simply went and did it, but she listened to it. Mandatory training meant attending, not liking the material presented. When they broke for lunch, Reese drifted over to her. "And you are?" he asked with an almost bar-pick-up tone in his voice, flashing his bright teeth in a broad smile.

"Getting ready to eat," she said grabbing the box chicken salad lunch.

"Your name.... What is your name?" he pressed, securing a box for himself and following her.

"Caylee Leatrom."

From her sideways glance, she saw his eyes flare. "I've heard of you. You have a bit of a reputation."

"Don't we all?"

He followed her to her seat, taking the chair that Michelle had been using. "You know, there's nothing on the agenda for tonight. Why don't we grab a ride into Yorktown and have a few drinks, swamp notes and war stories?"

How incredibly forward and arrogant. He doesn't even know me, and is trying to pick me up! She eyed him carefully. "I don't think so."

"Don't you want to get to know me better?" he said; clearly his pride was injured.

"Not particularly."

"Ah, I see."

"You see what?" she asked with a crisper tone of voice, pausing at unwrapping her lunch.

"You prefer women," he stated. "I should have known with that short haircut. Sorry for wasting your time."

His level of presumptiveness made her hot with anger. "It's not a matter of the sex I prefer next to me at night, Mr. Reese. You just aren't my type."

Clearly her words infuriated him. "What? You have something against LatinX people?"

"It isn't your race either. I just don't socialize with people who do the same thing I do," she said in a lower tone of voice.

That seemed to satisfy him. Nodding to her, he flashed his grin again. "You don't know what you're missing." Before she could rebut his point, Reese got up and left.

Present day ...

"Now I remember him," Caylee said to Charli. "Last name Reese. They used to call him the Rumbler—I have no idea why. His first name is Thiago I think. He's an operative. His specialty was deep embedded ops. Word was he's the guy you sent in to topple governments and undermine regimes."

"Shit!" Charli spat back. "I was hoping my gut feeling was wrong."

"He was with the Agency before being an operative, heavy counter-intel background if I remember correctly. I can't remember his first name. I will say this: He is dangerous."

Charli said nothing for a few moments. "Any advice on how to take him down?"

"Shoot first; don't give him a chance to get away."

"Not exactly by the book. I have to adhere to the law, Caylee."

"He won't, so you shouldn't. If he is there, he's there to take down the government—that was his area of expertise, if I remember correctly. That means the whole gambit, ruining the economy, causing dissent, spycraft, and even assassinations. Those nations he didn't help topple, he hamstrung them."

"I could use your help on this."

"You know I'm tied up here," she said. We are looking at a week or so—depending on the Army."

"Is there anything you can tell me that might help me deal with him?"

"He's cocky—arrogant. He likes women and isn't afraid to toss around his heritage when it fits his needs. I suspect his ego comes from his string of successes in the field. He'll be armed and always have a fallback plan."

"Roger that," Charli responded. "Is Andy with you?"

"Not yet."

"Okay," she said. "Anything else you can share with me that might help?"

Caylee wished there were, but none came to her. "I'm sure you have a tail on this guy. Chances are he will spot them and have a plan to evade them. You can't beat this guy one-on-one. He's used to being under surveillance and still pulling off his missions. To take him down, you are going to have to think big and be creative. You can't frighten or intimidate him."

"Thanks … I think."

"Good luck," Caylee offered. Charli hung up. Deep in her own thoughts, she stared at the muted television. *Charli is good. She's more than smart. She took down one hostile operative already. This Reese guy is a step above a mere presidential assassin.*

She found herself longing to end this camp breakout and return to Nashville to help her friend.

White Mountain National Forest
New Hampshire

Su-Hui Zhou stood next to Tate Palmer who had volunteered to lead in the harassment attack and lure the Newmerican forces into the trap hidden in the White Mountain National Forest. Tate had been angry when he came to after Su-Hui had incapacitated him and driven him away from his motor lodge. The two finally reconciled, though Su-Hui knew their relationship had been damaged. From his perspective, he had little choice. Letting the man fight and die was a waste, one he could not tolerate.

Tate had been the first to volunteer for the mission. "I used to come up here all the time. We would four-wheel on the logging trails." As they trudged through the dense forest, the burly man had clearly been telling the truth. He seemed to have an instinct for where he was and where he was going.

Tate's scouting skills had led a mobile recon company to a road about a mile back, where they were positioned, waiting for Su-Hui to lure the enemy to them. Lieutenant Boothe of the New Hampshire National Guard had accompanied them as they got closer to the enemy.

Crossing a creek, they climbed a steep embankment of nearly fifty feet. At the top, Tate went low and held up his hand for the rest of them to stop. As the others hunkered down, Su-Hui climbed up the embankment, slipping slightly on the wet, dead leaves. There were still spots of wet snow under the massive pine trees. The rest of the ground was slick with mud, and the air hung with a cool dampness as spring slowly tightened its grip on the forest.

As he slid up next to Tate, he looked out on the other side of the ridgeline. At least a platoon of troops were there, parked on a dirt roadway. Several were smoking cigarettes, and a few were walking slowly along the perimeter. Five Humvees were parked, fanned out to provide cover. Their wheels were muddy, a testimony as to how hard it was to travel through the forest, even on the trails. One was topped with a TOW missile launcher; the others bristled with machine guns. An officer held a map up and two others were pointing at it. While he couldn't hear their exact words, their murmurs reached him. Both he and Tate backed down the hills a few feet.

"Most of these trails aren't on the maps," Tate whispered. "They're out of road. They are trying to make heads or tails of where they are."

Su-Hui nodded. "Our ATVs are about a mile back with the recon company under Major Segal. If we hit them here, hard, we can fall back to them and convince them to follow us."

Lieutenant Boothe nodded in agreement. "We are set up on two hilltops. If you can convince them to follow you down the middle, where we walked in from, we will flank them. No matter what, we need to let a few of them get away, if only to lure the rest of the enemy to follow."

"Oh, I'll convince them," Tate assured him with a smile. "I'm all about convincing the enemy to die."

"No heroics, my friend," Su-Hui said.

"Not an issue today. I actually can't wait to see what happens when they come at us with everything they have." There was glee in the man's whispered voice, which gave Su-Hui some degree of tense pleasure. Motioning to his people, the two squads crept up the ridge and huddled.

With all eyes on him, Su-Hui laid out his plans. "We will form up along the ridge, pick targets, and open fire. I want the grenade launchers to concentrate on the trucks. The rest of you, target the officers first. We will engage, then fall back to the ATVs. I want claymores positioned so that when they follow, we take them down. This isn't about wiping out the enemy, but getting them to summon reinforcements and follow us. Once we fall back, it is to be done orderly, but fast. They need to believe they have us on the run. They need to believe we are bigger than just two squads. That means grenades and a lot of gunfire. Does everyone understand?"

There were silent nods. Several of the troops went down and set the claymore mines. Everyone else moved up in a long line at the edge of the ridge, double-checking their weapons. One man crossed himself; another woman wiped the sweat from her brow. Su-Hui watched them all and could not escape the pride he felt. Next to him, Tate Palmer pulled out a grenade and laid his hunting rifle out in front of him.

Slowly Su-Hui climbed with his elbows up the hill where he could see the Newmerican forces. This time he saw their New York National Guard logo on the side of one of the two trucks that were there. In his ears, his heart pounded like a bass drum. No one jumped the gun; they waited for him to take actions. *They are all professional soldiers now. They may be insurgents in the eyes of the enemy but now, after all of the actions we've done—we are as good as any professional military unit.*

Su-Hui slowly brought his assault rifle around. Adjusting the scope for the range, he carefully took aim at the officer that was holding the map. Switching off the safety, he drew his bead on the enemy, drawing a long breath. The weight of his next movement made him hold, if only for a millisecond. *When I pull this trigger, it starts a much larger battle. Men and women will die.* Slowly he let the air out of his lungs as he aimed carefully and slowly squeezed the trigger.

The kick and crack from the weapon happened in the same moment. The officer flew back, the map still clutched in his hands. Every head of the New York Guardsmen whipped around to see where the shot had come from.

Gunfire blazed from the entire ridge as the Sons of Liberty rained hot, full metal death down on the troops below. A truck was hit by a grenade launcher and exploded in a ball of fire. Another was rocked hard by a blast; its right front tire turned into a twisted mass of blasted steel-belt, rubber, and the remains of the hub.

Su-Hui aimed again, this time at a soldier that was climbing into the driver's seat of one of the Humvees. The shot hit the base of his neck and a splatter of gore covered the windshield as he dropped, half in and half out of the vehicle. Another explosion rocked the scattering New Yorkers.

Sporadic gunfire came back at them, kicking up the dead leaves and twigs as the bullets had only small targets to hit. One of the Humvees below roared to life, belching black smoke as the vehicle backed up. The rapid fire of machine guns joined the fray, forcing Su-Hui and others to duck. Tate threw his third grenade in a long arc over the ridge, followed by another *whomp* as it went off.

"Let's move out!" Su-Hui barked. His people didn't have to be told twice. They skidded down the ridge side. The pair of SOL soldiers with the grenade launchers fired some shots over the hill crest, just to maintain the illusion they were still present.

Looking back he saw that one of the SOL was still on the ridge, lying flat on his face. A part of his head was open and bits of his brain, mixed with blood, made his camouflage look dark and wet. *Damn!* He knew they would lose people, but that didn't make it any easier for him.

They ran past the claymores as the two soldiers that rigged them set the trip wire. Splashing across the creek, the SOL started up the other hillside when the Newmerican forces crested the ridge they had abandoned.

The machine guns on the Humvees purred, and three of his people went down in a spray of blood. Some fired back wild shots that slapped into the windshield of the lead Humvee and sparked off the hood. Su-

Hui's head pounded with adrenaline as he rose over the far hillside; bullets stitched the ground right behind him.

In the distance, they could see the recon company and their own ATVs. Lieutenant Boothe sprinted ahead of him, barking out orders as the recon vehicles on the two hilltops buttoned up. Su-Hui's breath was strained as he sprinted for the four-wheelers. Behind him came the distinct bangs of the claymore mines going off, followed by a scream that could be heard despite the intervening terrain.

Two dark, green, enemy Humvees raced over the hill, machine guns blazing. The drivers must have spotted the recon force because it skidded down the hillside with its brakes locked up as the driver tried to slow the momentum of the up-armored vehicle. It was a battle of physics that it would lose. The other Humvee raced straight at Su-Hui's people, as if it were intent on running them over rather than shooting them. For a heartbeat he wondered if the driver might be successful.

Then the armored vehicles opened up.

They hit the lead Humvee with a missile that snaked and twisted in the air just before impact. The explosion was so violent that it almost knocked Su-Hui down. Bits of blasted Humvee rained on the dead leaves and the remnants of the melting snow, sizzling in their dampness. Machine guns, this time from the New Hampshire troops, blazed at the vehicles and at their infantry support as they came over the hill.

Thankfully, Su-Hui and his people were forgotten in the skirmish. They made their way to their ATVs and started off, bullets cutting the air all around them. As they passed one tree, he heard several rounds chew into it … a near miss. Tate sat next to him, grinning broadly. His green fatigue jacket was cut on the sleeve by a bullet, exposing his white long johns underneath. Su-Hui reeled the ATV side to side to make it harder to hit as the banging and booming of the firefight drifted behind them. Overhead was the sound of helicopters in the distance, no doubt called in for support. The whooping of their approaching rotors was enough to force the New Hampshire forces to fall back as well.

"We stirred up a hornet's nest," Tate yelled over the roar of the engine and the sounds of the battle.

"Let's hope so. The General wants the fight brought to him—and it looks like that's exactly what we've done," he said weaving the ATV again and almost hitting one driven by other volunteers from the SOL.

As they raced and jumped over the next hillside, he reminded himself of his own military training back in Taiwan in his youth. *It was always easier to start a fight than to win one. I hope we have not brought about our own doom with this engagement.*

CHAPTER 13

"The enemy could be your neighbor, a relative, or your barista. Be vigilant!"

Abiquiu, New Mexico

Raul smiled broadly when Caylee arrived, driving a lumbering, olive, drab, school bus into the long-abandoned gas station that they were using for a rendezvous point. It was painted to look like a National Guard vehicle with stenciled, white identification numbers and the insignia of the 720th Transportation Company. She came out of the driver's seat and gave him back a nod and grin.

"You stole one of the Army's buses?" Travis asked.

"They had them parked in a staging area. No fences, no guards, just camo netting over them," she replied. "They were practically inviting me to take one."

"We saw a lot of troops coming over the border," Raul said. "If they were staging the vehicles, isn't that an indicator that they are preparing for something?" Raul and Travis had noticed the increase in patrols when they had come over the border into New Mexico.

She shrugged. "Probably. The military kicked off their offensive a few hours ago—it's on all of the networks. Some sort of big battle is unfolding around Tucumcari."

Raul and Travis had seen that on the television. It was their trigger point for starting their operation. Breaking the prisoners out of the camp was one stage of the mission. They were counting on the military offensive to provide them the diversion needed to get the people back to Texas and safety.

A truck pulled up, a battered Ford covered with a thin layer of New Mexico dust. A large man with a portly stomach got out and started over. Raul found himself moving, on instinct, to spread out from the group. The man adjusted his big, gray Stetson and strode right up to the group. "I take it you are the folks I'm looking for," he said in a deep voice.

"And you are?"

"Chris Luke," he said, "Maricopa County Mounted Posse," he proclaimed with a sense of pride. He extended his hand to Caylee who gave it a shake. The planning for the operation included the mounted troops, but their planning had been done virtually. Now that he saw Mr. Luke, he could tell that he was someone who could more than handle a horse. "We've got our mounts outside of town with the Texas Rangers. Captain Kenyon said he will be along shortly."

"It's good to meet you face-to-face," Caylee said, introducing everyone. The leader of Hell's Tarheels joined them as well. Raul could feel the almost sandpaper-like callouses on Luke's hands, making his own skin feel soft. Another vehicle pulled up and a man and woman got out. They were Gwen Holtz of the Witches of Wichita and Jefferson Morris of the Little Rock Irregulars—both SOL groups that had volunteered to help with the mission. Raul was impressed with Gwen Holtz. Her jet black hair was curly, and he could make out her broad chest muscles even under the gray T-shirt and unbuttoned Hawaiian shirt she wore.

When the pair met Raul, they both recognized him, and vigorously shook his hand. Gwen said it was an honor to meet him. "I saw you on TV. I thought you'd be taller."

"My reputation is bigger than I am I guess," he said with a smile.

Caylee unfolded a map of the camp and moved over to the car that Gwen and Jefferson had arrived in. Another truck arrived with Captain Ross Kenyon, of the Texas Rangers, who joined the huddle. She spread the map out on the hood of the vehicle so that everyone could see it. Andy stood at the far end, holding down the map as the breeze tried to take it away.

"Our goal here is to get the prisoners out. Getting them back across the border will depend on the fighting along the front. In other words, flexibility will be the key for that phase of the operation."

Raul saw her make eye contact slowly with everyone, one at a time;

then he continued. “We will need to scout the camp first. While we have data from our recon a few weeks ago, things often change. Those scouts will be responsible for dealing with the guard towers as we approach.”

Chris Luke spoke up. “Maricopa County will gladly serve in that capacity,” he said with pride. “The Texas Rangers would be honored to join you in that assignment,” he said. Luke gave him a single nod of acceptance. Men on horseback … it’s almost like fighting a war in a different century.

Mr. Luke looked over at Caylee. “Some night vision gear would be most appreciated.”

“That can be arranged—we have some … not a lot.”

“Are we just going to drive through the gate?” Jefferson Morris asked. “No offense; our vehicles aren’t exactly bulletproof.”

Raul caught a glimpse from Travis who nodded to him. He spoke up, attracting the gaze of everyone there. “We used a diversion at Valley Forge. We used fireworks, something they couldn’t ignore. It works. The guards are SEs. They are armed, but not trained, and in the middle of the night, they won’t be organized.”

Andy spoke up. “We have to be careful,” he said. “Fireworks with all of that brush out there could start a fire.

Gwen Holtz weighed in. “My Witches can get their attention. You just tell me where you want us and give us some time to get into position.” Raul looked over at her and saw a dark resolve wash over her face.

“Excellent,” Caylee said. “You’ll come in from the north and deploy some eight hours before we make our move. Our earlier recon demonstrated that they don’t patrol out of the camp. There were no trails to show patrols there. They probably presume that no one would be probing their defenses. The rest of you will plow through the front gate and establish a perimeter inside the compound. Remember, our goal is to ensure they don’t turn their guns on the prisoners before we get them out.”

“Los Alamos is in the vicinity,” Travis said. “If they get word out, that will bring NSF and possibly military resources in our direction.”

“That is why you are going to blow the cell towers within range of the camp. I doubt seriously that they spent the money to run a landline up there. No cell towers, no cries for help. We should take them down in the afternoon, just before the attack.”

"Count me in," Travis said. "Any day I get to blow stuff up is a good day." There was child-like glee in his voice.

Caylee offered a thin smile to his words. "We will drive through the main gate, preferably with the dump truck first. We will deploy out of that vehicle, then follow in with the bus and the other transports. Eliminating the enemy is the first priority."

"The prisoners are likely to stay in their barracks," Raul said. "Some might panic though. We just need to be careful of the targets we fire at."

"Good point," Caylee said. "Once we have the guards disposed of, we need to load up. Having been in a few of these camps, you need to know that some of these people can be pretty feeble. We need to check every building. We don't leave any of them behind."

"What about that plastic recycling center they are running there?" Andy asked. "If we leave it, they will just re-staff the camp and ship in new prisoners."

Caylee paused. "We destroy it. Travis can whip up something to ensure it won't remain."

"It would be my pleasure," Travis said.

"We will need to bring back evidence of their crimes," Andy pressed. "We have pictures, but they can be disputed. We need something tangible."

"What do you have in mind?" Raul asked.

"Those bodies they have dumped in that area with that waste residue—we need to bring at least one of them back. It is the best way to show the world what they have been doing." Andy's words were gruesome yet filled with resolve.

Caylee shook her head. "Andy, I know where you are coming from—but we have a lot in play with this rescue. I'm not sure we will have time to chisel out one of these victims."

Raul heard her words and knew she was right—but so was Andy. His mind went again to his sister and her struggles since she had been rescued. *It's wrong not to try. These people have to be held accountable for their crimes.*

"I disagree," he stated firmly. Caylee glanced over at him and cocked her left eyebrow in a look of genuine surprise.

"Andy is right. We have photos, but they will claim they are fake. We need to show the world what is happening in these camps."

"I'll handle that part of the mission," Andy said.

Caylee looked at Andy for a moment, then to Raul. She silently conceded with a nod. "Very well then. We'll have a few hours before the authorities can figure out what has happened, and even then, they aren't going to know who we are or where we are going. We'll work our way to the Texas line and establish communications with the Army to get back to safety."

"Assuming everything goes our way," Gwen Holtz said firmly.

"Exactly," Caylee replied. She spent the next few minutes reviewing what vehicles the team had at their disposal, discussing the timing and sequencing of their actions. For the next hour and a half, the hood of the Ford truck was active with discussion, fingers pointing to places on the map, and the team aligning on what needed to be done—and when.

When they were finished, Gwen Holtz sided up next to Raul. "I want to thank you," she said.

"For what?"

"I was in a camp outside of Wichita. It wasn't a death camp like they are now—but in some ways it was worse. The guards ... well ... they had their way with us. They sold us out by the hour to the locals and their friends." She didn't have to say what they were sold for; everyone understood.

"That's terrible," Raul said. His mind immediately went to his sister. *These people are monsters.*

"After Valley Forge and the swearing in of the President, the local SOL cell liberated us. There were only about a hundred of us at the camp. I ended up forming my own SOL cell from the survivors. The Witches of Wichita are those survivors." Clearly Gwen was holding back tears ... her eyes were watering as she spoke.

"I'm glad you got out of there," was all he could say.

"If it hadn't been for you at Valley Forge, they might not have even tried to save us."

Raul opened his mouth to say something, but couldn't find the words. He stammered for a moment, then finally spoke. "Everywhere I go people tell me I inspired them, or that what I did was great. I wasn't even in charge at Valley Forge. I was just the one that got plastered on the internet and targeted by the NSF."

"You're the only prisoner ever broken out of the Supermax," she countered.

"Because of my friends, the ones who are here today."

"You don't understand the nature of heroes Raul." Gwen smiled. "You are who *we* believe you to be Raul." She reached up and squeezed his upper arm. "Don't fight our version of reality—embrace it."

East of Tucumcari, New Mexico

The M1 Abrams tank next to Trip's command Bradley exploded with such fury and force that its turret blew clear of the body, thudding into the ground in front of his own vehicle. Oily, black smoke rolled through his vision slot and bits of hot shrapnel rained down onto the Bradley's top armor.

It had to be a Javelin or another missile that made the kill shot. Either way we are too damn close to the front. "Watney, back us up," he barked to Bradley's driver. Above him, the gunner for the Bradley unleashed a rapid volley of two three-round bursts from the M242 Bushmaster chain gun. It made Trip's headache throb, but he was glad they were firing back at the enemy.

General Reager hated ordering his vehicle back, but he also had no desire to die. Overhead he heard the roar of a fighter jet and cringed. Chances were it wasn't one of theirs. Explosions followed further down the line. The banging and purring of machine guns mixed with the explosions of mortar rounds. Some were far too close for his liking.

The offense into New Mexico had not gone as Trip had planned. The Newmericans had been perfectly poised to blunt their assault. They were also in prepared positions and had far more forces deployed than Harnessy's intelligence estimates thought possible. He didn't blame his G2. Trip knew that up to this point, Harnessy had delivered good intel. *You don't throw an officer under the bus for one shortfall.* Paul had left the command Bradley to personally assess the front lines.

Trip's invasion had been along two axis of attack. The northern thrust that he was on, was aimed at driving towards Santa Fe. The southern axis was aimed at Cannon Air Force Base. Both had been blunted by strong defenses, bristling with anti-tank missiles and the Newmericans concentrating their air assets. The drive for Cannon had been stopped short, but American artillery had shelled the base extensively, rendering it inoperative as a forward airfield, at least for the time being. When the Newmericans counterattacked, Trip had ordered his force there to fall back to a position right on the Texas border where they could take advantage of their own defensive positions.

"Where's our air support?" Trip called over to Captain Hall.

"We just got our runway repaired. Friendlies are inbound," she replied. "ETA is three minutes."

Another explosion nearby, this one from artillery, sandblasted his Bradley as it backed up. *Let's hope that we have three minutes.*

Trip contemplated his situation. His instinct was to pull back and attempt to flank the Newmerican forces. That was his preferred way of dealing with stubborn opposition. *Somehow the enemy knew our plans. They also know me, which means they know how I am likely to react.* General Reager also knew his opponent, General Rinehart, or at least he thought he did. *He prefers diversion and long, sweeping actions. Assuming he is true to form, this defense is not his only plan. He must be planning to strike at me somewhere else, where I am not prepared.* That realization was unnerving more so than the resistance his attack force was facing.

A part of him wanted to push forward, drive the enemy from their positions, but such battles of attrition used the warfighters as fodder. Trip knew that his ego wasn't big enough to cost troops their lives. *This is a worthless piece of ground; it was a pathway to Santa Fe. That path is blocked. It's time to rethink things. I'll be damned if I send troops to die for something that isn't even a strategic objective.*

The Bradley lurched hard to one side, and rapid metallic pings of machine gun bullets ricocheted off of the front armor. He held on tight to a support loop on the side hull as the armored vehicle lurched hard in one direction. A muffled explosion in the distance boomed and seemed to make the entire Bradley throb with concussive vibrations as it continued to fall back to better ground. It stopped after two more minutes of reverse, adjusting slightly behind what Trip hoped was suitable cover.

The roar overhead signaled the arrival of an airstrike. Unlike the artillery and mortars, the big bombs that were dropped didn't just make the vehicle vibrate—they shook every bone in his body. His joints in his knees and elbows ached in protest. His eyes swept the rear of the vehicle, and he saw that his command staff were shifting in their seats, shaking off the nearby explosions as well.

The side hatch opened, and Captain Harnessy entered. When he pulled off his helmet, a thin wisp of dust came off with it. He was breathing heavily and took a moment to get his breath.

"Alright Paul," what's the word?" Trip asked.

Harnessy shook his head. "Not good. They have multiple lines of trenches running north and south. I got a motorcycle and headed north. Behind a low rise, they have a platoon of light armor. Word from the south is that infantry is dug in. In front of us is a well-entrenched position—razor wire, probably minefields from the looks of it. We push forward, and it will be costly." He paused for a moment, sucking in a deep breath.

"And the flanks are protected too," Trip said.

"Yes sir, from the looks of it."

"They are using helicopters to the south of us for ground support operations. We think Cannon has shipped their aircraft to Luke Air Force Base and are flying out of there."

"I thought Luke was staying neutral in this fight."

"I can't say for sure. It might be they are only using one runway, one designated for the National Guard. Someone over there is bending the rules enough to let them operate there. The only god news so far is that while we are bogged down there, we continue to render Cannon as ineffective. The problem is that advancing there is as bad as it is here."

"They knew we were coming ... and where," Trip said coolly. Outside, there were the thumping explosions of mortar rounds in the distance.

"It does at that," Harnessy said, bowing his head slightly as if he were ashamed of the reality they were now facing.

"It's not your fault, son," he said. "We can worry about how they got their intel later. Right now, I have to try to salvage what we can here."

Harnessy nodded. "We still have our reserves."

"You know Rinehart as well as I do Paul, probably better. What's his next move?"

"He has our attention here, so he's going to hit us somewhere else—somewhere that we are not prepared."

"That could mean to the south, or up north—maybe Oklahoma or even Kansas. My gut tells me to the south."

"Why is that?"

"Texas was a thorn in their side for a long time, even before this war." Memories of the fighting in San Antonia at the Alamo came back to him in that moment, and he felt his face redden at the violence he had been forced to unleash there. "It also has the oil reserves and facilities that make it a more viable strategic objective. Hitting Kansas or Oklahoma would be easier, but it wouldn't really give the enemy anything tangible. Deep down, I think the Newmericans want to hurt Texas. It is personal with them, not strategic."

"I haven't had any indications of an offense anywhere, General."

"Yet—you haven't seen it yet. Rinehart likes offensive ops with big sweeping end-runs. He tried that with Knoxville. He's under pressure by Washington to deliver a victory; you can bet on that."

"What are your orders, sir?"

Trip frowned. *I've never given a retreat order before, but I won't waste my troops lives on my hubris.* "We are going to fall back. Not a retreat, a redeployment. If they are in prepared positions, I want them to have to crawl out to come at us. And I will need a force waiting for them that can make them bleed."

Harnessy nodded, understanding the gravity of his words.

Trip continued. "I want our reserves on the road—heading south. Let's send them to San Angelo. That puts them in position to prevent a thrust at Fort Worth, or to shift and block a run on San Antonio or Houston."

"Sir, with all due respect, that may not be enough."

Trip understood completely. "I know. We're going to have to get creative."

"Creative?"

"You know we've been approached by several PMCs. Maybe the time has come to start using them. If nothing else, they can reinforce General Ricketts when he engages the enemy."

The mention of Private Military Contractors, corporate mercenaries, garnered a cocked eyebrow from Harnessy. "Sir, you've been opposed to using them."

"True, but desperate times call for desperate actions." Trip had held back on hiring them because he didn't trust them. He had worked with several PMCs in the Middle East and had been stunningly disappointed with their lack of discipline and tendency to break the rules. In Ukraine and the Central African Republic, the Wagner Group that the Russians employed had committed war crimes they had never been held accountable for. The PMCs kept pressuring him, offering a wide range of services for an even wider cost. He wanted people that wouldn't break the rules, individuals that would solve problems, not create them. In the pit of his stomach, he felt that PMCs introduced as many risks as they solved. He didn't have much choice. *We may regret it down the road, but for now, I don't have much of a choice.*

"Are there any you prefer I engage with?"

He considered Harnessy's question for a moment. "There's one group out of Florida—Mission Ready. There's another, operating in South Carolina—Lock Jaw I think was their name. They have some pretty high-tech stuff that might help. Get them under immediate contract and make sure we have people working with them that can keep them on a leash."

"Yes sir."

"Lock Jaw has some air elements, but they will need more."

Harnessy nodded. "I will get whatever air assets I can shifting south along the southern border to see if we can spot any enemy movement short-term."

"That's going to be a challenge with their drones operating in our airspace."

Harnessy nodded. The Newmericans had been using nearby Cannon Air Force Base to fly drone sorties against his forces. They had shot down one with a Stinger, but that had only driven the drones to higher altitudes. "Agreed. We are stretched thin as it is. Especially with the shifting of resources to support Defiance."

The mention of New Hampshire weighed heavily on Trip. That battle was likely to erupt at any moment. It was a grim reminder of the scope of the war he was waging. *We are thin as a rail right now. I hope this setback ends here. If we lose New Hampshire and part of Texas, the entire nature of this war may change.*

"We have one uncommitted unit here that should be enough to bounce them back if they decide to try and pursue us."

Harnessy nodded. "The Purebloods."

Trip grinned at the mention of their name. It was a company of former Marines. When COVID hit, they had been forced out of the service for not taking the vaccine. The TRC had made political hay out of their dishonorable discharges, making them an example to anyone that refused the jab. When the war had started, they volunteered to fight against the Newmericans. "They should be more than enough."

"Sir, that's just a company of Marines."

"I know there are a lot of Army personnel that will dog the Marine Corps. I never bought into that inter-service rivalry bullshit. I saw them fight overseas. There's no such thing as "just" a company of Marines. Nothing is meaner or tougher than Marines with a purpose. If the Newmericans decide to push against them, these guys will tear them a fresh asshole, piss on their dead bodies, and laugh while they are doing it."

"I hope you're right, sir."

A distant artillery blast reverberated throughout the Bradley. *Falling back isn't going to be easy, but I'm not going to throw good money after bad in this fight. I need to trust my instincts and what I know about my enemy. I just pray that I'm making the right call.*

Jal, New Mexico

Darius thought the tiny town of Jal was little more than a speed bump on State Road 18. The Dollar General was the busiest place in town, and that wasn't saying much. When their trucks arrived, Captain Aguilar called for an immediate deployment, fully armed. He wondered what they would be fighting near such a worthless little town.

They were not the only military unit that showed up in Jal. There was a company of the California National Guard and another from Washington State. Darius saw them milling around their transports and he gave them a friendly nod, but all he got back was cold shoulders. "What's their problem?" he asked Private Jaxson.

"They don't think much of us. Clearly their shit doesn't stink like ours," he quipped back.

Darius felt slighted, but let it pass. *Chances are they don't see us as real military despite the fact we are all veterans. It's hard to blame them. All we've been used for is rounding up squatters.*

South of Jal was Texas—just over a mile down the dusty road. The highway was a two-lane affair, flanked by patches of green scrub brush and a few blooming yellow wildflowers that were just signaling the start of spring. The Veteran Corps spread out perpendicular to the highway. Behind them were additional troops, piled in pickup trucks. There was one bus marked Youth Corps. Darius had seen them and was stunned to see through the windows that the young people were armed. *I thought that the Youth Corps was all about public service—now they are arming them.* For a moment, he was unsure what to think about what he saw. It felt wrong, but someone must have approved the idea.

Another bus had a platoon from the Rainbow Brigade. Newmerica's push for diversity and inclusiveness had formed an all-volunteer unit of LGBTQTI+ troops. Darius almost laughed at the fact that they excluded everyone not part of their alphabet community. *In being inclusive, they excluded everyone else.* The TRC had pushed stories out that they were the most potent unit in the Newmerican forces because of their diversity. Darius knew better. *Bullets don't give a shit what gender you call yourself or what sex you are. Inclusiveness doesn't stop shrapnel. We will have to see how these troops fare when the shooting starts.*

"Here's the situation," the captain barked. "There's a checkpoint down there. We need to secure it. First and second platoons will approach the Texans on the sides of the road. Once we are in range, we will send a third platoon down in trucks. They will emerge to inspect the vehicles. When they do, I will give the order to fire.

"This checkpoint needs to be taken down quickly, before they can get word out and call for reinforcements. Once we secure the checkpoint, we will reload in our transports and proceed to our next objective."

Darius understood what the Captain didn't say. We are dealing with the locals, while the National Guard are here to fight military objectives. We are getting the table scraps. He didn't mind that approach. *I've been in real combat. Some of these kids in the National Guard are weekend warriors at best. I'm content with them doing the real fighting if it comes to that.*

Sergeant Ingersoll barked orders rapid-fire as to where he wanted Darius's platoon. It was only a mile, but they would move low, from brush to brush for cover. Everyone was ordered to be quiet until the Sergeant gave the word. The words of caution and warning from the sergeant made Darius wonder just how many enemy they might be facing. Looming just beyond the checkpoint was a large sign with the words, "Welcome to Texas!" *They may regret having that greeting up after today.*

Their approach was slow. The undulating ground and brush broke up the platoon's line, turning them into small fire teams that were just in sight of each other. They moved in slow, fluid spurts five to ten yards at a time, hunkered low. Darius clutched his rifle in front of him, double-checking to make sure that his safety was off. His trigger finger was extended straight over the top of the trigger guard to avoid accidental firing. The scrub bushes and desert-like ground gave him an eerie reminder of his time overseas. *If I'm getting a sense of déjà vu, then I'm sure some of the others are as well.*

The Sergeant raised his left arm for them to halt. He then pointed ahead with his thumb down—the signal for the enemy in sight. Darius could hear his heart start to pound in his head as the two trucks of the third platoon came down the highway off to his left. The anticipation of what was to come was almost as bad as being in the firefight itself; that much he knew from experience.

Rising slightly, he saw the checkpoint. A few concrete road walls were laid out to block the highway, forcing vehicles on the shoulders. There was a small sandbag bunker on either side of the road. Milling around were Texas State Troopers, in body armor, assault rifles at the ready. There was a black police Humvee pulled over on the northbound side of the highway—and while it wasn't armed, it could be holding additional troopers. It didn't look like much of a defensive position, but Darius understood that often there were things you didn't see at first. *Once the shooting starts, who knows what will pop up.*

The trucks squeaked to a halt in front of the southbound barricade. Out of one of the sandbag bunkers, two more troopers emerged, weapons at the ready. Darius felt his body tense as he squinted out at his potential targets. Sergeant Ingersoll extended his arm in front of him, palm down, making a side horizontal arc repeatedly. *Commence fire!* Raising his rifle, he brought the person furthest back of the trio into the crosshairs of his scope; he poked his weapon through the bush that concealed him.

His finger drifted from the guard down to the trigger. Halting his breath, he squeezed slowly. The weapon recoiled into his shoulder hard, three times, as he unleashed a trio of rounds in rapid succession.

His target lunged backwards under at least one hit. The other border guards were hit as well. One dropped prone, unleashing a spray of return fire on full auto. Darius flinched, going flat behind the bush. Gunfire broke out everywhere as the third platoon jumped from the trucks and were laying down a deadly fusillade of full metal jacketed chaos. There were screams over the crack-pops of the guns on both sides. Someone hit the lead truck, destroying the windshield with gunfire.

Darius rose and saw that the man he had hit was prone and crawling back towards the sandbag bunker. Four more guards emerged from a slit-trench that no one had detected, and they blazed away in controlled bursts. One threw a grenade which went off on an advancing fire team, taking three of the Veterans Corps down.

He drew a bead on the man he had hit earlier, catching him as he reached the sandbag bunker. One of his shots hit the booted foot of the target; through his scope, he saw a squirt of blood go straight up in the air. Another round thudded into the man's chest, probably not penetrating his blast plate, but effectively knocking him flat on his back.

Another pair of explosions destroyed the front driver's side tire of the police Humvee. A man bolted out the side door, running back towards greater Texas, only to be shot in the back by several of Darius's comrades.

The gunfire dwindled after another grenade went off near the slit trench. Wisps of smoke and kicked-up dust swirled over the Texas force positions as the order was barked out to hold fire. Darius didn't stand up quickly; he knew better from experience. A few minutes later, Ingersoll moved closer to the enemy positions and signaled that it was clear.

They walked over to the skirmish site and saw the dead whose blood was soaking into the sandy soil. Moving to the man he had shot, he saw that the color was already fading from the man's face. His boot had been shot from the bottom and had blown out the top. The man had a wound on his right arm as well, and he was unsure if it had been one of his shots or someone else's.

A handful of teenagers from the Youth Corps mingled with the veterans. They were joking and laughing about the carnage. One of them kicked a dead men, only to have Darius put his hand on his shoulder to stop him from further desecration of the bodies. "We don't do that."

"Whatever, old man," the kid sneered, walking away.

"We kicked these redneck cop's asses!" Fax said gleefully, even throwing in a bob and weave of a dance move.

"Never brag about taking another man's life," he said solemnly.

Glancing back down at the man he had shot, his eyes became strangely transfixed on the insignia of the Texas State Troopers. His father always scorned the police. Darius had tried to be impartial. Only once in his life had he been intimidated unjustly by an officer. He and two friends had been harassed by an Hispanic officer who claimed they fit the description of three boys that had shoplifted from a local grocery store. He had handcuffed them, patted them down, and held them while his white partner contacted the store owner. The owner cleared them, and the police released them, but Darius had never forgotten the overwhelming fear and dread that he felt during those tense minutes. His father's words had rung in his ears. "You do what they say, when they say it. Keep your mouth shut. Don't give a cop any reason to pull a cap on your ass."

Before his father died, Darius had tried to pry the source of his disdain for the police. The old man wouldn't tell him any of the details, other than, "Stay the hell out of southern Georgia." It was cryptic; yet it told a story all on its own.

From the New Mexico side of the border, a long line of Humvees and trucks appeared with more troops. A few trailer trucks carried Bradley fighting vehicles, painted in desert camouflage—no doubt from the last time they had been used overseas. Newmerica was invading Texas—and the Volunteer Corps was leading the way. While that should have given him a sense of pride, it didn't.

As he stood over the dead officer, those memories tore at him. This officer wasn't harassing anyone—he was just doing his job. They never stood a chance. *We slaughtered them.* While Fax and Julius were laughing and nervously celebrating their victory, another member of the corps was using his phone to snap pictures of the dead—until Sergeant Ingersoll ordered him to stop. To them, they had won some sort of glorious battle. To Darius, it felt like murder.

They are all acting like this was some sort of game that we just won—and we did. But what did we really do? Shoot up some folks that were just protecting their border. All we did was murder some folks for no reason. The driver of the Veteran Corp's lead vehicle was dead, and a few troopers were wounded. For Darius, it didn't seem like a triumph worth celebrating ... certainly not for the driver that had died in the ambush. He diverted his eyes from the dead man at his feet and started back to the highway.

CHAPTER 14

"Definitions matter. That is why we create them."

Social Quarantine Camp NM028, New Mexico

Caylee huddled behind a clump of desert growth. While the chilly night air didn't penetrate to her skin, the sand she lay on seemed to find a way in, regardless of how much she wrapped herself. She had chosen her position well, with a view of the main gate and a clear line of sight to the north of the facility. She was hidden approximately ninety yards from the camp, close enough that she could smell the chemicals in the air from their plastics operation. With her Nightvis binoculars, Caylee surveyed the perimeter fence of the Social Quarantine camp, pausing and taking in the tall watchtowers with great interest.

She heard the footsteps near her and quickly rolled over to validate who it was. The figure of Gwen Holtz of the Witches of Wichita knelt down next to her. "Any changes?"

"All is quiet. The Rangers and the Posse dismounted a while ago. I can only assume they are crawling up on their objectives. How are your people?"

"Nervous—excited—all of the things you'd expect," Holtz replied. "They are all looking forward to extracting some Witch-style vengeance on these misguided SE assholes."

Revenge was a powerful motivator, but often could be misguided. It needed to be tempered, focused, to be effective in her experience. "Remember, your job is diversion. We want them to see and react to you."

"Oh, don't worry, they'll be looking in our direction."

A part of Caylee wanted to know the details of what Holtz had planned, but she also knew that it was best to not micromanage such a large operation. When it was a small op, she and a handful of people, things were different. With larger missions, like this liberation, things were different. *You have to trust people to do the right thing.*

"There will be time later for your Witches to extract appropriate justice. The mission comes first."

"Understood."

"Alright then. Head back to your people and listen for my signal." She checked her watch, and seeing the time, she felt her body tense, if ever so slightly. As Gwen scurried off into the darkness, Caylee reached up to her shoulder mic and squeezed it. "This is Jophiel," she said, using the call sign that Raul had devised for her. "Alright Philistine One and Two, are you in place?"

The deep-intoned voice of Chris Luke of the Maricopa County Mounted Posse came back first in a whispered voice. "This is Philistine One. We are right under their noses, and they don't see us yet. You bet we are ready.

Captain Kenyon of the Texas Rangers responded next. "This is Philistine Two. We have the baddies in our sights." There was more than a glint of cowboy intoned in his voice which Caylee found oddly comforting. "Hold your fire until the Witches get their attention."

She turned her focus to Raul. "Gabriel, this is Jophiel. What is your status?"

The pause of a few seconds was too long for her liking. If they had a comms failure or if the main assault force under Raul had been discovered, then the mission would be at risk. He rallied her patience and said nothing. After another few seconds, Raul's voice came back. "We are in position. A car passed near our position, but we were far enough off of the road that they didn't spot us."

It was a game of chess and all of the pieces were in place. Once this starts, it will be hard not to push ahead. Timing was everything. It was 0128 hours—two minutes to their push off time. *If I want to abort, this is it.* Caylee could not come up with any reason to do so other than she knew that when the shooting started, innocent people might get hit and die. There was no way to avoid that. Breakage was bound to happen.

"Uriel," she spoke in a whisper, so that her voice wouldn't carry. "You are to go silence them."

Travis Cullen's voice came on with a hint of glee. "Understood. Setting off in three, two, one."

There was no sound. The cell phone towers that covered the remote camp were far enough away that she wouldn't be able to hear the explosions that Cullen had set off to take them down.

A half a minute later his voice came back. "Check your phone."

She threw a hand over the screen to shelter the light so she couldn't be spotted by some guard. "No bars."

"Bingo."

Another check of her watch, and she sent the signal to Holtz. "Witches—you're up."

Turning her head, she looked out into the darkness of the desert to the north. The clouds were obscuring most of the stars, and the sliver of moon only illuminated the clouds themselves. She saw a light come on, brighter than a flashlight … *probably a lantern.* Another, then another came on, shining brightly into the night like lighthouse beacons.

Then came the blare of music, loud, echoing out across the cold desert sands. It took Caylee a moment to identify the song—AC/DC's *Highway to Hell.* She could see the trucks out where the Witches had set up their diversion, barely visible in the darkness. *Whoever has those speakers has a damn big set.* As she watched for a moment, she could see that several of Holtz's people were out in front of the lights, silhouettes in the night—dancing as if some sorority party was going on in the desert. A few of them whooped and hollered as they gyrated to the music.

As she looked away, it was hard for her not to smile. It was a perfect diversion, one she admired. There was no threat, and the guards in the towers would be compelled to look. They'll assume it's some college kids having a party. It was loud, visible, and would lull her targets in with a false sense of annoyed security.

Checking her watch she saw that they were right on time. "Philistine One and Two, this is Jophiel. You have a green light. Take them out!"

Caylee turned to look at the camp through the Night Vis binoculars. Flashes appeared all along the perimeter of the camp, followed a second or two later by the crack-bang of the guns going off.

It's on! "Jophiel to Gabriel, you are up. Take the prize."

The battle for Social Quarantine Camp NM028 was underway. Lowering her binoculars, she grabbed her ruck sack and pulled out her Sig Sauer M18 and started to move towards the front gate.

The Southern White House
Nashville, Tennessee

Charli could tell that Jack Desmond was relishing her plan. It had been all but impossible to get to meet with him during the day. It was late in the evening before Charli had been able to get in to explain what she was proposing. He leaned back in his chair and cracked a rare, wry grin. "So, you know we have an operative in our midst, spying on us, and you want to use that to feed the enemy misinformation … did I get that right?"

"More or less. We stage some fake meetings in the room; Reese records them; sends that information onto the media and the enemy."

"You don't want to just pick him up?"

"Don't be crazy, of course I do. Right now though, we don't have enough to make a case on this guy. We do this, and we can confuse the hell out of the Newmericans and will have evidence that we can use in court on this guy."

For a few minutes, Desmond said nothing. "He's an expert in toppling governments—how do you know he won't do something a little more, dare I say, *dramatic*?"

Charli nodded. "He might. I have people shadowing him though. We have tracking devices on his car and even some we had sewn into his clothes in his locker while he was at work. Electronically we have very discreet teams listening in on him wherever he goes. It is already revealing how much some members of the media are conspiring to undermine us."

"That is far from surprising."

"Tell me about it. Bit by bit we are constructing our case against Reese. I want this guy brought up on treason charges. Right now, all we have is him leaking information to the media." She knew that Jack was asking the necessary questions. He had her job at one point in time, and it looked like a part of him wanted to step back into it with this revelation.

"Operatives are dangerous. I don't have to remind you of that. What did Caylee recommend?"

"Shoot first."

That made Jack chuckle. "No surprise there. She might not be wrong in this case."

"Killing people without a trial or putting them in front of some tribunal that has no legal standing, then stringing them up—that's what the enemy does."

"You were a vigilante of sorts when I tracked you down," he reminded her.

Charli felt her face redden at his comment. *He's right—I took the law into my own hands, but I only did it when the justice system failed utterly ... when it put the rights of the criminal over those of the victims.*

"That's a low blow boss," she replied as she managed to regain her composure.

"My bad. My point is that you've changed ... and I think it's a change for the better. You are right; we *are* better than the Newmericans. You'd be surprised at the number of people I interact with that say we need to lower ourselves to their level in order to win. I feel like I'm fighting it every day. I have to admit, it's refreshing to hear from you that it isn't the right course of action."

The compliment removed some of the blush from Charli's cheeks. "I hate this guy, Jack. He's an enemy agent, sent here to take us down. I've tangled with operatives before ... our would-be assassin, Julius Bernstein. Putting the NSF and their operative program under a microscope and making it public is a huge step in the right direction."

Jack leaned forward, resting his elbows on the desk. "The media here covers it, but he's getting zero air play in Newmerica. The TRC takes down every post mentioning the guy, and the media that they control doesn't talk about the assassination. All that matters to them is their false flag attack on the Capitol."

"I can only control the things I can control," Charli replied. "I've got eyes on this Reese. I believe that we have him contained without him knowing it. In the meantime, we can use him. Stage some fake meetings where he has his listening device planted. Seed him with things that, when revealed, embarrass the Newmericans. Doing that will give us a chance to figure out how he is getting intel to the District and tighten the case on him like a noose."

Desmond nodded. "Fair enough. For the sake of counter-intel, I'll have some of my staff craft some wonderful little nuggets that your spy will think are perfect—things we can easily prove and refute when they are made public. I'll give you the rope for that noose. Just make sure you tighten it at the right time."

Over Port Jervis, New York

The C-5 Galaxy heavy transport seemed to vibrate as it hit another wave of turbulence. Each bump made Judy Mercury nervous. There was no turning back at this point, no aborting the mission. They were past the point of no-return for the mission parameters. Her butt hugged the seat cushion on her jump seat in the rear of the cockpit. It was for a second pilot for long flights, but she had taken it … though there were moments when she wished she hadn't.

They had gotten the go-signal four hours earlier. The Newmerican forces were starting to engage the Defiance forces in New Hampshire's White Mountain National Forest. The initial reports were sketchy, only that they were beginning artillery and aerial bombardment of the Americans dug in there anticipating of an all-out assault. That meant that the move to seize the Stewart Newburgh Airport was imperative. Once that was done, strikes could be directed at the air bases that the Newmericans were using. Assuming they would be successful in seizing the base, Judy knew that she was getting very little sleep and would be dealing with constant pressure. While a part of her dreaded it, a greater part thrilled at what was coming. *This is going to make what we did in Illinois look like a trip to your local Starbucks.*

First, they had to take control of their base in the middle of enemy territory. She had immersed herself in studying similar raids, especially the Israeli raid on Entebbe Airport in 1976. Seizing an airport was a dangerous proposition. Targets such as the tower, TSA offices, airport security, and the military objectives were spread out. Taking and holding them was tricky. The intent was to secure the airport before word could get out to the NSF or the National Guard that the raid was happening. It was a stretch, but Judy was hopeful. Every hour that the locals stayed in the dark was useful to her raiding force.

Operation Green Lantern had called for the American assault force to fly low, dangerously low, on their journey to Stewart Newburgh, New York. The aircraft roared over the trees and structures so closely that she feared they might hit the upper limbs. Flying in the darkness of night, they were barely visible except from ambient light. The pilot joked with her that they were actually well above them, but that wasn't enough to quell the clenched knot in her stomach. When Lieutenant Colonel Mihalek saw the consternation on her face, he grinned, and put on some music—the Air Force band's rendition of the "Battle Hymn of the Republic"—reminding her of watching *Dr. Strangelove* days earlier. That music made everyone in the cockpit crack a grin except for the pilot. He was concentrating on hugging the earth.

One of the crew spoke up, and she could hear his crisp voice in her headset. "We are fifty miles out—no sign of detection. No intercepts on plot."

Those words were reassuring. The big transports were vulnerable and almost defenseless. A single enemy fighter could wipe out Operation Green Lantern before they got a chance to secure the airport. Judy was nervous but strived to hide it. *Everything depends on us securing the airport quickly—and I am going to be sweating until we are boots on the ground.*

The minutes seemed to drag by. The co-pilot called out a few minutes later. "We are beginning our approach. They will pick us up any second. Piping you in to listen in."

"I have a visual of an aircraft on the primary runway," the voice of the copilot called out.

"Shit," the pilot muttered. "Well, I guess we'll have to get them to move it.

A few seconds later, the pilot spoke up from his left-seat position. "KSWF this is a classified military flight OES one-zero-zero, coming in on final approach."

"Um ... standby OES one-zero-zero," the tower signaled back. "We have no flight plan for you."

"KSWF, recommend you clear runway 9–27 immediately. We are starting our approach."

Another voice, a little older, a little more seasoned came on. "OES we have an Atlantic 337 taxiing right now. Recommend you go to holding pattern while we work this out."

"Negative KSWF. We are a priority mission and landing immediately. Recommend you move that plane now. We are dropping gear."

"OES, we are ordering you to divert," the air traffic controller said firmly.

"Negative KSWF. We are starting our run now."

Mihalek leaned back, covering his microphone, yelling loud enough for her to hear over the din of the engines. "They are shitting bricks down there."

"They'll be shitting more once we land." She could hear the whine of the landing gear dropping, and Judy tightened the grip on the folding arms of the jump seat. *Would the plane move in time? What would the pilot do if it didn't?* She knew there was only one runway at the airport that could handle the C-5s. She stretched up a little to see if she could see the airplane in question, but to her, it was a confusing blur of lights illuminating the airport.

"OES one-zero-zero, runway 9-27 is clear. Be advised we are going to report this incident to the FAA."

There was a small pop in her headset. "He's going to report us," chortled the pilot. "I'm so scared!"

Another snap came on as the pilot changed channels. "This is your captain speaking, we are coming in hot. Standby for a bump and run." The speakers carried his voice throughout the aircraft.

Looking forward Judy could see the runway lights and the tower. The big aircraft came down fast on the massive runway. The pilot didn't slow the plane appreciably; instead he roared down the runway, heading for the debarkation point near the Marine Corps Reserve Refueler Transport Squadron building. The second plane, coming down behind them would move on the New York Air National Guard facility.

Judy knew that the troops behind her were listening in. "Captain Olsen, prepare to drop the ramp as soon as we stop." The word were not necessary, Judy knew that, but she said them more for herself than for Olsen.

"Roger that Lantern Actual."

The plane braked hard, the engines counterthrusting to assist with the stopping. It came to a jerking halt and the large, rear door opened immediately. The sound level increased throughout the aircraft as the troops deployed out the rear. The crew of the Humvee started their engine, adding to the cacophony of noises, and it rumbled out.

Judy hit the release on her belt and bolted for the rear of the aircraft, opening the door to the rear compartments. A rush of cold air hit her, along with the smell of jet fuel and exhaust from the Humvee. She moved past the pair of helicopters; and secured her rifle and headed out to the ramp.

As she hit the tarmac, she saw the other planes taxiing into position near hers. More troops rushed out from them as well. *Getting here was half the battle.* Each squad moved out to their designated targets with remarkably little noise other than their boots hitting the ground as they ran. Judy followed Rampage Squad heading for the Marine's building.

There were no guards, but the door was locked. A battering ram was brought forward, and the squad slammed the door right at the reinforced lock plate hard, three times. Each hit was a loud, booming noise. The big, metal door buckled to the point where the lock was superfluous. They pushed it open and immediately gunshots fired from the inside. Their cracks echoed into the night as the aircraft shut down their engines, amping up the tension that Mercury already felt. The trooper holding the battering ram fell and was dragged to the side, out of the line of fire as the rest of the squad fired into the first floor of the two-story structure. He was moaning, but eventually got to his feet—a sign that his injury was not likely fatal. Judy crouched low and aimed her own M4 carbine at the windows—watching for a defender to appear there.

Another team rigged a breaching charge further down the building. The explosives were placed on the red brick wall in rectangular shape in a matter of a few moments. Her breaching team used hand signals to coordinate with the team at the door that had come under fire.

The breaching charge went off at the same time a flash-bang was thrown through the open door. Glass shattered the surrounding windows, spraying shards everywhere. The blast had blown a man-sized hole in the brick façade, and four infantry burst through. A few moments later the flash bangs went off at the door, and that opening was rushed. It took a lot for Judy to keep her focus on the windows.

There were the distinctive crack-bangs of gunfire inside the structure, slightly muffled, but identifiable. There were yells, commands being barked out. Mercury wished she had tied in with the squad's comm channel to listen to it live, but her responsibilities were larger than just this building.

Her ear piece did chirp with an incoming message. "Tower is secure." That was a sign of some relief. She looked some fifty yards away to the team that had rushed the National Guard building, and there was no gunfire coming from there. The continued gunfire from the building in front of her told her that the Marines were not prepared to give up without a fight.

"Terminal and TSA are secured." The voice came in Judy's ear from a female team member. "We are closing the main gate to the airport now."

That left two objectives still unaccounted for—the building she stood in front of and the Defense Investigative Services office at the perimeter of the airport complex. More gunfire, sporadic and angry, sounded again in a concentrated burst from the building in front of her. She kept looking at the windows, looking for any sign of what was going on. The flickers of muzzle flashes on the second floor bounced off of the glass presenting little more evidence of the struggle going on inside.

"The Defense Investigative Services building was a bust—no one at home," came the voice of Ric Clifton, the sergeant in charge of that target. "We are sweeping it now to remove anything that might cause us a problem, and then we are going to secure it."

The Department of Defense's tacit support of Newmerica was the well-known starting the night of The Fall. Since the Civil War had broken out, the DoD had provided personnel and assistance to the enemy, while publicly claiming they were staying out of the fight. Judy was happy that no one was present or had been killed because it might have given the Pentagon an impetus to give more support to the Newmericans.

A breathy voice reached her ears from the Rampage Squad leader, Lieutenant Douglas: "Marine Refueling secured. We have three wounded, one dead."

She didn't press for details. The fact that the enemy had mounted any defense was impressive and spoke to their training. "Roger that," was all she replied as she gathered her thoughts. Mentally she checked off the list of targets, just to validate that they hadn't missed any.

"OES one-zero-zero, transmit the success code and get a confirmation. "Tower, inform ATF control that this airport is shut down for military operations, effective immediately. Let's tighten our perimeter, get our defenses set, and get those helicopters unloaded," she ordered.

Lieutenant Colonel Mihalek came up beside her. "The whole thing took less than twenty minutes—almost as fast as our training exercises."

"This isn't over. We've got civilians that need our attention. The local NSF is bound to show up at some point and will eventually start to piece together that we are a hostile force. This is just the start."

"It's a hell of a start, though. Good work."

"Thank you. I'll feel better once we get those helicopters tracked and balanced and ready to execute their missions." *For now, we have the upper hand. That can change any minute.*

Social Quarantine Camp NM028, New Mexico

Raul rushed through the brush alongside members of the Little Rock Irregulars. Gunfire filled the desert night air as he reached the main gate. It was a chain-link affair, well mounted and secured. Looking through the holes, he could see flashes from the gunfire all along the perimeter. *If we don't get through this gate, it's all for nothing.*

The deep roar of the dump truck's diesel engine sounded behind him, its headlights finally reaching him. "Make a hole," he commanded, and they cleared the roadway as the big vehicle sped up and aimed for the locked gate.

Some shots rang out from inside the camp, from one watchtower especially, pinging into the dump truck as it loomed ahead. Sparks from the ricochets showed where the vehicle was being hit, and the cracking noise showed that a few were hitting the windshield. *If they take out that truck, it will clog the road, and it will cost us more time to get into the camp.*

Jefferson Morris of the Irregulars barked out orders. "Get fire on that tower!" He didn't have to give the order twice. A dozen weapons opened up on the watchtower, riddling it with a steady barrage of bullets. Raul raised his own Sig Sauer and fired two rounds at it as well. The driver of the truck lurched the vehicle into a higher gear and roared past

Raul, slamming into the camp's main gate with a crunching and metallic grinding sound.

The main gate tore off of its hinges, falling under the truck's big tires with a loud whomp as the vehicle plowed on into the camp some one hundred feet away. Brakes hissed loudly as it skidded to a stop. More gunfire hit the side of the big truck, metallic thunking and ringing sounds added to the noises.

"Get in, get to whoever is firing those shots and take them out," Raul called. The Irregulars rushed in through the gate, fanning out around the buildings. The one tower that had been shot up began to fire again. This time, it was hit from three different angles at once. There was a cry in the night, a female voice, coming from it this time—a wail of pain followed a few moments later with, "Hold yer damned fire! I surrender!"

Raul's head was pounding as he raced in beside the truck, checking each building corner he passed. The silhouette of a figure stepped out, rifle in hand, leveling it at him. Raul lowered to one knee for a good firing stance as the training that Caylee had given him kicked in. The figure fired a rapid succession of rounds; the shots passed close enough for him to hear the bullets cut the air by his head.

He aimed at the center mass and squeezed the trigger twice. The first shot made his target twitch. The second round a moment later made it topple backwards, collapsing on the ground. An audible moan rose from the figure; then deep and agonizing sounds were followed by a strange almost choking noise.

Rushing at the fallen man, his intent was simple—disarm the shooter. Reaching down he grabbed the AR 15 that had been fired at him. The person he had hit was male, a large man, who gasped for air, then coughed. He felt for his chest as he finally got some air, and Raul realized that the blast plates on his tactical vest had likely stopped his bullets but had knocked the breath out of his lungs.

The man sat up and Raul leveled his Sig Sauer at him. "Put your hands behind you!" In the dim light, the man saw the pistol aimed at his head, coughed again, and nodded. Raul got behind him and zip-tied his hands tightly together.

"Hey," the man said. "That hurts."

Raul saw the knife that the man wore on his belt and pulled it from its sheath. More gunfire rang out from all around the camp as the guards tried to fend off the assault. The attacker's bus came in and squealed to a stop behind the dump truck. Raul told the man to stand and helped him get to his feet.

"Stand here," he ordered, picking up the AR 15 and slinging it over his shoulder.

"Who are you people? You can't just come in here shooting the place up. This is a sanctioned camp."

"Shut up," Raul commanded. *You want to know who we are? We're the good guys. How many innocent lives are you responsible for killing here?* A torrent of rage hit him, and he struggled to keep it from controlling his actions. "Stay here and be quiet and you live. Talk, and I will shoot you." Off across the roadway, Sam Patheal's Hell's Tarheels busted into one building with a battering ram, barking out orders. Gun flashes flared from inside, visible through the windows … a reminder that things could quickly get out of hand.

Turning, Raul moved to the next building, which appeared to be a barracks. Travis Cullen came up alongside him as he leaned into the side of the structure. Raul slowly peeked around the corner and saw a figure dart up the short steps and dive inside, slamming the door behind them. "What have we got, Raul?"

"One just went inside."

Travis leaned back and surveyed the structure. He checked the side they had passed. "Looks like one way in or out. If this is a barracks, it is filled with innocent people."

"Hostages," Raul corrected his friend.

"Yup. If I was that guard, I would hold my gun at the head of one right now."

Raul looked at the plain clapboard building made from cheap lumber and shoddy workmanship. It was raised off the ground by two feet. From the other side of the wall, he heard the muffled cry of a young woman. He tried to suppress the images of terror that the people inside must be feeling … gunfire everywhere, a panicked guard coming in.

"There's windows on the back side," he muttered. A dim, yellow light trickled out of the curtain-less windows.

"What are you thinking?"

"I'll go in at the door. The guard will focus on me. You get something to stand on; come up on the window; and take the shot."

Travis said nothing for a moment. "Maybe I should go in the front. I have a little more experience with that."

"No," Raul said. "You're a better shot than me … we both know it. You need to take the shot through the window."

Travis nodded. "Alright. When you open that door, don't do it aggressively. That guard might jump the gun and take a shot at you. Go slow; let the guard think he has control of the situation. Move slow; don't threaten; just talk." As he spoke, more gunfire echoed off of the building they stood by.

Raul gave him a nod of assurance, crouched low, and maneuvered around the side of the barracks to the steps. The Sig Sauer was still in his hand as he crept to the door, stood beside it, and opened it.

As he rose and drifted into the doorway, he got his look at the barracks. In many respects they were just like those he had seen at Valley Forge. Long rows of crude wooden bunk beds. The aroma hit him next, the mix of filthy humans. Three utilitarian lights hung in the barracks casting shadows.

They huddled the prisoners along the walls or behind their beds. Standing near the center of the barracks was the guard with his gun pressed to the temple of a young woman. Tears streaked her cheeks as she sobbed. The guard was a young black man, skinny, wearing a T-shirt. "Hold it right there," he said, pressing the muzzle of the weapon tighter to the woman's head.

Travis's words echoed in his mind. He held his gun angled slightly away, raising his other hand and opening it so as to not look like an immediate threat, even though he was fully prepared to dive for the floor and shoot if he had to. "Hey, lower that gun. Nobody has to be hurt here," he intoned as he took a step off to one side.

"Who are you people?" the young man demanded.

"We're here to liberate these people," Raul said. "That doesn't mean anything bad has to happen to you."

Sweat rolled down the man's face and into the hair of his hostage. "I want out of here," he demanded in a crisp tone. "Anybody messes with me and I splatter this kid."

"You let her go, and I will make sure no one messes with you." The gunfire outside was not helping deescalate the situation in the barracks—even if its tempo was diminishing.

"No way," he said, tightening his arm that was under her chin, hugging her closer. "She's my insurance."

The young woman made fleeting eye contact with Raul, and in that moment, he knew she was going to do something. Opening her mouth, she twisted just enough to sink her jaw into the flesh of his forearm, biting hard. Blood sprayed her head, and he recoiled, letting her free. The woman dropped to the floor and, in a blur, Raul swung his gun around.

There was a crack, shattered glass, and the head of the young man became a crimson cloud, splattering all the way to Raul. Bits of gray matter hit his shins as the dead, headless body, toppled over on the plywood floor with a dull thud.

The young woman, covered in gore, cried—as did several of the prisoners who emerged from their hiding places and rushed forward to help her. For a moment, Raul stood there, mute, not quite sure what to do next. Glancing up at the window, he saw Travis give him a wave, then drop.

Valley Forge had taught him that the prisoners would be frightened. I have to assure them. "We are here to get you out. We have vehicles outside, near the gate. Form up in a line and follow me." As he gestured for the door, he noticed that his voice sounded eerily like that of Caylee Leatrom.

CHAPTER 15

"Fear is normal. Fear is good. It means you are aware."

The District

The Vice President leaned in towards the screen on her desk, double-checking to make sure her face would dominate General Rinehart's view at the other end of the video conference call. He looked perturbed; a hint of pink in his cheeks told her he did not appreciate being interrupted with her input. The booming in the background told her he was near the front and that big guns were doing their job—killing the rebellious army of New Hampshire.

"General," she began with his title since she knew it meant so much to him.

"Madame Vice President. I am afraid we will have to make this short. I am in the middle of an operation at the moment."

"Which is why I called. I understand you have the enemy trapped in the White Mountains Park."

"I wouldn't use the word 'trapped.' We have identified a substantial base in the forest and are maneuvering to ensure that any rebels in that area are unable to escape." For a few moments, the artillery going off beyond him seemed to pause.

"General, I understand you haven't launched an assault yet. Why is that?" Veronica Hinkley, the People's Warden assigned to Rinehart, kept her abreast of what was going on in the ranks of the Army. It gave the Vice President the ability to offer her guidance and leadership to the military—an organization that desperately needed it.

"That is correct. Per the perimeters of Operation Star Burst, we are bottling up the enemy and leveraging our air and artillery superiority to suppress and destroy the enemy. We are laying siege to them, whittling away at their defenses, forcing them to concede their positions."

"That will take far too long."

Rinehart shifted in place; she saw his image move side to side in slight frustration. "If I may, those were in the strategy plans that were submitted to you, and you and the President approved."

"I know what you wrote, General. Things have changed. A political announcement is planned. We would prefer to make it after you have defeated this so-called Defiance movement. Getting it done fast meets political objectives."

"I understand that," he grumbled. "I am trying to factor in the PR implications of a lot of dead sons and daughters being sent home by rushing in."

"You say you understand, but this has been dragging on for weeks. We have them trapped. Let's wrap this up, so we can move forward on the political front."

"With all due respect," he started. *When I hear those words, they never have anything to do with respect.* "We can't run military operations based on you issuing a press release. The strategy I outlined is necessary to minimize our losses."

"General, the military answers to the elected political leaders, such as myself. This is not a 'press release.' It is an announcement that will set the future direction of our country. We desire to do this on the heels of telling the world that the resistance in New Hampshire has been crushed. To do that, we need you to do your job." She tried to use little words, convinced that Rinehart, like most military officers, didn't fully appreciate her role in such matters. *They think we are unimportant, that they are the actual power in the nation. The military is just a tool to implement policy. In reality, they are on leashes that we hold.*

"I am doing my job. Sieges are complicated affairs. We are poised to destroy the bulk of the resistance in one fell-swoop, if we do it correctly. If I rush in before we have weakened them, there will be losses. As much as you and the President want a fast victory, you will be forced to deal with dead sons and daughters being sent home, a lot of them. The images of coffins coming back from war will erode popular support."

Rinehart paused for a moment, then continued. "All I am asking for is the proper time to do the job right."

She didn't appreciate that Rinehart was explaining things to her as if she were a child. *Mansplaining.* He wants to make his job seem more complicated than it really is. "I understand fully what you are trying to avoid. No one wants to see the images of dead loved ones coming home. What you seem to forget is that I control the TRC. We determine what is allowed on the air and on the net. Families will grieve, as is their right, but I won't allow this to become a public relations nightmare. Those images and stories will never see the light of day."

"I need time to do this right."

"The longer it takes, the more it makes it look like we are weak. People lose interest. We saw that with Atlanta. The attention span of our people is weak at best. If this drags out, even a victory will not mean much. They expect things fast … as do I."

The expression on Rinehart's face told her that she had won. A mix of dejection and frustration tore at the older man. "I do this under protest."

"Of course you do," she replied in a flip tone. "Newmerica requires you to do your duty, nothing less."

He gave her a nod and logged off the call. Alex smiled to herself. The People's Warden Program is proving itself a great success. *It has given me control of the military without all of the burdensome laws and regulations.* Bullying Rinehart … that was merely a bonus, another blow against old white men.

Once New Hampshire falls, we will announce the Constitutional Convention. The basis of law will change to validate everything we have done. After that, we will erase the foundation of what made old-America and ensure our dominance over the continent.

White Mountain National Forest
New Hampshire

Stark terror and sleep deprivation marked the night for Su-Hui. The Newmerican forces that he had antagonized had pursued them right to where the Defiance forces were dug in. The ambush that caught the enemy was spectacular and stunningly short. Caught in a murderous kill box, the Newmericans had tried to fall back, only to find their egress blocked by their own blown up vehicles. Su-Hui had watched it from inside the defensive cordon and was amazed at how quickly the enemy had been devastated. They thought they were chasing SOL or local militia, only to find themselves pinned in. He saw two people successfully surrender from the enemy force—he also saw three that raised their hands, only to be mowed down.

The enemy had learned from their debacle, and had shifted their forces around the White Mountain defenses in a broad arc. The Newmericans did not have enough to completely encircle them, but around 75 percent of their position now faced the enemy. As Su-Hui walked through the positions, he could not help but feel they were trapped.

Then came the artillery. Indiscriminate death in the form of mortar and artillery rounds pummeled the Defiance position. The enemies' air power came in as well as the sun was about to set. One of their precision bombs perfectly hit and destroyed one of the faux bunkers and vehicles set up for just such an attack. A trio of fake tanks—little more than plywood, cardboard boxes, green paint and deception—had been hit so many times there was little remaining where they had been buried other than a deep series of craters. The amount of firepower dumped on the fakes gave Su-Hui a moment of humor. Bits of wood and churned earth, co-mingled with searing hot shrapnel, rained down everywhere in the defensive zone. The artillery would stop for a few minutes, only to open up again with a sickening rumble of death and carnage.

Real bunkers, deep and completely concealed, held armored vehicles, ammo, drones, and other supplies of war. Su-Hui had seen one of them, holding six armored fighting vehicles. On the surface, there were scrub pines, but below, the Defiance had hidden a deadly punch.

The worse were the aerial attacks. Those bombs made every bone in his body throb when they went off. His head ached from the concussions. They were rare, but they came and when they did, they scooped out massive craters in the forest. C-130 gunships made strafing runs that chewed up vast tracts of forest on each horrific pass. Smoke from trees and burning pine needles were set ablaze by the blasts and hung like a fog.

From what Su-Hui could see, for all of their exquisite and devastating firepower, they were not hitting actual targets. That was part of the genius of General Griffiths' defenses. Many of the bunkers were deep, deep enough that the artillery couldn't harm them, and they were concealed with an almost artistic flair. Even the tanks and vehicles were protected under layers of logs and dirt, hidden deep enough to survive the bombardment.

His own position was a hidden concrete bunker, made up of layers of former road barriers that formed the walls and ceiling. It held twenty-four people, most from his Sons of Liberty forces. A narrow tunnel that you had to crawl through led to two more buried bunkers where other forces were huddled. A single, slender, concrete-lined shaft led upward. Su-Hui used it from time-to-time to get a visual surveillance of the bombardment. The dim light came from a pair of lanterns that cast long shadows in the dark space. While chaos and carnage raged above, down below was little more that the stink of fear.

He crawled down from his surface perch into the depths of the reinforced hole. The air was muggy and the temperature was warm. The aroma of unbathed people was something he had gotten used to, but could not ignore. He saw his wife, Hachi, motion for him to come sit near her, sharing an ammo crate. There was barely enough room for the two of them, but somehow they sat and held each other close.

"Will it stop soon?" she asked as a rumble above shook tiny bits of dirt on them.

He could not resist looking up at the concrete above them as the blast thudded off in the distance. "Probably not for a while," he confided to her.

"It reminds me of home … when the Chinese came."

Hachi rarely spoke of Taiwan. Much like the assault of their daughter, it was simply a subject that she refused to discuss. Su-Hui knew enough not to raise the subject with her. Her silence spoke volumes about what they had been through. "Those were difficult times," he said loud enough for her to hear over the rumble. "There were times when I thought we might not get away."

"We did," she said, taking his hand in hers and squeezing hard, "because of you."

Another blast resounded around them. "You are wrong, my dear wife. We made it because of you. You kept the children calm, even when the helicopters came in."

Hachi grinned, blushing slightly. "We did it together."

A young woman sitting in the bunker next to his wife leaned in, "You have been through this kind of thing before?" she asked Hachi.

"Oh yes," she said, offering a thin but firm smile. "The Chinese attacked Taiwan, our homeland. They were vicious. They didn't care if they killed children. All that mattered to them was a swift victory." A muffled blast went off above them, showering them with more tiny bits of concrete dust and dirt.

The young woman's eyes welled with tears. "I'm not sure that I can take much more of this."

Hachi took the woman's hand as Su-Hui spoke. "You will be fine. These are the times that test us. They challenge who we are. We have endured many ordeals, but as long as you remain strong and don't give in to your fears, you will come through this storm even stronger. If we can come through such things, you will too."

His words elicited a nod in response, a thank you. Major Segal, his liaison, shuffled over to him, holding a walkie-talkie in his right hand. "I just got word," Segal said loudly enough for him to hear the words. "They are moving on us."

The words made Su-Hui pause momentarily. "I thought they would hit us for more than just this bombardment."

"We all did," Segal replied. "But they were sending in troops to support armor to the west of our position. We are being asked to move to our firing positions."

A part of Su-Hui wondered if this was some sort of trick, a desire to lure them out into the open to attempt to finish them off. There was a time to challenge orders, but this didn't feel like it. Turning to the SOL volunteers in the bunker, he locked gazes with Valerie Turner. "It looks like we're up."

She rose, grabbing her hefty M248 light machine gun and a pack filled with four belt canisters of ammo. Valerie was well seasoned, and her New Yorker Sons of Liberty cell had been instrumental at swearing in the new President. "I'll take my people to the right. You have the left." Su-Hui nodded and motioned to the rest of his people to join him.

They moved down a narrow tunnel, coming up under a pile of fallen logs. From the surface, the pile looked like a jumble of erratically felled trees. The Newmericans had taken no chances; they had dropped a few artillery rounds on the pile to be sure. While their efforts had screwed up some firing positions, new ones had been created. The light of morning reached him as he came upon a suitable spot. It gave him a decent view down a gentle slope to a muddy ravine some 150 meters at the bottom. Despite the artillery barrage, there was still a lot of old growth pines and oaks standing, though the number of shattered limbs on the ground created a twisted wooden carpet. Paths had been cleared by the Defiance defenders, perfect roadways that led into the ambush corridors. Su-Hui's position was set up to take advantage of such a venue.

The enemy armor was barely visible through the haze of the bombardment and the burning trees and thick beds of needles and dead leaves. Four Abrams tanks were poised at the top of the low ridgeline across the creek, some 350 meters away, sliding in between several large trees. They were not rushing in; instead they paused, their machine guns banging away at targets perceived and real. Their big guns fired as well into the heart of the defenses, adding to the carnage and seemingly endless rumble.

Charging out of the forest was a moose, a handful of deer, and other small animals—driven into the Defiance positions as if they were herded by the approaching vehicles. It was a strange sight as the panicked animals darted about, seeking cover. One deer exploded in a mist of crimson gore, either on a landmine or because of a mortar round. Su-Hui had never seen a moose before, let alone one charging through the middle of battle. *They are uglier than I thought they'd be ... and braver than I could have imagined.*

In that moment, Su-Hui came to grips with the fact that this was the battle that the war had been building up to in New Hampshire. There had been insurgents, ambushing vehicles and columns. There had been raiders, attacking barracks and bases and then fleeing into the icy darkness. This was a different war, the kind of war that people prepared for their entire lives. Newmerica had the seductive chance to wipe out the Defiance and reclaim the state. The Defiance had the potential to crush the Newmericans and free New Hampshire from their rule. That realization made Su-Hui's stomach clench as he settled in and cleared a good firing port between limbs.

Su-Hui turned to his people. "Remember the plan. Hold your fire until I give you the word. We engage for just a few minutes, then go down and move to the next position." He and the other defenders knew the enemy would respond with devastating firepower. Silent nods of grim understanding came back to him. Each person he made eye contact with, even the redoubtable Trudy, looked weary from the bombardment and had bags under their sullen eyes.

Turning to the hill, he watched as the trees next to the tanks exploded a few feet above their trunks. The blasts went in unison, offering a cracking sound of shattered wood to the cacophony of the surrounding battle. The hills had been rigged with explosives, mostly wraps of det cord, just for this moment.

The old trees fell, toppling sideways along the top of the ridge, right onto the tanks next to them. Some missed entirely; others fell on the turret or the engine compartment; one hit the massive 105mm barrel of a tank with a sickening thud.

Most of the tanks moved forward, primarily to shed the trees. The one that had been hit in the barrel retrograded down the back side of the hill, out of sight. No doubt the gunner didn't want to risk firing after the tree had hit his main gun.

From another adjoining hill, came the distinct *whomps* of Carl Gustafs firing. The thin white streaks marked their flight paths into the sides of two tanks. The explosions engulfed the tanks in a wreath of flames and rolling, black smoke. As it cleared, one tank advanced, but its damaged tread fell off, disabling the vehicle after a few more meters down the hillside.

A roar overhead came down and a purring *bbbrrrttt* of 30mm gatling cannon fire from the diving New York Air National Guard A10 Warthog tore into the positions that had fired the anti-tank rounds. Flare sprayed out from the rear of the aircraft as it dove in, unleashing its deadly ordnance. The strafing run churned the ground near the hidden position. Trees were chewed into a spray of deadly wooden shrapnel, and the ground was tilled and cratered. The crippled tank turned and fired its main gun and machine guns at the position as well. *I hope those poor people got out of there.* For Su-Hui, it was a warning. *We need to attack and move fast.*

From behind the tanks, their supporting infantry moved forward, quickly taking positions to lay down fire and protect the tanks. Their appearance brought bursts of fire and a rain of mortar rounds near their positions, enough to make them cower in place.

The lead tanks continued down the slope towards them. Su-Hui turned to Corporal Abernathy, one of the New Hampshire National Guard troops in his command. Looking at the distant tanks, he realized he was seeing their top armor as they came down the hill … thinner, more vulnerable. "How many Javelins do we have?"

"Two," the younger man replied.

"Stow one, and get ready to fire the other." He turned to the others in his command. "The rest of you, don't waste time firing at the tanks. Put suppression fire down on their infantry support. We shoot and scoot—l got it?" Nods and two thumbs up came back to him. Abernathy took one Javelin back into the tunnel, and emerged again a few minutes later and prepped the other one.

Su-Hui turned to the advancing tanks. Explosions went off around them, but the three remaining vehicles were still moving forward—their enormous guns booming loudly, throwing high explosive rounds into the forest. The Newmerican supporting infantry advanced as well in controlled and perfectly orchestrated spurts. Bit by bit, they were getting closer.

"I'm ready," Abernathy called. "Clear my rear."

"SOL—lay down your cover fire on those support troops. Give us a few moments of fire; then take out the lead tank." Abernathy nodded.

"Fire!" Su-Hui barked. He raised his own rifle and aimed shots at the enemy infantry. He wasn't sure if he hit anyone, but he saw two of them crumble and drop as the SOL engaged. Further down the line, he heard the cracks of gunfire from Turner's position. The distinctive short bursts from her machine gun tore at the advancing troops, forcing them to whatever cover they might be able to find.

Off to his right he heard the *swhooh* followed with the bang-roar of the Javelin as it cleared the disposable tube and ignited. The entire bunker lit up orange from the launch, if only for a moment. The air stung with spent propellant as the missile stabbed out at the lead tank, a wispy blur in the air.

From the light contrail, he saw it rise slightly in its flight arc, then stab downward at the lead M1 tank. The explosion was devastating. A glorious, bright yellow and crimson spray of flames threw bits of quasi-molten armor into the air all around the tank. A plume of black smoke rolled past the tank as its drive forward continued. A few moments later there was another explosion, this time from deep within the tank. The concussion was a ripple in the air, throwing the turret off the vehicle and turning the tank slightly. It crashed in front of another Abrams, cutting it off, and then lurched to a halt as flames roared like a blast furnace skyward from where the turret had been.

A muffled cheer came from the troops in the small bunker as they continued to fire at the supporting infantry. Su-Hui saw the face of Corporal Abernathy, who had a smile from ear to ear. "We need to get moving!" Su-Hui called out. As if to accentuate his point, one of the remaining tanks turned its massive barrel right at their position and fired. The explosion hit in front of their position, raining in bits of hot sod and rattling the limbs above them.

"Move! Move!" he commanded, though he could barely hear his own voice over the ringing in his ears. His ears slowly popped as he reached the tunnel. Then he heard the distinct and distant roar of an A10 jet incoming. Su-Hui fell on his knees and crawled rather than trying to stand.

The air around him throbbed and thundered as the Warthog unleashed its deadly barrage. Incoming fire tore into the bunker. The concrete road barriers that made the tunnel sprayed a fine gray dust that stung his eyes as he fumbled in the darkness, trying to get away from the deadly fusillade. He felt pain in his left shin, and as he tried to crawl further, he found that leg pinned—unable to move.

The concrete barrier above him shattered, raining heavy bits of debris on him and a cascade of dirt. The air was knocked from Su-Hui's lungs, and he struggled to breathe, almost in a panic. His mind went to his wife and their children. *I cannot die here ... not after all that I have been through. I have to make it out, if only for them.* The weight of the dirt and concrete felt as if it would squeeze the remaining air from his lungs.

CHAPTER 16

*"There is no such thing as propaganda.
There are only unquestionable truths."*

Nashville, Tennessee

Thiago Reese grinned to himself as he hit the Send button on his iPad, blasting away the latest data dump he had gotten from his surveillance in the Southern White House. He had a lot to be proud of. His little bugging device, hiding in a flash drive, had monitored several meetings where details of the war effort, troop placements, and even economic data were covered. No doubt the VP would take that material and find ways to use it to put the screws to the American government.

The American nation, under the Pretender's rule, was stronger than Reese had initially expected. It wasn't just their victories in the war so far; there was a belief that they were right. The citizens felt they had been oppressed by Newmerican rule, and being part of America again lifted that perceived burden. Objectively, looking at the two sides in the conflict, that was one of the biggest differences that Thiago Reese saw. The Newmericans were not as passionate about their government. Their people didn't believe that the people in power were right or even just. They simply desired to preserve what they had in place. People profited from reparation points. Those who perceived that they had been oppressed, real or not, liked the fact that they benefited from the government … even if the new systems weren't fair. In reality, fairness had become an early victim in the rise of the Newmericans.

The concept of fair wasn't as important as equity; at least that message was pounded into people's minds. Others liked not having to think as much. There was only one side of the news—even if they didn't trust it. Tensions and strife were reduced. Sure it meant sending millions into Social Quarantine, but as long as it didn't affect individual citizens directly, they were comfortable with that. People were oddly comfortable with their neighbors disappearing and with reparation points awarded for turning in disloyal citizens; people were encouraged to find reasons to call in their friends and family.

He put the device down on the small table in the apartment and grabbed his jacket. It was time to go for a walk—perhaps pick up something to eat. He earned it. *Everything is going exactly as planned. The information I've been gathering will make its way to people that can use it. TRC stories about it will run, highlighting all the negative aspects. The Americans will start to question their rulers; they will doubt their government. When that happens, the collapse is simply a matter of pushing things along at the right time.*

He already had that push planned out. Reese had followed his target discreetly, enough to see a simple pattern in his behavior. His actions would hamstring the American leadership. *They will distrust their president, question his decisions. I will give the people what they secretly yearn for, controversy and excuses to doubt their leaders. Deep down, people want to hate their leaders. The old United States was built on disdain for King George. America loves to take down successful people. A part of their psyche hopes that once they are down, they will rise again ... but sometimes people are just taken down. Their love of the underdog can be exploited, and that is what I intend to do.*

Getting up, he went to the couch where the box was. It had been delivered from the District through nefarious means and dropped at his door in the middle of the night. Inside was what he needed to transfer the fingerprints he had lifted from the conference room. There was a handgun as well, complete with a perfectly crafted and registered serial number linked to the person he intended to take down. The disguise kit that was in the box was perfect as well, the wig, the nose piece, the chin ... no one would recognize him, probably not even his target.

The assassination he had planned was exquisitely timed. The TRC-media and even the American free press were reporting on a battle along the Texas, New Mexico border. It had become bogged down. There were unconfirmed reports of Newmerican advances into other parts of Texas. Combined with the recent uprising in northern parts of the state, it created the image that the war was not necessarily going American's way. If Texas were at risk, would they all be at risk? Already the TRC was circulating stories about how the District would be dealing with those that backed the American Revolt. Images of Social Quarantine camps had the desired effect; they generated fear in the population. *Fear will drive them into silence ... it almost always does.*

Tomorrow would be the big day. *With a squeeze of the trigger, I will nudge this government down the road to collapse. Combined with the media thrust and the fighting out west, the dream of a restored America will become an obscure footnote in history.*

Andrews, Texas

The Newmerican attack force reached Andrews and was immediately confronted by the local and state police and a hailstorm of gunfire. Darius and the Veterans Corps had bounded out of their vehicles and scrambled for cover, though there was little to be found on the flat ground. The police vehicles had blocked State Road 385, their approach to the city, forming a wall that made circumventing them difficult, if not impossible.

"What the hell?" Jaxson said as he flopped onto the ground next to Darius. "It's almost like they don't want us going into town."

"You can't blame them after what we did when we came across the border," Darius replied, holding his assault rifle up and attempting to get a bead on a target. Shots were being returned by the Veterans Corps, but they were mostly hitting the police vehicles erratically. He knew that it was best to conserve ammo until he had an excellent target, something that his peers seemed to have forgotten. *Maybe they just like shooting up cop cars.*

A bullet hit the ground ten feet from where Darius lay, spraying him with dust, some of which got into his left eye. It took a moment to wipe out the particles, during which Jaxson fired a few shots towards the officers that had fired at him. "If you don't have a clean shot at a human target, stop wasting ammo," Darius said as he returned to a firing stance.

Andrews was not the task force's destination; Captain Aguilar had revealed that much, but it had to be moved through. Darius knew enough to not ask the location of their final destination. In many respects, it didn't matter. If they didn't suppress the police in front of them, it was all for nothing.

A Humvee wheeled in behind him, then opened up with its M2 heavy machine gun. The weapon hit the vehicle that blocked the center of the road and seemed to devour it, chewing up the plastic, metal and glass with each round hit. The police behind—those who were still alive—dove for cover behind other vehicles.

Then came back automatic fire from the police—concentrated on the Humvee. Bullets slapped into the armored windshield and the front of the vehicle. Darius finally saw a target, an officer in body armor, lying flat on the ground just like him, huddled behind a tire. While he couldn't see all of the trooper, he could see his torso and legs. Drawing a long, deep breath, he adjusted his sights and aimed at the extended legs of his target. Breathing out slowly, he squeezed the trigger.

The rifle kicked and banged, and he saw a squirt of blood from the thigh of the trooper. His target rolled over, out of the line of sight, no doubt attempting to cope with his wound. For a moment, he felt a strange sense of satisfaction, one that was quickly followed by shame. *I just shot a man for defending his home town.* It felt wrong, terribly wrong.

There was an explosion as another Humvee blasted a police cruiser, rupturing the gas tank and turning it into a bright yellow and orange ball of flame. Ugly black smoke rose in the brisk breeze, blowing back towards the town. It made seeing details even more difficult.

A line of trucks came up the highway, heading for the roadblock from Andrews-proper. *What in the hell is this?* Pickup trucks of every size and make … and through the haze of the smoke, he saw that they were loaded with people—armed people. The locals, armed to the teeth, bailed out along both sides of the road. A few moments later, the intensity of the gunfire directed at the Newmerican forces was amplified. This was no longer a police standoff. This was a battle.

Several shots came near their position, throwing more sand and dirt on them. Darius elbow-crawled for cover behind a piece of scrub brush. When Jaxson saw him do it, he moved away, duplicating the move. *This bush won't stop bullets, but you can't hit what you can't see.* Scanning the flat desert-like scrub brush in the distance, he could not see the enemies firing occasional flashes from gun barrels.

That will have to do. The time for conserving ammo had passed. This was not a skirmish; this was an actual battle. Aiming at the flashes, he fired shots at them. There was no way to know if he was hitting the enemy, but he was forcing them to move—or at least he hoped he was. Some locals fired full auto sprays. One burst was enough to force the first Humvee to reposition, shifting to the right, attempting to flank the small army. A truck that had brought the local in exploded in the middle of the road, and while the blast was not flashy, the flames roaring skyward were like a spectacular furnace fire. He spotted a handful of the Rainbow platoon break and run, some even throwing down their weapons in flight. They were fulfilling his earlier prophesy that their diversity would stand up to combat.

There were a few cries from wounded, painful wails that reached his ears and tore at him. On the far side of the road, he heard the *thunk* of a grenade launcher going off and more explosions blasted the police line. They returned fire with tear gas canisters, then fell back to where the citizens were digging in.

The brisk wind blew some of the irritant into his eyes, making them water uncontrollably. Snot rolled out of his nose for a moment, and he silently cursed his enemies. The people of Andrews, Texas did not yield for long minutes; if anything, it looked as if they were going to entrench there.

Suddenly, off to his right, a crack was loud, closer—definitely not a military weapon. Looking over at the Humvee, he saw that the M2 gunner was lying limp over the side, blood drizzling down over the tan camouflage of the vehicle.

There was another crack and Jaxon cried out. "Aw shit! I'm hit … I'm fucking hit!" *They are flanking us. Whoever was doing it was a deadly shot—a sniper.*

Darius bent low, ran over to Jaxon, and dropped flat behind his comrade. "He got me in the leg!" Jaxon cried out, attempting to stop the squirting blood with both hands.

It was bad. Darius could see that. The bullet had punched in the back side of his thigh, tearing out a big piece of flesh that dangled on the torn camouflage pants. Pulling off his belt, he wrapped it around Jaxson's leg and pulled it tight. Doing so made his friend go ashen for a moment, wincing in a sweat-drenched wave of pain.

"You have to hold this tight, or you will bleed to death," Darius told him, handing the end of the belt to Jaxon's trembling fingers.

"You have to get me out of here, bro," Jaxon said with a wavering voice.

Another gunshot cracked off to the right of Darius and the bullet hit the ground very near his own knee. Pivoting, he moved perpendicular to Jaxon, using his wounded friend as momentary cover. "Goddamn sniper," he muttered.

"You gotta get me out of here. I don't want to die here."

"You aren't gonna die," Darius muttered, searching for a sign of where the shot had come from. Squinting, he looked for anything that might give him a hint.

Then it came, a muzzle flash from behind a tree that was barely big enough to hide a man. The crack followed the flash.

He heard the bullet slap into Jaxon's side. It passed through his body and dug into the ground right near him, close enough that Darius feared he might have been hit. Jaxon's body went limp, and his grip on the makeshift tourniquet released.

Darius rested his weapon on his fallen friend and aimed at the tree where he had seen the flash. A figure leaned out, weapon at the ready, moving slow and steady. Darius fired before the citizen's weapon could be brought to bear—hitting the figure, sending it flying backwards.

Satisfied that the immediate threat was down, he reached up to Jaxon's neck and felt for a pulse. There was none. Jaxson's eyes stared upward, blankly, at the blue sky. He was gone, and there wasn't anything that Darius could do to bring him back. For a moment, he tuned out the sounds of explosions and gunfire around him. One of his people had died. It could have been him. He understood that. *At least you weren't alone brother. I was here with you right up to the end.*

Gripping his weapon, he checked the magazine to make sure it was still loaded, and crawled towards the burning blockade across the road.

Two hours later ...

A few of the civilians and police finally broke and fled back towards Andrews. Only two civilians had surrendered as the battle drew to an end. They had been led out of the brush and onto the road. There, members of the Youth Corps shot them both in the head. Darius had been stunned with the violence that the young people had shown in the executions, but a dark part of him understood. He had lost Jaxson, which had numbed him to the violence.

Walking across the scrub brush, he went to the tangled mesquite tree that had served as the sniper's protection. He wanted to see the man that he had killed, the man that had killed Jaxon. Somehow, Darius thought that seeing the shooter's dead body would help him with the emotional wave that was swelling within.

When he reached the spot, what he saw didn't make sense. It was not some burly man with a rifle. The body was that of a young woman. She wore hunting attire, and in the center of her chest was a dark maroon spot where his bullet had hit—ending her life. Her red hair was tossed out on the light sandy soil. The rifle she had used was a high-end hunting weapon, with a deadly sight on it. Her blue eyes stared skyward ... *like Jaxson's.*

She's just a kid. Why did she come out here to fight? What would her parents think? Seeing that it was a young woman wracked him with guilt. He tried to mentally justify the fact that he had shot her. *If I hadn't, she would have killed me.* Still, the sense of guilt lingered with him. *I joined the Corps to protect California. I joined because if I didn't, I would have lost all of my welfare. They made me do it. Now I'm in Texas killing civilians. A few years ago, we were on the same side. Now I'm supposed to think of them as the enemy.* None of it made sense to him.

Captain Aguilar came up beside him. "You okay, Darius?"

Am I? Unable to form the words to describe his state of mind, he simply shook his head.

"I saw Jaxson."

"I was with him. This is the one that shot him," he nodded at the dead body of the young woman.

"Geez, she was just a kid." Looking down at her seemed to drain any energy he had from his body.

"She was a killer."

"She was fighting for her home," Darius muttered. Memories of All Jacked Up Coffee came rushing back at him like a speeding-out-of-control semi on a slippery road. *There was a time when I was willing to fight to protect what was mine. Was she any different?* Shame wrapped its grip on him tightly.

Captain Aguilar shrugged off his words. She really didn't have a choice; he understood that. Being in command meant doing nasty, dirty things during war ... *and we are at war.* "I just got the word. We are going into this town and burn the place to the ground."

Her words hung in his ears for a few moments as he processed them. "What will that accomplish?" *It won't bring Jaxon back.*

"It sends a message to the rest of this damned state. If you want to fight us, we will burn you out of house and home. Anyone thinking about picking up a gun and using it against us will remember what happened here and think twice about it."

Or it will give them a bigger motive to fight. Memories of the Presidio came back to him. Unconsciously, he reached up to his left breast pocket and felt the medal that came from the woman that had died there that day. It was a reminder of the same carnage that he had waged before. "All that's going to do is piss people off more. We've killed the troublemakers. We should move on." A part of Darius wanted to be as far away from Andrews, Texas as he could get.

"You'd think that killing a bunch of them was message enough."

"We have orders," Aguilar said firmly. "They are bringing up a TRC film crew to capture the retribution and to film our dead and wounded—you know—craft the proper narrative."

Is that what we've become—forced actors in some skit? We are the justification for war crimes—that's all. No narrative can change reality. "What about Jaxson?"

"They've tasked some of the Youth Corps to bury our dead."

"He wouldn't want to be buried here. This isn't where he's from."

"We don't have the logistics to take our dead home right now. And you know California's laws on the matter."

California had recently forbidden banned cremation and burials. They had a new composting order where the remains of the dead were converted to fertilizer. They did it under the auspices of being a "green" initiative. Many families defied it, secretly burying their loved ones in private ceremonies in the dark of night. The thought of Jaxon being used as fertilizer was despicable to Darius, even more than him being interred in Texas.

"Maybe leaving him here is better than sending him home," he muttered, reconsidering and changing his previous position." *Even the regular Army made sure that their honored dead were returned to their families.*

"Once the war is over, I'm sure the Army will take care of things like our dead."

Darius heard those words, but wondered who would remember a battle in some obscure Texas town—or the people that died there.

East of Tucumcari, New Mexico

Trip Reager watched through his enhanced binoculars as a pair of Marines from the Purebloods slowly crawled under a stubby pinon tree. One carried a Carl Gustaf recoilless rifle; the other carried three rounds of ammunition. The pair huddled behind the short, scraggly tree, carefully loading the weapon as the sun slowly crawled up behind them. As they prepared to fire, Reager looked out over the flat terrain at the positions held by the Newmericans.

The fighting on the Texas/New Mexico border had been brutal. Offensive operations had given way to both sides, digging in, turning the space between them into a deadly, free-fire zone. Looking out across the no-man's-land of the desert, he could barely make out a few of the vehicles that the enemy had poised behind makeshift berms of sand. A few Bradleys, a number of Technicals, and a few M1126 Strykers, and even a pair of antiquated M113s. Through the night, the gunfire had come in sporadic bursts, except for two nasty thrusts by the enemy at his lines. Both times had been costly, this time for the Newmericans.

His holding force had less, but enough to make it count. Twice the Newmericans had pushed forward, and the result was the burned-out hulks of smoldering black wreckage that lay blasted between the two firing lines. Several charred, dead bodies lay splayed out on the desert floor not far from their blasted vehicles. The smell of burned metal and plastic stung his nose as he turned his attention to the two Marines. Trip stood next to his own command Bradley, which was hull down in a dugout position.

They had crawled precariously forward towards the enemy to the west, using the smoke from a destroyed Humvee for cover. He admired them for their daring. All the Purebloods had been Marines before COVID. They had refused to take the jab and had been forcibly mustered out of the service. When the new president was elected, they had volunteered once more, forming their own unit in the American military. Now these Marines were holding the Texas line. Trip's offensive had been shattered.

After several long minutes, the weapon roared and boomed, sending the projectile downrange. One of the Strykers was instantly engulfed in an explosion. Trip could barely make out the crew bailing from the damaged vehicle as flames roared from the rear of the armored target. Glancing back at the Marines, they were already quickly redeploying, falling back to their trench line, while their comrades cheered. Machine gun fire tore at the pinon tree, shredding its trunk and sending the upper portion toppling over.

"That was gutsy," Captain Harnessy said, looking through his own binoculars.

"They are making a point," Trip replied. "The Marine Corps turned their backs on them over the damned vaccine. Now they are showing that they are every bit the Marines they were trained to be. Hell, I admire it."

"I just got word from Major Mercury and Task Force Green Lantern. The Poughkeepsie branch of the NSF has shown up at the airport and started issuing demands."

Trip lowered his binoculars, turned, and met Harnessy's gaze. "And?"

"You know the Major," he replied. "She responded with her usual brute force. They are still having some security issues on the perimeter, but she says that they should be ready to move on their targets soon."

That was one bit of good news. "Word from the Defiance?"

"Not much. We have some satellite coverage, but not much. The bits and pieces I have stitched together indicate that the Newmericans have them surrounded and are moving in."

"As planned."

"Yes sir."

The fighting in New Hampshire worried Trip. While Griffiths had prepared his position well in the White Mountains National Forest, it was a risky proposition. The Newmericans coming at them had as much to prove as the Marines fighting beside Trip. They had been flummoxed by the SOL and their use of IEDs and vicious raids. They had never been able to engage them in the fighting they were best at, a straight-up military battle. Griffiths was handing them the exact battle they desired, using it as bait to lure them in for the kill; but there was always the chance that the entire plan might backfire and the Defiance forces get overrun. *At least with Mercury's force in position, the odds might shift to our favor.* "What about the word from further south?"

"Reports are incomplete. The Texas State Police have been feeding me intel that the enemy engaged troops near Jal, New Mexico at the state border. We have reports of fighting at Andrews and some place called Monahans. I'm hoping to get some word out of Andrews, but so far it is quiet, which can't be a good thing. I can't confirm if this is one force, or two prongs of an offensive at this time."

Trip nodded grimly. "Are our troops on the way to engage them?"

Harnessy nodded. "Everyone is on the road. From the looks of it, the enemy could be targeting either Austin or Fort Worth as their ultimate objective, though it is too early for me to confirm that."

"Austin would make sense. There's a lot of support for the Newmerican government there. Let's look at the map." The two walked over to the dug-in Bradley and entered through the rear ramp. The map of Texas was pulled out and Harnessy pointed to the cities he had just mentioned.

Trip eyed the sparse roads and vast emptiness of the map. "I think we should direct our forces to block them there, at Big Springs. Is ground good for us to hold there?"

"It's as good as any. The problem will be speed and lack of roads to get there. There's a good chance that the enemy might get there before we do."

Trip nodded. "If they do, let's bottle them up there. Their supply lines are going to be stretched pretty far at that point."

"Yes sir," Harnessy replied. "I hate to bring it up, but that raiding force that went into New Mexico to liberate that Social Quarantine Camp? They are still in there. They were counting on Operation Diamondback to give them an open road to get the prisoners back to safety."

Shit! If Trip could have kicked his own ass, he would have. He was glad that Harnessy had remembered. "With all the action, I forgot about them. Send them the no-go code … let them know we cannot give them passage."

"According to their timetable, they may already be in the process of liberating that camp, sir."

Trip winced and thought back to the details of their mission. "Damn it. I wish there was something we could do, but we can't." *My offensive has ground to a halt, and the enemy is now counterattacking in southern Texas.* "I wish we could help them, but we have colossal problems of our own right now."

"Understood, sir."

Trip sighed heavily. *Diamondback is a bust. I had hoped to be in Santa Fe by tomorrow; instead I'm on the defense out here and trying to get the genie back in the bottle to the south. New Hampshire is fighting for its life, and their best hope is for a raiding force that is trying to hold an airport behind enemy lines.*

The weight of the war was heavy on his shoulders. *Tomorrow has to be better ... it has to be.*

CHAPTER 17

"No one is dependent on the government. They simply recognize the benefits of accepting assistance that is owed to them."

Social Quarantine Camp NM028, New Mexico

As the brilliant orange and yellow sun inched into the desert sky, Caylee saw the handful of surviving guards. There were eight of them, men and women, on their knees on the roadway that cut to the center of the camp. Standing behind them, weapons at the ready, were the Witches of Wichita. Most of the guards showed signs of beating, ugly purple bruises that were invisible in the dark, early morning hours were now clear. One couldn't hold a hand over his head because his arm was clearly broken, the bone poking painfully at the sleeve of his shirt.

Raul came up alongside her. "We've got the prisoners loaded."

That only leaves a few loose ends. Andy, with the help of Sam Patheal's people, had loaded two of the bodies recovered from the desert wastes and moved them outside of the camp. They were encased in several inches of what appeared to be a dark greenish plastic—a byproduct of the recycling facility inside the fence wire. Caylee saw the anguish in Andy's face. He wore a blend of fury and sadness. *He saw all of the dead out there—he knows what these so-called guards are responsible for.*

"There are hundreds of dead people out there," Andy said grimly.

Raul intervened before Caylee could. "We saved a lot as well, Andy."

"Someone needs to be held accountable."

Gwen Holtz held a beat up old .44 caliber Desert Eagle magnum aimed at the head of the camp's director who knelt on the ground in front of her. She shoved his head back with the end of the barrel of the weapon, grinding it into his brow for effect. "How about we implement the justice right here and now, starting with him?" As she spoke, the portly man wet himself, forming a puddle of urine around his knees. Fear, stark and consuming, washed over his face. "I didn't do anything I didn't have orders to do."

"Too many crimes in history have been committed with the words, 'I was just following orders,'" she said, pushing the gun barrel in another inch, forcing him to lean back.

Caylee watched and for the first time in a long while, she wasn't sure how to respond. The guards served no purpose that she could see. For all of their planning to take the camp, they had overlooked what to do if they captured any of the SEs running the place. They will be a burden if we bring them with us. There was something appealing in what Holtz was proposing. Counterbalancing those thoughts was that Caylee was rarely in favor of killing people out of general principle. Yes, they had committed what could be called war crimes, but shouldn't they simply face justice?

Raul spoke up. "We take them with us," he said firmly.

"I don't think so," Holtz replied angrily; her face was flushed with rage.

Andy held his hands out as if to pat down the tempers. "Look, I get it. The SEs did some horrible things to you—but it wasn't *these* SEs. If we bring them along, they can testify about what happened here."

Raul weighed in quickly. "They can do more damage to the Newmerican government alive than dead."

"Tell that to the dead people out in the desert," Gwen replied, as several of the Witches raised their weapons from the guards to the gathered rescue party. "Tell that to my people. They used us as sex slaves up in Wichita. They tied us to the beds and raped us over and over. They sold us to the locals."

"These people didn't do that to you," Raul said. "You want revenge. I understand it. Take it out on the SEs up in Wichita."

"They are responsible for all the dead people out in the desert," Holtz said, tears running down her cheeks. "They are mass murderers."

Caylee knew that to be the truth. There was no denying it. Looking down at the eight guards that had been captured, she wondered if they needed all of them. It was a cold calculation, but a realistic one. *Bringing these people along means having to post guards on them. They may try and escape or warn others. How many of them do we need if we do take them with us?*

Andy continued to try to diffuse the situation. "They are mass murderers," he conceded. "They killed all of those people out there. If you kill them now, the *real* criminals, the people that gave the orders, will get off. If we can bring them with us, they can tell the world what is going on in these camps and point the finger at the people behind all of this."

"It never works," Holtz said with a sob. "The people guilty of atrocities rarely get the justice they deserve. Sometimes a bullet in the head is the only justice that matters."

Caylee saw that Holtz was unstable. *She wants revenge and most people who do that are blind to logic. This may still go down poorly.* Once the bullets started to fly Raul, Andy, and the others were in danger. That helped her arrive at a decision—a course of action. Her hand slowly drifted down to her holster, and she removed the weapon.

Raul walked slowly over to Holtz, his hands low and open to show that he was no threat. Caylee moved so that Raul was between her and the Witches, using him to block her movements. "I know how you feel. We all do. You are better than they are. The blood on your hands is justifiable. Killing these people in cold blood is not. You are better than this."

"You don't know what we went through!"

"I do," he said. "I was at Valley Forge. I know what the Newmericans did to me at the Supermax. I was beaten, regularly. My life was threatened. They took my mother and sister hostage just to get to me, and they killed my madre—just like these people were worked to death. I know how you feel, most of it anyway.

"I want to take them down—not just this camp, but all of them. I want justice, real justice, for those responsible for these deaths. Bringing these guards back will do that."

Holtz paused, sobbing slightly, then lowered her weapon. Raul stepped over to her and hugged her. It was then that everyone noticed that Caylee had her weapon drawn and aimed at Holtz. For a moment, all eyes fell on her. She lowered her pistol and slid it into her holster. "There was a chance he wouldn't be able to talk her down," was all she said in justification. One by one the Witches lowered their weapons as well.

The guard that had wet himself glanced over at Caylee. "I promise, I'll testify about everything."

"Shut up," Caylee snapped coldly. "Gag all of them."

At that moment, Travis approached. "We have a problem," he said.

"What is it?" she asked.

"I just got a message from the Army. Our exit route doesn't exist. There's a battle being fought at the border right now. We can't just drive out of here."

Damn it! Glancing at Raul, Caylee could see that Travis's word had been a gut punch. She knew she had to get their thinking focused on the problem at hand. "Don't worry Raul. We planned for this. Travis, get Kidder on the radio. Tell him we are going to need him to get us out of here."

Raul gave her a silent nod as Holtz walked up to her. "You were going to shoot me, weren't you?"

Caylee said nothing for a moment, then responded. "Ms. Holtz, if you were going to put my friends in jeopardy, yes, I would have shot you."

"I would have thought you'd understand … being a woman."

"I do understand. By the same token, who I am is not defined by my sex. I don't have some 'special bond' with other females. I look at situations based on what is happening in that moment. If you had defied Raul and Andy and shot that guard, I probably would have shot you only because there was a risk of this turning into a free for all. I protect my people."

Nashville, Tennessee

Charli got the call early on a Sunday. It didn't bother her; sleep had been elusive. The worries about Andy made her unable to get more than a few minutes of slumber. She had hoped the call was Andy, but it had come in on her work phone. "This is Kazinski," she said, stretching her arms and shoulders as she rolled to the side of the bed.

"This is Agent Chester," the voice said. "We may have a problem."

Her brain amped up a notch in intensity. Chester was on the detail tasked with watching Thiago Reese. "Explain."

"We ran our hourly IR sweep of our target's apartment and detected no heat from inside."

Aw crap—we've lost track of Reese. "I thought you had all the exits covered," Charli snapped, rising to her feet and looking for her jeans.

"That's it, we did," Agent Chester replied. "So we went to the tapes of the people leaving the building, comparing it against our tracking of the individuals that went in. We came up with a person leaving that we have no record of entering. We suspect that this was our target, in disguise."

She held the phone with her raised shoulder as she struggled to get her jeans on. *A disguise—that's just great.* "So he's slid past you?"

There was a brief pause. "That's correct ma'am. If you want my resignation, I'll tender it."

She actually appreciated the fact that Agent Chester was willing to accept responsibility for the failure. *We have had far too many members of the Deep State that spent their lives dodging accountability. That was one problem with Washington DC—personal responsibility, specifically the lack thereof. We cannot afford to lose someone who owns his mistakes.* "That won't be necessary. How long ago did your target depart?"

"One hour … forty-four minutes."

"We know he doesn't have a car. That means he's walking or using public transportation. Leave an agent there in case he returns, but get out there and see if you can track him." She paused for a moment. Her mind raced through scenarios and options. "He wouldn't have gone so far as to put on a disguise unless he knew we were tailing him, or he was planning to execute a plan. Do you have a good image of him in disguise that you can send me?" she asked, buttoning her jeans.

"Sending encrypted now. I've got work to do."

"I'm going to the office—you can get me there," she replied, looking for a hoodie to put on. Thankfully it was a Sunday; the staffing would be light. *I need to be in the office, so I can lay hands on the resources we need. I will need to let the President's detail know we have a potential threat on the loose.* She was thankful they had a photo of Reese in his disguise. Her phone chirped after she got her hoodie on.

She opened the photo and was stunned. She knew the face all too well. *Caylee! He's disguised himself as Caylee.* A sinking feeling came down on her shoulders. The real Caylee was out of pocket, with Andy and Raul in New Mexico. He had to have a reason for such a specific disguise, possibly to frame Caylee for something … but what?

What the hell are you up to Reese?

White Mountain National Forest
New Hampshire

Su-Hui struggled to open his eyes as his lungs surged in a deep gulp of air. Hovering over his field of vision were several faces, all of whom seemed overjoyed that he was alive. He coughed, blowing out some dirt that had gotten into his mouth. His ears rang with a dull, tinny sound, and his brow ached. For a moment, he was disoriented and trying to recall where he was. *Wait, I was in the bunker, wasn't I?* He tried to sit up, but several hands coerced him to lie flat. The light came from a portable lantern and a small hole in the bunker's roof above him. "Take it easy," Hachi said, tears running down her dirt-smeared cheeks.

"What happened?" he managed as he flexed his arms and legs. He could feel his limbs, which was a good sign. Reaching up, he felt his chest. Under his shirt, he felt the empty shell casings that he wore in a necklace. *I'm still in one piece.*

"The bunker got hit," Abernathy said, wiping off some of the dirt that covered his jacket. "You've been out for an hour or so."

"My head," he said reaching up and touching it. For the first time, he felt a bandage there."

"One of the logs hit you pretty hard," the voice of another national guardsman said. "You need to take it easy—chances are you have a concussion."

As he sat up, a wave of nausea washed over him. A hot sweat gripped him and slowed his movements. "How goes the battle?"

Before a human voice could respond, an explosion went off nearby, only making his head ache more. Dirt from the remains of the tunnel splattered down on him. "It's nasty out there. They have pushed two more times with armor and made it as far as the second line of trenches, but they got bogged down there," Abernathy said.

I am needed in this fight. Clenching his teeth, he drew a deep breath through his nose, and tried again to sit up. The dizziness was mild, but still there, along with the sweat, but he made it to an upright position. Hachi moved a ruck sack behind his back to help brace him. "You need to rest," his wife urged as the muffled purr of machine guns roared in the distance.

"I must tend to my people," he said.

In the dim darkness he saw Trudy move in next to him. "You took quite a bonk there," she said. "We've got this. Valerie's position got shelled too. We are shifting to a new spot further down the line."

"I'm fine," he lied. When he flexed his legs, pulling them closer to his body, his knees and hips ached, protesting his movements. *I am no good lying here. I need to be able to shoot—to take the fight the enemy.*

Hachi looked over at Trudy. "You will attend him with me," she ordered in a polite but firm tone. Trudy nodded, sliding one arm in his armpit to help him stand.

It was a struggle in every way, mentally and physically, but he rose—mostly with the help of Hachi and Trudy. Abernathy moved in front of him, ready to assist. "Are you sure that this is a good idea?"

"No," he said cracking the thinnest of smiles. *I only fired a few shots at the PLA when we fled our homeland.* Memories of that came with deep regrets. A part of him always wanted to not flee on his sailboat, but to dig in and fight. *I know it would not have changed the outcome of the struggle for my homeland, but I still desire to go back to that moment and set it right.* Making a stand in New Hampshire would have to fill that hole in his life.

Each step was hard, but slowly became easier as the small group bent over and made their way through the narrow tunnel. After several twists and turns, they emerged in another bunker position. The flood of daylight made him squint as he pulled himself near an opening where he could see the battlefield.

Smoke obscured much of the forest. Easily half of the trees were blasted into splinters. Smoldering fires threw more white smoke in the air, which stunk of spent ammunition, burning pine needles and boughs. It took a moment to orient himself. What was he looking at? The terrain had changed so much. Several tanks were ablaze, and he was stunned to see how close they were … proof that the Newmericans were pressing hard to break the defenses. Explosions went off along the ring of hills around where the Defiance were dug in, throwing more dirt into the cratered landscape. Flashes from gunfire showed where the positions of the assaulting infantry were—almost 200 yards away. *I barely recognize this ground ... it has been pounded so much.*

There was a roar overhead, that of a jet. He didn't have to see it to know that it was Newmerican; the Defiance did not have air support. The A10 Warthog's rotary cannon chewed an angry swath through the defensive lines, seemingly not aiming at any target in particular.

Su-Hui ducked slightly. He heard the swish of a Stinger missile fire and saw the gray contrail as it snaked around skyward. The purring and churning roar of the Warthog ceased with a cracking boom in the air above him. He didn't see the hit, but parts of the aircraft slammed into the ground, adding to the carnage and debris. A cheer rose from the SOL and National Guard in the bunker.

Trudy moved up next to him. "He totally deserved that," she said.

Abernathy was not as joyous. "That was probably one of our last Stingers," he said in a low voice, just loud enough for Su-Hui to hear.

Before he could reply, bullets dug up the ground in and around their position, forcing them to duck. He heard several rounds *thunk* into the tree trunk that helped support the roof. "I need a weapon," he said. Abernathy turned away for a few seconds, then came back with an AR-15.

"We need to put fire on their supporting infantry," he said firmly, drawing a deep breath that seemed to give him a burst of energy. On the count of three, rise, take aim and fire. Steady your weapons on the limb laying there—it will improve your aim."

Looking at the dirty and weary troops, his eyes fell to his wife. Hachi gave him a single nod of support. *It is so fitting that she is here with me. This is the definition of love.*

"Three, two, one," he said, turning and rising, bringing the barrel of the weapon to bear. The bangs and cracks of gunfire from the bunker were muffled by the dirt, but were only adding to his throbbing headache. "Come on—pour it on!"

Stewart Newburgh Airport, New York

Judy Mercury dived for cover in the lobby of the Marine Aerial Refueler Transport Squadron 452. The glass from the lobby door shattered into thousands of shards, raining in around her as she crouched behind the desk. Another shot slammed into the far wall a few feet behind her. *This guy isn't a pro; that shot was off by a wide mark. Then again, he doesn't have to be that good to wreck more havoc.*

The seizing of Stewart Newburgh Airport had gone well at first. She had released most of the civilian personnel that were captured—keeping guards on them would have taken far too many personnel. She had kept the civilian air traffic controllers just in case they were needed … that and holding some civilian hostages was better than none. The military personnel—that was a different matter entirely. They were zip-tied and gagged in four different locations.

She knew when she released the civilians that it would lead to a response by the local NSF forces, and they didn't disappoint. They had started with issuing demands for her to surrender over a bullhorn. After an hour of being ignored, they attempted to bull-rush the closed airport gate with a Bearcat armored vehicle. Why the Poughkeepsie NSF would need an armored vehicle was something she never understand—but they had it and seemed happy to try to use it.

One rocket from a battle-prepped, old-school Cobra attack helicopter had ended the glorious assault. The Bearcat now blocked the roadway leading to the tarmac, its burned out husk still belching smoke into the night air.

The sniper had been taking potshots at her people for the last half-hour. One dead, three wounded. Her patience was running out. The helicopters were almost done with their track and balance checks—but getting the crews out there meant they had to do so under fire. *This one little NSF prick is holding up my entire operation.*

She grabbed her shoulder mic. "Anybody got a bead on that sniper?" As she finished, there was another crack in the darkness. No bullet came her way, showing that their sniper, no doubt a member of the NSF, was seeking other targets of opportunity.

"Stand by," came the voice of Sergeant Clifton. Another shot rang out into the early morning darkness.

"Bingo," the Sergeant replied. "There's a small metal structure outside of the fence line, due southwest of your position. Looks to be a garage of some sort. I got a faint heat sig from there and a momentary muzzle flash of heat. It looks like the target is on the roof."

"Does anyone have a shot?"

"None here," Clifton replied. "He's flat and even from my spot on the roof, I only get a glimpse of the guy."

A deep south Texas accent came over her earpiece. "I reckon I can take care of this," said Captain "Lariat" Paredes, leader of the helicopter attack force.

Paredes was from the Texas National Guard and had earned distinction in the Battles of Stone Mountain and Knoxville. A man of few words, he had shown his bravery many times for the American cause in the war. Before she could ask what he intended to do, she heard the crack of gunfire from the sniper and the pinging ricochet of bullets hitting the tarmac. Creeping forward on the broken glass, she saw him sprint to one of the Black Hawk helicopters, climbing in on the right side of the chopper, opposite of the sniper.

Shots continued, hitting the armored side of the helicopter with a deep *chunking* sound. The rotors of the dark black chopper began to spin up, kicking up anything loose on the tarmac as Paredes ignored the gunfire.

The shooting stopped, most likely because the sniper was fighting the down-draft gusts from the rotors. Paredes brought the Black Hawk up a few feet, then pivoted towards the structure that Sergeant Clifton had spotted. The pair of forward mounted 12.7mm guns roared, lighting up the area as their bullets devoured the target structure in a hail of hot tracers and death.

There was a momentary pause after the blast with no gunfire coming back. Paredes brought the Black Hawk back down on the tarmac gently. "I'd say that he now understands the error of his ways."

"If he's still alive," she replied. "That was a bit of overkill."

"There's no such thing as overkill. I know this; his superiors will have a hard time getting volunteers to take shots at us from now on. Now then, with your permission, Major, I'd like to get this show on the road."

"Permission granted," she said, rising and moving out of the office where she had taken cover.

"You heard the lady. The bad guy is paste. This is Lariat to the attack force, mount up," he said, talking as if he were an announcer at a rodeo rather than commanding the helicopter strike force.

"Good hunting Lariat," Judy said as the crews rushed out to their helicopters. *We're behind schedule ... hopefully not too far behind.*

CHAPTER 18

"There are only accepted narratives. Anything else is dangerous misinformation."

Midland, Texas

Darius eyed Midland with a strange sense of dread. There was no reason for it, nothing that might hint at danger, but he could not shake that feeling when he was looking at the outline of the buildings against the Texas sky. Andrews had been a town, a speed bump in the road. Midland was a city with tall buildings. *There's got to be over 100,000 people there.* The Newmerican force seemed large when they passed through a small town, but in a big city, they were dwarfed by the concrete and steel.

The road to Midland had been slow. Three times, gunshots came from the desert forced the troops to stop and deploy. Each time, the source of the shots was not found. What should have been a one-day trip to Midland had turned into two and a half days thanks to the harassment. Worse yet, two soldiers had been wounded. There had been more than one shooter, and the rumors they had heard, that everyone in Texas had a firearm, apparently had some validity. *I can see why the FedGov ordered all personal weapons rounded up. In the hands of civilians, they are dangerous.*

Their force had doubled in size, joined by another prong of the Newmerican thrust into Texas. It was mostly Oregon National Guard with Social Enforcement units from California and Washington State. They had several older Humvees, no doubt pulled out of some National Guard depot. The most welcomed addition was two howitzers.

They had come in via State Highway 349—a dull, flat stretch of road flanked by a barren landscape. They came over a shallow hill, and Darius saw Midland—its buildings lighting up the bleakness of Texas. Two police cars blocked the road ahead with their bright red and piercing blue flashing lights. Several troopers were standing in front of them, no weapons in their hands. *This isn't going to be like Andrews. This is something different.* The Newmerican column, which the Veteran Corps was leading, slowly stopped.

"What is it?" Fax asked from the rear of the truck, unable to see. Darius had the driver's seat next to Captain Aguilar, who had told him to stop.

Darius looked and the two state troopers, along with a civilian, were approaching them. "I think they want to talk."

"They're afraid of us," Fax replied. "Probably pissing themselves."

"Can it," Aguilar ordered. "Thorne, come with me." She opened the door to the truck and climbed down, as did Darius.

As they walked down the stretch of roadway, Darius couldn't help but think back to the western movies he had watched as a kid. This had all the hallmarks of an old-fashioned gunfight … the local sheriff and his men coming to hold off the bad guys. It was not lost on him that in this case, the Newmericans were cast as the villains.

He kept his right hand on his pistol grip, but kept the weapon in his holster as they came to a stop some twenty feet apart. For a few tense seconds, the two groups looked at each other, saying nothing.

The man, in his fifties, tall and lean, wearing a Stetson on his head and cowboy boots, took two steps forward closing the gap between the two groups. "I am Randolph Howard, Mayor of Midland," he said firmly, with a slight accent and a hint of pride in his title.

Thorne's captain took a single step forward. "I'm Captain Lauren Aguilar of the Veterans Corps of Newmerican Army."

"Captain," Howard allowed a momentary pause, acknowledging her title. "We hope that you and your forces are just passing through our fair city. If that is the case, we will offer no resistance and see you on your way."

Darius knew this would be a point of contention. In a few hours, it would be dark. While they could pass through, it would force them to camp out in the Texas scrub brush. *Aguilar won't go for that, not with comfortable lodgings right in front of us.* She spoke crisply, but directly at Mayor Howard. "Your offer is appreciated, but we will likely be using several of your local hotels for the night."

The mayor was unshaken by her words. "We would much rather you and your people move on to wherever you are heading."

"If we opt to stay, there's not much you can do about it. I've got wounded that need medical attention, and the rest of us are tired of Texas hospitality." Her words seemed to ratchet up the tension. One of the state troopers shifted in place slightly.

"The good people that I represent would not take kindly to an invading army camping in their city."

"What they want and what we will do are two different things," she replied, crossing her arms.

"Your being in the city might bring about fighting, should the American forces come after you. I am attempting to avoid damage and bloodshed in Midland."

"If your people let us go about our business, there won't be any bloodshed. We will move out when we desire it."

Mayor Howard looked down for a moment, then back at her, locking his gaze. "Captain, I cannot be held accountable for what happens if you set up operations in Midland."

"Is that a threat?"

Howard shook his head. "No. It is a statement of fact."

"Tell your people to tune into the news. They can see what happened when the locals of Andrews decided to stand up against us. We have artillery, armored vehicles, and a lot of troops. You need to remind your locals of that. If any of them get trigger-happy, we will not pull punches."

The mayor was unshaken. "I see your little invading army. It's intimidating. I'll give you that. By the same token, this is Midland—not Andrews. It would behoove you and your people to stay the night and move on."

"Again, that sounds like a threat. May I remind you, we are not 'invading,' we are simply taking things back that belong to our nation."

"You lost the election. Texas is not a part of your traitorous government—it is American." He said the last word with pride, going so far as to puff out his chest slightly.

"We could argue about the election validity all evening. I'm tired, as are my people. I suggest you step aside, and let us secure some warm food and our lodging for the night. We will be out of your hair soon enough. If you are worried about your people, I suggest you tell them to stay home and off the streets while we are here." While she used the word, "suggest" it was clear that she was expressing an order.

"Very well, I will order a curfew—for your safety." The way the mayor said it, Darius wondered just how concerned he really was for their safety. *Is he protecting us, or the citizens?*

"That is appreciated." Aguilar replied. "If your people are peaceful, we will be too."

"We will greet you with appropriate Texas hospitality." Those words didn't give Darius a sense of comfort. *All of the hospitality of an invading enemy; that's what he means. The mayor chose those words carefully. We are going to need to proceed with caution.*

Turning around, the mayor returned to the police vehicles and a minute later, they sped off. Darius stood with the captain, watching them slowly drive back to the city. "Staying here is a mistake; you know that, don't you Captain?" he said as she turned and walked next to him, pausing for a few seconds.

"There's some hotels on the southwest side of town. We will need to set up there," Aguilar replied, refusing to acknowledge the threat he raised. "We'll set up patrols around them, and position some teams on rooftops. I want teams organized to go to local grocery stories and forage supplies." She paused for a moment, then turned to face him. "These people are arrogant and proud. If we just bypass Midland, it only emboldens them. Texas needs to return to the Newmerican fold. We are only here overnight, but being here is a reminder of who is really in charge … who they are accountable to." With that, she turned and started walking back to the column.

Darius followed, secure in the belief that sleep was likely to be elusive in the coming night. *We are in enemy territory, and they know it.*

Nashville National Cemetery
Nashville, Tennessee

Thiago Reese had gotten off the bus a block south of the National Cemetery, near the Home Depot. He had little doubt that the bus's camera would record him as a passenger; in fact, he welcomed it. Wearing the disguise that made him appear as Caylee Leatrom, he knew the footage would further implicate the rouge operative in the crime he was about to commit. *They will turn on Leatrom. She will go from a sympathetic traitor to a wanted criminal. Questions will be raised about why the President had embraced her. TRC-approved stories would imply that the American President was incompetent, and the people would devour it.* The investigation and chaos will eat at the American government from within. It was better than simply killing his former colleague. He was using her for the Newmerican cause.

The walk in the early Sunday morning sun was warm. He could feel his face perspire under the prosthetics that he wore. The wig made the top of his head feel like an oven, but he was used to that sensation. The skin-tone-colored latex gloves he wore made sure he didn't leave unwanted fingerprints. Disguise was part of his effectiveness as an operative. Thiago had wished that Caylee had worn a dress … a dress was perfect for concealment of weapons. It had taken him some time to find clothing that matched what she wore when in the Southern White House, but he knew that would help in framing her.

As he approached the open gates of the National Cemetery, the long, low rows of white marble grave markers snaked through the first hints of emerging spring grass. Parked near the entrance was a pair of vehicles and two black-suited Secret Service agents. Clutching the grocery-store-purchased flowers that Thiago had brought with him, he walked towards the gate. To anyone seeing her, he would look like someone coming to pay respects to a lost loved one. Holding the pistol behind the flowers was both part of the disguise and perfect obstruction.

One agent looked over at her as she walked on the driveway where the vehicles were parked and gave her a nod, turning away once he was sure Thiago was no threat. He flashed a thin smile, something to reassure the agent. As he passed them, he reeled about quickly, stepping forward, dropping the flowers, and jamming the pistol's suppressor in the back of the Secret Service agent. He pulled the trigger. The crack of the gun was muffled by the suit as the bullet shattered the agent's spine. His partner spun and was in the middle of drawing his own weapon when Thiago fired once more. The shot hit the face of the Secret Service agent; his head exploded in a brilliant red spray. Bits of brain from the muffled bang hit the black SUV.

Thiago moved fast, dragging the bodies into the vehicles. He was wet with sweat when done, but didn't care. *His guards are out of pocket; now comes the easy part.* Picking up the flowers, he walked to the north end of the cemetery. Cold calculations ran through his mind. How long would it be before someone came through the gate? Would they notice the blood on the pavement, or the vehicles—or just curiously spot the dead bodies in the back of the SUV? Prior to his arrival, he had walked the ground, so he knew the possible escape routes.

Pausing for a moment at the SUV, he glanced up at the camera mounted at the gate. *I want them to see my face, the face of Caylee Leatrom. I want there to be no doubt who pulled the trigger.*

His target had not seemed to react to the shots. The ground, trees, distance, and bustle of the surrounding city, along with the suppressor had been more than enough to muffle the shots Thiago had fired. He moved carefully, almost casually, so as not to raise any suspicion should his target hear him.

Jack Desmond was kneeling in front of a small grave marker, as he had every Sunday morning, no doubt coping with grief. Lowering the bouquet of flowers to the ground, the plastic wrapper made just enough noise to get Desmond's attention. Rising, he turned and looked at Reese with a mix of anger and confusion in his face.

"Caylee …" he started, then his face tensed. "Shit!" *He saw through my disguise!* Reese didn't overreact—his weapon was already aimed.

Reese fired, the bullet hitting Desmond's shoulder as the Chief of Staff sprang to the side. Desmond pulled his own weapon—something that Reese hadn't considered. He moved, firing another shot—this one hitting one of Desmond's knees.

Jack Desmond fired two shots rapidly. Reese's right arm seared as if it were on fire, almost to where he would drop his weapon. His left hand took the gun, leveled and aimed at Desmond, firing the final round into his target's right chest.

Desmond toppled backwards with an audible groan, landing next to the grave marker he had been kneeling at. Reese turned and walked to the north side of the cemetery, glancing at his wound. One bullet had hit his right shoulder; blood stained the shirt he wore, oozing down into his padded bra. It wasn't an arterial wound, but it still complicated matters.

A few yards from the gate, he tossed the gun he had carried. The weapon had been licensed to Caylee, courtesy of the NSF. Reese had transferred the fingerprints of Leatrom to the weapon as well. When the American Secret Service and FBI checked the recovered weapon, they would be led right to Caylee Leatrom.

Desmond was the actual power behind the Pretender President; killing him was a devastating blow all on its own. Satisfaction almost made the gunshot to his shoulder worth it. *Desmond is dead—and their prized traitor, along with the President, would be blamed for it all.*

Stewart Newburgh Airport, New York

Judy Mercury watched the small, flat screen with the feed from one of the attack forces, the one led by Captain Paredes. The three Black Hawks were coming in low and fast, closing in on Barnes Air National Guard Base in Massachusetts. She saw the flicker of the runway lights at the Westfield-Barnes Regional Airport in the early morning light. Lieutenant Colonel Mihalek stood beside her, arms crossed, eyes locked on the same images.

"Target in-sight," came Paredes's voice. "Commencing our attack run."

Several A10 Warthogs and a pair of C-130 gunships were parked on the runway near the National Guard hangers. Their positioning was sloppy; they were close to one another. It made sense; they didn't have much to fear. The New Hampshire Air National Guard existed more on paper than anywhere else, and thus far they had not made an appearance. *They don't have much to fear and it shows.*

The trio of choppers unleashed a torrent of gunfire. The tracers were like a solid beam of light on the display as Mercury watched. They tore into the C-130s first. One of them exploded, throwing blazing debris into the air and on some of the other aircraft. One of the Black Hawks unleashed several missiles into the row of hangers, adding to the explosion and flames. More shots riddled the Warthogs on the runway—chewing up their targets.

Paredes angled to the tower of the airport, sending three bursts of fire into it. The lights inside the tower flickered off as the rounds ate up the facilities. A missile was sent into the center of the runway. It flashed brilliantly as the cratering charge did its job.

A few more missiles were fired into support buildings and the refueling farm. The resulting explosion of the airplane fuel looked like a tactical nuclear strike. An enormous ball of crimson and orange flames rolled skyward; then seemed to pop—sending a black, mushroom cloud rising skyward.

The firing stopped and Mercury saw the helicopters banked away from the airport. "Target destroyed. Moving to our secondary objective," Paredes stated coolly.

"This is Lantern Actual. Good shooting Lariat," she said into the handheld microphone.

Judy pursed her lips and let out the breath that she had been unconsciously holding during the attack. Mihalek broke the moment of silence. "The force that hit Bradley Air National Guard Base had similar results. So far, so good."

"They still have to hit the National Guard Joint Force Headquarters in Hanscom AFB," she reminded him. "We had surprise on our side for the bases we've hit. They may have advance warning when Paredes shows up."

"He's coming in low, below their radar. The attack group is about to hit the base in Falmouth soon. We've already hamstrung the Newmerican's air support. Clearly, they didn't expect us to hit them at all. Their air defenses were nil."

"What you're saying is that we have been lucky so far."

"I'll take good luck over bad any day of the week."

"Hitting their bases is only one part of this plan," she said. We will need to recover our choppers, refuel, and rearm them. They may try to come at us here."

"We have anti-aircraft teams in place," he reminded her. "Let them come. I think you may be overreacting. Right now, they are not sure where we are striking from. Their upper command will be in chaos trying to figure out how we got helicopters this far north."

"I won't feel good about this until we can offer support to the Defiance," Judy stated firmly. *I only hope our luck continues to hold ...*

East of Tucumcari, New Mexico

"Midland?" General Reager asked as he and Harnessy huddled behind his command Bradley. There was only sporadic gunfire the last few days. Both sides were dug in. The Pureblood Marines were proving themselves adept at creating the illusion that there were more forces in front of the enemy than there ever were. For Trip, it was good to keep them focused on his position. *They think they have stolen a march on me, hitting us in southern Texas. That's fine by me, for now.*

"Yes sir," Harnessy said. "They rolled in a few hours ago."

"That's a big damn apple for them to try and take a bite out of."

"The locals didn't put up immediate resistance, pursuant to our recommendations."

"And our forces?"

Harnessy grinned a little. "A few units of SOL and the Texas Rangers are moving in on the outskirts of the city as we speak. The biggest unit is Belle's Bama Deplorables." The mention of Darcy Belle's SOL unit brought back fond memories of their performance during the battles for Atlanta.

"If Darcy's people are on their way, that's a bit of good news."

"Agreed. She's not alone. The PMCs we hired, Lock Jaw and Mission Ready, have linked up with them. The Newmericans have the numbers on their side, but fairly soon, they are going to find Midland a difficult city to hold onto."

Trip rubbed the stubble on his chin. The Texas grit clung to his skin as if it were part of him. It was everywhere, making his skin itch where it acted like sandpaper under his tactical gear.

"Where is General Rickett's current position?"

"He's anchored in Abilene with his forces spread out in an arc to Coleman. His intent was to block moves on Austin and Fort Worth."

We still don't know the destination of these enemy troops. While letting them run into Rickett's force might make sense, Trip wanted to take away their initiative. *I have been dancing to their tune since they blunted Diamondback.* "So the question is: Is Midland where we want to make our stand?"

"We may not have a choice. Two of their three assault prongs converged there."

Trip knew the city well. He had a cousin that lived there and had visited it often in his youth. *Midland gives them an interstate to Fort Worth and puts Austin and San Antonio within striking distance. Fighting them in a city will be brutal. Innocent people are going to be killed in the process.* A part of him preferred to catch them in the open. *Less civilian casualties that way, but we risk them breaking off some of their force and hitting more cities.* "I don't like it, but that's the cards we've been dealt, and I intend to play this hand. We can bottle them up in Midland, cut them off from supplies and reinforcements. That will allow Ricketts to do what he does best, go at the enemy."

"Excellent idea, sir. The mayor indicated that a lot of locals are armed and are looking to unleash a little payback on the invaders."

Trip allowed himself a dry-cracked grin. "They are about to learn that most Texans didn't turn in their weapons when the FedGov ordered them to after The Fall. I almost pity them."

"Almost."

Trip grinned a little more. "Naa. Send the word Captain. Get them under a single commander to coordinate their actions—then tell them to bleed these bastards."

"With pleasure."

"Talk to me about Clovis."

"The Newmericans are dug in pretty tight there. Oregon National Guard, some from Washington State and Californians. They are formed up outside of the city in a fairly wide arc. They have been flying drone strikes out of Cannon AFB against us too."

Trip pondered the situation. *The DoD likes to claim they are neutral in this civil war, but they are more than willing to help the enemy every chance they get.* "If we strip most of our force in front of them, what will they do?"

"They are likely to push into Texas. Why sir, are you thinking of redeploying?"

Trip nodded. "I don't think we have a choice. We are stalemated here and there. If we push into them, it will cause a lot of deaths for ground that is of little value. The only target worth our attention along this border is Cannon Air Force Base, which the enemy is using."

"Yes sir."

"I'm tired of being forced to play defense. I think it's time to shake things up. That may mean surrendering some worthless ground for something that is worth taking."

"Agreed. I stand by for your order, sir."

This wasn't the offensive operation that Trip had planned on. The enemy had caught him off guard, but now he intended to make them pay for it. *They are about to get a good dose of Texas hospitality.*

CHAPTER 19

"Policies before people."

Rio Rancho, North of Albuquerque, New Mexico

Raul insisted on riding in the dump truck with the people they had liberated. Every bump they hit on the road reminded him of that decision. The suspension of the truck was almost nonexistent. Each time they hit a bump or made a turn, a groan rose in the vehicle's bed from the passengers hiding there.

They arrived at the abandoned Target that had been arranged as a rendezvous. Parking at the rear, he helped the riders get down. A chance to stretch their legs was welcomed by most. Many scrambled inside the store to relieve themselves. Bottles of water and protein bars were distributed. It wasn't much of a meal, but from the looks of the emaciated former prisoners, anything would be welcomed. They were led into the back entrance of the abandoned store and given a chance to spread out. The building had power and some running water, so many had an opportunity to clean themselves. Most of the florescent bulbs were broken; a few flickered with a creepy strobe effect. The store displayed were eerily abandoned, some thrown over by looters or vandals. Spray painted graffiti covered some walls; gang and Social Enforcement tags marked the Target as their territory. There was no sign if the Target had been looted during the riots at the time of The Fall, or if it had simply closed because of the economic downturn that followed the rise of the Ruling Council. To Raul, it didn't matter. *It will be a long time before the country rebuilds, if ever.*

Raul joined Caylee, who concentrated on establishing perimeter security. They had been listening to the TRC radio program, and there had been no indication that their prison break had been detected yet, but it was only a matter of time.

Faust Kidder arrived in a beat up Dodge RAM pickup that belched black smoke as it came to a stop. Kidder had been the helicopter pilot in Raul's prison breakout from the Supermax. He and Travis gave a cursory hug and back pat, and Raul came over to join them as they moved inside the target. Andy joined them, dark bags showing under his eyes. *None of us have slept for two days ... we're all tired.*

"You made good time," Faust compliment them.

"So far, there doesn't seem to be any word about us out there," Travis said.

Kidder shook his head. "Oh, they know. About an hour ago, I picked up some chatter on my police scanner. Lots of NSF units are being shifted up to that camp you liberated. They just aren't releasing the story to the media because it's bad news. The TRC protects its narratives carefully, and getting a quarantine camp liberated doesn't fit their story."

It was sobering news. *We thought we had gotten away with it ... in reality; they are afraid to tell people that truth.*

"What's the word with the Army?" Andy asked.

"There's a big battle going on near Tucumcari and another near Cannon Air Force Base. If you believe the official hype, the American Army was surprised and is getting its balls waxed in the process. They are claiming they have invaded southern Texas a well."

"That's bullshit," Travis said. "Or plain stupid. The Texans aren't likely to take that laying down."

Kidder shrugged. "When all you are fed is lies, it becomes impossible to know what is the truth, even when it's right in front of you. The Army is slugging it out—that's the key thing."

Caylee crossed her arms. "So how are you going to get us out of here, Mr. Kidder?"

Glancing at Caylee, he grinned, clearly flirting with her. "Well Sweet Cheeks, I've got a plan. It's risky, but it may be our best bet."

Caylee's eyes narrowed and Raul could see that she didn't appreciate the nickname that Kidder had chosen for her. "It is Caylee, Mr. Kidder.

Call me Sweet Cheeks again, and you'll be wearing two eye patches."

Her threat only made Kidder grin more broadly. "Roger that."

"The plan, Faust?" Travis spoke up.

"Right," the pilot said, refocusing his attention. "Going out by plane here is the best choice. The runways up in Santa Fe were big enough, but not rated to handle the weight of a big jet.... and we're going to need big equipment to get these folks out at once. Of course, flying out of here comes with some risks too. Kirtland Air Force Base is attached to the airport."

Andy reacted to that information with trepidation. "Wait, you are going to have us fly out from an airport that is an Air Force base?"

Kidder nodded. "Kirtland is still tied to the DoD. Yeah, there's some National Guard forces there, but on paper they are neutral. Kirtland is a nuclear base—so the Department of Defense is not willing to hand those resources over to either side in this little civil war. If we do this right, we aren't going to have to worry much about their interference."

"That seems like a big 'if'" Travis interjected.

"What is the plan?" Raul asked, wanting to hear the details of the operation.

Kidder seemed to appreciate his words. "We can't just march these folks in through the main terminal. Security there is too tight. They are prepared for hijackings. Moving all of these people would be problematic too."

"I trust you have a plan," Caylee pressed.

"Their biggest weakness is the freight terminal. Security is paper thin there, and they have aircraft that are large enough to accommodate all of the passengers ... Airbus A300F equipment. If you don't load the cargo containers, there's plenty of room for people. No seats, but we don't need them."

Raul's mind reeled. *We are going to fly out on a freight plane?* He knew little about airplanes, but the sound of it seemed fraught with risk. "So how will this go down?"

"Simple. I was able to get the flight schedule for Fed Ex at the freight terminal. They have a flight scheduled to go out at 1745 hours, with loading taking place at 1615. We will force our way through their security at 1600 hours. Rather than loading cargo, we load our people.

I will request an early departure, and we will take off and head to safe territory in Texas."

"Do you have details of their security?" Caylee asked.

"I have what I've been able to observe," Kidder replied. "We are talking five guards, two at the gate, three assigned to patrol the freight area. These are not your typical TSA guards."

"Worse?" Travis asked.

Kidder chuckled. "Not from what I've seen. These guys are rent-a-cops ... big, slow guys. Apparently TSA isn't too worried about the freight terminal. The terminal building is big enough for us to get our people in and secured should *real* security shows up."

Raul focused on the airplane. "So you've flown this kind of an airplane before?"

Kidder's one eye winced slightly. "Not exactly. I've flown similar aircraft over the years. It shouldn't be a problem."

Raul's stomach clenched at the words. "Not exactly? That isn't making me feel very good about this."

"Look kid," Kidder went into rebuttal mode. "I'm not rated on this Airbus, but I've flown their equipment before. I went over the PDF for the flight manual last night just to refresh my memory. I can fly anything. The principles of air flight are the same, even if the equipment isn't. I know enough to get us where we need to go." He spoke with confidence, which helped. He had heard the story of him coming in with the helicopter at the Supermax, which helped Kidder's credibility.

Glancing over at Caylee, she made eye contact with Raul, and gave him a nod. *If she trusts him, I need to.* "Alright then, what do you have in the way of plans?"

Kidder pulled out a pile of printouts. "I did a lot of the surveillance when you asked me to prep as your fallback. Here's the layout of the freight terminal ..." He put the printouts on one of the dusty store display racks. Raul leaned in studying the building layout. *We have no choice. If this doesn't work, we're trapped here, with a war between us and safety.*

Nashville VA Medical Center, Nashville, Tennessee

Charli had only seen Jack for a few moments when they transferred him to the VA hospital from the Vanderbilt University Medical Center where he was initially taken. He was in the ICU now, clinging to life with three gunshot wounds. That he was still alive was testimony to his toughness.

The doctors and nurses bustled past her as if she were little more than an obstruction as they entered the ICU. She didn't mind—as long as they were working to help her former boss. She had ordered identity verification on every person working in the facility. No one was going to get near Jack who shouldn't.

I should have increased his security, no matter how much he protested. Her people were already poring over the evidence. When she had seen the security camera footage, her heart had dropped. It had been Caylee … no, one operative cleverly disguised as her friend. The disguise was convincing at first glance. When she saw the wrists of the shooter taking down the security detail, she noticed how thick they were. Those are the wrists of a man, Thiago Reese.

Staring at the door to the ICU, Charli fought back the tears, as she had for the last few hours. There had been some resistance to moving Jack to the VA hospital, but security was her primary concern. Reese was still out there, and if he learned that he had been unsuccessful in killing Jack yet, he would want to finish the job. Secret Service agents had sealed off the building, but she wondered if it was enough when going against a Newmerican operative. Charli heard the shuffle of shoes on the floor of the hospital hallway. Looking up she saw a man in a suit next to her.

"Director Kazinski," he spoke in a formal tone. "Special Agent Prescott, FBI." He pulled his credentials.

Charli took the time to review them for a moment before responding. "What can I do for you?"

"We just got back the preliminary info on the recovered weapon. We got two good and two partial prints off of it, from Caylee Leatrom. While we don't have access to the national registry, what we do have shows the weapon as registered to her as well."

"I know you're trying to tell me you believe that Jack's assassin was Caylee Leatrom. Well, it wasn't. She is out of the country on a classified operation."

"So I've been told." Prescott replied. "But the evidence is overwhelming."

Carli narrowed her gaze. "We were tracking a known operative, Thiago Reese. Apparently Reese used a disguise, dressing up as Leatrom. The agents running the surveillance didn't know it at the time. We hadn't expected that from him. I'm willing to bet he transferred the prints to the weapon."

Her words didn't change the expression on Prescott's face. "I was briefed about this on the way over. To be honest, it's all too convenient. You have someone that you claim impersonated Leatrom, but you have no proof that it wasn't her. In fact, the evidence overwhelmingly points to her and her alone."

"I *know* it isn't her, Agent Prescott," Charli snapped loudly. She glanced around the hallway, realizing that her voice was carrying. She tried to temper the flames of anger raging in her, but it wasn't easy.

Prescott spoke in a softer voice, just above a whisper. "Ma'am, I understand what you are saying. But the Attorney General has to do something. What do you expect her to say? "We have evidence pointing to this person, but we are going to ignore it on a theory?" No one is going to buy that. Someone shot the Chief of Staff. Actions have to be taken, if only to give the people a sense that we are in control of the situation."

"Caylee is innocent."

"If that is the case, she will get the chance to prove it. In the meantime, we have to take action based on the data we have. What we have points to her."

"I hope you don't mind if I bump this up over your head," she warned. It wasn't an idle threat. *I'm the Director of the Secret Service. I Goddamn will go over your head. This wasn't Caylee!* Charli rarely threw her weight around, but this time was an exception.

"I assumed you would. But you should know in the next hour we have to go public with this. The people don't know that Mr. Desmond was shot yet, but somehow the TRC got word about it and are going to run it. That means the Attorney General needs to get out in front of this before it becomes a runaway train. You know how the media can be."

Shit! "If he goes public with this, it tells everyone he wants information on Caylee; she'll be playing into the hands of Reese and the Newmerican government. Worse, when she has to reverse it all, she's going to look like an idiot."

"That's above my pay grade. It's her call to make."

"It's a bad call." Charli gained some measure of composure. "No doubt you are going to relay this conversation to your boss. Fine. Let the Attorney General know that I am on the way over. You may as well have the FBI Director join us. This is the kind of bullshit that plays into the enemy's hands."

Glancing once more at the door leading to the ICU, Charli stormed down the corridor to the elevator bank. *This would be a hell of a lot easier to prove if Caylee was here.* In the meantime, she had put out word to find Thiago Reese. *Jack fired his gun. If he hit Reese, he's a wounded animal in a potentially hostile city. As an operative, he's dangerous. As a wounded operative, he's even more so.*

White Mountain National Forest
New Hampshire

The enemy M1 tank looked as if it were driving right at Su-Hui. It churned through the mud and blasted ground, heading right for his firing position. It's supporting infantry was lagging, struggling to keep up with the M1. He had moved so many times, from one location to another, to avoid bringing in enemy artillery on them. They would pop up, firing for a few minutes, then trudge on, only to pop up and fire again. Time had no meaning in the White National Forest. The only thing that had meaning was the battle, and for him the tank heading towards him dominated his entire focus.

The vehicle was some thirty-five yards away and heading towards him far faster than he had expected. *The commander of that vehicle does not know how close he has come to our infantry—a mistake that he will pay for.* He knew he should move further down the trench line, but he found himself transfixed on the flat, green tank that seemed to charge right for him. The Newmericans had launched so many waves of attack; he had lost count. Each one had devoured more of the defensive positions. *Is this the wave that is going to push right through us?*

A hand grabbed him and jerked him to the left. It was Corporal Abernathy. The younger man was covered with a dull brown layer of cold, wet mud, just like Su-Hui. "We need to redeploy," he yelled. Su-Hui nodded, then turned to Hachi, who was crouching low. She had heard Abernathy and nudged Trudy, who popped up for a moment, firing two quick shots at a target he didn't see. The entire group of SOL troops shuffled down the covered trench as the sound of the tank got closer. Even with the crude slabs of concrete and dirt covering every ten feet of the trench, there was a feeling that it would not protect them.

Su-Hui rose just enough to see that the tank was almost over where they had been in the trench when an explosion washed over the vehicle. Hot shrapnel splattered the wet ground, leaving wisps of steam rising from where it had torn the forest floor. There was an immediate metallic grinding noise from the vehicle and through the smoke, Su-Hui saw that the front drive bogie of the tank was gone. The tank spun in place for a moment as the driver attempted to figure out what was happening; then he stopped. With a thrown tread, it was now unable to advance or retreat.

Pausing momentarily, the Abrams' massive cannon fired, making the air roar all around him. The ground throbbed under the blast. The driver attempted to back up and was able to back up slightly, but soon the tread was off entirely and the tank was completely stranded. Its machine guns blatted out bursts with deafening efficiency, adding to the cacophony of the battle raging around him. Someone further down the trench line threw a Molotov cocktail at the tank, wreathing it in flames. While the improvised weapon would not be enough to destroy an Abrams, it gave even Su-Hui a burst of enthusiasm. The smell of the burning gasoline wafted down around the SOL team as they continued to move further down the line. The tank's support infantry had its own problems in terms of incoming mortar fire, driving them back, further stranding the tank.

Reaching another uncovered portion of the trench some eighty yards downrange, the unit opened up again on a fresh wave of Newmerican infantry that were moving in to provide support to the burning tank. Valerie's M249 caught two of them as they tried to crawl forward, sending a spray of red mist into the air. Su-Hui rose and fired as well—unsure if he had hit the trooper he was aiming at.

The Abrams turret turned side to side, but its massive gun didn't fire. It hit him in that moment that the fire still burning on the vehicle was obscuring the gunner's ability to find a target. Taking aim, he fired again at the Newmerican infantry. This time he was sure that he at least wounded his target. The infantryman rolled several times, diving for cover.

Valerie was reloading two people down, snapping down the barrel locking lever on the M249 as Hachi rose and fired off three short bursts of gunfire. "I think they are retreating," she said as she reloaded her assault weapon.

Rising, a pair of bullets splattered the ground in front of him, throwing dirt in his face. He dropped back down, safe again, and secure that his wife was right—their infantry was once more falling back. Better yet, in doing so, they were stranding the hulking tank, leaving the crew to their fate.

In the skies above, he heard the roar of an airplane, then the deadly purr of the AC-130 gunship unleashing another strafing run. The ground in front of the tank was devoured in the spray of rapid gunfire that raced from in front of the vehicle right across the trench that Su-Hui and others were huddled in. The shots hit the concrete they had dived under, but it did little to stop the rounds from punching through. Dust from the blasted concrete irritated his eyes for a moment as he tried to maintain some degree of composure. *Blasted gunships ... where is our air support?*

The gunship swung out of the combat zone and Su-Hui checked Hachi to make sure she was alright. Though covered with bits of dirt, she was fine. Valerie lay on the floor of the trench, slowly stirring under the dirt that had been thrown on her.

Abernathy was pale. Moaning, he held his leg. Where his right food had been was now a pulverized meaty paste. If it hadn't been for the concrete slab over the trench, he might have lost the entire leg, but that was of little condolence to the wounded man. As tough as he was, his face was awash with fear. "They got me."

"Hachi, take him to the rear. Get him to the medics," Su-Hui barked. His wife moved without hesitation, sliding under one of the corporal's arms and helping him up.

Valerie rose, and her eyes widened. "The tank!" she snapped.

Su-Hui turned and saw that the crew had opened the vehicle and were climbing out, attempting to get away. That was why the gunship fired on us, to allow them to escape. One crewman was jumping down off the engine compartment; one was half-in and half-out of the turret hatch; another was batting at the flames. The driver opened his top hatch to the remains of the flaming Molotov cocktail. He hesitated, unsure how to proceed, then tried to climb out. He fell, no doubt it hurt to put his hand on the hot metal armor. Grasping one hand in pain, he tried to roll off of the side of the tank, managing in the process to ignite some of his uniform. When he hit the mud near the good track, he rolled more to put out the fire, exposing himself.

The M249 purred two bursts. The first cut the person climbing out of the turret almost in half; the other downed the one running for the safety of the Newmerican lines. Su-Hui aimed at the driver and fired. The shot hit the shin of the man, sending him face-first into the mud. Crawling, desperate to get to safety, he never stood a chance. Su-Hui aimed carefully and fired, hitting him in the upper neck right below his helmet. His head exploded as he lay in the mud.

His mind raced at the new opportunity. The tank was disabled, but still had an operable weapon. Wheeling about to Valerie, he called out, "We can turn that turret around and fire on their line."

"I've never fired a tank cannon before," she countered. Both of them had been given a cursory orientation months earlier by the New Hampshire National Guard. Now it was being put to the test.

"Neither have I, but it can't be too hard."

She looked at him, saying nothing for a second. "You get up there and get in first. I'll cover you."

Su-Hui nodded. This was something he never would have done if Hachi were at his side. She never would have approved. He had seen the inside of a tank before, during his service in Taiwan. *We don't have to be accurate; we just have to keep firing in the general direction of the enemy.* Gathering his resolve, he drew a long, deep breath, then nodded to Valerie who rose and sprayed towards the Newmerican line in full automatic mode. Su-Hui sprinted down the trench, putting the tank hull between him and the enemy, then rose. The flames were dying down as he climbed up. *I must be mad to try this ...*

CHAPTER 20

"To question government policy is to ignite the flames of treason."

Nashville, Tennessee

Thiago Reese's wounded shoulder and arm throbbed every time his right foot hit the pavement. Only one of Jack Desmond's bullets had hit him, blasting his right shoulder and blasting out the rear of the arm. He had stopped several times to apply pressure to the wound. While an artery hadn't been hit, he was fairly certain that the shot had damaged his shoulder joint. Any movement he made with his right arm was met with a flaming, hot, stabbing pain.

Reese had shed the Leatrom disguise, leaving it in a dumpster behind an apartment complex. He had used the padded bra to rig a sling for his arm, and material from the dress to wrap the wound and keep pressure on it. He had pre-positioned a go-bag behind the dumpster, with a burner phone, some cash, and another handgun with four magazines. There were emergency supplies there, including a first aid kit with some antiseptic which he used to douse his wounds. He also had a pair of pliers, a knife, and a screwdriver.

The gunshot wound was a problem. Going to the hospital would immediately involve local law enforcement who no longer had ties to the NSF. There wasn't much that he could do other than rest and hope the bleeding stopped. The damage to his bones wasn't the kind of thing that could heal on its own, not well.

For him, that meant that the only viable option was to secure a vehicle and head for Newmerica. Moving through the parking lot of the CVS, north of the cemetery where he had been shot, he eyed a few vehicles that would serve well. One in particular was driven by an elderly woman. It took her five minutes to walk into the CVS, which meant he probably had plenty of time to hot-wire the vehicle. He climbed in the older, gas-burning car, a dull maroon Buick, his arm throbbing in protest as he moved. With just one hand, it would be difficult to do the work, but not impossible. His body was sweat-drenched from pain as he pulled the screwdriver out of his go-bag.

Reese realized he was breathing hard; he slowed it out of fear that he might slip into hyperventilate or go into shock. Taking in air slowly through his nose, he held it and released it through pursed lips to maintain some control. Passing out here and now would land him in the hospital and the waiting hands of police. *I've never hot-wired a car one-handed, but I sure as hell can try.*

Shifting in the driver's seat so he could use his left hand, with a hard thrust, he jammed the screwdriver into the ignition. That motion alone made his vision tunnel, if only for a moment. Reese had been in dangerous situations like this before. He had barely gotten the leadership of Ukraine out of the country when the Russians invaded. That time he had been shot in the left lung by some Wagner Group thugs on the tarmac of the airport. He had thought he was going to die from that, but had survived. *If I can overcome Ukrainian robber barons and Russian mercenaries, I can beat this too.*

With a forced turn of the screwdriver, the car started up, giving him a sense of relief. He pulled out, wheeling it with his only free hand, merging into traffic. It was tempting to go back to his apartment, but operational protocol required him to avoid it. Luis Fernando, the identity he had used to infiltrate the Southern White House, would disappear. It was better that way. Safer too.

He drove for thirty minutes, then pulled off the highway to rest at a gas station, parking behind it to be out of public view. His wounds were still seeping blood, soaking his makeshift bandage and the leather of the car seat. Reese needed the rest, but he still had work to do. Picking up the phone, he considered how to best leverage the call.

Reese pulled up one of the three numbers he had stored on the phone and waited for someone to pick up. "Pat Templeton," the MSNBC reporter answered.

"This is Luis, your 'friend' at the White House."

"Now isn't a great time," she said, clearly distracted by something else.

"I have a tremendous story for you, and it can't wait."

There was a pause. "Alright then, go ahead."

"Jack Desmond, the Chief of Staff, was the target of an assassination attempt today."

"No shit," she said flatly.

"If you haven't been watching the news, I was just on the air talking about it. He's lucky to be alive."

Alive? Damn! Reese had not planned on that. *I hit him with three shots. By all rights, the man should be dead.* "I know who did it. If you do what I ask, you can get the exclusive."

"You have my attention."

"It will cost you. I need you to drop off some things at a Shell Station at the north end of town."

"Alright. First, tell me who pulled the trigger."

"Caylee Leatrom," he said coolly, even allowing himself his first smile since shooting Desmond.

"The rogue operative? The one that the Americans have been courting?"

"One and the same. She shot up Desmond's detail. I'm sure they have footage of it. They are covering it up because of her ties to the administration. For all I know, this could go all the way to the President." The truths were spun in tightly with the exaggerations and outright lies. Reese knew the press. He knew that Templeton would take the bait if his lies were elevated to something that would get her great ratings.

"Wow," she replied flatly in amazement. "This is huge. Do you have proof?"

"Do I need it? No, I don't. But there is security footage of Leatrom near Desmond. I'm pretty sure of that. My source tells me they recovered her gun, registered to her, and that her fingerprints are on the weapon. The fact that they aren't releasing it to the press means that they are in the early stages of this cover up."

"I need to go on the air with this."

"As you should. The people have a right to know that their leaders are misleading them, hiding the truth from them. It begs the question: 'Why?'"

"Does anyone else have this story?"

"I only brought it to you. You are my favorite reporter." The lies came easy in his line of work, and Reese knew how to stroke egos. "You mentioned some supplies—I can't bring them, but my assistant can. I need to get in front of the camera with this. What do you need?"

Reese grinned, and for a moment the throbbing of his injured arm didn't seem as bad. "Some gauze, a few Ace bandages, a sewing kit, a bottle of alcohol, cotton balls, a few bottles of Gatorade, and some Tylenol," he rattled off the list of supplies from memory. It wouldn't solve his problem, but it would tide him over until he got back to the safety of Newmerica.

People will always believe there is a cover up ... one of the beauties that Watergate and the JFK assassination gave the nation. They will always suspect that their leaders are doing something behind their backs and will become angry about it. The weaker their minds, the more they crave conspiracies, regardless of how farfetched they are. It is a trait unique to our people. The media can always be manipulated too. The more they claim it is a conspiracy theory, the more people believe it to be the truth. A scandal like this will bog down any progress that the Americans might make. My actions will plant seeds that their leaders cannot be trusted.

It is the start of their downfall ...

Midland, Texas

Darius walked in the shadows of the Hampton Inn where some of the Newmerican force was bedded down. He had volunteered for the patrol simply because he knew he wouldn't be able to sleep. Captain Aguilar seemed confident that the locals would leave them alone, but to Darius the opening of the proverbial gates to the city seemed far too convenient. Everywhere else, even on the highways, the Texans had resisted, taking pot-shots at the column. He didn't trust them. Even when they were part of Newmerica, a lot of locals resisted. The TRC didn't run a lot of stories about Texan holdouts after the Liberation, but the ones it ran showed them as wild, defiant rednecks with guns.

The Newmerican forces were spread out over five hotels, all within two miles of each other. The transports used by the forces housed at the Hampton Inn were in the parking lot with some distance between them. Two old M113s were angled outward with their backs to the parked transports. On the surface, it was a good deployment, but everything felt painfully exposed. *We are close enough to support each other if we are attacked, but fighting in an urban environment is not something anyone wants.* Tall, nearby office buildings surrounded the hotel. He was thankful that there had been no signs of enemy air support.

Vixen walked beside him as he clung to the shadows of the building, seeming to sense his hesitation. "You seem all jacked up."

As they moved out, his eyes scanned the rooftops of the nearby buildings. "I don't like this place," he said with an icy stare.

"You don't like anyplace."

"We are in enemy territory."

"Yeah, and the Captain knows that."

"We should have gone outside the city, camped out in the wild."

She shook her head as he spoke. "Remember the drive here? The locals were taking shots at us out in the flatlands. That is where they operate best. Why would anyone trade sleeping on the sand for sleeping in a comfortable bed?"

He heard a sound that was high pitched, almost like a mosquito, though it seemed to be distant. The noise drifted in and out, echoing off of the buildings. He looked around, trying to find the source, but the noise disappeared as suddenly as it arrived. "What the hell was that?"

"Don't know. You are way too edgy. You need to relax."

"Texans have guns, and we are acting like we are frightening them with all of this hardware we brought. I know people from Texas, you can't intimidate them."

"Your PTSD is showing, big time. The FedGov rounded up all of their weapons, remember? Talk to the doc and see if you can get something for it."

He ignored her comments. Yes, he had PTSD, but he knew when it was showing itself, and this wasn't it. This was experience coming back to haunt him. Memories of his last deployment were chewing at his brain, heightening his senses. *She thinks she understands, but she's way off.* Rather than debate the matter, he let it drop.

They stepped away from the building into the white lights from the parking lot. As they moved down along the driveway leading to the Hampton Inn's parking lot, they took a momentary position near the bright sign that was mounted in brick at the entrance.

Vixen leaned against the big sign, her eyes glancing down the street while he looked up. It was dead quiet, no traffic at all. *The mayor's call for curfew was useful.* Maintaining security with passing vehicles would have required a lot more in the way of resources. "This place isn't all that bad," she commented.

He heard the buzzing sound again. It seemed to be coming from the area near the hotel proper. "There that is again."

The noise seemed to be in the air over the parking lot. He spotted a tiny, pulsating white dot of light in the air. "That looks like one of those toy drones," he said.

"Where?"

He gestured with the barrel of his weapon. "Look over there; you'll see a flicker of light."

"Oh yeah. Some kid is probably just having fun."

Who flies a toy in the middle of the night? A sinking feeling hit him, the knowledge that something was dangerously wrong. Darius's mouth opened to respond, but an explosion cut him off.

Under the drone, the bus that they had come in on exploded in a brilliant blast lighting up the parking area. Bits of bus rained down on the parking lot as the vehicle was destroyed. *It was the drone—it must have dropped something!* He raised his weapon to shoot at the drone, but it was obscured by the black, oily smoke that rose skyward.

All of the lights went on in the hotel. "Shit," he muttered, taking several steps back towards the parking lot. Vixen followed a few feet behind. "What do we do?"

Then a sharp trio of cracks came from the sign across the street. Vixen muttered a dull, "oomph," then fell face-first on the pavement. Darius dove behind the Hampton Inn sign as a shot came at him, ricocheting off the brick top of the sign.

Grappling with his shoulder mic, he barked off a quick report. "This is bravo patrol. Drones are dropping explosives on the parking lot. We are taking fire near the entrance." He looked over at Vixen and for a moment thought she was dead. Slowly, her head turned towards him, and her arms shifted.

More gunshots went off from a different direction. The lobby glass exploded inward from the gunfire, and several rounds hit windows where soldiers were moving to see what was happening in the parking lot. A secondary explosion went off with the bus, throwing more debris skyward and illuminating the parking lot with a fresh ball of crimson flames that rolled skyward.

Darius gestured to Vixen to keep down. "Are you okay?" he called to her.

She winced. "No," her feeble voice replied. Gone with the rough expression she usually wore. What remained was a woman desperate and afraid.

More shots rang out, this time from the north side of the hotel, farthest from his position, shattering more windows. Again he heard the buzzing sound over the parking lot. To get a clear view, he pushed aside a hedge that was a few feet from the sign. He saw the tiny dot of light on the drone; then he could make it out. It was black, barely lit up by the parking lot lights. Under it was something bulbous. As Darius raised his weapon, he identified what it was … *a mortar round!*

The drone released it over one of the trucks; they darted away into the night. The round dropped with eerie precision on the vehicle, blowing it apart, adding another fireball in the Midland, Texas night sky. There was another, off in the distance. *They are hitting our folks at the Holiday Inn too!* The truck closest to the one hit by the mortar round exploded next—not from a drone but by its mere proximity.

His mind rapidly went over his options, and he settled on the best course of action—getting Vixen to safety. Turning back to her, he spoke loud enough for her to hear over the popping and cracking of gunfire around them. "Vixen, I am going to get you out of here," he said, shouldering his weapon. Can you walk?"

She shifted her body slightly, wincing in pain. "No."

Darius knew he could drag her, but it was a long distance to the hotel, and they were under fire. He glanced around at possible cover along the way. Going through the parking lot was best, but the risk of the drones was still present. Some cover was better than no cover. His heart was pounding as he squatted, ready for the run. "I'm going to drag you. Stay with me, don't black out."

Vixen nodded.

Drawing a deep breath of cool night air, he sprinted to her, grabbing her tactical vest at the shoulders and started to pull her. Shots rang out the moment he got his grip, but he ignored them. At his side, the asphalt was pockmarked from near misses, but he pulled her backward, ignoring them. He reached the parking lot and moved behind one of the boxy M-113s as several rounds pinged off of its armor near him.

Now that we're safe, I can shoulder her and move faster. Bending down in the dim light of the parking area, he looked at her face. Vixen's eyes stared skyward, open, unblinking. *No!* The relaxed expression on her face, devoid of life, was something that he had seen before ...

Two years earlier ...
La Verne, Los Angeles, California

Darius's home was made of green and blue nylon. The tent had an ugly brown smear on one side, and no matter how much he tried, he couldn't clean it off. The tent and their sleeping bags had been provided courtesy of the California government's, "Roofs for the Displaced," program. For him and John, it meant they had a roof over their head for those rare, rainy days, and a hint of privacy.

John had been interred for a year and a half in the California Transformation and Development Facility, the new fancy name for the old California Institution for Men. The TRC news pieces about the prison claimed that participants, their new word for inmates, got a good education and trade skills. John had told him that the shop where they were supposed to learn was more of a weapons factory, so that the gangs could protect themselves and go after each other. Gangs ran the place, with the guards simply doing their best to keep the 'participants' inside. Darius had been there when John had gotten out, taking him under his wing.

Living on the streets was rough, rougher than the nights he had spent in the desert on deployment. Drugs and the people that dealt them were those in charge. Some dealers organized the housing disenfranchised into robbery gangs that would travel out to the nicer neighborhoods at night and rob the locals. Drug stores, Target's, and Nike stores were favorite targets for fencible goods. There was a running joke that the homeless had better shoes than the people living in homes around them. Darius managed to stay away from the drugs. He made some money at odd jobs. The garbage service that worked the neighborhood gave him a part-time job three days a week riding a truck, picking and tossing residential garbage cans in the back. It was filthy work and hard lifting, but there was a sense of accomplishment. He was paid in cash, under the table, which also helped.

He had tried to get John to do it, but his former partner didn't have the drive for it. Losing their business had devastated him; then had come the humiliation of prison. Yes, he had been released after eighteen months, but his time in the facility had done something to him. John seemed like an empty husk of a man, devoid of the drive and energy that Darius always liked about him. *He's my brother still; somewhere deep inside him, the man I knew is still there.*

As he approached the tent on the sidewalk, he saw Crazy Maxine from the tent in line, standing by the door flap. Her stench greeted him before he made eye contact. That was what was odd about living on the street. You never smelled yourself or your tent mate, but the stink on other people could be overpowering. "Dar – John isn't doing good," she muttered. "I heard him moaning. I tried to wake him. He ain't moving." She stepped away from the tent slowly, tentatively.

Darius moved in and threw back the flap. John was lying there before him, shirtless, wet with sweat. Kneeling by his friend, he felt his forehead. *He's burning up.* "John, John … hey brother, how you feeling?"

John didn't respond; his blank eyes stared up—even his blinking was slow. Darius took his hand and squeezed it, but it was limp in his grip. Rifling through the dirty clothing thrown about the tent, he found the cheap flip phone that the state provided the homeless. He called 9-1-1. The woman that answered was so casual, so calm; it bothered Darius. She asked the nature of the call, and he cut her off.

"My friend is sick. He needs to get to the emergency room."

"I see this as a state-issued phone," she said, meaning that she knew he was homeless. "What is your location?"

"B Street and Bell, right on the corner." He could hear the click of her fingernails on the keyboard.

"Very well, and your name?"

"Darius Thorne," he replied, giving John's hand a squeeze of assurance. "My friend is John Livingston."

"I have you in the queue," she replied. "Help should arrive in the next hour and a half."

"That long? Look, he's really sick, not responding."

"I will note that. They will contact you at this number when they are close."

Darius felt a wave of anger wash over him. I should have known better. The Newmerican FedGov had nationalized healthcare. There were priorities, queues, and processes. The housing disenfranchised—they were low on everyone's lists. *If we die, it helps them get rid of us as a problem.* He became lost in his rage, and only the woman's voice on the phone shattered it. "Did you hear me, Mr. Thorne?"

"Yeah," he said.

"Help is on the way," she said, no doubt reading off her script. Then the call went dead.

Darius drew a breath to try to calm himself, but a gurgling sound next to him shattered that. Looking down at John, he saw his chest was no longer rising and falling. His eyes stared skyward, blank, devoid of his soul.

Darius hammered his chest as he had been trained to do, administering CPR, but it was to no avail. He cried, alone in that tent, stopping and cradling his brother in arms close to him. *This was all so wrong, all of it. You shouldn't have had to die like this, on the street. You deserved better.* "I'm so damn sorry, John," he sobbed. "I should have been here with you sooner." Guilt, rage, and sorrow consumed him in those moments.

Three years later ...
Midland, Texas

Darius tried CPR on Vixen, but something deep inside told him that the effort was more for him than for her. He blew into her mouth, pressed her chest, but nothing changed. Another distant explosion jarred him back to the reality that she was dead. He had seen men and women die all over the planet, but that did not numb him from the mental agony that came with each loss. Another bullet pinged off of the M-113 above him. He had thought he was safe there, but knew he was not.

I'm not leaving her here ...

Grabbing her, he threw Vixen over his shoulder, then rose slowly from a crouch and eyed the lobby of the hotel. His muscles protested, but he didn't care. He broke into a run, aiming for the shattered window frame of the lobby so he would not have to deal with the door. Shots cracked around him, and he heard the distinct pings of ricochets. There was a tug on his back but no pain, which he was thankful for. He half-jumped through the shattered window, landing in the lobby and running fast off to a side hallway to get out of the line of fire. He almost slipped on the marble tile floor as he skidded to a stop.

Helpful hands from another member of the Veterans Corps grabbed onto Vixen, pulling her off of him. It was then that he saw she had been shot again during the sprint in. *That shot was meant for me.... She saved my life.*

"What do we do?" Private Snow asked him.

"What's the word from the Captain?" Darius panted out.

"The officers are pissing themselves," Snow replied. "These damned Texans are all armed." Another explosion out in the parking lot drove the point home.

Texans and their damned guns. "We need to get in some hard cover positions; get eyes on where they are firing from."

"We need to bug out."

Darius saw the flames from the destroyed vehicles lighting up the night. Sergeant Ingersoll appeared with his tactical gear thrown on over his white T-shirt. His mere presence was enough to shake the panic from those troops in the hallway. "We are not playing their game," the sergeant muttered. "That's what they want. If we rush out there, they will pick us off, shoot us to pieces. Thorne is right; we need to get eyes on them—shoot at them."

Darius nodded as the sergeant barked out orders. *This is going to be a long, damn night ...*

South of Clovis, New Mexico

General Reager stared through his binoculars at the artillery rounds cratering Cannon Air Force base along the Texas border. The American forces were stalemated to the north, and to the south, the Newmericans had punched into Texas, taking Midland. Clovis had been a bitter battle, with Oregon National Guard troops digging in against them. They had been fighting for days with no progress. His analysis of the battle was simple—they wanted the Americans to try to pry them out; then they would fall back into Clovis. Urban fighting always favored the defenders. If we get drawn into that, we'll bleed troops for a pointless objective.

Trip's solution was to swing wide around them. There was a risk that the Newmericans would push off into Texas, but he knew they would be cut off if he was successful. Their supply lines would be severed, leaving them easier to eventually pick off. It was a risk, but one he was willing to take. He understood better than most that war was about logistics more than tactics.

His troops had shelled the base for the last half hour, cratering the runways. He had spared the hangers and ammo storage, knowing that those facilities were worth more intact. The base's Air Force security was putting up some resistance, but Trip was keeping his forces at a distance—out of their range.

Weaving around the explosions, he saw a desert camouflage-painted M-1008 Commercial Utility Cargo Vehicle (CUCV), with a bed sheet hung as a white flag, driving towards the chain link perimeter fence. Well, this should be interesting. "Cease fire," he called out to his communications office. "Hold all fire."

Trip called for a Humvee to take him forward. Sitting in the passenger seat, he directed the driver to close on the vehicle. The Humvee stopped some fifty feet from the fence. Trip stepped out alone. He wasn't concerned about this being a trap. *They shoot me here—my people will level this place.*

As Trip walked to the fence, An Air Force Colonel stepped out. His duty uniform was covered with a thin layer of dust. Reager planted his fists on his hips defiantly as the older man approached. "General Reager, I presume."

Trip nodded and the colonel continued. "I am Colonel Spires, USAF."

"What can I do for you, Colonel?"

"You are shelling a Department of Defense facility," the Colonel said. "Your fight is with the Newmericans, not with us. I demand you cease this attack now."

Trip admired the bravado. It made him want to chuckle, and he did.

"Did I say something funny?"

Trip nodded. "In fact, you did … starting with the word, 'demand.' You are not in a position to issue demands from where I stand."

"The Department of Defense's official policy is to not take sides in this civilian conflict."

Trip still smiled as he spoke. "There's plenty of blood on the DoD's hands, Colonel. Generals Donaldson and Rinehart both were on active duty before they were given command of the Newmerican forces. Plenty of DoD facilities are assisting Newmerica in this civil war, not to mention troops."

"A lot of our people, and a few of our bases have joined your side as well."

"True. But the DoD chose sides when it refused to come to the President's aid the night of The Fall. You ignored the orders of the Commander-in-Chief and left him to die."

His words hit with precision. Trip could see the crimson color fill the colonel's face, highlighting his gray hair. "We could discuss policy decisions all day, sir. I want you to stop shelling this base."

"I will, with your surrender."

"I am not authorized to surrender this post."

"Colonel Spires, we both know you provided vehicles and support to the Newmericans. We both know that the DoD policy is a fallacy that you are trying to hide behind. You've been assisting the Newmericans by letting them fly drones off of your runways."

"The Newmericans leased that permission."

"If you hope that hiding behind some technicality is going to save you, you are mistaken. Those are Air Force drones. You're aiding and assisting my enemy, which makes your little base a legitimate target."

"I disagree."

"And I don't care. If you know anything about me, then you know I don't pussyfoot around. I hope you're smart enough to know that your paltry security force is too weak to defend against my armor and infantry if push comes to shove. I also don't give a hot wet shit about what you are authorized to do or not do. I'm fighting a war, and your base is going to fall. If you choose to fight, a lot of your people are going to die, and for what? Holding a base that's going to be worthless rubble in a few minutes?"

"I know your reputation. You, sir, are no gentleman."

"I'll give you that," Trip replied with pride. "I'm trying to end this civil war as quickly as possible with as little loss of life as I have to. If you know my reputation, you know I am not kidding around."

The colonel fumed in silence for a few long moments. His light blue eyes locked with Trip's when he finally replied. "I do this under protest."

"Noted. Have your people assemble and stack arms until you can be processed."

"Can I assume we will be treated as noncombatants?"

"Hell no," Trip smirked. "You gave up that right when you started letting the enemy use your base and personnel for drone attacks."

"When this is over," Colonel Spires said through gritted teeth. "I will see you hang."

"Maybe. In the meantime, you'll be spending your days in a POW camp."

CHAPTER 21

"The patriarchy is always lurking in the shadows, waiting to take away what is equitably yours."

Air Freight Terminal, Albuquerque International Sunport, Albuquerque, New Mexico

Caylee entered the small FedEx terminal office, which was little more than a few chairs and a counter with an opening and a scale to weigh incoming packages. The girl behind the desk seemed downright chipper, smiling broadly when she stepped in, followed by Raul, Faust Kidder, Sam Patheal, Travis, and Andy. Patheal had remained with the prisoners, but the Rangers and the other SOL units had debarked outside of the camp and were each working their way back to their respective homes or their next assignments. It had been tempting to keep them with the party, but it only made their group larger, possibly attracting more attention

"What can I do for you?" the young woman asked.

"My friends and I need to talk to someone about the security here," Caylee said, casually checking her watch. "I have something I want to ship, and I want to make sure that it is safe."

She smiled. "Let me get our head of security," she said. "I assure you, Federal Express takes security of our packages seriously, she said, punching several buttons on her desk phone. "I will pull up our insurance options for you, just to give you more protection."

She's upselling the wrong person. "Thank you."

The security person came from the back, waddling slightly as he walked. When he saw Caylee, he tried to suck in his gut, but it was a losing proposition. He wore a dark blue shirt and black pants that were straining to hold his girth just above the beltline. He had three chins and no neck that was discernable. This is a man that couldn't get hired by the TSA, which is amazing on its own. This might just be easy.

"Howdy, ma'am. How can I help you?" He paused and stroked his light red mustache.

She eyed his badge, "Clint Lubben." Her eyes drifted to his Glock, worn on the left side. If it came down to shooting, where he drew from would be a factor. She eyed the exits and calculated what it would take to get out, if she had to. Old habits die hard.

"Mr. Lubben, my friends and I have some cargo to ship. We were curious what kind of security you have here to ensure our shipment."

The portly man smiled. "Well, ma'am, there are four of us here at all times. We train at the TSA facilities. I can assure you, whatever you are shipping is going to be safe."

"And where are your other security personnel?"

"One is at the intake, the other two are outside with their eyes on the cargo containers."

"If you have problems, the regular TSA personnel can be brought in, correct?"

"They can. We have a radio frequency that we can signal if needed. So far, we have never needed it." There was a bit of pride in his comments, and she was looking forward to deflating it.

In her mind, she mapped out the best course of action. *Two people here in the lobby, one armed. One landline phone and Mr. Lubben had a belt worn walkie-talkie. They will need securing right after he is disarmed. There are bound to be a few loaders we will have to round up. Then we can load our people, and Faust can get us in the air.*

She turned to Travis. "Travis, what are your thoughts?"

"Talk to Raul."

That was unexpected. Travis was as close to an operative as anyone, but he was differing to Raul to make the call. For a moment, Raul got a bump in terms of respect. "Alright, Raul?"

"I think we can make this work," he said, cracking a smile.

Indeed we can. "I agree." In a fluid motion, she reached to the small of her back where her holster was poised. She pulled her weapon and aimed it right at Lubben, only a few feet from his nose.

He was stunned, and she used that to lean in, unhook his weapon, and pull it from his holster. "There was a commotion behind her, no doubt with the others securing the front desk. Caylee tucked his Glock into her pants and then pulled the walkie-talkie out of its holder. "Mr. Lubben, I suggest that you not panic or overreact. I definitely would not call out for help."

He nodded so quickly that his chins couldn't keep up with the motions. Stepping back, she glanced over and saw that Travis and Sam had secured the counter clerk, who was whimpering with fear. Andy moved forward with a zip-tie and moved behind Lubben to secure his wrists. It took some effort given the rent-a-cops girth, but Andy knew it was necessary.

"Travis, you and Raul are with me. Let's go secure the others," she said in a low, tense tone.

The first guard she came across was sitting at a table playing Candy Crush on his phone when she came up behind him, and pulled her weapon first. He turned and Caylee kicked his chair out from under him, sending him topping to the floor. She planted her knee in the small of his back and zip-tied him quickly. His voice spoke up, to call out, but the pressure of her handgun barrel was in the space where his skull came to rest on his neck. It silenced him. "Ah, ah, ah," she whispered to him. "The last thing you want to do right now is try to be a hero." He nodded silently in agreement.

She didn't see the start of Travis's encounter with another guard, but she saw the results as he lifted the young man up and threw him on the floor. Travis came down on top of him. Sam found the last guard, a young woman, coming out of the employee restroom. He disarmed her quickly as she kept asking who he was.

The baggage handlers were in the employee lounge, a grungy white room with a television, a sofa, a small table and chairs. When faced with weapons pointing at them, none offered resistance. Caylee checked her watch—eight minutes. *Not great, but certainly not bad.* "Alright, Mr. Kidder, you get aboard and start your job. Raul, you go out with Andy and get these people in here. We will stage them here in the cargo area and then load them once we're sure the plane is good to go."

Normally she would calm herself at this stage of a mission, but glancing out the back of the freight terminal, she saw the distant Air Force base. *We have a commercial freight hauler that will be full of people—no match for anything they might throw in the air.* It was sobering enough for her not to let her nervous energy fade.

Until we are in American air space, we are at risk.

The Southern White House
Nashville, Tennessee

The security team ushered Charli into the Attorney General's office, and she entered briskly, with purpose. Jack Desmond clung to life still in the ICU which was a sliver of good news. Beyond that, things looked grim. Thiago Reese had framed Caylee for his crime, at least in the short term. *I have to convince the AG that Caylee is innocent. It would be a hell of a lot easier if she were here and had an alibi.* Charli had an ace up her sleeve, and had him on his way over, just in case he was needed.

The Attorney General was an older woman, and she had steel-tinted hair streaked with white. Her wrinkles were deep and well-earned. After The Fall, she had been a Democrat who had stood up to the progressives in her own party when they seized power. Social Enforcers had rounded her up and thrown her in front of a Tribunal, and they had sent her off to Social Quarantine. She had spent almost five years there, released just a few months before the former VP had been sworn in. Charli presumed he had picked her for the job to show that he could be bipartisan, with the right people. That didn't mean that Charli fully trusted her. "I assume you are here because of the assassination attempt on Jack Desmond," the AG said, gesturing to a chair for her to sit.

"That's right."

The Attorney General rested her arms on the desk between them and locked gazes with her. "Is it safe to assume that your interest in this is because a known associate of yours, Caylee Leatrom, is implicated in this crime?"

Charli appreciated the bluntness. "Yes. I know you have video footage of someone pretending to be Caylee Leatrom being involved in this crime, but I came to assure you it wasn't her."

"It's more than video footage. We have her gun, with her fingerprints on the weapon. Ballistics has already confirmed that it was the weapon used in the crime."

"It wasn't her."

"And how do you know that for sure?"

"She is on a special operation. That, and we had the actual shooter under surveillance at the time. If he hadn't disguised himself as Caylee, we could have stopped him." To make her point even stronger, she pulled out a file with reports and photographs of Thiago Reese and put them on the desk between them.

"Really? That seems remarkably convenient. And who approved this operation that Ms. Leatrom is allegedly on?"

"Jack Desmond," she said, realizing that saying his name would not help her argument.

The Attorney General paused for a moment. "I understand that this woman is your friend. You need to understand that I can't make decisions based on that. I have to execute the law based on the evidence in hand."

"She will be back soon," *I hope.* "She'll be able to clear herself."

"Look, Ms. Kazinski, we both have jobs to do. Even if I were inclined to help you on this matter, it has already spilled into the media."

Oh God! "It has?"

"MSNBC started running the story an hour ago … coming right out and naming Leatrom as the killer and implying that we are covering it up, hiding it from the public."

That was news. *Reese has to be behind it.* "As you will see in that file, we believe the shooter was Thiago Reese, another NSF operative. His specialty is toppling governments, and that is likely what he was doing here, attempting to sow discord in our ranks—have us turning on each other. We were tailing him, but when he put on this disguise, he slipped right past my people." It wasn't easy admitting mistakes were made, but Charli was not about hiding facts or distorting the truth.

The Attorney General flipped open the file and spent several silent moments looking at the reports and photographs. Charli's phone chirped, and she checked it. Good, he's in the lobby. "Ma'am, I understand everything points to Caylee, but she is on a mission. I can prove that."

"How?"

Charli walked to the door of the office and opened it. Ted came in, flashing a smile under his beard. “Hello Tulsi,” he said. “It’s good to see you.”

“Ted,” she said, rising and shaking his hand. “I hadn’t expected you here today.”

“Charli told me there was an issue about Caylee, and I thought I might help validate that it couldn’t be her. You see, I’m nominally in charge of planning this little operation. Caylee and a select team are out of the country; specifically, they are in New Mexico. I can’t go into the details for security reasons, but we know she is still there. She isn’t the trigger-person who shot the Chief of Staff.”

Charli hated having to call in Ted for reinforcements, but she was glad she did. The Attorney General leaned back in her chair, crossing her arms. “This puts me in a bit of a quandary.”

“How so?” Ted asked.

“The media is eating this up. MSNBC is claiming we brought in Leatrom, and she flipped on us. It makes everyone, right up to the President, look ignorant if not worse. Factor in that Jack Desmond is the man behind the Sons of Liberty—he’s a damn hero, and the pressure is there to make sure that we pursue Leatrom with the full weight and authority of the DoJ.”

Charli weighed in. “That’s the game they want us to play. He probably was the person who leaked this to MSNBC to force us down the wrong path. We can’t let him call the shots on this. He’s done enough damage already. If you go public and tell the world that we are going after Caylee, you are helping the enemy.”

“She’s right,” Ted said. “You don’t have to dance just because the media is playing the tune. In fact, responding to them only gives them more power.”

She pursed her lips slightly in deep thought. “This hasn’t been made public, but we found fresh blood near where the gun was recovered.”

Bingo! I knew Jack fired his gun; I didn’t know he hit Reese. “We can have that tested against Caylee’s DNA that she submitted for her security clearance.”

“DNA tests take time. I still have this as a problem. The American people want to know that we are actively investigating this case. They will want answers, and with the TRC and all of the nasty outlets out there painting a dark picture, I need to be able to respond and respond firmly."

Ted smiled. "You were in politics long enough to know that sometimes the best answer is deliberately vague, Tulsi. Tell the public you are pursuing several persons of interest. Don't mention Leatrom by name."

"In the meantime, if you can engage your forces in looking for Reese, that will help immensely. I'd hate to see that son of a bitch slip out of the country and back to Newmerica," Charli added.

"You're asking me to place a lot of trust in you, Director Kazinski."

"That's why I brought Ted with me. My people had this guy in their sights, and he slipped by us dressing as a friend of mine; then he shot my former boss and tried to frame the wrong person for it. He's dangerous. I know he's responsible. He's got to be brought to justice."

"She's right, Tulsi. Keep your eyes on the prize. This Reese is the prize."

"Agreed," she intoned. "I will have our law enforcement double-down on the border points—making it harder for him to get back to safe territory. He's been wounded, so we can get word out to hospitals and physicians to be on the lookout for him. I'd love to plaster his face all over the news, but that could easily bite us in the ass. For now, our hunt for this Reese is going to be under their radar. When Caylee Leatrom gets back from this little mission, I want her brought in immediately so that we can rule her out, if indeed, she has nothing to do with this."

Charli nodded. "She's done a lot of things in her life, but she's innocent of this crime. Reese is the real threat. We need him, preferably alive."

"Alright. I'll handle the media; buy us some time. You had better be right about this. If it turns out that it was Leatrom, we are all going to find ourselves hauled up in front of Congress and having to explain our actions."

Charli gave her a silent nod in response. *It's not Caylee. It can't be. We need Reese, so we can prove it.*

White Mountain National Forest
New Hampshire

Getting into the crippled tank had taken the better part of two hours, mostly to wait for the sun to set and the right angle of approach to minimize being shot. Even with that planning, bullets had pinged on the open hatch as Su-Hui and Valerie climbed down. They had to push out the bloody remains of the loader, then close the hatch. Blood streaked down to the floor of the turret where it began to thicken and dry.

He had assumed that loading and firing the tank's weapons would be easy. What he saw was a dizzying array of levers and controls, and he was in the loader station. He felt overwhelmed until he looked at the gunner's position, which Valerie had slid into. It was even more complicated. The air stunk of munitions propellant, sweat, and the metallic aftertaste of copper from the blood in the turret.

"What do we do first?" he asked.

"I've never done this before. That overview they gave us on this thing was minimal. I'm counting on it being easy."

Touching the duel yoke controls and turning them, she made the turret jerk slightly—then she stopped. "Pop the top hatch," she said.

"We just got here," Su-Hui protested.

"We're not leaving. I need a cell signal."

He pushed up on the hatch and could hear the Newmericans firing at it. "Alright," Valerie called up. "I got it."

Moving down next to her, he looked over her shoulder at the YouTube video of a loader slamming a shell into the chamber of the big gun. *I can't believe we are going to be firing at tanks using an online video.* "You think you've got it?" she asked. "Because I need you to put an HE round in."

Su-Hui shrugged and tried to mimic the moves he saw in the video as Valerie looked at how the gunner fired. There was a color-coded chart next to the blast doors, which helped. He accessed the shells and immediately discovered they were heavy—ungodly heavy. For a few moments, he feared he might drop it, which seemed deadly. Flexing all of his upper body strength, he managed to get it into the firing chamber. Then, after a few moments, he could close the breech.

"Loaded," he panted.

"Alright," Valerie said, putting her forehead on the padded surface in front of a small green targeting screen. "Hang on."

She seemed to fidget with the screen and controls for long minutes. Su-Hui leaned over for a moment. "Can I help?"

"No," she growled. "The damn video only went so far. It's hard as hell to sort out what is a target and what isn't, and how do I get the aim right. Look at this shit—atmospherics, earth rotational. They don't pay these gunners enough." Clearly she was frustrated, and Su-Hui leaned back and returned to the loader's seat.

"Okay—here goes nothing!" she yelled.

The turret lurched into motion again, turning away from the Defiance forces and back over the rear of the tank, towards the Newmerican lines. The breech flew back, almost hitting him in the arm and making him wary of it the next time they fired. The air stunk of propellant and his own nervousness. Su-Hui led in behind her, trying to see what she saw. It took long minutes, but she finally said. "Okay, I think I have a target."

"Okay."

She put on ear protection and tightened the strap of her helmet. It took Su-Hui a few moments to find his own ear protection and even longer to get it adjusted to his head. Valerie double-checked her iPhone, watching part of the video again. "This is a shot in the dark," she yelled. With the protection on, her muffled voice was barely discernable. *I pray that this doesn't kill us both.*

The world around him roared and rocked. He hit his helmet on the side of the turret hard as the cannon fired. The spent casing ejected, but he didn't hear it because his ears were still ringing from the shot.

"Load again," Valerie yelled. He barely could make it out, and gave her a thumbs up. Loading the second round was easier and faster. This time he took the loader seat rather than standing hunched over. He patted her on the shoulder to let her know it was ready to fire.

Valerie adjusted the turret slightly, with far less jerking this time; her eyes were fixed on the tiny, green screen at her station. "Here we go again!" she called.

The turret roared once more. Su-Hui quickly loaded again, and once more, she fired.

"Are we hitting them?"

"It's HE. I can only assume that when that shit goes off, people are dying. If nothing else, I'm scaring the shit out of them."

Suddenly a concentrated staccato of bullets slammed into the tank. "Is the machine gun loaded?" she asked.

Su-Hui rose and checked the belts of ammunition. "As far as I can tell."

She tried to fire, but nothing happened. "It's not working."

Su-Hui pulled the belt and saw that it wasn't fed in. He struggled with it, and Valerie rose up next to him to help. She finally pulled a lever that gave a metallic click as it chambered the round. "Alright, they are moving up on us. Let's spray them with this." Returning to her seat, she adjusted the turret and fired.

Compared to the main armament firing, the machine gun purred in his aching ears. She adjusted the turret several times, firing short bursts. The weapon ate the ammo belt incredibly fast. He had to reload after a few minutes.

An explosion went off outside of the tank, rocking it hard, sending Su-Hui half-falling into Valerie. "Shit—I think we pissed them off," she yelled.

"Time to go?"

She nodded. "There's a smoke launcher on the outside. Look for how to trigger it. They both crawled over the controls in both stations, and it was Su-Hui that found it. "This or nothing."

"Punch it."

He did and heard a thunking outside, but we did not know what happened. Another explosion rocked the tank, killing the big turbine engine with a sickening metallic grinding sound. He helped Valerie up to the hatch, and she slid away. Then he followed her.

The two of them darted for the firing trench, diving in head first. The white-gray smoke stung the back of his throat, but it obscured their movements as they ran away from the tank. Every muscle in his body protested as he rolled over. He was still wearing the ear protection, and he fumbled with his helmet to get it off and remove the gear. When they came off, the universe around him was a hundred times louder, adding to his headache.

Rising slightly from cover, he saw a missile hiss in and slam into the already crippled tank. It exploded, tossing him backward in the trench. A bit of twisted, hot metal, either from the tank or the exploded missile landed next to him. It sizzled on the moisture of the dirt.

Inching up the trench again, he saw the burning tank; the heat ripples were so intense that he could feel it even as far away as he was.

Another artillery round went off near the tank, forcing him down. Su-Hui followed Valerie and squatted down into the trench. They almost stumbled into an intersection in the trench line heading to the rear, and they darted under the concrete slabs to put some distance from their former position.

He arrived in a bunker some 200 feet back from the trench he and Valerie had been in. Hachi was there, and when she saw him, she wrapped her arms around him. He was fairly sure she said, "I love you," but it was muffled and fighting the competition from mortar rounds going off outside the bunker. He spoke back loudly, "I love you too," hoping he had chosen the right response given his temporary deafness.

A New Hampshire National Guardsman fired an M248 light machine gun out one of the firing ports of the bunker. Trudy approached him. "You were lucky to get out of there. They are moving into that trench you were in."

Su-Hui had given Hachi his rifle, and she handed it back to him. As he rose, an artillery round hit right in front of the bunker they were in. The thunderous explosion threw Su-Hui flat on the floor. The ground throbbed and made his own body quake as the shock waves passed. His headache surged anew as he heard the echoes of the explosion ripple across Defiance's defensive zone.

Dirt and smoke filled the air and stung at his nostrils as he tried to get his bearings. Pushing himself upright, he checked Hachi, who lay a few feet away. She grabbed at her left thigh, and he saw a six-inch splinter of wood from the roof the bunker, sticking out of her camouflage pants. The dark maroon stain of blood marked where it had punctured her body.

Memories of the fear he had felt at Lisbon surged in his brain. He had feared that Hachi had been killed in the bombardment that leveled the town. It was a miracle that she had survived. He hugged her tight and didn't want to ever relax.

"I'm fine," she whispered in his ear between explosions.

"I need to get you to the medics."

She relaxed her grip on him and looked at the splinter. Reaching down, she jerked out the fragment of wood. There wasn't a lot of blood, nothing showing that an artery had been hit, but Su-Hui did not want to take chances. "I will carry you."

She cocked her heard at his words. “You can’t.”

“I will surprise you,” he replied. Sweeping his arms under her, he lifted her small body and held it tight to him. She wrapped one arm around his neck. “Valerie—you are in charge.”

“Get her to safety,” Valerie snapped, rising to fire at the approaching troops.

Safety? Where in this carnage is that?

CHAPTER 22

"Doubt in your leaders is doubt in yourself."

Stewart Newburgh Airport, New York

Major Mercury watched as Captain Paredes slammed back the coffee, wincing as he did so. The small flight break room was in the Marine refueling offices. It could have been at any airport, the look was so familiar and so dull. "You want more?" Judy asked. There was little for her to do at this stage, and she found that frustrating. Taking the airport was a big job; holding it was tricky, but Judy wanted to be in the thick of the fighting.

They were still an hour or so from sunrise. It had been a tense night with the helicopters out waging their deadly secret war against the air forces of Newmerica. The worst part of it was that she had been forced to sit, watch, and listen to the attacks. Judy felt worthless back at the base. *It was a lot more interesting during the Illinois raid. At least I was in the action.*

"Thank you—but no," he said, putting the liberated Marine Corps coffee mug down and rubbing the beard stubble on his chin. He was tired. Judy could see that from the sunken look of his bloodshot eyes. Paredes wasn't the complaining type. He's only happy when he's flying a chopper. Everything else has little meaning to him. "Any word yet on our missing bird?"

Judy shook her head. One of their helicopters, a National Guard Cobra, had gone off the grid during the attack on Hanscom AFB. The base had air defenses that engaged, if only for a few moments before being laid waste. "Nothing yet. We are using the Air National Guard's communications to monitor the Newmerican forces—but they haven't said much since the attack."

He glanced out the window to the hanger where the ground crew and armorers were busy prepping his Black Hawk. "The pilot was Lieutenant Poire. His gunner was Warrant Officer Galbreath. Good people—damn good team."

"We don't know their status," she replied, attempting to soften the loss.

"It's 10,000 pounds of helicopter coming in at over a hundred miles per hour. Add in gravity, and it's not hard to fill in the blanks." The grim form of mathematics played out in his words.

"We can always hope."

Paredes nodded. "Indeed, we can."

"You readying for the next wave?" she asked, hoping to move onto happier subjects.

"That depends. Do we have good comms and air-to-ground support people up there that can guide us in?"

"They have assured me they can paint your targets and call the shots. They also advise that there are still enemy air assets in their battle zone."

Paredes shrugged. "Not entirely surprised. As I stated during the planning sessions, we can plaster the airfields and their equipment on the ground. Anything they had in-flight will find a safe place to land, eventually."

"Helicopters are better at hiding from fighters than engaging them, but the Apache loadouts we have include the modified AGM-122 Sidearm missiles. If any of their flyboys want to go toe-to-toe with us, we will give them a damn good run for their money." He fondled the coffee mug for a moment. "How hot is that battlespace?"

"Hot—very hot," Judy replied. "I haven't gotten a full picture, but the Newmericans are pressing in on all sides. They are trading bodies for yards of ground, though. From what I gathered, their losses are so great that they should have broken off. Apparently they are going all-in."

"Desperation makes people do stupid things. Let's hope that's what we are dealing with."

"Once you take off, I'm getting the transports fueled and prepped.

We will package your folks up and get out of Dodge."

"Much appreciated."

Lieutenant Colonel Mihalek entered the break room and walked over to them. "You doing okay there Lariat?"

He gave a tired nod. "So far. We passed the midterms, but I hear the finals may be brutal."

"You've got this," Mihalek assured him.

Glancing over his shoulder at his Black Hawk, he started for the door. "We're going to dust off and get this shit taken care of. Keep the home lights burning for us."

"Roger that," Judy replied as he walked out.

Mihalek stood next to her, watching Paredes begin to do his visual check of the helicopter in the morning light. "They are going to be flying into a hell of a battle."

"Yes, they are," she said solemnly as Paredes finished his walk-around and climbed aboard the Black Hawk.

"Some of them won't be coming back." His voice was like that of her own conscience.

She drew a long breath of air in through her nose, then spoke. "I know. I have known that since we started planning this mission." She hated speaking the words out loud, but there was no choice. "We did all we could to minimize losses."

"This is war. People die. You've lost people under your command before. You've done your job; you've minimized the risks as much as humanly possible."

"What I hate about this job is the numbers," she confided, not lifting her gaze from the helicopter. "If we didn't come here, a lot more people would die up in New Hampshire. Our choppers are going to fly through hell, but the damage they inflict will hopefully be enough to tip the scales in our favor."

"That's the part of being an officer that sucks ass," Mihalek said. "You aren't just looking at the calculus of a battle—you are playing with the numbers, trying to get better results each iteration. I would be more worried if you didn't understand the realities of this kind of operation—if you lied to yourself about what was about to go down. We can always fudge things, add in variables to the equations, but in the end, the math always wins." As he finished, she heard him walk away, leaving her alone to watch the helicopter.

"How's our perimeter?" she asked, simply to change the subject.

"Good so far. The NSF knows something is going on here, but they're keeping their distance. Blowing up an armored vehicle will do that. They have probably reached out to the military, trying to figure out whose job it is to intervene. That's the advantage we have—bureaucracy. We aren't likely to hear from them until later today."

Judy nodded in response. That was what she thought as well. *We've got enough firepower to defend ourselves if we have to. If they blast our transport aircraft though, we are going to be stuck here—behind enemy lines.* It was a sobering thought.

The engine began to whine and roar to life, and slowly, the rotors started their scythe-like cutting of the air. Judy stiffened as she saw Paredes glance over at her and give her a thumbs up. She returned the gesture, forcing a smile to her face.

Please God—bring them all back.

The District

The Vice President waited as the call went through. The fighting in New Hampshire had her in constant contact with her People's Warden assigned to General Rinehart, Veronica Hinkley. Reports coming to her only confirmed what the VP felt about the military. *For all of their machismo, they are cowards. So he's taken losses; that is what the military is for. What good are they if they turn tail and run every time some of them are hit?* Rinehart was talking about pulling back from the White Mountain Forest, something that the Vice President refused him permission to do. "No retreating!" had been the words she had barked to the General while Hinkley held the phone.

Now she faced another problem—Midland Texas. Starting the night before, the locals had been sniping at the Newmerican invasion force that had taken refuge there. With the sunrise, the citizens were joined by elements of an American military group. Now they were trapped in Midland—surrounded, with many of their vehicles knocked out of commission by improvised drones. Their infantry was pinned by local snipers with guns.

The armed civilians infuriated her. *We should have gone door-to-door in every state, rounding up every gun and bullet we could find and dealing with the violators. We relied too much on the gun registration system to hunt down weapons. We were too soft on these gun owners. We arrested hundreds of thousands of them, but most paid fines and went home. We killed the more fanatic holdouts in sieges, which was just fine. Now we are paying a price for not just taking the guns, but dealing with people that would own them.*

Guns kill people and only enemies of the state own such weapons. I will make sure the TRC plays up on this. When we have our new Constitution, no citizen will be allowed to own any weapon ... that is best to maintain order. We will go out looking for guns and their owners. When we find those violators this time, they will go to the camps, and never come out again. It would tie up large parts of the NSF, but she was convinced that this was the ultimate solution to the gun problem.

Leaving the attack force to die in Texas was a disaster she did not want to contemplate. That meant being creative in order to break the siege … hence the phone call. On the fifth ring, there was a crackle; then a suave voice rose in her ear. "I did not expect to hear from you, madam Vice President," Juan Carlos García said, concealing much of his accent.

"Can't I pick up the phone and call an old friend?" she said with a faint smirk.

"I did not know we were friends. I saw us as merely having a mutually beneficial arrangement."

"Such arrangements create the bonds of friendship."

"Yes, but in this case—not so much."

Soon after the Ruling Council had secured power in the District, they had opened dialogue with the Mexican drug cartels. It made perfect sense. The Mexican government only held a thin grasp of power in the nation—not much beyond the city limits of Mexico City. When she and Daniel had first come to power, the cartels wielded the actual power and authority in Mexico.

Daniel had insisted on backing one cartel, García's, as the means to bring stability to the border. There were three large cartels and dozens of smaller ones. The Ruling Council had provided García's people with the firepower needed to consolidate and remove their competitors. There had been a year of vicious mob-like war down in Mexico, with no one being the wiser as to who was arming García's people. Eventually, one cartel, one friendly to them, was the true power in the region.

The tradeoff for that was a slowing in the flow of drugs and displaced refugees into Newmerica. The drugs were the true target, especially fentanyl. Controls were put in place, and the cartel was provided safe routes across the border for the drugs that they shipped. It allowed the FedGov to cut the budgets to the NSF forces patrolling the border. It was a perfect agreement from where the Vice President sat, controlled and stabilized. "Come now Mr. García," she said. "We have had an arrangement in place between us for years now. We are neighbors. From time to time, neighbors ask each other for assistance. That's all this call is."

"So you need our help."

"Yes. Some of our troops are currently surrounded in Midland, Texas. I hoped that you would come and help get them out of that situation."

There was a pause for a few moments, when the head of the García cartel said nothing. "My people have been monitoring the events in Texas. Your people are facing a great deal of resistance."

He's been monitoring what is happening—that in itself is intriguing news. "The situation there is why I am asking for your help."

"The Americans don't know about our little arrangement. If I send my people north, into your country, it will be like when Pancho Villa raided the US. It will cause a reaction. I am not sure I want to deal with that kind of problem. The American President is likely to see this as an invasion and respond in some way that neither of us can anticipate."

"That man is a Pretender to the Presidency. He does not represent that legitimate power in our nation. He is a traitor, and his government is one of revolt."

"So you say. He might say the same thing of you."

He needs the stick before the carrot. "Consider this, Juan. If the Americans prevail in this conflict, our arrangement will be thrown out the window. You would be returning to the old days of walls being built on the border of the DEA blocking your supplies. If this Pretender and his allies are successful, a great deal of what we have built together will be lost."

"Your concern for my financial well-being is touching," García said. "Of course, if they win, you and your President will be imprisoned—or worse. We will find a way around what the Americans put in place, should they be victorious. I doubt you will be as lucky."

She ignored what he said. It was far easier to disregard the implications, than to mentally process them. *We can't afford to lose; Daniel and I both know that.* García's words were goading her, despite her efforts to keep her frustration in check. *I need to offer him something that makes this easier, more palatable.* "I prefer to think in terms of the positive. We are both reasonable people Mr. García. If you were to help us in this matter, I think it might be possible for us to make some adjustments to our existing arrangement to compensate you for the minor risks that you are taking."

"What did you have in mind?"

"Why don't you tell me what you think will help you cope with your conscience on this request."

Another momentary pause came back at her. "We would need your assurance that our involvement would not cause retaliation by this so-called Pretender."

"Done."

"You are fast to say that, especially when you are calling for us to relieve your invasion force," he quipped back.

She refused to take the bait. "This is a minor reversal at best."

García was unimpressed with her confidence; she could hear it in his voice. "We would want to increase our shipments across the border. I would estimate a 25 percent increase."

"That seems high, given that we are asking for a one-time favor."

"I am putting the stability of the country that I control in jeopardy by giving your people aid. This is not something that I intend to negotiate."

"Agreed. For a year?"

"Going forward, madam Vice President."

She felt a tinge of anger rise in her, and her skin was hot with his words. "I may be able to convince President Porter of this arrangement."

"We also have been flooded with refugees lately from Cuba and Venezuela. I have little need for such people. Newmerica has always been willing to accept people and give them homes. I will be passing these people on to you at your border. They are not wanted back here in Mexico. We have our own problems that must be addressed."

"We would be honored to give them a taste of Newmerican freedom."

"Then your terms are acceptable," García replied coolly.

"I will provide a point of contact with our people in Midland, the People's Warden, for that force. He will coordinate with you on how you extract our force there."

"That is acceptable. We will be there in, shall I say, two days."

The Vice President paused for a few moments. "May I ask how you are going to pull this off?"

"You may ask, madam Vice President. I assure you, you do not want to know those details. Being in the dark provides you with a degree of deniability. I suggest you embrace it." There was something ominous about his words.

"Very well. Thank you for your enlightened leadership and assistance."

"Thanks are unnecessary. Simply adhere to the terms of our bargain." With that, the line went dead.

He has me over a barrel. That may very well be the case for the moment, but that will change over time. García is entitled to his arrogance. When this war is over, I will deal with him. For now, one war is more than enough for us to deal with.

CHAPTER 23

"Devotion to your religion is potential treason. You do not need a church to give you morals, the FedGov can do that far more effectively."

Albuquerque International Sunport, Albuquerque, New Mexico

Raul helped the last of the freed prisoners climb up into the belly of the FedEx aircraft. The late night rescue, combined with their deteriorating state of heath and the long ride to the airport, had left many of the party exhausted. Add in the tension, and the former prisoners could not hurry. Travis and Andy had positioned some of the cargo containers between the jet and the freight terminal to block anyone that might see them loading people into the aircraft.

The hardest cargo to get in was the encased bodies that Andy had recovered. They had jagged edges from where they had been chiseled out of their burial spot. He had made sure they were wrapped in moving blankets, both out of respect and to make them easier to handle.

Raul and Travis remained on the ground to supervise loading while the rest of their team was aboard the aircraft. Travis had secured them some FedEx shirts and ball caps. While Raul's shirt was far too big for him, putting it on made them look like slovenly cargo loaders.

Things had gone well so far, which was something that Raul had come to believe was deceptive. The guards and ground crew had been captured and tied up in a break room. Sam Patheal helped Raul with the last of their precious cargo; then he pulled down the big doors that secured the aircraft. "This has been too easy," Raul said out loud. He wasn't bragging, it was the voice of concern.

Travis looked around the tarmac. "Yeah. I hear you Raul. Keep sharp."

Faust Kidder signaled from the cockpit. "The fueling truck is on its way over," he transmitted to Raul's radio. "You two had better get up here. I don't plan on hanging around long after we get gassed up."

Travis went up the roller passenger boarding ladder, a set of steps, leading up to the aircraft. Raul hovered for a few moments at the bottom as the refueling truck arrived. Kidder waved to them as they went about pumping the fuel, and Raul remained at the bottom of the steps; his eyes darted around the terminal, looking for threats.

As they finished the fueling some ten minutes later, Raul saw a Cushman cart approaching with a trio of men in TSA uniforms heading right for the aircraft. He slowly pulled the radio up and pressed the transmit button. "We have company coming."

"Roger that," was Kidder's voice.

Glancing up the stairs, he saw Caylee standing at the door. There was no sense of tension in her face. There was an air of strange calm in her eyes as she gave Raul a single nod. Just knowing that she was nearby gave him a surge of confidence. As the cart pulled up near the foot of the walkway to the airplane, Raul stepped forward a few long strides to meet them.

"Hello," he said plainly.

"I don't recall seeing you here before," the tallest of the TSA agents said, walking towards him.

"I just started here."

"Well, we had a strange report from the tower," the tall man said. "They said they saw you loading people in your cargo hold."

Raul forced a laugh that was downright authentic. "People? That's crazy. We were loading cargo."

"Regardless," a portly TSA agent said, sliding out of the front passenger seat of the Cushman. "We are going to need you to open those hatches and let us check the aircraft."

Raul's mind was alight with focus. If bullets started flying toward the aircraft, the people they were carrying would have little protection. The thin skin of the aircraft would puncture easily. The training that Caylee gave him kicked in. He walked to the flank of the man, away from the aircraft. If they start shooting, the plane doesn't need to be behind me.

There was another reason to put the aircraft off to their rear. Caylee was no longer visible, but he had no doubt that she was on the move. His repositioning would give her some cover.

"I'm not sure I'm authorized to do that," Raul replied lightly. "I will have to check with my supervisor."

The portly TSA agent put his hands on his belt. As he tried to puff out his chest, the race between that and his stomach was easily won by his gullet. "You go ahead and do that."

Raul lifted the radio slowly and pressed the transmit button. "Hello, Mr. Kidder. These TSA agents say that they need to check the cargo of this aircraft."

"Is that so?" Faust replied. "Well, you can tell them that we don't have time for that bullshit." Raul was fairly certain that Kidder's voice carried far enough for all three men to hear him.

"He says, *no*," Raul told them regardless.

"Now son," the tall main said firmly, taking another step toward him, closing to about five feet. "You are new at this, so I will cut you a little slack. We are NSF-TSA. When it comes to the safety and security at airports, we are the final word. I suggest you walk over there and open that aircraft hatch. If you don't, we will." His voice wasn't as much demanding as it was resolved.

Raul didn't want to kill these men. He hated taking lives unless it was necessary. Balancing that was the fact that he would not put the entire mission at risk. *I can take one of them without using my gun, perhaps two. Taking all three, I will be in trouble.* The pistol he carried was stuffed in the small of his back in his beltline, and the urge to grab it grew with each pounding of his heart in his ears. The tallest one, clearly the leader, was the most important to disable.

"I don't want any trouble," he said, raising his hands slightly to show they were empty and stepping closer. "Especially with the TSA." As Caylee had taught him, the best way to keep your enemy from pulling their weapon was to make yourself as little a threat as possible.

The taller man didn't sense any danger. With Raul's words, he even cracked a smile. "Good," he replied, grinning.

Raul's mind mapped out his attack just as he had trained with Caylee. He stepped into a jab at the man's throat, hitting it hard, collapsing his windpipe. Stepping straight in, the tall man's body blocked his actions from his counterparts, buying Raul a few moments. The TSA agent was stunned; his eyes were big, round, and full of panic as he gasped for air and reached for his throat. Raul took another swing, this time coming around with a haymaker aimed at the man's side. The impact was hard, sending ripples in the flesh as his fist dug deep towards the man's kidney.

The other two rose, sensing something was wrong. The tall man doubled over. His face was red with startled pain and terror.

Raul jumped over him as he fell, coming down on the portly man's right foot with his own shoes. The round man reached for his weapon, and Raul punched him in his cheek and the side of his jaw—colliding hard with the boxer's sweet spot. For a moment, the blood was cut off to his brain, and his eyes rolled back in his head as he toppled backwards.

The remaining TSA person fumbled to undo his holster clasp and pull his weapon. Raul did not hesitate in pulling his own. Leveling the aim of the gun, the TSA agent pulled his gun free. As he raised his eyes, he saw that Raul already had aim at him.

He hesitated. It was perfectly natural. If the situation had been reversed, Raul would have probably responded the same way. Then a blur of motion and color swept in at the man striking him in the head from the rear. *Caylee!* Three fast blows to the man near his jaw and ear disabled him, dropping him hard face first onto the tarmac.

"You okay?" she asked. Her fists were ready for more action as she eyed the three men.

Raul's breath was heavy, but he nodded quickly. "I had him."

"I know," she replied, cracking a grin that he interpreted as pride. Bending down, she zip-tied the man as he did the same with the gasping tall man, who finally was getting air. They pulled their weapons and radios, smashing the latter on the tarmac under their shoes. As Caylee tied off the portly man, she glanced over at Raul whose hands were starting to tremble as the adrenaline flushed through his system. "Whoever trained you did a heck of a job," she smirked.

"She's not only good; she is modest."

"Come on," she urged. "We need to get out of here."

Raul looked at the three men near the Cushman cart, tied and either in pain or unconscious. He finally felt as if he had somehow graduated. He was still a student, and Caylee was the teacher, but he was able to apply what he learned in real life. As he followed her up the steps to the airplane, he could not hide his glee.

White Mountain National Forest
New Hampshire

The trek to the heart of the Defiance defenses took Su-Hui and Hachi nearly an hour. It involved hunkering down through dim tunnels, winding through snaking trenches in the darkness and through crowded pillbox positions packed with people. Su-Hui carried his wife, despite the aches in his lower back and arms, never once wavering. When he was momentarily exposed, he saw the tracers stitching through the darkness, incoming and outgoing. Smoke, invisible in the darkness, was illuminated by fires and distant explosions, casting strange and eerie shadows over the field. He could taste the gunpowder and smoke from burning fires as he carried his beloved wife to some place safe—as if such a place existed. Once he got her to the aid station, a medic gave her a shot to ease the pain, then cleaned and stitched her wound.

Sandwiches were handed out. While Su-Hui was no fan of tuna, he was so hungry he gulped it down, barely tasting it. He got Hachi to a cot where, hopefully, she could get some sleep; then he sat next to her on a muddy plank that served as a floor. Sleep took him, despite the rumbles and murmurs of those around him.

He was jerked awake in a moment of near panic when someone's boot hit his foot. Hachi was still sleeping next to him. He looked up, and saw the owner of the offending boot, a National Guard trooper. "Are you Su-Hui Zhou?" he asked in a whisper so as not to disturb those sleeping around him.

Su-Hui wiped the crust from the edges of his eyes and slowly rose, "Yes."

"I've been looking for you for a while. The General wanted you to join him."

How long have I been asleep? The aches from his joints did not offer answers other than at least a few hours. The sun was coming up, marking the passage of the night, giving him a sense that he had gotten a few hours' sleep at least. The bright morning clouds were tinged in a reddish hue. The crack and bang of gunfire was diminished, but still present, surrounding him as a deadly reminder of where he was and the risks he faced. The one thing he did notice was that the aerial bombardments and strafing attacks weren't happening. *Maybe they have run out of ammo or things to blow up.* He followed the corporal through a long maze of tunnels and trenches to a bunker deep underground.

The bunker was lit by several LED lanterns. When he arrived, he saw General Griffiths at the large table that dominated the room. His face seemed to sag. The bags under his eyes were dark and fearsome. The other officers and militia members were all as filthy and weary as he was. Valerie Turner was there as well; her black hair was mixed with mud, and dried dust gave it a gray tint.

"I'm glad they found you," Griffiths said, seeing Su-Hui. "We were getting worried that you might be a casualty." The older man turned to the table where a map showed the current positions of both the Defiance defenders and the Newmerican forces. It was a sobering image. The Newmericans had pressed in on three sides with a blocking force to the south in case the Americans tried to break out there. Easily half of the defensive positions were either under their control or dangerously close to the enemy forces. *We've lost a lot of our forward bunkers and trenches—paid for in blood.*

"As you can all see," Griffiths said, pointing to the map. "We are getting squeezed into a tighter space. This has come at a cost for the enemy, however. We estimate they have lost half of their vehicles, including their tanks. They tried to overrun us, using their armor to break our lines. It was sloppy and stupid against fixed positions, and they have paid a high toll to get as much ground as they have. Our drone strikes with mortar rounds have torn up their infantry support."

Major Segal had led the harasser force that lured the Newmericans into their trap. He spoke up with a question. "How bad *are* their losses, sir?"

"Best estimates say Rinehart's people are at almost 30 percent, some units more. Frankly, with these numbers, I'm surprised he hasn't fallen back. You take a modern combat unit and inflict far less than those kinds of casualties on it, it ceases to be combat effective. He just keeps pressing in on us, though."

"Someone is pressuring him," Valerie offered. "He's probably being pushed by the District. They know we are here, in force. This is their first and best chance to bag us all at once in a proper battle. They must be pushing him, regardless of losses."

Griffiths nodded. "That was my thinking as well. I intend to turn this to our advantage. He can't let go, which means he is stuck. For now, I'm willing to trade every yard of ground for a few more of his people. We are going to bleed him, and bleed him badly. We will pretend to be falling back. Then, we go on the offensive—when he's at his weakest."

"Are we able to?" Su-Hui asked.

The General grinned, albeit a small one. "We are, and we will. I have an ace or two up my sleeve, something I've kept secret until now. You've probably noticed that we haven't had a lot of air strike activity overnight. Well, there's a reason for that. A strike team has secured an airfield in striking distance of our position. While we have been fighting here, they have been bombing their airfields and aircraft on the ground. Now they will provide us some much needed air support."

Su-Hui's mouth slowly fell open with those words. It was the first real good news they had since the start of the operation. *If we get air support, we can beat them!* Griffiths continued, "They are going after a couple more of the enemy airports; then we get them overhead. When they arrive, we launch out of here, go right at the jugular." His fingers traced the path of intended attack out of the Defiance defenses, to the north, where the bulk of the Newmericans were poised. "They are not dug in or entrenched. If we hit them hard enough, they will break and run."

"Is it possible?" asked another officer that Su-Hui didn't know.

Griffiths nodded. "This is all about logistics. We are sitting on our stockpiles. They have to trek fuel and munitions quite a way to reach us here. They fired off most of their switchblade drones in the first day of fighting. Their logistics lines have to be thin already, and they have burned through a lot of fuel and ammo for the ground they have gained. They also believe we are incapable of mounting an offensive. We've lost around 25 percent of our tanks and armored fighting vehicles, but the rest are still hidden in concealed positions, waiting for the word to roll. Our main force will strike north, which is where I believe their command and control is based. Major Segal, you will take a strike force and head west. We have word they have a supply hub in Carroll. Your mission is to take that out."

Segal nodded in agreement. "It would be a pleasure, sir."

Su-Hui spoke up. "You said we would be gradually falling back, sir."

"That's right. We need to let them think they are winning, even if the cost to them is high."

"We should rig our trenches and tunnels with improvised explosives—booby traps. It will make them afraid to use our defensive positions against us, and might take a few of them with us."

Griffiths gave him a single nod. "Not a bad idea. Your SOL troops have a lot of experience with IEDs. Can I leave that tasking up to you?"

Glancing over at Valerie, who gave him a supportive nod. "You can count on us."

Looking at the map, Griffiths rubbed his temple momentarily. "We are going to have to be ready to move on a moment's notice. I will give you a pre-determined code phrase. When that hits, we will flip the tables on the Newmericans and let them see what it is like to be on the defensive. You will need to stay in tight communications—coordinate with the units near you. Get to know them, work through the frequency list we provided you. I don't want people to get shot up with friendly fire."

He paused, sweeping the room with his gaze, then continued. "We have been preparing for this fight for months. A lot of good people have died along the way. Everyone in this room has lost someone to this war. I want this to be the last fight here in New Hampshire. I have no intention of letting the enemy get away. The threat to this state by the usurpers needs to come to an end. This is the last battle here, and by God, we will win it."

The older man's words seemed to electrify the air. Despite his weariness, Su-Hui felt renewed—new strength and determination. *This is what we have all been waiting for, an end to this part of the war.* His mind went to images of his son and daughter, and his beloved Hachi. *I have to win; the thought of losing is far too frightening to contemplate—not for me, but for my family.*

Nashville, Tennessee

Charli glanced at the desk of Kiffin Renner, Director of Cybersecurity for America. She was amazed at the toys he had on his desk, action figures, and model starships. *How old is this guy?* His office was dark, no doubt intentionally. He looked every bit the geek, wearing a long sleeve T-shirt with the Hulk on it, chewing on a red Twizzler.

"How exactly can I help you, Director?" he asked, leaning back in his chair.

"I'm a good friend of Jack Desmond and Caylee Leatrom."

The mention of the two of them made him toss the Twizzler stem onto the desk and sit upright. "How is Jack? I tried to go to the hospital, but they wouldn't even confirm he was there, let alone let me in."

"He's in a medically induced coma."

"Damn."

"Someone framed Caylee with the crime. That's why I came here."

Renner's eyes narrowed. "It wasn't Caylee. It couldn't have been."

"I know—but how do you?"

"If it was her pulling the trigger, Jack would be dead."

He certainly knows Caylee. "I agree. Look, what I'm about to tell you is classified; it can't leave this room."

"Everything I do is classified. Caylee is a friend. Whatever you need, you've got."

Charli held back a smile. *Everything I've been told about this guy sounds accurate.* Caylee had gone with Renner into Texas and had hacked the rebels up there, exposing their Newmerica and Chinese ties. "The guy that took the shots was disguised as her, right down to the fake fingerprints on the gun. His name is Thiago Reese, an NSF operative. The problem is that they have framed Caylee pretty well. If I can deliver Reese to them, prove that he did it, well, it saves us from hunting down and arresting Caylee."

"What do you have on this guy?"

She handed him a flash drive. Renner loaded it up and opened multiple windows on his monitor, squinting at each one. "He's on the run?"

"Yes. We think Jack managed to wound him."

"Good. When and where did this go down?"

Charli provided the details. Renner pulled up satellite feeds, etc. "Alright. So we got a super-secret agent assassin, master of disguise, who shot the Chief of Staff and is on the run."

"That's the gist of it."

His fingers flew so fast, it was like watching a professional pianist play. She could only see a little of his screen, but it was clear he was focused, pulling in data sources. "Did this guy have a car?"

She shook her head. "None we found."

"Any known associates?"

Charli thought that over. "No one. Wait. MSNBC broke the story. It was that reporter that General Reager punched … what was her name? Templeton—Pat Templeton."

"You think he had contact with her?"

She shrugged slightly. "Unknown—but just a hunch."

"This Reese-guy will not use a traceable phone—but whatever he has will still ping a tower if he uses it. We know he's not in any hospital or clinic with a gunshot wound because that would raise a red flag with the authorities. I assume he's not at his place; you would have that staked out, which means that he is going to be on the move—looking for help or safety. Let me check car thefts in the region, and I will pull drug stores that might have sold some of the stuff you'd need to treat a gunshot wound."

"You can do that without a warrant?"

Kiff grinned, but his eyes never left his screen. "When Tennessee was part of Newmerica, the NSF got access to all of the security cameras and cash registers, mostly for tracking down undesirables to send off to their camps. While we closed down those programs, I kept some back doors to the access portals, just in case I needed them."

"Not exactly legal."

Kiff nodded. "No it isn't. Then again, the Director of the Secret Service isn't exactly authorized to have me do this kind of search, is she?" He let the question hang in the air between them for a few moments, then spoke up. "Rhetorical question. No, this isn't legal. This is for Jack and Caylee. I'm counting on you not telling and I know I won't."

Charli understood. *Extraordinary times requires extraordinary measures.* After a few long minutes where the only noise was that of Kiff breathing and the sound of his fingers hitting the keyboard, he finally spoke. "Alright, after the attack three cars were stolen in that vicinity. One of those has been recovered by the local cops. That leaves us two that may be in his possession."

Turning in his chair, he looked at his other monitor. "I'm running a routine looking for this car on traffic cameras—let's see if anyone picked him up."

Charli moved around behind his desk, pausing simply to make sure that she was not encroaching on his privacy. He seemed to welcome her gaze. She was stunned at the flurry of numbers and the nearly dozen windows, all seeming to have some sort of activity on them.

One window paused with the image of the car. "There we are. Seen an hour after the incident, at Gallatin Pike and Due." He zoomed in on the license plate. "No good view of the driver, but we got the plate. He's heading north."

Probably trying to get out of town and heading for the border, especially if he's wounded. Charli pulled out her phone and took a photo of the image. "I need to get this out to the State Police and FBI," she said.

Kiff reached over and picked up the stub of his Twizzler, taking a bite. "Go do that. The algorithms I am running are going to take a little while to work."

It was Kiff's way of saying that he needed some time and space. Charli respected that. "Thanks for this," she said, heading for the door.

"Keep close," he said, offering her a Twizzler from the pack. "I don't show this car having crossed any of the borders heading to Newmerican territory."

Albuquerque International Sunport, Albuquerque, New Mexico

Caylee sat in the jump seat in the back of the Airbus A300F cockpit. Faust Kidder maneuvered the big aircraft in a tight arc out of the freight terminal. Her eyes were constantly scanning the distance, looking for law enforcement to make their move, if they had one. The arrival of the trio of TSA agents had been unexpected. *By now they may have pieced together that things are not quite what they seem.*

"Tower, this is FEDEX 211, requesting departure runway," he said into the headset that he wore.

She could hear the murmur of response to Kidder as he continued to creep the aircraft along. While she couldn't make out the words, she could tell that they were tense.

"I have no idea what you are talking about. We have an authorized flight plan, and I need a clear runway tower."

More terse words came back to him. Faust reached down and shut off the headset. "They are asking us to pull back to the terminal."

From the copilot's seat, Travis shook his head. "They suspect something is wrong with those TSA agents."

"Can you take off without clearance?" Caylee asked.

"Yeah," Faust replied, craning his head slightly so she could hear him better. "There's always a risk that we will hit another aircraft. And they can try to block the runway."

Caylee paused for a moment, considering the options. *If we go back to the terminal, the entire mission is scrubbed. They don't likely know who we have in the cargo hold, only that we weren't loading cargo containers and their agents aren't responding.* There was no real choice in her mind. "We have to take off."

"Tell those folks in the hold to lie flat," Kidder said. "This is likely to get bumpy."

Caylee unhooked her belt and went to the cargo door. Opening it, the big open bay of the cargo hold was filled with people. Raul was there, and immediately locked gazes with her. "Alright everyone, lay down. Takeoff is going to be a little rough."

Raul worked his way to the doorway, climbing up the ladder to join her in the cockpit. As he closed the door behind him, he turned to her. "What is up?"

"They think something is wrong," she replied.

"What's our plan?" Raul pressed as the plane accelerated.

"Something dangerous."

Faust turned the headset back on. "Tower, this is FEDEX 211, we are declaring an emergency. We cannot return to the freight terminal. We are diverting to runway three. Have emergency vehicles move to the parking ramp at the end." He then shut off the headset and tossed it to the floor of the cockpit. "They will scramble fire and law enforcement there. We are going onto runway five and punching our way out." Kidder grinned at his ploy.

Caylee took her seat and buckled up, and Raul lowered himself to the floor next to her. She stared at the back of Kidder's head and the realization came to her that she was powerless in the situation. *I hate this. On the ground, I have some control. Up here, I can't do anything.*

She could see the flashing red lights of the fire engines and rescue vehicles moving off to the far end of the tarmac on the parking ramp, fully expecting the Airbus A300F to pull over. Instead, as they got closer, Faust gunned the engines. The turbines roared behind her, and the cockpit was deluged with their sounds. The plane lurched as he turned at a fast speed onto the main runway and immediately sped up. For a moment she almost feared that the plane would tip over; that was how forceful the turn was. Raul lurched over to one side, and she held onto the seat.

"A little fast there," she called up front. Then she felt another surge of acceleration as the jet roared down the runway, pushing her back in her seat.

"I told you, I can fly anything. I just need to get a feel for this girl," he yelled in response.

His diversion seemed to work, at least for the moment. From where Caylee sat, the police and fire vehicles were caught off guard, and the plane passed them. Faust pushed the big jet down the runway, and at the far end, wheeled it around—again almost tipping it over.

Looking down the long stretch of runway, Caylee saw two police vehicles racing straight at them. The engines picked up in intensity and tempo as Faust lurched down the runway at them, preparing to take off.

The police cars didn't swerve or break off. Instead, they seemed to head straight at the jet. Travis spoke up from his seat. "The tower is calling for us to stop immediately."

"Screw them," Kidder replied as his jaw set.

"You do see the police cars, don't you," she said as the jet picked up even more speed.

"I do, pretty lady. Trust me, this is a game of chicken they are unwilling to play."

The jet felt as if it reached the speed for takeoff, but didn't. For a moment, Caylee wondered if there was a problem, or if Kidder really didn't know how to fly it. Then, at the last minute, the plane's nose started to rise. The police cars dove for the sides of the runway, disappearing behind them as the jet began a tight turn and slow climb skyward.

"Jesus," Travis loudly called out. "That was close."

"I knew they'd break off," Kidder said, adjusting his eyepatch as he leveled out.

"So we're clear?" Raul asked, finally sitting upright after the turns and takeoff.

The plane wasn't climbing as fast as what Caylee expected, but was completing its turn and leveling off. *I need to trust that Faust he knows what he's doing.*

"We're in the air," Kidder replied. "That's not the same thing as being clear."

Nashville, Tennessee

It took almost an hour and a half, but Kiffin Renner broke out with a big smile. "Got the asshat," he said with pride. Charli came around his desk and looked at the myriad of windows. "The cell tower data was cross-referenced with the calls that went to the reporter—that gave me his signal. I mapped the highways near there and pulled the local cameras."

"I didn't know you could get the cell data that easily."

"Most people can't," he said with pride. "Don't judge me."

"Where is he?"

"He's at a rest area in Franklin, Kentucky, on I-65. He pulled in there about thirty minutes ago. From the parking lot camera, it looks like he's asleep there."

"How far?" Charli asked.

"Fifty-six miles."

Charli's mind was a flurry of options. This guy is an operative. Even wounded, he's going to be dangerous. *I need to contact the KSP—have them stop traffic so he can't drive away. We need him contained, not panicked. If they stop traffic north of the rest area, he will assume it is an accident. "Thank you Kiff,"* she said, starting for the door of his office.

Renner bounced to his feet. "Oh, no, no, no!" he said.

"What?"

"Jack's my friend too, so is Caylee. I did the grunt work. I want to be there when you bust this asshole."

Charli looked at him and nodded. “Come on.”

“Can I have a gun?”

“Can you handle one,” she said, stepping out in the hallway.

“Oh yeah,” Kiff replied, grabbing the package of Twizzlers as he hit the door. “I’m going to need some Diet Mountain Dew too.” He reached for the small refrigerator under his desk.

Charli headed for the elevator and jabbed the button. *I can see why Caylee liked this kid.*

CHAPTER 24

"There is nothing insignificant about microaggressions."

Midland, Texas

From his third floor hotel room, Darius lay on blankets on the far side of the bed. His window had been shot into shards of shattered glass the day before when he had stepped out of the bathroom. Bullet holes dug deep into the wallboard, passing right through into the bathroom, littering the floor with bits of tile and shattered mirror. With the bed blocking his line of sight to the surrounding buildings, he felt a twinge of safety.

Of course, feeling completely safe in Midland was impossible. Their hotel had been surrounded, as were the neighboring structures. The California National Guard troops tried a breakout to link up with them and get everyone out. Snipers had caught a lot of them, making a rush for the vehicles that were operational. Almost all the buses and the trucks were damaged or destroyed. The drones had dropped mortars on them. A few hit open hatches on armored vehicles, blowing them up as well. A few remote-controlled toy trucks came in at one point, running under vehicles and exploding. One vehicle went up in a ball of orange fire. Darius assumed the others were crippled.

In the end, the National Guard troops made it to the nearby Holiday Inn and had been forced to fall back into that besieged structure. They had gone from being an unstoppable invading army to a trapped and besieged force faster than most could imagine.

The stories that were coming in claimed that the locals were now reinforced by the Sons of Liberty. *That's all we need, a terrorist organization shooting at us.* The Sons had a reputation that was undeniable. There were allegedly other American military units that had joined in on the siege. He had tried to ignore the rumors, but these were backed up by more intense gunfire.

The long night of gunfire had left him ragged and exhausted. *The FedGov should have gone door-to-door, rounding up guns when they banned them. If they had, we wouldn't be in this situation.* He crawled to the hallway door and opened it, which brought another two shots tearing into his already ruined hotel room.

Even the hallway didn't feel safe. There were holes where rounds from the outside had punched through the walls, leaving white powder on the low plush carpeting of the Hampton Inn. The hallway was crowded with members of the Veteran's Corps, mostly sitting, some laying down. Sergeant Ingersoll was squatted low, and shuffled slowly over to where Darius hunkered down. "Not easy getting sleep in those rooms," he commented.

"I could hear them taunting us all night, telling us to surrender or die," Darius said, keeping his voice low. "Have our snipers had any luck?"

"Some—it's hard to tell. Every time we think we take out one of their people, a few more start firing back," he replied, sitting down next to him with his back against the wall. "They've got us penned in here pretty good. If we try to make a break for the vehicles that we do have that are operational, they will cut us apart. That's what happened to those SEs that came in with us. Half of them are dead or wishing they were—and they didn't get fifty feet from the door."

That was one rumor that just got confirmed. "Sergeant, how are we going to get out of here?"

Ingersoll's face tightened with the question, almost as if he knew something. "Help is on the way."

"We've been trapped here for two going on three days. We've lost some good people," he paused, thinking about how Vixen had been the first to fall to the enemy bullets in Midland.

"Help is coming." He said it loud enough for others nearby to hear. "All we have to do is not panic or overreact. We've got allies that the

Americans don't even realize. They are on their way, and when they come, we need to be ready to move out." The sergeant's eyes swept the hallway, giving a spark of energy to the otherwise exhausted troops.

Four hours later ...

Darius heard the battle suddenly intensify outside of the hotel. There was a rumble of artillery, which he hadn't heard up to this point. So far the Americans had not shown a desire to blow up the buildings where he and his comrades were hunkered down, and the Newmerican forces couldn't get to their surviving armored vehicles to dish out heavy fire.

The Hampton Inn didn't shake from impacts—which meant someone else was using big guns to join the fight. *Good, maybe we are going to get out of this after all.* He made his way down the stairwell to the ground floor, but he couldn't get to a vantage point to see what was happening.

"What's all that fire Lucius?" he called out to a member of his squad who was further in the lobby, hunkered down behind some furniture that was overturned and made into a barricade.

"They are hitting that office building across the parking lot, the one the damned snipers were using."

"Who is hitting it?"

An explosion echoed through the blasted front windows. "I don't know, but I'm sure as hell glad they showed up."

The distinct *thunk* of mortars sounded in the distance. Darius braced for the explosions, but they did not sound like the typical anti-personnel rounds. These went off with a loud *whoof.* He raised himself up just enough to see that the parking lot and surrounding buildings were being hit with exploding rounds that threw a white fog into the air.

Chemical weapons—shit! Memories of training in MOPP (Mission Oriented Protective Posture) gear came rushing back from his days in basic. *We don't have any of the gear for this kind of stuff.* "We need to fall back if that is a chemical attack," he said.

His words hit everyone in the room at once. They rose, rushing for the interior of the hotel, pushing and shoving. The hallway became jammed with the rush of those near the lobby. Darius was aware of that, trying to get somewhere less exposed.

The person who stopped the panic was Captain Aguilar. She took out her sidearm, pointing it up, and fired a single shot. "Stop this shit right now!" she roared. Everyone froze.

"They are using chemical weapons out there," someone from the rear of the group called out.

"I know," she said. "They are bringing us some gear, so we can get out of here. If you don't go outside, you'll be fine." Darius doubted her words. *That's not how chemical weapons work, not at all.*

The sound of gunfire died off outside. Then, through the low misty white haze, a figure wearing a mask emerged with two big duffels over his arms. He wore desert camouflage, not Army, or at least, not their army—the pattern was one that Darius had not seen before. He came in and opened the duffels. His gloved hands pulled out masks and gloves, and he started distributing them.

When he handed a set to Darius, the experienced soldier cocked his head. "How is this going to help with a gas attack?"

The man's Hispanic accent was thick, muffled by the mask he wore. "It's not gas. It is powdered fentanyl."

"Like the drug?"

The man continued to distribute the masks and gloves as another person joined him. "Si. It is weapons grade—very fine." He then turned to the group and pulled off his mask. "You cannot touch anything with the white powder. Don't let it on your skin or breathe it in. Just a little bit and you will be, how you say, incapacitated."

They are using weaponized fentanyl? Darius was stunned at what the man was saying. *They fired off a lot of profitable drugs for this attack.* It made sense. From living on the streets, he knew that just a bit of the drug was enough to overdose someone. *These guys have to be from one of the cartels to come up here and use that kind of weapon.* Fumbling with the straps of his mask, it took a few moments to put it on and make sure it sealed around his face … no straightforward task given several days of stubble face growth. He helped Lucius get his mask on, and both pulled on the latex gloves.

There were still a few erratic shots firing outside, but the men that had brought in the masks formed them into fast-moving lines that raced through the parking lot. Armored crews got to the surviving vehicles and fired them up. Darius and the others were led past the carnage from the attacks in the parking lot—the burned out and smoldering husks of trucks and a bus. Everything was lightly coated with a fine, white dust.

They made their way quickly past three badly damaged buildings beyond what they had seen from the Hampton Inn. Clearly, these had been the targets of artillery. Then they were put aboard waiting gray, unmarked buses. He saw several teams carrying out wounded on stretchers, racing to get away from the combat area.

One of the masked men spoke up as the bus roared into motion. "You can take your masks off now. Be careful. That powder is deadly."

The fresh, cooler air hitting his sweaty face felt good. The bus headed southwest, out of Midland. Darius was glad to be away from that town. *I knew going into Midland was a mistake.* Now that they were speeding away, there was a sense of relief. He did not know where they were going, but it didn't matter.

In the seat ahead of him, Sergeant Ingersoll sat rigid, leaning up against the window. "Sergeant," he said tapping him on the shoulder. "Any idea where they are taking us?"

Ingersoll didn't respond. Darius rose up slightly as the bus turned, and looked. The sergeant's eyes were huge, wide open, staring blankly up. His mouth was slightly agape, unmoving. "Aw shit! Hey, the sergeant here is having a reaction!" Darius had seen it before while living on the streets of LA. This was an overdose.

One of the men that had helped them evacuate Midland rushed down the center aisle of the bus, pulling out a Narcan shot, slamming it into Ingersoll's neck. For a few moments, the sergeant didn't seem to respond at all, and Darius was worried that it was too late. Without warning, Ingersoll seemed to jerk violently. His breathing became rapid. His hands went up, grabbing the back of the seat in front of him, and he started to quake. Slowly he was able to close his mouth and blink his eyes.

"Watch him," the man with the Narcan said. "He should be okay." Captain Aguilar moved the man out of seat next to Ingersoll and took that spot. She rolled up her jacket and used it to cushion his head against the window of the rambling bus.

Darius saw the beads of sweat forming on the sergeant's face and the look of raw terror that gripped him. He put his hands on Ingersoll's shoulders to try to calm him, but it did little to relax the man as he coped with his unexpected overdose. *Shit, that could have been any of us.* He carefully pulled off his latex gloves, turning them inside out, dropping them to the floor.

The look in Ingersoll's face tore at him. It reminded him for a moment of John and of Vixen. The blank look in his eyes was slowly being replaced with terror, but Darius had seen it all before. For a few moments, he wasn't on the bus; he was back in Los Angeles cradling John as he died.

"He'll be okay," Aguilar said, snapping Darius back into reality.

"Will he?" he asked. "He got overdosed. This shit is going to mess with him. I lived on the streets. I've seen stuff."

"I lived on those same streets," Aguilar said in a low tone. "I know when someone is going to die and when they are going to make it. He's going to make it."

"Who are these guys?" he said in a low tone, nodding to the men that had rescued them.

"I don't know. I'm just glad they came when they did."

"I don't think the sarge feels that way," he said, glancing over at the still semi-rigid Ingersoll. Darius looked up at the men that had gotten them out of the Hampton Inn. He saw they wore military gear, but the way they held their weapons wasn't like that of professional soldiers. One had his finger on the side of the trigger, something that a professional never would do. They dressed well, but their shaggy, unkempt, black hair and poor grooming made them either militia or something else. He settled on some sort of cartel connection, given their use of fentanyl.

While he was thankful for their rescue, a part of him was suspicious. *Who have we crawled in bed with? Why would a Mexican drug cartel be in the country? These dickweeds have killed thousands of people with the drugs they smuggle across the border. What kind of bargain have we struck with these criminals?* Before the Liberation, the news had talked about the need to secure the border and the drug problem from smugglers in Mexico. That had all stopped when the TRC had taken control of the news. Now he understood why—we have been working with the cartels.

Anger gripped him. He was mad that the Ingersoll was struggling still with his exposure to the drugs. He was more furious at the Newmerican government for having a covert alliance with the cartels that controlled Mexico. They covered it all up. Media moguls at the TRC made sure that the story never saw the light of day. The people that had coerced him into joining the Veterans Corp were the same ones working with the cartels. The depth of the corruption of the Newmerican government was slowly becoming clear.

They played me—hell, they played all of us. They made me reenlist and fight for their cause and convinced me it was for my own interests. It was never about me—it was about them, holding onto power. Looking at the men that had gotten them out of Midland, his rage continued. *Now they are siding with people that are murderers. My mom told me you were judged by the company you keep. We are tainted by these criminals.* It took long miles on the road before he could reel in his anger.

For a few moments, he felt dirty ... not just from the fact he had now showered for days, but from what he had been a part of. *I never wanted to return to fighting a war and killing people.* He reached up to his pocket where he carried the service medal that he had been carrying since the skirmish at the Presidio. *I have become a tool for evil men and women, and never even knew it was happening.*

The rocking of the bus and the fact that Ingersoll seemed to be slowly regaining his senses allowed Darius to succumb to sleep. There would be plenty of time for the answers to his questions whenever they got to their final destination.

Franklin, Kentucky

Thiago Reese was awakened by the sunlight hitting his face. He needed the slumber after his loss of blood and the flight from Nashville. As she shifted in the car seat, where he had dozed off sitting up, his wounded right arm throbbed, reminding him of the damage it had been dealt. He wiped the sleep from his eyes with his left hand, checking his watch for the time. *I slept for nine hours ... I don't remember the last time I slept that much.*

Looking around his vehicle in the rest area parking lot, he saw that no other cars were close. From what he saw of I-65, traffic going north was at a dead stop—bumper to bumper. There must be an accident or something to clog up the road like that. For Reese, it meant he had time to raid the vending machines in the rest area for something that could pass for breakfast.

Most people would have panicked and pushed themselves too far too fast after an assassination like he had performed. When he trained operatives in his craft, he told them to take things slow and steady—it attracted far less attention. It didn't bother him that the roads were backed up. Reese was in no rush. Besides, by now, Caylee Leatrom was going to be who the FBI and local police would be looking for—not him. Thinking of the turmoil around Leatrom that he had created was enough to bring a grin to his face.

Checking his wound, he saw that no blood had soaked through the gauze or the Ace bandage he had used to wrap the wound. That was a good sign. Walking around with a bloody shoulder was the kind of attention grabber that he didn't want. While he had staved off an immediate infection with an agonizing flush of alcohol, he knew he would need surgery to repair the shattered bones. *When I get back to Newmerica, I'll get all the medical care I need.*

Standing was painful, not just from his shoulder, but every joint and muscle seemed to protest his movements. He put his smaller PPK pistol into his front jeans pocket hoping that it wouldn't draw unwanted attention. The shoulder was the worst. It seemed to burn hot, and he was sweating after the first few steps.

When he reached the rest area, he entered the men's room and stood in front of the mirror. His face reminded him of his time in Brazil. His eyes were slightly bloodshot; his hair was a mess and looked almost oily. He ran his left hand through it a few times, acting as a makeshift comb. Even those movements made his other arm ache. *Once I'm into Kentucky, I will head northwest into Illinois.* It wasn't his first choice—he would have preferred going to Virginia, but that was much farther, and his wound was not getting any better. *In a few days' time, they'll have me in a government-run hospital, and hopefully on the mend.*

A man passed him at the door of the men's room as he was leaving, bumping him slightly. He cringed at the pain and the man turned and said, "Sorry," as he continued inside. *Damn idiot.* His body was still struggling with the damage that had been inflicted on it.

At the vending machines he cringed at the options, finally settling on a package of blueberry Pop-Tarts. That was one of the good things about being in American territory, there were no restrictions on what kind of food was for sale. Pop-Tarts had been banned as unhealthy two years ago, making them highly desirable on the black market. *These will tide me over until I find a Waffle House or some other place to get some protein.* He fed the machine old American money. There was no point in carrying a wad of Newmerican bills while on an op in the traitor nation. Seeing George Washington on the one-dollar bill was so odd. He was used to Jimmy Carter's face on the Newmerican equivalent.

Bending over to the pull out the Pop-Tarts with one hand hurt, he knew he would be better once he returned to the car. As he rose, he saw the man who had passed him at the men's room door. "Not much to choose from," he commented as Reese walked to his car.

Instinct kicked in. Two close encounters with a stranger … was he being tailed? He narrowed his gaze as he entered the parking area, looking for cars with people in them. None seemed to stand out as potential threats, but that didn't mean they weren't. Reese started looking towards the exit onto the highway. Escape and evasion became his goal. *If I gun the engine, I should be able to cross the median and get in the southbound traffic.*

Passing a rearview mirror, he saw the man he had encountered start to make his way into the parking lot as well. Normally, he would prepare, let the man make the first move, confirm he was a threat, then eliminate him. Reese could not afford such a plan given his wound. *I will get to the car, shoot him, then get out of here. If he's tailing me, chances are good that he's not alone.*

A nagging voice in his brain wanted to know how they had found him. *My disguise was perfect. Everything pointed to Leatrom—not to me.* He suppressed those thoughts. *Focus on getting out of here alive—that's what matters now.*

He reached the maroon Buick and opened the door slowly. Using his body to block his movement, he drew the weapon from his jeans and turned around, holding the gun in his left hand. His eyes tracked onto the man, who suddenly saw that he was looking at Reese's gun.

Squeezing the trigger, the gun kicked hard adding to Reese's agony. The shot hit the man low, toppling him backwards onto the pavement.

There was no time to see if he had killed him. Reese knew he had to get away. He slid into the car, slamming the door, and used the screwdriver to start the vehicle up. Reese jammed the gun into his crotch in case he needed it again. It wasn't optimal, but his right arm was out of commission.

He had backed into the spot, so he simply aimed for the exit ramp to the highway. He heard three bangs, guns firing in rapid succession. The passenger window exploded into tiny bits of glass. One shot hit the windshield and was deflected, cracking the glass. Reese swerved the car from side to side, cringing with each lurch. His eyes stung with the sweat that was hitting them, but he ignored the pain and his body's reaction. Overhead, he heard the distinct sounds of a helicopter, adding to his growing list of problems. *They think they have me trapped. That is a mistake on their part.*

The car lurched as he drove onto the grass, and he heard three more rapid cracks of gunfire. The back window of the Buick was punctured, the shot going just past him, into the dashboard, throwing bits of plastic everywhere. A tire pressure indicator flashed, but he kept focused.

More shots rang out; he could hear them punching through the thin metal of the Buick. He struggled for a moment—as if he had just received an electric shock to his chest. There was no way that he could look down to see if he had been hit. All that mattered was getting away.

Whipping the Buick into the southbound lanes, he nearly collided with an SUV—the driver laid on the horn. A semi-tractor trailer in the other lane hit the rear of his car at an angle, performing an ad hoc PIT maneuver (precision immobilization technique). The big Buick swerved hard to one side and pivoted to where he could see oncoming traffic. Another car hit him, sending him turning even faster in a tight spin, back onto the median.

The car dug into the lush green grass of the strip between the north and southbound lanes as he fought to regain control. His gun had gone flying onto the floor. He could hear it moving near the brake pedal.

Realigning the car to head south took effort and it seemed to slow, clearly getting bogged down in the grass. *Come on, get on the road—I can still get out of this.* He coughed, and a splinter of blood rose to his lips and hit the steering column. *I was hit. Damn!*

At this point, adrenaline and training was piloting the Buick. He came up on the shoulder as more gunshots rang out. The distinctive puncturing sounds of the rounds penetrating the vehicle didn't shake him; nor did the fact that he was struggling to get air. *I trained for this ... I can do this!*

The Buick roared as he jammed the accelerator down, but it wasn't moving hardly at all. *I'm stuck! Shit!* For the first time since his assassination of Jack Desmond, things were out of control. The tires were spinning so fast that he could smell the rubber burning in the soft sod. He bent down to find the pistol, and the moment he did, his vision tunneled. Darkness came at him from all around. The sound in his ears was a ringing noise as his left hand groped trying to find the weapon.

It can't end like this. I'm an operative. He struggled to get air. Panicked, he tried to sit back up, but the darkness that had been surrounding his field of vision took him and pulled him down far and fast as he slid into unconsciousness.

South of Tucumcari, New Mexico

The battle for Tucumcari had been raging for days. Operation Diamondback was supposed to have raced through the town in a matter of minutes. As much as he hated to admit it, the Newmericans had gotten the drop on him. The enemy had dug in with field fortifications facing east. They had brought in troops, arms, and armor. They had turned his lightning fast war plan into a mirror of WWI trench warfare.

General Reager didn't play their game. He had positioned some troops in front of Tucumcari, led by the Marines of the Purebloods. They had kept up the illusion that Trip was still bogged down while he sent a flanking force to take Clovis and Cannon Air Force Base. He had wanted to swing around earlier, to flank the enemy, but had waited. He had sent the bulk of his force south to deal with the Texas incursion. Timing was a key component to victory, and he prided himself in knowing not just *where* to strike, but *when*.

He had heard the reports from Harnessy about how the Purebloods were driving vehicles back and forth along the lines, kicking up dust, creating the illusion that exaggerated the number of troops. The Purebloods wanted a more straight up fight—*hell, they have earned it.*

Now it was time to deliver them the victory they had earned.

Reager had swung north to Clovis after he secured Cannon AFB. His troops now were raining artillery and mortar rounds on the defenders from the south. An armored platoon had swung in behind Clovis, cutting off the supply lines on I-40 and securing a small convoy of munitions and food that had been destined to the Newmericans.

He stood outside of his Bradley armored fighting vehicle and listened to the roar of the artillery as they rained death and destruction down on the small New Mexico town and its defenders. He hated this part of war, the carnage. If there were civilians still there, he knew many would be killed. Common sense would be for them to have evacuated days ago, but there were always people that avoided rational thought and stayed. *They already call me The Butcher. Today I may earn that.*

The barrage had been slow and steady for almost two hours. The Newmericans had tried counterbattery fire, but their targeting was off and they had blown up nothing but New Mexico desert before their own guns were silenced. Trip put himself in their heads as best he could. *They know now they are flanked; their primary retreat route is cut off. They are calling for help, but the rest of their army is down in Texas.* He knew that their isolation and the pressures of the fighting a prolonged battle against the Purebloods was eating at their nerves. *Fear is as potent a weapon as any artillery round.*

"Comms, signal the Purebloods. Tell them we are about to commence our advance. Once fully engaged, they should move in from their positions," Trip called out.

"Yes sir," his comms person in the Bradley replied.

There would be critique and criticism of each of his decisions. Some would call his failure to seize New Mexico a debacle—Trip understood that. Other were bound to say that his attack on Clovis was an attempt to salvage his reputation. That was a lie that had not happened yet, but was destined to come. *The time has come to restore some order here.* "Artillery is to continue until we are close. My order is simple: Envelope Clovis."

Thirty minutes later ...

Smoke rolled out of what was left of Clovis as the Marines moved through the rubble, pulling out each surrendering enemy trooper. Trip walked over and saw that almost every structure in the small town had been leveled. He stood in front of the rubble that had been the Route 66 Museum and felt terrible that a bit of nostalgia had been destroyed at his order. *Some of this will never be rebuilt. That is the price tag of a civil war.*

The commander of the Purebloods, a burly and bearded Marine Captain in his mid-40s, walked up to him. "General Reager, I'm Captain Dolio," he said, giving him a weary salute that Trip returned, waiting for the gesture back which Trip gave him. "We have most of them rounded up. A few platoons struck off to the northwest into the desert when we hit them. No doubt they are still running."

"Damn fine work," Trip replied.

"My people are dragging ass, but you get us transport, we will round them up."

Trip drew a breath. A part of him wanted to let them go. *There is no place for them to run, just flat ugly desert.* By the same token, he didn't want them to get away and fight another day against him. "Your people have to be pretty exhausted. I can task another unit to do it."

"No offense, sir, but we came here to win a victory. We are Marines, despite the fact they kicked us out for not taking the poke. Let us finish what we started." It wasn't a plea, it was a solid request from a professional soldier to his superior.

"Very well Captain," Trip replied. "Round 'em up."

Dolio smiled and started away as Captain Harnessy stepped up and took his place in front of Trip. "What's the word from Midland?"

"The Newmerican force is gone—broken out. Some sort of chemical attack."

His mind reeled at those words. *This is a damned ugly escalation. Hell, it's a war crime!* "Chemical weapons? What in the blue blazes—"

"Sir, there's more. They had help."

"Help from who?"

"A relief force came in from Mexico," Harnessy reported, handing his pad over to Trip so that he could see the details.

The García Cartel ... the criminals that controlled Mexico. His mind raced with questions and possible decisions that needed to be made as he looked at the images of a caravan crossing into Texas from the south. "I'm going to need to talk to Jack Desmond," he said out loud—realizing that the implications of this were far beyond his pay grade.

"Sir, I didn't tell you this earlier. That isn't possible."

Aw crap, what now?

CHAPTER 25

"Chances are your neighbors are hiding something. Be vigilant and earn Reparation Points for your loyalty."

Franklin, Kentucky

Charli moved up on the maroon Buick that Thiago Reese was in as the paramedics and FBI pulled him out. He looked dead; his face was waxen; his clothing wet with sweat, and there was a growing splotch of blood in his lower torso. A part of her hoped he *was* dead after all the chaos he had sown. She tempered those emotions with a grim calculus. *He's worth more to us alive than dead.*

Reese coughed and a drizzle of blood trickled down his chin as the paramedics worked on him. "Cuff him up, ankles and wrists. He's an operative. Cut his clothing off of him, he probably has a weapon hidden. Don't think for a minute that he's wounded and can't get away," she ordered as Kiffin Renner came up by her side, weapon in hand.

"Is he dead?" Kiff Renner asked, gasping from his sprint to catch up with her.

"Not yet," she replied as the FBI agents heeded her warnings. One of them at the car called out, "Gun," and emerged from the floorboard of the vehicle with a PPK.

Another ambulance was across the median at the rest area where one of the FBI agents had been shot by Reese. People stranded in traffic got out of their cars and stood, watching in amazement at what had unfolded next to him. Southbound traffic was now blocked as well by the accidents that Reese had caused.

As Charli looked around, she knew that the mess had to be straightened out, and fast. "Someone let the KSP know that they can start letting northbound traffic through. We are going to need more troopers down here to get those accidents cleared in the southbound lanes." The FBI didn't question her orders, in fact, they relayed them almost verbatim into their walkie-talkies. A helicopter flew overhead. *How in the hell does the media get to these scenes so fast?* It hovered for a few moments, but found itself sharing the airspace with a KSP helicopter that persuaded it to depart.

The paramedics hooked up an IV to Reese and she could tell that some color was returning to his face. They began to move him to the ambulance that was on the shoulder of the highway, followed by four FBI agents that looked as if they came out of central casting—from their skin-tight golf shirts right down to their khaki trousers and cheap sunglasses.

"We need to go," she said to Kiff as she holstered her weapon and started back to her car. "The bureau and the KSP can handle the cleanup and evidence gathering here. We need to stay with Reese."

"Gotcha," Renner said as he followed her. "You think you can get him to talk?"

She reached the car and opened the door. "No. But sometimes what you don't say is as revealing as what you do speak." It was a lesson that she had learned a long time ago and embraced fully.

"This will clear Caylee, right?" Kiff asked.

"It's a big step in that direction," she said as she fired up the engine and made the turn to come in behind the ambulance.

Over New Mexico ...

Raul had only flown once before in his life, and it was nothing like this. Kidder was keeping the plane low, almost dangerously low, over the ground. They were flying fast as well, and as he rose enough to see through the cockpit, he could see the blur of the desert racing at them.

"Why are we so low?" he asked loud enough to be heard.

Kidder kept his hands on the yoke and didn't respond. Travis turned and spoke to him. "We're coming in under the radar. Kirtland just scrambled fighters to find us and divert us back."

Raul immediately tensed on hearing those words. "Will they catch us?"

"Not if I have anything to say about it," Kidder sneered from the pilot's seat. "You may want to let the Americans and Texans know we are coming in and possibly bringing friends with us. Tell them I am going to make for Rick Husband International."

Travis turned back and worked a panel, barking off a jumble of words into his headset microphone. Raul slid back down to the floor, sitting next to Caylee. Looking up at her, she seemed perfectly calm, almost bored.

"Aren't you a little worried?"

"Would it help?"

"How do you do that—just sit there and be calm?"

She cracked a smile. "This is out of my hands at this point. Mr. Kidder, and to a lesser degree, Travis can influence the outcome of this. I cannot. I trust them to do what is necessary."

Her words made sense, but still required something that Raul had not fully mastered yet, suppressing emotions. *I'm afraid; she isn't.* "What about fear? Aren't you the least bit afraid?"

"Raul," she said in an almost instructional tone, "Death has been on my trail for years. I'm not numb to it. I simply accept that at some point, it will come for me. In the meantime, I worry about the things that I have control over. This isn't one of those things."

Raul shook his head. He understood the concepts she spoke of, but could not shake the trepidation that gripped him. *This is something I can only master with experience.* What helped him cope was that Caylee was still teaching him. *If I am going to die, the cause is the right one, and I am surrounded by good people.* Those thoughts gave him a strange sense of security.

The aircraft banked abruptly, tossing Raul to the side. There was a bump, and while he assumed it was turbulence, there was some doubt. From the cargo hold, he heard a cry, not of pain, but fear. *If I am afraid, those people must be experiencing it even more.*

He crawled to the hatch down to the cargo bay and down the short latter. The floor of the Airbus was covered with people lying flat or huddled in small groups. He saw one woman rolled up in a fetal position, rocking nervously. There were several people crying, men and women alike.

"We are almost to Texas," he called out to the former prisoners. "We are flying low to avoid radar; that is all." The plane buffeted again.

"Are we safe yet?" one younger man called out.

"We will be soon," he assured them. "Our pilot is one of the best."

"Is he the man with the eye patch?" an older woman asked.

"Yes," Raul said. "And he can fly better with one eye than most pilots with two."

"He's right," Andy added from where he was comforting an older gentleman leaning against the rear bulkhead. "He's one of the best I've ever worked with." There was a sincerity in his words.

Andy's words helped, but Raul was plagued with nervousness that the escapees had as well. How much of an exaggeration as to Kidder's skills he had voiced was still yet to be seen. Caylee had told him how he had flown a helicopter over the Supermax prison to deliver her to his rescue. *If she is comfortable with his skills, then I am.*

He could still feel the fear from the prisoners. He had seen the same thing in those that were freed from Valley Forge. It would take days, if not months, for some of them to return to normal. *That is the price for being a dissenter in Newmerica—a bit of your life and a chunk of your soul. No matter what evidence of what we show is happening in the Social Quarantine camps, there will be people that will deny it and claim that these people are paid actors. The people in the cockpit, they are focused with getting out through this alive. These people need more—they need hope. I need to find that for them. That is something I can do.*

An idea hit him, one he latched onto instantly. "Does anyone know a song? One we could all sing?"

For a moment, no one answered Raul. *Singing can calm them.* A woman in her 30s raised her hands. Her prisoner uniform was gray, covered with streaks of dirt and filth that would defy DNA tests. The red hair on her head was a tangled mess of curls and lack of care. The woman's blue eyes locked onto Raul's. "I know one," she said just loud enough for him to hear over the rumble and roar of the cargo bay.

"What is it?"

She sat up straight, drawing a deep breath, closing her eyes as if to summon the strength to sing. The words and tune rose from her, not from her throat, but from much deeper. "Oh beautiful for spacious skies. For amber waves of grain …"

Other voices joined her. "For purple mountain majesties. Above the fruited plain!" then more sang until the whole of the cargo bay filled with voices. They sang a song that had been banned for half a decade. "America! America! God shed His grace on thee …" Raul joined them in the chorus, struggling to remember the words. He knew that getting them right didn't matter. What mattered was the spirit that they sang in.

"And crown thy good with brotherhood. From sea to shining sea." He could see it in their faces—the fear ebbing away. The song carried them from terror to a sense of resolve, of purpose. In their eyes he could see the memories of the nation they once had, of better times. Some shed tears as they broke into the second chorus; others simply hummed when they didn't know the words. The bucking of the airplane meant nothing; nor did the sounds.

Raul glanced over his shoulder and saw Caylee at the top of the ladder. She smiled and gave him a nod and in that moment, he knew he had done his part in the mission. More than leading the attack to free the prisoners, this moment was something that proved to them that no matter what followed, they really were free again.

White Mountain National Forest
New Hampshire

Su-Hui was hunkered down in the trench as an explosion made his body throb and vibrate and dirt rained down on him. Trudy was curled up next to him in a size that seemed impossible given her body mass. The Sons of Liberty were fanned out in the twisting trench, every one of them waiting for the right moment to emerge.

The sound of distant airplane props sent a chill up his spine. *A C-130 gunship!* He knew that sound all too well. When that plane flew over, people were going to die; it would blow vehicles up. It had happened far too often. "Get down!" he yelled, but he didn't have to; his people were making themselves as small as they could. Su-Hui stiffened, waiting for the inevitable purr and roar of the gunship making its pass.

Then he heard it, another sound. This was something new, something different. It was a helicopter racing from the south. He raised his head just enough he saw the black-gray chopper bank upward. A missile unleased from one of its weapons pods, turning and twisting skyward right at the distant gunship.

The C-130 banked and climbed sharper than he imagined as the missile closed the gap. There was a flash as it went off, a brilliant orange ball of destruction. The explosion came a few seconds later, but by that time the deadly gunship was already plummeting towards the ground, one wing peeling off as it collapsed downward. It hit the ground out of his line of sight, but the rising black and crimson ball of fire marked its ultimate resting place, somewhere at the far edges of the White Mountain National Forest.

Turning back to the helicopter, he saw it unleash another missile, this one at a tank that was barely visible on a hillside. The distant Newmerican vehicle erupted like a volcano, its turret blown off, and it landed behind the now-burning hulk. Orange blobs of melting interior and tank splattered all around it.

Another helicopter appeared off to his right, its forward chain gun humming, the tracers lighting up an almost solid beam of yellow as they tore into the infantry positions. Shots came down at him, peppering the ground near him, forcing Su-Hui to duck. This was it, the long awaited help. *The cavalry has finally arrived!*

Another helicopter roared over their trench, firing rockets off in the distance. In a strange unified move, the Sons of Liberty rose from their trench to watch as their airborne angels unleashed rockets, missiles and gunfire on the Newmerican forces. Valerie Turner led the cheer that the rest of the SOL joined in, including Su-Hui.

His walkie-talkie crackled; then came a voice. “Live free or die! Repeat, live free or die!”

That was the code phrase that General Griffiths had given them. Su-Hui turned to his people. “Sons and daughters of Liberty,” he howled at the top of his lungs. “The time has come. Attack!”

They didn’t have to be told twice. Rising out of their trenches, the SOL surged forward. Members of the New Hampshire National Guard charged forward, blurring their formations. It didn’t matter. The counterattack had begun. It was as if the whole of the Defiance positions erupted, with forces surging outward at the enemy that had hemmed them in.

Running was hard: The forest floor was cratered, churned, filled with exposed rocks and bits of trees that no longer existed. A helicopter from behind him sent a pair of rockets racing over their heads at the distant hilltop, bathing it in explosions and death. Su-Hui aimed for that spot, running with his rifle in his grip.

Gunfire came from a foxhole off to the left. He dropped low, firing several shots at the helmets he saw poking up from the cover. One was hit and disappeared. Trudy moved up beside him and threw a grenade. It went on a high arc as he continued to shoot, landing to the left of the foxhole, only a foot or two from the edge. The explosion rocked those troops in the hole. Hands rose as they threw down their weapons and started the crawl out.

"See to the prisoners," he ordered. Trudy took two steps forward but someone fired at the surrendering men in a quick burst of automatic fire. They dropped, dead. Su-Hui looked to see who had pulled the trigger, but could not tell who the perpetrator was. It seemed dishonorable to kill surrendering troops, but that happened in war. Refocusing, he charged towards his objective hilltop.

A Newmerican Bradley Fighting Vehicle backed away from the rushing troops, its 25 mm cannon banging away as it raced backwards for safety. It was erratic fire, panicked. A burst of gunfire from one helicopter tore into it. Smoke rolled from the hatches as the crew opened them, climbing out, trying to run for safety. Bullets tore the air around them, chewing up all but one of the crew.

Su-Hui stepped in a hole as he ran and twisted his ankle, sending him falling face first in the dark dirt. His ankle throbbed as he rose to his knees. Trudy came alongside him. "You hit?"

He shook his head. "No. I twisted my ankle."

"Stay here boss," she assured him. "We've got them on the run."

"No!" he barked. "Help me up." *I need to be there ... now, more than ever.*

Trudy slid her arm under his and helped him to his feet. He gingerly tested the ankle, and it screamed in pain. His jaw set as he focused on movement over the pain. "We go together," he commanded.

Trudy didn't protest. The beefy lumberjack from the UP of Michigan started forward, holding him up, acting as his bad leg as they rushed in pursuit of the rest of the SOL. Each time he lowered the foot it hurt, but just a little less. By the time they reached the bottom of the hill, he could limp along on his own, albeit slowly. Trudy stayed with him.

The Newmerican resistance crumbled. Many simply surrendered; their exhausted faces looked strangely like those of his own people. Others tried to run for safety. A small drone with an explosive chased a pair of men, hitting the back of one, exploding both men in a mist of crimson and smoke. Many of those fleeing were shot in the back, where others threw away their weapons and sprinted like wild animals attempting to flee hunters emerging from their blinds.

The Defiance forces went up the hillsides and ridges that flanked their position. He saw his people crest the hill before he did, and heard the staccato of their gunfire barking from the other side.

Limping heavily, he and Trudy reached the top as a helicopter roared past him, firing rockets down the other side. What he saw from the hilltop was a sight that would forever be etched in his mind. Several burning vehicles were belching black and gray smoke skyward. The flaming hulls of several armored fighting vehicles dotted the hillside as well. One M113 was so badly crumbled and mangled that he barely could tell what it had been. Amidst the stench of the smoke, he caught a hint of feces, no doubt from a dead person. Dead Newmerican troopers lay in every conceivable position along the muddy hillside—while others were huddled in clumps, their arms up in the air. A few clung to what was left of blasted trees, doing what they could to prop themselves up. Those that were still running were being pursued by the New Hampshire National Guard troops, running in full sprints.

This is victory! In all of his time fighting for the Sons of Liberty, he had never allowed himself to imagine what it might look like. They had won battles, ambushes and raids, but this was different. It was larger, more vicious, more earned. Victory was dirty, ugly, smoke choked, death and a strange feeling of jubilation. His people moved down around the clusters of the surrendering troops, disarming those that still had weapons.

Valerie Turner moved up next to him. She had a cut on her left cheek, not deep, but it streaked her dark skin with blood. "You're hurt," he said.

She touched the wound and looked at the blood on her gloved fingers. "So are you." She nodded to his cocked leg and injured ankle.

"We won," was all Su-Hui could say.

"Yeah," Valerie replied as a helicopter banked away from their position and headed to the north, probably looking for more targets. "What a mess."

"We need to get this organized. If you can, get these prisoners assembled, and I will reach out to General Griffiths as to what he wants us to do with them."

"Don'tcha wanna savor this moment?" Trudy said, her UP accent more prominent than usual.

She was right, it was a scene worth savoring. The smell of burning vehicles stung at his eyes and nostrils. The smell of the churned forest almost had a manure-like aroma. He watched as the filthy enemy National Guard were being forced to succumb to searches. Their faces were blank, stunned, as if they didn't believe they had lost. Despite their losses, they thought we were defeated. Some of them wept, others looked infuriated. *Good ... you have been hunting us like wild animals for months. Now you know what it is like to suffer genuine loss, true defeat.* Memories of those that had been lost and of his predecessor Randy Birdsell all came to the forefront of his mind. *Would they be happy with what has happened today? Yes. They would be proud of what we have accomplished.* The satisfaction of the moment was intoxicating.

Two hours later ...

The New York National Guard Colonel was the highest ranking officer that had been captured. Su-Hui watched as he was presented before the gathering of officers of the Defiance. The man was old, clearly out of shape, with short, silvery hair. There was a bloody smear on one of his uniform sleeves, but it wasn't his own. His bright blue eyes still showed his rage at the humiliation that he felt he was being put through.

"Colonel Strother," Griffiths said.

"General."

"Where is your General Rinehart?"

"I wish I knew. Last I saw was his M1130 burning rubber heading southwest. He left me holding his bag."

"We will deal with him in good time. For now, there is a formality I think needs to be done."

Strother's face got bright red. "You want to take what dignity I have so that you can gloat about what transpired."

"I could care less about our dignity. I would say that we've earned a little formality on an occasion such as this."

"Your people played dirty. Where in hell did those choppers fly out of?"

"Shangri la," he said with a chuckle. The gathered officers joined in with his laugh, only adding to the crimson on Strother's face. "Suffice it to say that your grip on this part of the country isn't as firm as you thought."

"Let's get this over with," the Colonel muttered.

"Hold on for just a moment," Griffiths said. "The fight for New Hampshire's freedom was not just the citizens of the National Guard. We had help, brothers and sisters in arms. People that came from all across the country to fight for this moment. It is only fitting that your surrender be to not just me, but to them as well."

The crowd murmured in agreement. He gestured to where Su-Hui stood, still favoring his good foot. "Leaders of the Sons of Liberty, step forward."

He stepped out, as did Valerie Turner and a half dozen other men and women. He limped next to General Griffiths and stood as erect as possible. Strother rose to his full height, taller that Su-Hui. His eyes made contact with each one of his adversaries, one at a time in a long moment of silence. *He is a proud man, and this hurts him deeply.*

"On behalf of the Newmerican Armed Forces, I surrender our forces. I only ask that you treat us respectfully and with the respect we have earned."

Griffiths smiled. "Earned? You killed innocent civilians, blew up towns, killed elected legislators, and stole from the people of this state. You ask for respect. I demand justice. I accept your surrender and you and your people will be held accountable for your war crimes." With a nod, Colonel Strother was put in handcuffs and taken away.

"It's a great day for the people of my home state," the General said to the SOL leaders. "We couldn't have done it without your help. You have given us a debt that is going to be difficult to repay. Know this, however, wherever you go, you are honored heroes of the Granite State."

Su-Hui bowed his head slightly. "I only wish we had caught Rinehart."

"We may yet," Griffiths replied. "We are still rounding up a lot of fleeing enemy troops. Even if he does get away, I can't imagine that he will be warmly welcomed back in the District after losing New Hampshire."

Those words made him feel happier. As he glanced in the crowd, he saw Hachi, on crutches, smiling broadly at him. In that moment, he knew he had avenged the attack on his daughter. *I paid back the Newmericans for what they did to her—no, WE paid them back. This war is not over, but this battle is and it is our victory—together.*

West of Rick Husband Amarillo International Airport

Caylee looked over and saw the fighter jet maneuvering about a football field's length off of the left of the Airbus. Travis was working the communications while Faust concentrated on flying. "This is all a big misunderstanding," Travis said. "We will land at Rick Husband. Then sort it out."

The fighter began to drift back, out of Caylee's field of vision. *He's maneuvering to get behind us and fire.*

The Air Force had sent a jet out after them, and it had managed to catch up with them as they crossed the border into Texas. Travis looked nervous, which was far from encouraging. "He says he's going to shoot us down if we don't divert back to New Mexico."

"Mr. Kidder," Caylee said.

"Hang on tight," he said. "Keep your hands and legs in the ride while it is in motion."

The Airbus was already flying low and fast. Kidder pulled the yoke, and the plane rose sharply, pushing Caylee back into her seat. He banked the plane at the top of the sharp climb, hard to the left. The seatbelt dug into her abdomen as her stomach pitched.

After a few moments of stomach wrenching, Kidder dove down, pulling up just before she thought they would collide with the rugged terrain. A warning sounded, a British sounding female voice, "Collison alert—collision alert." She could hear some panicked screams coming from the cargo hold where Raul was, a sharp contrast to the singing that they had been doing a few minutes earlier.

"Jesus, Faust," Travis cursed.

"Don't bring the Lord into this just yet," Kidder replied, turning again, this time to the right.

Suddenly there was a flash of crimson lights flickering on the consoles. "We've been hit," Kidder cursed, banking the Airbus again hard and climbing. Caylee never heard the gunfire over the roar of the engines. *We have no armor, no weapons ... this might not end well.*

"How bad?" Caylee asked.

"He didn't fire missiles—if he had we'd be dead. We're leaking fuel and I have some hydraulic issues. Nothing I can't cope with ... I hope."

He leaned over to Travis. "Tell Husband we are declaring an emergency and to clear all traffic," Kidder spat as he used every muscle of his body to twist and turn the cargo aircraft around.

Raul struggled up the ladder from the cargo bay, fighting the laws of physics as the plane rocked wildly. "What is going on?"

Caylee opened her mouth to respond, when Kidder cut her off. "Hot damn!"

Everyone looked forward as two F-16 fighters roared straight at and past the Airbus. "Friendlies? she asked Travis.

"Oh yeah, the baddie is breaking for New Mexico," Travis replied. He muttered some words into the microphone. "I told Husband we are coming in hot."

"Raul, tell them to hold on to anything they can down there," Kidder called back. "I've got a brake light warning here."

Raul took off for the cargo bay as the plane leveled out and slowed. She saw the airport looming ahead and could hear the landing gear drop and lock under her. "That runway looks awfully damn short," Travis said to the pilot.

Kidder nodded, but kept his single-eyed gaze on the runway. "Alright people—it's show time." He began the last of the descent smoothly, though at the last moment, there was a short rise upwards that he quickly compensated for. Caylee was unsure if was because of the damage or the atmospherics. To her it didn't matter. She wanted to be on the ground.

At least there I have some control.

The plane came down with a hard bump and the engines quickly began thrust reversal, pushing everyone hard forward in their seats. There was a skidding sound from the rear of the aircraft, and she could see that Kidder was struggling with the controls. The Airbus shifted to one side of the runway, and Faust was clearly attempting to keep it centered, and fighting a losing battle.

They were still moving when they reached the end of the runway and ran into the ground beyond. The plane throbbed, rocked and the front landing gear gave way, crashing the fuselage down on the ground. They skidded for a good fifty feet before the plane lurched to a stop.

Caylee half expected Kidder to brag about what he had just done; instead he rose quickly. “Open the emergency doors and get everyone out.”

There was a flurry of motion. It was going to be impossible to open the cargo doors, so the former prisoners were brought up to the cockpit deck and helped onto the slide out. Firefighters arrived and began dousing the airplane. Sam Patheal, wet with what Caylee assumed was his own vomit, helped Andy get them up, while she and Raul assisted them onto the emergency ramp. It took twenty minutes, and finally Kidder ushered them to the ramp and down.

When they reached the ground, the firefighters came over to them and walked them away from the battered and beached aircraft. Kidder glanced back at the airplane and grinned. “Any landing you walk away from is a victory.”

Caylee felt compelled to agree. “A lot of these people needed medical help before we took off. They are going to be needing more after that flight. We need to let the paramedics know they were prisoners and to keep them together in the hospital.”

Travis added to what she said, “We also have those bodies that Andy got from the desert. They are still in the hold. We need those extracted as well—they are evidence of war crimes.”

Andy nodded, “I’ll handle that,” he responded, heading over to one of the senior firefighters who was directing their evacuation.

“There’s more,” Raul said to her. “We need to get word to Ted. We will need the media to come.”

"You thinking of putting on a show?"

Raul nodded. "The world needs to see what is happening in these camps." There was a determination in his voice, a maturity, that she admired and respected. He was no longer the young man that she had extracted from Pennsylvania. Raul had aged far more than the months that had passed.

"I wholeheartedly agree," she replied.

CHAPTER 26

"The enemies of fairness and equity will stop at nothing to achieve their evil goals."

North of Angeles, Texas

The convoy of evacuated Newmerican troops stopped a mile short of the Texas/New Mexico border on State Highway 285. Darius looked around and saw nothing but a long stretch of desert—a flat road leading back to New Mexico and Newamerican territory. The cartel members ushered the Newmericans out of their buses and trucks. The smell of filthy, sweaty people was not new to Darius, and the bus reeked of perspiration.

Sergeant Ingersoll was able to move on his own, but he was still quasi-zombie-ish as far as Darius was concerned. His steps were wary, unsteady, and his balance seemed messed up by his overdose. The only medics they had were either wounded or dead back in Midland, so Ingersoll's recovery was dependent on street skills with overdoses. He was also assisted by Captain Aguilar, who had been remarkably quiet since their talk on the bus earlier. The ride was one of disgrace—they had been trapped and had to be rescued by the cartel.

The biggest change that Darius saw in the faces of the personnel was in the Youth Corps members that had come along. When the campaign had started, they had been full of bravado. Having spent time under siege, having the enemy shoot at you, killing your friends—it was sobering. *They have aged ten years in a matter of a few days.*

The journey had been bumpy, quiet, and for Darius, filled with contemplation. He knew the cartel for what it was, criminal killers. They had devastated Mexico and had sent their poison north into the United States with greedy glee. He acknowledged that without them, their entire force might have been killed or captured—but that didn't mean that he liked or trusted the cartel members.

The trip had given him time to search his soul. *Since the riots and we lost the coffee shop, I've been used by the system. They labeled me, classified me,* gave me programs they said were for my own good. Even when they had given him housing in a Tiny Town, he now saw it for what it was. *They were not being kind or trying to help us—they were just getting us out of their way, off of their sidewalks.*

Being in the Veterans Corp was like being drafted. It was worse to him; it was government sanctioned coercion. It forced him to sacrifice his freedom of choice; something he thought was unforgivable. Memories of the clearing of the Presidio tore at him. During the ride, he had fondled the medal that he had taken from the woman that died during that assignment. It was his anchor, a tangible reminder of what he had done to a fellow veteran. *It was wrong. I should have left then. I convinced myself I was doing the right thing, when really I was just a pawn in someone else's game.*

No more.

He took a bottle of water that the cartel members handed out and listened to them. "We are letting you out here. A mile north is a border crossing. We have taken care of the Texans there. You just need to walk into New Mexico, and they will arrange to get you back to California," one of them proudly announced.

Darius took a deep slow sip of the cool water, and turned his eyes back towards Angeles, the tiny town they had just driven through. *It isn't much, but a few miles of walking, and I can get there and maybe get shelter for the night.*

He started walking down 285 heading away from Newmerica.

Captain Aguilar rushed up next to him. "What are you doing, Darius?"

"I quit."

"You can't just quit."

"The fuck, I can. This shit is worse than during the COVID outbreak. They are using me … all of us. They are twisting us into a fight we have no business being in. The Veteran Corps is a lie; we aren't volunteers;

we're voluntold. If we hadn't been coerced into joining, we would have been left with nothing. Well, I'm done with this bullshit. I can quit, and so can you."

He saw the anguish in her eyes, but she maintained her composure. "You'll be a deserter. You'll lose everything."

"That's the thing Captain. I don't have anything to lose. I am through playing their game, putting my life on the line for people who have never done the same thing for me. They have taken everything from me except my body and soul. I still control those. They have made me a person that has nothing to lose, and people like that either thrive or die. Well, I ain't dying."

"Where are you going to go?"

"I don't know. It doesn't matter. I just know where I'm not going to go. If you want to stay with these criminals and do their dirty work, you can. Me, I have no intention of fighting their war for their twisted-ass causes. I was with Vixen when she died. I'm done seeing that shit for nothing more than a guarantee of more relief and reparations. If I am going to fight, it's going to be for something that is worth fighting for." Without saying it, he implied that he was going to America. *They at least have a cause that makes sense.*

"You'll be labeled a deserter."

Darius chuckled. "I've been called worse by better people. I'm not going to fight and die for a cause I don't believe in … for a government that has worked against me and never supported me. You know, the other side, they are fighting for their survival, for freedom, for their personal liberties. Newmerica? They stole their power and are forcing folks like us to fight so they can hold onto it. I say, *no*. For the first time in a long while, I know what's important in life. I'd rather take a stand with the people that think the way I do."

Aguilar could not form words. For a moment, she simply looked at him. When she spoke, she said, "Wait here," and headed back to the bus.

Darius waited. He was concerned that she might tell the cartel members that he was a deserter, but that did not compel him to shoulder his weapon. If it was a firefight, they would win. *No matter what happens from this point forward, I won't fight for these people.*

She came back with Sergeant Ingersoll, helping him keep steady as they walked. Aguilar had tossed on her ruck as well. Stopping in front of him, she looked him squarely in his eyes. "I'm done with this shit too."

"You?"

Aguilar nodded. "You're not the only one who has been misled. Fighting for people that think they are better than me was never in my plans either."

Ingersoll nodded slowly. "Fucking cartel nearly killed me trying to rescue us. I'm out too. I'd rather go with you than fight for drug smugglers or the people that hired them."

Darius did something he hadn't done in a long time. He smiled. "We need to get walking—it will be dark soon." The trio started down the flat dusty stretch of highway, away from their pasts, towards an uncertain future.

Stewart Newburgh Airport, New York

Judy Mercury watched as the last of the helicopters was loaded into the transports. They had lost two choppers in the operations, the fates of the crews were unknown still. Chances were pretty good that they wouldn't know if they were alive or dead until after the war was over. The Newmericans were not forthcoming with the status of their POWs.

"We're good to go," Lieutenant Colonel Mihalek stated as he moved next to her on the tarmac.

"I'll be glad to be on friendly soil."

"You'll be pleased to know that four of the Marine reservists have volunteered to come along with us."

"Can we trust them?"

He gave a slight shrug. "They seem sincere, but looks can be deceiving. I have some of our people keeping them under tight wraps."

Mercury looked around Stewart Newburgh one last time. Darkness had come an hour ago, and the field looked eerily quiet. She was glad that the NSF had decided to not try to retake the field. *If I ever see this place again, it is too soon.* "It's past time to go."

"I agree," he said, pausing for a moment. "You know, you did really well on this op."

"*We* did really well," she countered. "Let's not count the chickens until all the eggs are hatched."

"Still, you deserve a lot of credit for this mission."

Judy shook her head. "I planned. I didn't get to fight, not really. Next time out, I want to be in the action, like with Grab Ass. I felt like I had some control that I was contributing then. This time I was an observer." She walked to the lead C-5 with Mihalek at her side.

"Planning is usually the most important part of the mission. If you screw that up, people die, usually horribly."

"Still, I want to be in the fight."

"That will raise some eyebrows. Most majors are not on the line."

"Neither are Generals, but Reager pulls it off. If he can do it, so can I."

The Lieutenant Colonel smiled broadly. "Something tells me you are right." Together they walked across the dark airport as the planes fired up their engines.

BSA Hospital, Amarillo, Texas

Raul found himself in an uncomfortable situation, handling the media at the hospital where the escapees had been taken. Caylee had left abruptly, having gotten a phone call. She assured him she would connect with him in Nashville when he returned. *Something has come up to get her to take off like that.*

The hospital had set up a large room for him to talk to the media. Travis and Faust had taken off, doing what they could to avoid the media. He understood that. In their lines of work, anonymity was crucial. Andy had stayed with him, carefully guarding the sheet-covered bodies encased in the plastic waste that he had recovered. *They are an important part of the story ... proof of what the Newmericans are doing in the camps.*

Their hostages, the former guards, were in custody. Captain Kenyon of the Texas Rangers had made it back from New Mexico and had joined Raul and Andy. From what he had told Raul, Gwen Holtz and her Witches were on their way home as well as Jefferson Morris of the Little Rock Irregulars. The Maricopa County Mounted Posse had rode off into the sunset. Raul had little doubt that they would find their way home with no problem. It was comforting to know the fate of some of the rescue team; reassuring that they were alive and hopefully avoiding capture.

Raul had immediately called Ted and had relayed the results of their rescue mission. At Raul's urging, Ted had flown immediately to join him. He was a welcome arrival. As a former Senator he had a knack for handling the media. The two of them did a press conference, answering questions from the media. Most wanted the details of the rescue, but Travis had insisted that they keep those secret. "There's a lot of other camps out there that we are going to have to take and save."

The TRC-backed Newmerican media approached the questioning more viciously, lacing it with innuendos and casting doubt. "Why should anyone believe you, Mr. Lopez? Aren't you wanted for terrorist activities in Pennsylvania and other states? How many innocent people did you murder in the process of this so-called 'liberation?'" Ted helped in responding to those questions, but Raul also held his own.

When one reporter claimed that the report of dead bodies out in the desert were a blatant lie, it was Andy that spoke up. "You want proof? We have the proof!" He uncovered the remains of the two young victims that had been brought back with them, still entombed in a greenish, black, hard plastic coffin of sorts. Andy also shared photos of the other dead with the reporters.

When it was over, and the last member of the press left, Ted patted Raul on the back. "You did good kid—*real* good."

"I just did what I had to."

"No," Ted corrected him. "Most people go through life sitting on the sidelines. They talk a big game, but when it comes time to act, they stand back and wait for other people to do it. When the progressives overthrew the government, there wasn't a big uprising. Sure, there were incidents, but most people, for all of their bravado and bluster, did nothing. When their neighbors and friends were sent off to Social Quarantine, they kept quiet. Deep down, most people say they will take action, but they don't. They want other people to do it for them."

"Not you. You stood up in Detroit; you took a stand at Valley Forge; you didn't break when we were in the Supermax. When it came time to save these people, you never even thought about sitting it out and letting someone else do it."

"He's right," Travis stated as he approached the small gathering. "People look to guys like me, a SEAL, and think we are heroes. We are highly trained and precise in the execution of our work, but we are not heroes. Guys like you and Andy," he flipped his thumb over his shoulder at Andy, "you are the real heroes. Everyday people who are willing to step up to the plate and do what has to be done. You are inspiring a lot of folks Raul." Raul felt himself blush from the compliments. He had never thought of it quite that way. Now it made sense. *I finally understand my role in all of this ... in everything we've been doing.*

"To hell with the media and the propagandists that tried to paint you as a criminal," Ted said as he smiled. "Most people will see through that. When the prisoners here start getting well enough to talk to the press, people will see you for what you *really* are."

Raul drank in the words and nodded in agreement. "You make me out to be a hero. I am just a person. I have, however, surrounded myself with good people of strong character. I will not fail you, my sister, or my madre.'"

He had a family once more. They weren't normal, but what family really was? For Raul, this was the best life he could imagine.

The Southern White House
Nashville, Tennessee

Caylee was followed into the office of the Attorney General by Charli. She had wanted to come alone to clear her name, but Charli had insisted and from what Caylee knew of her friend, there was no point arguing about it. Charli had briefed her on the phone, and after she landed in Nashville, as to the situation. It angered Caylee, but didn't entirely surprise her. *Reese has had much of the same training I did. His only mistake is fighting for the wrong side.*

A pair of security people flanked them as they entered, no doubt concerned for the safety of the AG. Caylee could see that they were in good shape, armed, and ready for action should she move. By the same token, she also knew that if push came to shove, she could take them. The Attorney General gestured to the two seats in front of her desk, and they took them, though Caylee would have preferred to stand. "I take it you have been brought up to date as to the assassination attempt on Jack Desmond."

"Indeed, I have," she replied, glancing around the office. Her mind always processed possible evacuation routes, in this case a fourth-story window. *Taking the AG hostage would be a mistake; it would slow me down. Best to kill the two security people if I have to and take my chances on a good landing after I shatter the window.*

"What can you tell me about your whereabouts during the time of the crime?"

"I was in New Mexico, on a mission to rescue prisoners from a Social Quarantine camp."

"I see. I take it that was the one I just saw the press conference on?"

"I wasn't aware of a press conference, but I presume that is correct."

"And did you have anything to do with the assassination attempt?"

"No, I did not."

"Mr. Reese has been placed in custody and is out of surgery for his injuries sustained in the attack and his flight," she replied.

"You will need more than your normal guards on him," Caylee stated flatly. "He's a trained operative. Even injured, he's more than a match for your typical police officers."

"So I am to understand. Mr. Reese had his right arm amputated, the results of a gunshot would."

Amputated? That was something new that Charli hadn't relayed. "Good. Don't let that fool you, Madam. He will try to get away."

"How do you know that?"

"Because I would—arm or no arm."

For a moment, the Attorney General said nothing. "Reese has not confessed to anything. We got his blood to match the blood found at the crime scene. If it matches, he will be charged with the attempt on Mr. Desmond's life."

"Those kinds of tests can take a few days."

"Yes," she said coolly. "Based on the statements by Director Kazinski and a certain former Senator that vouched for you, I am quite confident that you are not responsible for shooting Mr. Desmond. I am faced with a problem, however."

"And that is?"

"Certain media outlets have linked you to the crime. We haven't gone public with Thiago Reese's connections yet, and I can't until we have the evidence to link him to this. As far as some of the public are concerned, you are the prime suspect in this case."

Caylee whetted her lips slightly in thought. "It seems you have a problem."

"If I let you walk out of here, the media will eventually catch wind of it. There will be talk of a coverup. Even if you are proven innocent in this matter, it will appear that the government is giving you some sort of pass."

"Ma'am," Charli chimed in. "You could always put out a statement that you have cleared her as a suspect. Now that the team is back from New Mexico, they can vouch that she was with them the entire time—that she couldn't have committed the crime."

"I understand that," the Attorney General replied in a clearly controlled tone of voice. "This isn't about the law or even justice. This is about public opinion. The legitimacy of our nation and our adherence to the laws is just a few of the things that separate us from Newmerica."

"So, you want to place me under arrest."

The AG nodded once slowly. "It is a formality. Technically we will refer to it as protective custody … just until we can prove that Reese was responsible for this."

Caylee said nothing as she contemplated this. The thought of her needing protective custody was a joke. *I can more than take care of myself.* She wanted to decline what the Attorney General was offering.

Glancing over at Charli, she began to reconsider. *After all I have done and been through, doing this will help erase some of the stigma I still carry as a former operative. She is right, this is bigger than me or this crime. I became attached to this cause out of a need for revenge. It has become something larger. I have Raul and Maria to think about. Jack Desmond has always been good to me. Is it too much to give him a few days locked up?*

"Alright, I agree."

"Are you sure?" Charli asked.

Caylee nodded. "For Jack, Raul, Maria, you and Andy—yes. I've spent days in far worse places during my career." *A few days to rest and regroup will help me. It also sends a message. I am not the same person who came out of Newmerica. I see the bigger picture now. And that makes me far more dangerous to those that tried to frame me for this …*

EPILOGUE

"If you are questioning a policy, you clearly don't see the big picture."

Arnold Air Force Base, Tullahoma, Tennessee

General Reager walked out to the airplane as it idled to a stop. The gangway came down, and Judy Mercury appeared. She looked tired ... *no, exhausted.* Her face was drawn, and she had dark circles under her eyes. Seeing him approach seemed to give her a little more energy. Walking up to him, she saluted. "General."

"If it isn't my favorite Green Lantern." He returned the gesture. "Can I get you a cup of coffee, Major?"

She smiled and nodded to him, following him into the ready-room. He poured her a cup from the dispenser. "I can't for the life of me, remember how you take it."

"Today—black."

She cradled the ceramic cup in her hands, as if she could draw strength from the contents just by touch. Finally she took a cautious sip and sat the cup down."

"I want to congratulate you on a hell of an operation."

"From what Lariat told me," she said, taking another sip, "The Newmerican forces broke and ran. I haven't heard shit since we got back to Wright Pat—and I caught the first flight down here."

"New Hampshire has been freed. The Newmericans are shitting themselves over it. A lot of National Guard troops are dead or POWs now. Vermont is ripe for the taking, and their governor has done the unthinkable and contacted our president. You showed up at the right time to tip the scales to our advantage."

Judy didn't talk for a moment, and then when she did, he saw a sadness in her eyes. "I lost two choppers and crews."

"I know—saw Mihalik's BDA. It's not your fault Judy."

"It *feels* like my fault."

"You performed brilliantly. Far better than I did."

"I take it we are meeting here because things out west went bad?"

"That's an understatement. Diamondback got bogged down from the get-go. The Newmericans tricked me, sent a force into southwest Texas."

"I heard they retreated."

"They had help. The Newmericans played a trump card we didn't know about. The García Cartel came across the border from Mexico to extract them. They used some sort of fentanyl-laced mortars as chemical weapons. There's over two hundred people dead or near dead from overdoses."

"Fentanyl? That's an expensive solution."

"Is it? They produce the stuff and set the price. Regardless, it worked. The President has kept his cool about it. He's going to go public tomorrow on the affair; use it to link the Newmericans to the cartels and the drug trade."

"Are we going down there?"

"No," Trip said. "He asked my opinion, and I told him we needed to be vigilant, but we need to fight one war at a time."

"Good," she replied, taking a longer sip. "I've been down to Mexico, years ago. It was a shithole then, and has to be a bigger shithole now."

"At least once you've rested up, you know one place you won't be going."

"So what is next for me?"

"I have plans for out west still, but I think you might be better suited to help resolve the issue in St. Louis." Since the election, St. Louis refused to accept the election results. They had declared the city an autonomous zone and had thrown their lot in with the Newmericans. Where Atlanta had been swiftly dealt with, the rebels in St. Louis had used the passage of time to fortify and dig in.

"Sounds charming," she said with a hint of sarcasm. "What about you?"

Trip grinned. "I have some plans in motion already for New York State, and I haven't quite given up on going west. But before all of that, I am fairly certain I will have my butt hauled up in front of Congress."

"You're kidding," she chuckled. "We are in the middle of a civil war."

"They are all armchair Generals," he replied. The President had warned him that an inquiry would be coming. As much as Trip wanted to tell Congress to fuck off, he knew he needed to go and take a bit of a verbal beating. *I probably deserve a little of that after New Mexico and Texas. My wife used to say I needed humility—well, a public flogging will have to do.*

"That was one campaign. What about Atlanta and Knoxville?"

"Defeat is an orphan. They want to grandstand a little at my expense. It reminds me of the old Irish saying: 'Critics are like eunuchs in a harem. They've seen it done, they talk about it, but are incapable of doing it themselves.'"

Judy chuckled again, and he was glad to hear that the joy had not entirely been squashed from her. "We will always have New Hampshire."

"Yes, we will Judy. That is in a large part because of you." With those words, he rose to his feet. "Pep talk is over. The time has come to kick this war into high gear."

Finishing the cup of coffee in two large gulps, she set it down hard on the table. "What, no medals?"

"Oh, there's bound to be a medal for the fighting up there. Medals won't win the war."

"No," she said, as she followed him out of the ready room. "They leave that kind of work to people like us."

The District

Daniel Porter, President of Newmerica, sat next to the Vice President at the small round table in his office. The news was not all bad, but some of it was inescapable. New Hampshire was a disaster. Not only had they lost, but the casualties were high and the governors were infuriated by the entire debacle.

President Porter tried to focus on the positive news from the war. The attack into New Mexico had been stalled. Despite the retreat from

Midland, Texas, the TRC was spinning the events along the New Mexico border as great victories. In some respects, they were.

"This information that the American press is running with about the camp in Santa Fe is troubling," he said.

"They have been stating for months that these camps were killing factories. We have several perfectly produced documentaries that show that the camps are anything but that. Children playing in the streets, cheerful people who have realized that their old ways of thinking are corrupt … that kind of thing."

"Good. Still, some people are not going to accept that. They will start showing interviews with these prisoners. And those bodies they brought back. That's a hard image to shake."

"We will play it up as fake. It's like those alien autopsies that get passed around on the internet. If you tell the people what they want to hear, they will accept it and make it their reality. That has been the hallmark of the TRC."

"What of these reports about the involvement of the García Cartel?"

"We deny that ever happened. My people have already come up with a good spin for it. They will say that the Americans are lying to cover up their military disaster. They are spreading these stories to justify their failures on the battlefield. You'll see," she assured him. "In a few weeks, they will move onto the next shiny object that gets their attention." *That is the best part of the electorate; they actually want to be played. Many want to be lied to. It is far easier to accept a lie than to have to cope with reality and the truth.*

A knock sounded, and Daniel looked at the door for a moment, then back to her. "That would be Rinehart."

She nodded. This is a lesson that the people in the Pentagon need. They must understand the price of failure. First was Donaldson. At least he had the decency to die, so we could martyr him. Rinehart just ran. If he had done his duty, he'd be dead. "We need to do this, to send a message about our intolerance."

"Enter," Daniel said. Rinehart came in. It was fairly clear that he had taken the time to put on his dress uniform. He stepped in, followed by Veronica Hinkley a half pace behind him. She was dressed in combat fatigues, filthy with dried dirt, the crust of dried tears. The two were in stark contrast of each other.

Rinehart saluted the President, who did not return the gesture. Instead, Porter waited until the doors closed. "General," was all he said, practically baiting the officer to respond.

"Sir, it is with great displeasure that I must inform you of—"

The Vice President cut him off. "We already know of your failures in New Hampshire. The whole world does."

Rinehart's face reddened with her verbal salvo. "If I may madam Vice President—"

"No," Porter cut him off this time. "You may not. You were sent up to New Hampshire to bring it into the fold. Do you know what I saw on TV coming out of America this morning? An American flag, flying over the State House in that damned state. A flag that we have banned and blocked—now flutters in the breeze over the Granite Staters. The Goddamn stars and stripes! You know what else I saw, I saw them rejoicing over their victory."

"Mr. President, I can—"

"I don't want explanations," he cut him off once more. "I wanted results. You failed to deliver. All that remains is what we do with you now."

"Sir, I have been a loyal supporter of the cause."

"Yet you failed us," the Vice President snapped.

For a moment, the General fumed but remained silent. It was the Vice President that shattered that silence. "Thanks, in no small part to the People's Warden assigned you," she nodded to Hinkley, "We have determined that you will face a People's Tribunal for your failures. Your fate will reside in the realm of social justice."

"I am an officer in the US Army," he growled through clenched teeth. "I should face military justice, not that of the mob."

"You should be thankful," Daniel Porter said. "The Vice President suggested a firing squad. I was able to convince her it would be better for you to atone publicly for your failure in a Tribunal." He paused just before Rinehart could speak again. Porter added, "If I were you, I would hold my tongue in case I am forced to change my mind."

Hinkley pulled out her sidearm and pointed it at the General. His face was caught in a torrent of confusion, fear, and anger—with each emotion attempting to gain control of his thought. The Warden led him out of the office before he could speak again, closing the door behind her.

"I won't miss him," the Vice President jibed.

"We will need someone ruthless on the battlefield."

"I have a person or two in mind."

"Good."

"We need to address the other big issues on the table, Daniel."

"Such as?"

"We need to start a draft. You've seen the numbers from my Warden program. People aren't volunteering at a rate that we would have expected. Our setbacks are making people, shall I say, hesitant to do their duty to the country."

"Drafts are unpopular. There could be protests. Probably riots."

Which I will have the NSF squash. "Our military his suffered losses and the desertion rate is alarming. We can rebrand a draft, make it easy to sell. Call it National Service Donation, or the Defenders of State Liberty program ... whatever plays best with the test groups. In the meantime, we can form up more penal units, emptying some prisons. Losing prisoners in battle costs us nothing. With the Warden program, we can make sure they don't break and run like they did in New Hampshire." *If they do, my Wardens will gun them down ... as a means of motivation*

"People will rise up against a draft. We've indoctrinated them into protesting every little perceived infraction."

He was right about that. Protests had been a tool to manipulate the public and generate fear since the election in 2020. Now it was something that might be used against the state.

"Alright, anyone caught rioting or protesting the draft will be labeled as seditionists. We will arrest them. After a few fast and highly publicized trials, people will see that speaking out against our actions is going to suffer."

"Let's get someone to put together a draft of how things might work. I don't want a random thing. This should focus on the segment of the population that has caused our greatest problems in the past."

"Understood. White males love the macho lifestyle. Let them shed blood to be part of the future. We can rig the draft so they are appropriately chosen."

Anything else?"

"Just the big one."

"The Constitutional Convention? I thought we were going to hold back on that for a while—at least until we had a major victory."

"That's what New Mexico and Texas was. That's what we told our people at least. Besides, we need to give the people something to look forward to. This is our big chance to throw out that worthless rag of a document the nation was founded on and recast it into something that reflects our new values and perspectives."

Porter gave her a single dip of his head in agreement. "If you think now is the time; then we should get things underway."

"Yes. We should announce a date. I think doing it in New York would be good, It will send a message that we are still solidly behind that state, despite what Rinehart and his military cronies did up in New Hampshire."

"Of course," Daniel replied.

"If we do this, it is the last line in the sand with these rebellious Americans. It will set the direction of our nation in the future. A new Constitution will keep that corrupt specter of our past and give us a new foundation of laws. It will be the beginning of the end."